Samantha's in love
with the boy next door.

"Jase?"

"Mmm-hmm?" He lifts up on one elbow, his face barely visible in the twilight.

"You have to kiss me," I find myself saying.

"Yeah." He leans closer. "I do."

His lips, warm and soft, touch my forehead, then slide down my cheek, moving sideways to my mouth. His hand comes up to press the nape of my neck beneath my wet hair, just as mine slips to his back. His skin's warm beneath the cool sheen of water, his muscles tight as he lies there, still balanced on one elbow. I curl in closer.

I'm not new to kissing. Or I thought I wasn't, but it's never been anything like this. I can't get close enough. When Jase gently deepens the kiss, it feels right, no moment of startled hesitation like I've had before.

After a long time, we swim back to shore and stretch out for a while on our towels, kissing again. Jase's lips smiling under mine as I kiss all over his face. My hands tightening on his shoulders as he nuzzles my neck and softly nibbles my collarbone. It is as if everything else in the world stops as we lie here in the summer night.

"We should go home," Jase whispers, his hands stroking my waist.

"No. Not yet. Not yet," I say back, sliding my lips along the willing curve of his.

OTHER BOOKS YOU MAY ENJOY

MY LIFE NEXT DOOR

by Huntley Fitzpatrick

speak

SPEAK
An imprint of Penguin Random House LLC
375 Hudson Street
New York, New York 10014

First published in the United States of America by Dial Books, 2012
Published by Speak, an imprint of Penguin Group (USA) Inc., 2013

THE LIBRARY OF CONGRESS HAS CATALOGED THE DIAL BOOKS EDITION AS FOLLOWS:
Fitzpatrick, Huntley.
My life next door / by Huntley Fitzpatrick.
p. cm.
Summary: When Samantha, the seventeen-year-old daughter of a wealthy, perfectionistic state senator,
falls in love with the boy next door, whose family is large, boisterous, and just making ends meet, she
discovers a different way to live, but when her mother is involved in a hit-and-run accident Sam must
make some difficult choices.
ISBN 978-0-8037-3699-3 (hc)
[1. Conduct of life—Fiction. 2. Love—Fiction. 3. Family life—Fiction. 4. Politics, Practical—Fiction.]
I. Title.
PZ7.F578My 2012
[Fic]—dc23
2011027166

Speak ISBN 978-0-14-242604-3

Printed in the United States of America.

13 15 17 19 20 18 16 14

MY

LIFE

NEXT

DOOR

Of course, to Colette Corry.
The words "best friend" will never say enough.

MY
LIFE
NEXT
DOOR

Chapter One

The Garretts were forbidden from the start.

But that's not why they were important.

We were standing in our yard that day ten years ago when their battered sedan pulled up to the low-slung shingled house next door, close behind the moving van.

"Oh no," Mom sighed, arms falling to her sides. "I hoped we could have avoided this."

"This—what?" my big sister called from down the driveway. She was eight and already restless with Mom's chore of the day, planting jonquil bulbs in our front garden. Walking quickly to the picket fence that divided our house from the one next door, she perched on her tiptoes to peer at the new neighbors. I pressed my face to the gap in the slats, watching in amazement as two parents and five children spilled from the sedan, like a clown car at the circus.

"This kind of thing." Mom gestured toward the car with the trowel, twisting her silvery blond hair into a coil with the other hand. "There's one in every neighborhood. The family that never mows their lawn. Has toys scattered everywhere. The ones who never plant flowers, or do and let them die. The messy family who lowers real estate values. Here they are. Right next door. You've got that bulb wrong side up, Samantha."

I switched the bulb around, scooting my knees in the dirt to get closer to the fence, my eyes never leaving the father as he swung a baby from a car seat while a curly-haired toddler climbed his back. "They look nice," I said.

I remember there was a silence then, and I looked up at my mother.

She was shaking her head at me, a strange expression on her face. "Nice isn't the point here, Samantha. You're seven years old. You need to understand what's important. *Five* children. Good God. Just like your father's family. Insanity." She shook her head again, rolling her eyes heavenward.

I moved closer to Tracy and edged a fleck of white paint off the fence with my thumbnail. My sister looked at me with the same warning face she used when she was watching TV and I walked up to ask her a question.

"*He's* cute," she said, squinting over the fence again. I looked over to see an older boy unfold himself from the back of the car, baseball mitt in hand, reaching back to haul out a cardboard box full of sports gear.

Even then, Tracy liked to deflect, to forget how hard our mother found being a parent. Our dad had walked away without even a good-bye, leaving Mom with a one-year-old, a baby on the way, a lot of disillusionment, and, luckily, her trust fund from her parents.

As the years proved, our new neighbors, the Garretts, were exactly what Mom predicted. Their lawn got mowed sporadically at best. Their Christmas lights stayed hung till Easter.

Their backyard was a hodgepodge of an in-ground pool and a trampoline and a swing set and monkey bars. Periodically, Mrs. Garrett would make an effort to plant something seasonal, chrysanthemums in September, impatiens in June, only to leave it to gasp and wither away as she tended to something more important, like her five children. They became eight children over the years. All approximately three years apart.

"My unsafe zone," I overheard Mrs. Garrett explain one day at the supermarket when Mrs. Mason commented on her burgeoning belly, "is twenty-two months. That's when they suddenly aren't babies anymore. I love babies so much."

Mrs. Mason had raised her eyebrows and smiled, then turned away with compressed lips and a baffled shake of her head.

But Mrs. Garrett seemed to ignore it, happy in herself and content with her chaotic family. Five boys and three girls by the time I turned seventeen.

Joel, Alice, Jase, Andy, Duff, Harry, George, and Patsy.

In the ten years since the Garretts moved next door, Mom hardly ever looked out the side windows of our house without huffing an impatient breath. Too many kids on the trampoline. Bikes abandoned on the lawn. Another pink or blue balloon tied to the mailbox, waving haphazardly in the breeze. Loud basketball games. Music blaring while Alice and her friends tanned. The bigger boys washing cars and spraying each other with hoses. If not those, it was Mrs. Garrett, calmly breast-feeding on the front steps, or sitting there on Mr. Garrett's lap, for all the world to see.

"It's indecent," Mom would say, watching.

"It's legal," Tracy, future lawyer, always countered, flipping back her platinum hair. She'd station herself next to Mom, inspecting the Garretts out the big side window of the kitchen. "The courts have made it absolutely legal to breast-feed wherever you want. Her own front steps are definitely fair game."

"But why? Why do it at all when there are bottles and formula? And if you *must*, why not inside?"

"She's watching the other kids, Mom. It's what she's supposed to do," I'd sometimes point out, making my stand next to Tracy.

Mom would sigh, shake her head, and extract the vacuum cleaner from the closet as if it were a Valium. The lullaby of my childhood was my mom running the vacuum cleaner, making perfectly symmetrical lines in our beige living room carpet. The lines somehow seemed important to her, so essential that she'd turn on the machine as Tracy and I were eating breakfast, then slowly follow us to the door as we pulled on our coats and backpacks. Then she'd back up, eliminating our trail of footprints, and her own, until we were outside. Finally, she'd rest the vacuum cleaner carefully behind one of our porch columns only to drag it back in that night when she got home from work.

It was clear from the start that we were *not to play with the Garretts*. After bringing over the obligatory "welcome to the neighborhood" lasagna, my mother did her best to be very unwelcoming. She responded to Mrs. Garrett's smiling greetings with cool nods. She rebuffed Mr. Garrett's offers to mow, sweep up leaves, or shovel snow with a terse "We have a service, thanks all the same."

Finally, the Garretts stopped trying.

Though they lived right next door and one kid or another might pedal past me as I watered Mom's flowers, it was easy not to run into them. Their kids went to the local public schools. Tracy and I attended Hodges, the only private school in our small Connecticut town.

One thing my mother never knew, and would disapprove of most of all, was that I watched the Garretts. All the time.

Outside my bedroom window, there's a small flat section of the roof with a tiny fence around it. Not really a balcony, more like a ledge. It's in between two peaked gables, shielded from both the front and backyard, and it faces the right side of the Garretts' house. Even before they came, it was my place to sit and think. But afterward, it was my place to dream.

I'd climb out after bedtime, look through the lit windows, and see Mrs. Garrett doing the dishes, one of the younger kids sitting on the counter next to her. Or Mr. Garrett wrestling with the older boys in the living room. Or the lights going on where the baby must sleep, the figure of Mr. or Mrs. Garrett pacing back and forth, rubbing a tiny back. It was like watching a silent movie, one so different from the life I lived.

Over the years, I got more daring. I'd sometimes watch during the day, after school, hunched back against the side of the rough gable, trying to figure out which Garrett matched each name I heard called out the screen door. It was tricky because they all had wavy brown hair, olive skin, and sinewy builds, like a breed all their own.

Joel was the easiest to identify—the oldest and the most athletic. His picture often appeared in local papers for various sports accomplishments—I knew it in black and white. Alice, next in line, dyed her hair outlandish colors and wore clothes that provoked commentary from Mrs. Garrett, so I had her down as well. George and Patsy were the littlest ones. The middle three boys, Jase, Duff, and Harry . . . I couldn't get them straight. I was pretty sure that Jase was the oldest of the three, but did that mean he was the tallest? Duff was supposed to be the smart one, competing in various chess competitions and spelling bees, but he didn't wear glasses or give off any obvious brainiac signals. Harry was constantly in trouble—"Harry! How could you?" was the refrain. And Andy, the middle girl, always seemed to be missing, her name called longest to come to the dinner table or pile into the car: "Annnnnnnnndeeeeeeeeee!"

From my hidden perch, I'd peer out at the yard, trying to locate Andy, figure out Harry's latest escapade, or see what outrageous outfit Alice was wearing. The Garretts were my bedtime story, long before I ever thought I'd be part of the story myself.

Chapter Two

On the first sweltering hot night in June, I'm home alone, trying to enjoy the quiet but finding myself moving from room to room, unable to settle.

Tracy's out with Flip, yet another blond tennis player in her unending series of boyfriends. I can't reach my best friend, Nan, who's been completely distracted by *her* boyfriend, Daniel, since school ended last week and he graduated. There's nothing on TV I want to see, no place in town I feel like going. I've tried sitting out on the porch, but at low tide the humid air is overpowering, muddy-scented from the breeze off the river.

So I'm sitting in our vaulted living room, crunching the ice left over from my seltzer, skimming through Tracy's stack of *In Touch* magazines. Suddenly I hear a loud, continuous buzzing sound. As it goes on and on I look around, alarmed, trying to identify it. The dryer? The smoke detector? Finally, I realize it's the doorbell, buzzing and buzzing, on and on and on. I hurry to open the door, expecting—sigh—one of Tracy's exes, daring after too many strawberry daiquiris at the country club, come to win her back.

Instead, I see my mother, pressed against the doorbell, getting the daylights kissed out of her by some man. When I throw the door open, they half stumble, then he braces his hand on the jamb and just keeps kissing away. So I stand there, feeling stupid, arms folded, my thin nightgown shifting slightly in the thick air. All around me are summer voices. The lap of the shore far away, the roar of a motorcycle coming up the street, the *shhhh* of the wind in the dogwood trees. None of those, and certainly not my presence, stop my mom or this guy. Not even when the motorcycle backfires as it peels into the Garretts' driveway, which usually drives Mom crazy.

Finally, they come up for air, and she turns to me with an awkward laugh.

"Samantha. Goodness! You startled me."

She's flustered, her voice high and girlish. Not the authoritative "this is how it will be" voice she typically uses at home or the syrup-mixed-with-steel one she wields on the job.

Five years ago, Mom went into politics. Tracy and I didn't take it seriously at first—we'd hardly known Mom to vote. But she came home one day from a rally charged up and determined to be state senator. She ran, and she won, and our lives changed entirely.

We were proud of her. Of course we were. But instead of making breakfast and sifting through our book bags to be sure our homework was done, Mom left home at five o'clock in the morning and headed to Hartford "before the traffic kicks in." She stayed late for commissions and special sessions. Weekends weren't about Tracy's gymnastics practices or my swim meets. They were for boning up on upcoming votes, staying for special sessions, or attending local events. Tracy pulled every bad-teenager trick in the book. She played with drugs and drinking, she shoplifted, she slept with too many boys. I read piles of books, registered Democratic in my mind (Mom's Republican), and spent more time than usual watching the Garretts.

So now tonight, I stand here, stunned into immobility by the unexpected and prolonged PDA, until Mom finally lets go of the guy. He turns to me and I gasp.

After a man leaves you, pregnant and with a toddler, you don't keep his picture on the mantel. We have only a few photographs of our dad, and they're all in Tracy's room. Still I recognize him—the curve of his jaw, the dimples, the shiny wheat-blond hair and broad shoulders. This man has all those things.

"Dad?"

Mom's expression morphs from dreamy bedazzlement to utter shock, as though I've cursed.

The guy shifts away from Mom, extends his hand to me. As he moves into the light of the living room, I realize he's much younger than my father would be now. "Hi there, darlin'. I'm the newest—and most enthusiastic—member of your mom's reelection campaign."

Enthusiastic? I'll say.

He takes my hand and shakes it, seemingly without my participation.

"This is Clay Tucker," Mom says, in the reverent tone one might use for Vincent van Gogh or Abraham Lincoln. She turns and gives me a reproving look, no doubt for the "Dad" comment, but quickly recovers. "Clay's worked on national campaigns. I'm very lucky he's agreed to help me out."

9

In what capacity? I wonder as she fluffs her hair in a gesture that can't possibly be anything but flirtatious. *Mom?*

"So, Clay," she continues. "I *told* you Samantha was a big girl."

I blink. I'm five two. In heels. "Big girl" is a stretch. Then I get it. She means old. Old for someone as young as her to have.

"Clay was mighty surprised to find I had a teenager." My mother tucks a wayward strand of newly fluffed hair behind her ear. "He says I look like one myself."

I wonder if she's mentioned Tracy, or if she's going to keep her on the down-low for a while.

"You're as beautiful as your mother," he says to me, "so now I believe it." He has the kind of Southern accent that makes you think of melting butter on biscuits, and porch swings.

Clay looks around the living room. "What a terrific room," he says. "Just invites a man to put his feet up after a long hard day." Mom beams. She's proud of our house, renovates rooms all the time, tweaking the already perfect. He walks around slowly, examining the gigantic paintings of landscapes on the white, white walls, taking in the so-puffy-you-can't-sit-on-it beige couch and the immense armchairs, finally settling into the one in front of the fireplace. I'm shocked. I check Mom's face. Her dates always stop at the door. In fact, she's barely dated at all.

But Mom doesn't do her usual thing, glance at her watch, say, "Oh, goodness, look at the time," and politely shove him out the door. Instead, she gives that little girlish laugh again, toys with a pearl earring, and says, "I'll just make coffee."

She whirls toward the kitchen, but before she can take a step, Clay Tucker comes up to me, putting his hand on my shoulder. "Seems to me," he says, "you're the kind of girl who'd make the coffee herself and let her mama relax."

My face heats and I take an involuntary step back. Fact is, I usually do make tea for Mom when she comes in late. It's sort of a ritual. But no one has ever told me to do it. Part of me thinks I must have misheard. I met this guy, like, two seconds ago. The other part instantly feels chagrined, the way I do at school when I've forgotten to do the extra credit math problem, or at home when I shove my newly laundered clothes into a drawer unfolded. I stand there, struggling for a response, and come up blank. Finally I nod, turn, and go to the kitchen.

As I measure out coffee grounds, I can hear murmurs and low laughter coming from the living room. Who *is* this guy? Has Tracy met him? Guess not, if I'm the *big girl*. And anyway, Tracy's been off cheering Flip on at his tennis matches since they graduated last week. The rest of the time, they're parked in his convertible in our driveway, bucket seats down, while Mom's still at work.

"Coffee ready yet, sweetie?" Mom calls. "Clay here could use a pick-me-up. He's been working like a hound dog helping me out."

Hound dog? I pour freshly brewed coffee into cups, put them on a tray, find cream, sugar, napkins, and stalk back into the living room.

"That's fine for me, sweetheart, but Clay takes his in a big ol' mug. Right, Clay?"

"That's right," he says with a broad smile, holding the teacup out to me. "The biggest you got, Samantha. I run on caffeine. It's a weakness." He winks.

Returning from the kitchen a second time, I plunk the mug down in front of Clay. Mom says, "You're going to love Samantha, Clay. Such a smart girl. This past year she took all AP classes. A pluses in every one. She was on the yearbook staff, the school newspaper, used to be on the swim team . . . A star, my girl." Mom gives me her real smile, the one that goes all the way to her eyes. I start to smile back.

"Like mother, like daughter," Clay says, and my mom's eyes slide back to his face and stay there, transfixed. They exchange a private look and Mom goes over and perches on the armrest of his chair. I wonder for a second if I'm still in the room. Clearly, I'm dismissed. Fine. I'm saved from the distinct possibility I'll lose control and pour Clay's still-hot coffee from his big ol' mug onto his lap. Or pour something really cold on Mom.

Pick up, pick up, I beg the other end of the phone. Finally there's a click, but it's not Nan. It's Tim. "Mason residence," he says. "If you're Daniel, Nan's out with another guy. With a bigger dick."

"I'm not Daniel," I tell him. "But is she really? The out part?"

"Nah, of course not. Nan? She's lucky she's got Daniel, and that's pretty fucking sad."

"Where is she?"

"Around somewhere," Tim offers helpfully. "I'm in my room. Have you ever wondered what purpose the hair on your toes serves?"

Tim's stoned. As usual. I close my eyes. "Can I speak to her now?"

Tim says he'll get her, but ten minutes later I'm still waiting. He probably forgot he'd even answered the phone.

I hang up and lie on my bed for a moment, staring at the ceiling fan. Then I open my window and climb out.

As usual, most of the lights are on at the Garretts'. Including the ones in the driveway, where Alice, some of her underdressed friends, and a few of the Garrett boys are playing basketball. There may be some boyfriends thrown in there too. It's hard to tell, they're all jumping around so much, music cranked loud on the iPod speakers perched on the front steps.

I'm no good at basketball, but it looks like fun. I peer in the living room window and see Mr. and Mrs. Garrett. She's leaning on the back of his chair, arms folded, looking down at him while he points out something in a magazine. The light in their bedroom, where the baby sleeps, is still on, even though it's so late. I wonder if Patsy's afraid of the dark.

Then suddenly, I hear a voice, right near me. Right below me. "Hey."

Startled, I almost lose my balance. Then I feel a steadying hand on my ankle and hear a rustling sound, as someone, some guy, climbs up the trellis and onto the roof, my own secret place.

"Hey," he says again, sitting down next to me as though he knows me well. "Need rescuing?"

Chapter Three

I stare at this boy. He's obviously a Garrett, and not Joel, but which one? Up close, in the light spilling from my bedroom, he looks different from most of the Garretts—rangier, leaner, his wavy hair a lighter brown, already with those streaks of blond some brunettes get in the summer.

"Why would I need rescuing? This is my house, my roof."

"I don't know. It just hit me, seeing you there, that you might be Rapunzel. The princess in the tower thing. All that long blond hair and . . . well . . ."

"And you'd be?" I know I'm going to laugh if he says "the prince."

Instead he answers "Jase Garrett," reaching for my hand to shake it, as though we're at a college interview rather than randomly sitting together on my roof at night.

"Samantha Reed." I settle my hand into his, automatically polite, despite the bizarre circumstances.

"A *very* princess-y name," he answers approvingly, turning his head to smile at me. He has very white teeth.

"I'm no princess."

He gives me a considering look. "You say that emphatically. Is this something important I should know about you?"

This whole conversation is surreal. The fact that Jase Garrett should know, or need to know, anything about me at all is illogical. But instead of telling him that, I find myself confiding, "Well, for example, a second ago I wanted to do bodily harm to someone I'd only just met."

Jase takes a long time to answer, as though weighing his thoughts and his words. "We-ell," he responds finally. "I imagine a lot of princesses have felt that way . . . arranged marriages and all that. Who could know who you'd get stuck with? But . . . is this person you want to injure me? 'Cause I *can* take a hint. You can ask me to leave your roof rather than break my kneecaps."

He stretches out his legs, folding his arms behind his head, oh-so-comfortable in what is oh-so-not his territory. Despite this, I find myself telling him all about Clay Tucker. Maybe it's because Tracy's not home and Mom's acting like a stranger. Maybe it's because Tim is a waste and Nan is MIA. Maybe it's something about Jase himself, the way he sits there calmly, waiting to hear the story, as though the hang-ups of some random girl are of interest to him. At any rate, I tell him.

After I finish, there's a pause.

Finally, out of the half dark, his profile illuminated by the light from my window, he says, "Well, Samantha . . . you *were* introduced to this guy. It went downhill from there. That might make it justifiable homicide. From time to time, I've wanted to kill people I knew even less well . . . strangers in supermarkets."

Am I on my roof with a psychopath? As I start to edge away, he continues. "Those people who walk up to my mom all the time, when she's with our whole crowd, and say, 'You know,

15

there are ways to prevent this.' As if having a big family was like, I don't know, a forest fire, and they're Smokey Bear. The ones who tell my dad about vasectomies and the high cost of college as if he has no clue about any of that. More than once I've wanted to punch them."

Wow. I've never met a boy, at a school or anywhere, who cut through the small talk so quickly.

"It's a good idea to keep your eye on the guys who think they know the one true path," Jase says reflectively. "They might just mow you down if you're in their way."

I remember all my own mother's vasectomy and college comments.

"I'm sorry," I say.

Jase shifts, looking surprised. "Well, Mom says to pity them, feel sorry for anyone who thinks what they think is right should be some universal law."

"What does your dad say?"

"He and I are on the same page there. So's the rest of the family. Mom's our pacifist." He smiles.

A whoop of laughter sounds from the basketball court. I look over to see some boy grab some girl around the waist, whirling her around, then lowering her and clenching her to him.

"Why aren't you down there?" I ask.

He looks at me a long time, again as though considering what to say. Finally: "You tell me, Samantha."

Then he stands up, stretches, says good night, and climbs back down the trellis.

Chapter Four

In the morning light, brushing my teeth, doing my same old morning routine, looking at my same old face in the mirror—blond hair, blue eyes, freckles, nothing special—it's easy to believe that it was a dream that I sat out in the darkness in my nightgown talking feelings with a stranger—a Garrett, no less.

During breakfast, I ask Mom where she met Clay Tucker, which gets me nowhere as she, preoccupied with vacuuming her way out the door, answers only, "At a political event."

Since that's pretty much all she goes to anymore, it hardly narrows things down.

I corner Tracy in the kitchen as she applies waterproof mascara in the mirror over our wet bar, prepping for a day at the beach with Flip, and tell her all about last night. Except the Jase-on-the-roof part.

"What's the big deal?" she responds, leaning closer to her reflection. "Mom's finally found someone who turns her on. If he can help the campaign, so much the better. You know how wiggy she already is about November." She slides her mascara'ed eyes to mine. "Is this all about you and your fear of intimacy?"

I hate it when Tracy pulls that self-help, psychoanalytic garbage on me. Ever since her rebellious phase resulted in a year of therapy, she feels qualified to hang out her own shingle.

"No, it's about Mom," I insist. "She wasn't herself. If you'd been here, you'd have seen."

Tracy throws open her hands, the gesture taking in our completely updated kitchen, connected to our massive living room and the vast foyer. They're all too big for three people, too grand, and make God knows what kind of statement. Our house is probably three times the size of the Garretts'. And there are *ten* of them. "Why would I be here?" she asks. "What is there for any of us *here*?"

I want to say "*I'm* here." But I see her point. Our house contains all that's high-end and high-tech and shiny clean. And three people who would rather be somewhere else.

Mom likes routines. This means we have certain meals on certain nights—soup and salad on Monday, pasta on Tuesday, steak on Wednesday—you get the idea. She keeps charts of our school activities on the wall, even if she doesn't actually have time to attend them, and makes sure we don't have too much unaccounted-for time during the summer. Some of her routines have fallen by the wayside since she got elected. Some have been amped up. Friday dinners at the Stony Bay Bath and Tennis Club remain sacrosanct.

The Stony Bay Bath and Tennis Club is the kind of building everyone in town would think was tacky if "everyone" didn't want to belong to it. It was built fifteen years ago but looks like a Tudor castle. It's in the hills above town, so there's a great view of the river and the sound from both the Olympic and the

Lagoon pools. Mom loves the B&T. She's even on the board of directors. Which means that, thanks to swim team, I was roped into lifeguarding there last summer and am signed up again this year, twice a week starting next Monday. That's two whole days at the B&T, plus Friday dinners.

And so, because today *is* a Friday, here we all are, Tracy, Flip, and me, walking through the imposing oak doors behind Mom. Despite Tracy and Flip's eternal quest for the gold in the PDA Olympics, Mom loves Flip. Maybe it's because his dad runs the biggest business in Stony Bay. For whatever reason, since Flip and Tracy started dating six months ago, he always gets to come along for Friday night hornpipe dinner. Lucky guy.

We have our usual table, underneath a gigantic painting of a whaling ship surrounded by enormous whales, stabbed by harpoons but still able to chomp on a few unlucky sailors.

"We need to outline our summer plans," Mom says when the bread basket comes. "Get a handle on it all."

"Moth-er! We've been through this. I'm going to the Vineyard. Flip has a sweet job teaching tennis for a bunch of families, and I've got a house with my friends, and I'm gonna waitress at the Salt Air Smithy. The rental starts up this week. It's all planned."

Mom slides her cloth napkin off her plate and unfolds it. "You've broached this, Tracy, yes. But I haven't agreed to it."

"This is my summer to have fun. I've earned that," Tracy says, leaning over her plate for her water glass. "Right, Flip?"

Flip has wisely attacked the bread basket, slathering his roll with maple butter, and can't answer.

"I don't need to be accountable to colleges anymore. I'm in at Middlebury. I don't need to prove a thing."

"Working hard and doing well are only about proving something?" Mom arches her eyebrows.

"Flip?" Tracy says again. He's still finding his roll fascinating, adding even more butter as he continues to chew.

Mom focuses her attention on me. "So, Samantha. I want to be sure you're all set for the summer. Your Breakfast Ahoy job is how many mornings a week?" She gives the waiter pouring our ice water her charm-the-public smile.

"Three, Mom."

"Then there are the two days of lifeguarding." A little crease crimps her forehead. "That leaves you three afternoons free. Plus the weekends. Hmm." I watch her split a Parker House roll and butter it, knowing she won't eat it. It's just something she does to concentrate.

"Mom! Samantha's seventeen! God!" Tracy says. "Let her have some free time."

As she's saying this, a shadow falls on the table and we all look up. It's Clay Tucker.

"Grace"—he kisses one cheek, the other, then pulls out the chair next to Mom, flipping it around to straddle it—"and the rest of your lovely family. I didn't realize you had a son."

Tracy and Mom hasten to correct this misapprehension as the waiter arrives with the menu. Kind of unnecessary to even offer one, since the B&T has had the same Friday night prix fixe dinner menu since dinosaurs roamed the earth in madras and boat shoes.

"I was just saying to Tracy that she should choose something more goal-oriented for the summer," Mom says, handing her buttered roll to Clay. "Something more directed than having fun on the Vineyard."

He drapes his arms over the back of the chair and looks at Tracy, head cocked. "I think a nice summer away from home might be just the ticket for your Tracy, Grace—good prep for going away to college. And it gives *you* more room to focus on the campaign."

Mom scans his face for a moment, then appears to find some invisible signal there. "Well, then." She concedes, "Maybe I've been too hasty, Tracy. If you can give me the names, numbers, and addresses of these girls you're sharing a house with, and your hours at work."

"Gracie." Clay Tucker chuckles, voice low and amused. "This is parenthood. Not politics. We don't need the street addresses."

Mom smiles at him, a flush fanning over her cheekbones. "You're right. Here I am, getting all het up about the wrong things."

Het up? Since when does my mother use a phrase like that? Before my eyes, she's turning into Scarlett O'Hara. Is *this* going to help her win in Connecticut?

I slide my phone out of my pocket under the table and text Nan: Mom kidnapped by aliens. Pleez advise.

Guess what? Nan types back, ignoring this. I won the Laslo for Literature prize! I get my essay on Huck Finn and Holden Caulfield into the CT State Lit for High School Students Journal!!!!! Daniel got his essay in last year and he says it totally helped him ace MIT!!! Columbia, here I come!

I remember that essay. Nan sweated over it, and I thought

21

the topic was such a strange choice because I know she hates *Catcher in the Rye*—"All that swearing. And he's crazy."

Gr8t! I respond as Mom reaches out for my phone, snapping it shut and tucking it into her purse.

"Samantha, Mary Mason called me today about Tim." She takes a deliberate sip of water and glances at me, eyebrows lifted again.

This can't be good. "About Tim" is always code for "disaster" these days.

"She wants me to pull some strings to get him a lifeguard job here. Apparently, the job at Hot Dog Haven didn't work out."

Right. Because if you have trouble putting ketchup and mustard on a hot dog, you should totally move on to saving lives.

"The other lifeguard job is available at the club now that they're opening the Lagoon pool. What do you think?"

Uh, catastrophe? Tim and lifesaving are not exactly a natural combo. I know he can swim well—he was on the team at Hodges before he got expelled—but . . .

"What?" she asks impatiently as I worry my lip between my teeth.

When I'm lifeguarding, I barely take my eyes off the pool for a second. I imagine Tim sitting in that lifeguard chair and wince. But I've been fudging what he's up to—to his parents, to my mom for years now. . . . "Mom, he's kind of—distracted these days. I don't think—"

"I know." Her voice is impatient. "That's the point, Samantha—why something like this would be good for him. He'd need to focus, get out in the sun and the fresh air. Above all, it will look good on his college applications. I'm going to sponsor him." She reaches for her own cell, giving me her end-of-conversation nod.

"So," Clay says, smiling at me, Tracy, and Flip. "You guys mind if your mom and I talk shop?"

"Talk away," Tracy says airily.

Clay plunges right in. "I've been looking at this guy's specs, this Ben Christopher you're running against this time, Grace. And here's what I'm thinking: You need to be more relatable."

Is that a word?

Mom squints at him as though he's speaking a foreign language, so maybe not.

"Ben Christopher." Clay outlines: "Grew up in Bridgeport, poor family, prep school on an ABC scholarship, built his own company manufacturing solar panels, getting the green vote there." He pauses to butter the other half of Mom's roll and takes a big bite. "He's got that man-of-the-people thing going on. You, honey, can seem a little stiff. Chilly." Another bite of roll, more chewing. "*I* know differently, but . . ."

Ew. I glance over at Tracy, expecting her to be as grossed out by this as I am, but she's preoccupied by Flip, intertwining their hands.

"What do I do, then?" A furrow forms between Mom's eyebrows. I've never heard her ask anyone for advice. She doesn't even find it easy to ask for directions when we're completely lost.

"Relax." Clay puts his hand on her forearm, squeezes it. "We just show what's there. The softer side of Grace."

Sounds like a laundry detergent ad.

He shoves his hand into his pocket and extracts something,

holding it up for us to see. One of Mom's old campaign flyers. "See, here's what I'm talkin' about. Your campaign slogan last time. *Grace Reed: Working for the Common Weal.* That's just awful, darlin'."

Mom says defensively, "I *did* win, Clay." I'm a little impressed that he's being so blunt with her. Tracy and I came in for our fair share of teasing at school about that campaign slogan.

"You did"—he gives her a swift grin—"which is a tribute to your charm and skill. But 'weal'? Gimme a break. Am I right, girls? Flip?" Flip grunts around his third bread roll, casting a longing glance toward the door. I don't blame him for wanting to escape. "The last person who used that in a political campaign was John Adams. Or maybe Alexander Hamilton. Like I say, you need to be more relatable, be who people are looking for. More families, young families, are moving into our state all the time. That's your hidden treasure. You're not going to get the common-man vote. Ben Christopher's got that locked. So here's my idea: *Grace Reed works hard for your family because family is her focus.* What do you think?"

At this point the waiter arrives with our appetizers. He doesn't miss a beat about Clay being at the table, making me wonder if this was planned all along.

"My, this looks mighty good," Clay Tucker says as the waiter tucks a big bowl of chowder in front of him. "Now, some would say we Southerners wouldn't know how to appreciate this kind of thing. But I like to appreciate what's in front of me. And this"—he tips his spoon at my mother, flashing a grin at the rest of us—"is delicious."

I get the feeling I'll be seeing a lot of Clay Tucker.

Chapter Five

When I get home from work the next day, sticky from walking back in the summer heat, my eyes immediately turn to the Garretts'. The house seems unusually quiet. I stand there looking, then see Jase in the driveway, lying on his back, doing some kind of work on a huge black-and-silver motorcycle.

I want to say right here that I am by no means the kind of girl who finds motorcycles and leather jackets appealing. In the least. Michael Kristoff, with his dark turtlenecks and moody poetry, was as close as I've gotten to liking a "bad boy," and he was enough to put me off them for life. We dated almost all spring, till I realized he was less a tortured artist than just a torture. That said, without planning, I walk right to the end of our yard, around my mother's tall "good neighbor" fence—the six-foot stockade she installed a few months after the Garretts moved in—and up the driveway.

"Hi there," I say. *Brilliant opener, Samantha.*

Jase props himself up on an elbow, looking at me for a minute without saying anything. His face gets an unreadable expression, and I wish I could take back walking over.

Then he observes, "I'm guessing that's a uniform."

Crap. I'd forgotten I was still wearing it. I look down at

myself, in my short blue skirt, puffy white sailor blouse, and jaunty red neck scarf.

"Bingo." I'm completely embarrassed.

He nods, then smiles broadly at me. "It didn't quite say *Samantha Reed* to me somehow. Where on earth do you work?" He clears his throat. "And why there?"

"Breakfast Ahoy. Near the dock. I like to keep busy."

"The uniform?"

"My boss designed it."

Jase scrutinizes me in silence for a minute or two, then says, "He must have a rich fantasy life."

I don't know how to respond to this, so I pull one of Tracy's nonchalant moves and shrug.

"It pays well?" Jase asks, reaching for a wrench.

"Best tips in town."

"I'll bet."

I have no clue why I'm having this conversation. And no idea how to continue it. He's concentrating on unscrewing something or unwrenching something or whatever you call it. So I ask, "Is this your motorcycle?"

"My brother Joel's." He stops working and sits up, as though it would be impolite to continue if we're actually carrying on a conversation. "He likes to cultivate that whole 'born to be wild' outlaw image. Prefers it to the jock one, although he is, in fact, a jock. Says he winds up with smarter girls that way."

I nod, as if I'd know. "Does he?"

"I'm not sure." Jase's forehead creases. "The image-cultivation thing has always seemed kind of fake-o and manipulative to me."

"So, you don't have some persona?" I sit down in the grass next to the driveway.

"Nope. What you see is what you get." He grins at me again.

What I see, frankly, up close and in daylight, is pretty nice. In addition to the sun-streaked, wavy chestnut hair and even white teeth, Jase Garrett has green eyes, and one of those quirky mouths that look like they are always about to smile. Plus this steady-on, I-have-no-problem-looking-you-in-the-eye gaze. *Oh my*.

I glance around, try to think of something to say. Finally: "Pretty quiet around here today."

"I'm babysitting."

I look around again. "Where's the baby? In the toolbox?"

He tips his head at me, acknowledging the joke. "Naptime," he explains. "George and Patsy. Mom's grocery shopping. It takes her *hours*."

"I'll bet." Prying my eyes from his face, I notice his T-shirt is sticky with sweat at the collar and under the arms.

"Are you thirsty?" I ask.

Broad smile. "I am. But I'm not about to take my life in my hands and ask you to get me something to drink. I know your mom's new boyfriend is a marked man for ordering you to serve."

"I'm thirsty too. And hot. My mom makes good lemonade." I stand up and start backing away.

"Samantha."

"Uh-huh."

"Come back, okay?"

27

I look at him a second, nod, then go into the house, shower, thereby discovering that Tracy's perfidiously used up all my conditioner again, change into shorts and a tank top, and come back with two huge plastic cups full of lemonade and clinking ice.

When I walk up the driveway, Jase has his back to me, doing something to one of the wheels, but he turns as my flip-flops slap close.

I hand him the lemonade. He looks at it the way I'm realizing Jase Garrett looks at everything—carefully, noticing.

"Wow. She even freezes little pieces of lemon peel and mint in the ice cubes. And makes *them* out of lemonade."

"She's kind of a perfectionist. Watching her make this is like science lab."

He drains the entire thing in one gulp, then reaches for the other cup.

"That's mine," I say.

"Oh, jeez. Of course. Sorry. I *am* thirsty."

I extend my arm with the lemonade. "You can have it. There's always more."

He shakes his head. "I would never deprive you."

I feel my stomach do that weird little flip-flop thing you hear about. *Not good.* This is our second conversation. *Not good at all, Samantha.*

Just then I hear the roar of a car pulling into our driveway. "Yo, Samantha!"

It's Flip. He cuts the engine, then strides over to us.

"Hey, Flip," Jase calls.

"You know him?"

"He dated my sister Alice last year."

Flip immediately says to me, "Don't tell Tracy."

Jase glances at me for clarification.

"My sister's very possessive," I explain.

"Hugely," Flip adds.

"Resents her boyfriends' past girlfriends," I say.

"Big-time," agrees Flip.

"Niiice," Jase says.

Flip looks defensive. "But she *is* loyal. No sleeping with my tennis partner."

Jase winces. "You knew what you were getting into with Alice, man."

I glance back and forth between them.

Flip says, "So . . . I didn't know you two knew each other."

"We don't," I say, at the same time Jase answers, "Yup."

"Okay. Whatever." Flip waves his hands, clearly uninterested. "So where's Trace?"

"I'm supposed to tell you she's busy all day," I admit. My sister: master of playing hard to get. Even when she's already gotten.

"Cool. So where is she really?"

"Stony Bay Beach."

"I'm there." Flip turns to go.

"Bring her *People* magazine and a coconut FrozFruit," I call after him. "Then you're golden."

When I turn back to Jase, he's again beaming at me. "You're nice." He sounds pleased, as if he hadn't expected this aspect of my personality.

"Not really. Better for me if she's happy. Then she borrows fewer of my clothes. You know sisters."

"Yup. But mine don't borrow my clothes."

Abruptly I hear a loud screaming, wailing, banshee-like sound. I jump, wide-eyed.

Jase points to the baby monitor plugged in by the garage door. "George." He starts heading into the house, then turns back, gesturing me to follow.

Just like that, I'm going into the Garretts', after all these years.

Thank God Mom works late.

The first thing that hits me is the color. Our kitchen's white and silver-gray everywhere—the walls, the granite counter-tops, the Sub-Zero, the Bosch dishwasher. The Garretts' walls are sunny yellow. The curtains are that same yellow with green leaves on them. But everything else is a riot of different colors. The fridge is covered with paintings and drawings, with more taped on the walls. Cans of Play-Doh and stuffed animals and boxes of cereal clutter the green Formica counters. Dishes teeter high in the sink. There's a table big enough for all the Garretts to eat at, but not big enough to contain the piles of newspapers and magazines and socks and snack wrappers and swim goggles, half-eaten apples and banana peels.

George meets us before we're halfway through the kitchen. He's holding a large plastic triceratops, wearing nothing but a shirt that says *Brooklyn Botanical Gardens*. That's to say, no pants, no underwear.

"Whoa, buddy." Jase bends down, indicating the naked half of his brother with a wave of his hand. "What happened there?"

George, still tear-streaked but no longer screaming, takes a deep breath. He has wavy brown hair too, but the big eyes swimming with tears are blue. "I dreamed about black holes."

"Gotcha." Jase nods, straightening up. "Is the whole bed wet?"

George nods guiltily, then peeps under spiky damp eyelashes at me. "Who's that?"

"The girl next door. Samantha. She probably knows all about black holes."

George eyes me suspiciously. "Do you?"

"Well," I say, "I, um, know that they're stars that used up all their fuel and then collapsed inward, due to the pull of their own gravity, and, um, that once anything falls into them it disappears from the visible universe."

George starts screaming again.

Jase scoops him up, bare bottom and all. "She also knows that there are none anywhere near Connecticut. Don't you, Samantha?"

I feel horrible. "Not even in our universe," I tell him hastily, although I'm pretty sure there's one in the Milky Way.

"There's one in the Milky Way," sobs George.

"But that's nowhere near Stony Bay." Reaching out to pat him on the back, I inadvertently touch Jase's hand, as he's doing the same. I snatch mine away.

"So you're completely safe, buddy."

George's cries descend into hiccups, then depart altogether under the influence of a lime Popsicle.

"I'm so, so sorry," I whisper to Jase, declining the remaining Popsicle in the box, orange. *Does anyone ever take the orange ones?*

"How could you know?" he whispers back. "And how could *I* know you were an astrophysicist?"

"I went through a big stargazing phase." My face heats, thinking of all the nights I sat on the roof, watching the stars . . . and the Garretts.

He raises an eyebrow at me, as though unclear why this would be embarrassing. The worst thing about being a blonde is that your entire body blushes—ears, throat, everything. Impossible to overlook.

There's another wail from upstairs.

"That'll be Patsy." Jase starts for the stairs. "Wait here."

"I'd better get home," I say, although there's really no reason to do that.

"No. Stay. I'll just be a sec."

I'm left with George. He sucks on his Popsicle meditatively for a few minutes, then asks, "Did you know that in space it's very, very cold? And there's no oxygen? And if an astronaut fell out of a shuttle without his suit he'd die right away?"

I'm a fast learner. "But that would never happen. Because astronauts are really, really careful."

George gives me a smile, the same dazzling sweet smile as his big brother, although, at this point, with green teeth. "I might marry you," he allows. "Do you want a big family?"

I start to cough and feel a hand pat my back.

"George, it's usually better to discuss this kind of thing with your pants on." Jase drops boxer shorts at George's feet, then sets Patsy on the ground next to him.

She's wearing a pink sunsuit and has one of those little ponytails that make one sprout of hair stick straight up on top, all chubby arms and bowed legs. She's, what, one now?

"Dat?" she demands, pointing to me a bit belligerently.

"Dat is Samantha," Jase says. "Apparently soon to be your sister-in-law." He cocks an eyebrow. "You and George move fast."

"We talked astronauts," I explain, just as the door opens and in comes Mrs. Garrett, staggering under the weight of about fifty grocery bags.

"Gotcha." He winks, then turns to his mother. "Hey, Mom."

"Hi, honey. How were they?" She's completely focused on her older son and doesn't seem to notice me.

"Reasonable," Jase tells her. "We need to change George's sheets, though." He takes a few of the plastic bags, setting them down on the floor by the fridge.

She narrows her eyes at him. They're green like Jase's. She's pretty, for a mom, with this open, friendly face, crinkles at the corners of her eyes as though she smiles a lot, the family olive skin, curly brown hair. "What naptime story did you read him?"

"*Mom. Curious George.* I edited it too. There was a little hot-air balloon incident I thought might be problematic." Then he turns to me. "Oh, sorry. Samantha, this is my mom. Mom, Samantha Reed. From next door."

She gives me a big smile. "I didn't even see you standing there. How I overlooked such a pretty girl, I don't know. I do like the shimmery lip gloss."

"Mom." Jase sounds a little embarrassed.

She turns back to him. "This is just the first wave. Can you get the other bags?"

While Jase brings in a seemingly endless series of groceries, Mrs. Garrett chats away to me as though we've always known each other. It's so weird sitting there in the kitchen with this woman I've seen from a distance for ten years. Like finding yourself in an elevator with a celebrity. I repress the urge to say "I'm a huge fan."

I help her put away the groceries, which she manages to do while breast-feeding. My mother would die. I try to pretend I'm used to viewing this kind of thing all the time.

An hour at the Garretts' and I've already seen one of them half-naked, and quite a lot of Mrs. Garrett's breast. All I need now is for Jase to take off his shirt.

Fortunately for my equilibrium, he doesn't, although he does announce, after carrying in all the bags, that he needs a shower, beckons me to follow, and marches upstairs.

I do follow. This is the crazy part. I don't even know him. I don't know what kind of person he is at all. Though I figure that if his normal-looking mother lets him take a girl up to his room, he's not going to be a mad rapist. Still, what would Mom think now?

Walking into Jase's room is like walking into . . . well, I'm not sure . . . A forest? A bird sanctuary? One of those tropical habitats they have at zoos? It's filled with plants, really tall ones and hanging ones and succulents and cacti. There are three parakeets in a cage and a huge, hostile-looking cockatoo in another. Everywhere I look, there are other creatures. A tortoise in an enclosure beside the bureau. A bunch of gerbils in another cage. A terrarium with some sort of lizardy-looking thing. A ferret in a little hammock in another cage. A gray-and-black furry indistinguishable rodent-like beast. And finally, on Jase's neatly made bed, an enormous white cat so fat it looks like a balloon with tiny furry appendages.

"Mazda." Jase beckons me to sit in a chair by the bed. When I do, Mazda jumps into my lap and commences shedding madly, trying to nurse on my shorts, and making low rumbling sounds.

"Friendly."

"Understatement. Weaned too early," Jase says. "I'm going to take that shower. Make yourself at home."

Right. In his room. No problem.

I did on occasion visit Michael's room, but usually in the dark, where he recited gloomy poetry he'd memorized. And it took a lot longer than two conversations to get me there. I briefly dated this guy Charley Tyler last fall too, until we realized that my liking his dimples and him liking my blond hair, or, let's face it, my boobs, wasn't enough basis for a relationship. He never got me into his room. Maybe Jase Garrett is some sort of snake charmer. That would explain the animals. I look around again. Oh God, there *is* a snake. One of those orange, white, and black scary-looking ones that I know are harmless but completely freak me out anyway.

The door opens, but it's not Jase. It's George, now wearing boxer shorts but no shirt. He comes over and plunks down on the bed, looking at me somberly. "Did you know that the space shuttle *Challenger* blew up?"

I nod. "A long time ago. They have perfected things much more now."

"I'd be ground crew at NASA. Not on the shuttle. I don't want to die ever."

I find myself wanting to hug him. "Me neither, George."

"Is Jase already going to marry you?"

35

I start coughing again. "Uh. No. No, George. I'm only seventeen." As if that's the only reason we aren't engaged.

"I'm this many," George holds up four slightly grubby fingers. "But Jase is seventeen and a half. You could. Then you could live in here with him. And have a big family."

Jase strides back into the room, of course, midway through this proposition. "George. Beat it. Discovery Channel is on."

George backs out of the room, but not before saying, "His bed's really comfortable. And he never pees in it."

The door closes and we both start laughing.

"Oh Jesus." Jase, now clad in a different green T-shirt and pair of navy running shorts, sits down on the bed. His hair is wavier when wet, and little drops of water drip onto his shoulders.

"It's okay. I love him," I say. "I think I *will* marry him."

"You might want to think about that. Or at least be really careful about the bedtime reading."

He smiles lazily at me.

I need to get out of this guy's room. Fast. I stand up, start to cross the room, then notice a picture of a girl stuck on the mirror over the bureau. I walk closer to take a look. She has curly black hair in a ponytail and a serious expression. She's also quite pretty. "Who's this?"

"My ex-girlfriend. Lindy. She had the sticker made at the mall. Now I can't get it off."

"Why ex?" Why am I asking this?

"She got to be too dangerous," Jase says. "You know, now that I think of it, I guess I could put another sticker on top of it."

"You could." I lean closer to the mirror, examining her perfect features. "Define *dangerous*."

"She shoplifted. A lot. And she only ever wanted to go to the mall on dates. Hard not to look like an accomplice. Not my favorite way to spend an evening, doing time, waiting to get bailed out."

"My sister shoplifted too," I say, as though this is some nifty thing we have in common.

"Ever take you along?"

"No, thank God. I'd die if I got in trouble."

Jase looks at me intently, as though what I've said is profound. "No, you wouldn't, Samantha. You wouldn't die. You'd just be in trouble and then you'd move on."

He's standing behind me, too close again. He smells like minty shampoo and clean, clean skin. Apparently any distance at all is too close.

"Yeah, well, I do have to move on. Home. I have stuff to do."

"You sure?"

I nod vigorously. Just as we get to the kitchen, the screen door slams and Mr. Garrett comes in, followed by a small boy. Small, but bigger than George. Duff? Harry?

Like everyone else in the family up till now, I've only seen Jase's father from a distance. Close up, he looks younger, taller, with the kind of charisma that makes the room feel full just because he's in it. His hair's the same wavy deep brown as Jase's, but shot with gray rather than blond streaks. George runs over and attaches himself to his dad's leg. Mrs. Garrett steps back from the sink to smile at him. She lights up the

37

way I've seen girls at school do, sighting their crushes across crowded rooms.

"Jack! You're home early."

"We hit the three-hour mark at the store with no one coming in." Mr. Garrett brushes a strand of her hair away from her face, tucking it behind her ear. "I decided my time would be better spent getting in some more training with Jase, so I scooped up Harry from his playdate and came on home."

"I get to run the stopwatch! I get to run the stopwatch!" Harry shouts.

"My turn! Daddy! It's *my* turn!" George's face crumples.

"You can't even read the numbers," Harry says. "No matter how fast or slow he runs, you always say it's been eleventeen minutes. It's *my* turn."

"I brought home an extra stopwatch from the store," Mr. Garrett says. "You up for it, Jason?"

"He has Samantha over—" Mrs. Garrett begins, but I interrupt.

"I was just leaving."

Mr. Garrett turns to me. "Well, hello, Samantha." His big hand envelops mine and he looks at me intently, then grins. "So you're the mysterious girl next door."

I glance quickly at Jase, but his face is inscrutable. "I am from next door. But no real mystery going on there."

"Well, it's good to catch a closer look. I didn't know Jase had—"

"I'm going to walk her out, Dad. Then I'll get ready to lift— that's what I'm doing first today, right?"

As we head out the kitchen door, Mrs. Garrett urges me to visit anytime.

"I'm glad you came over," Jase says when we reach the end of the driveway. "Sorry again about George."

"I like George. What are you training for?"

"Oh, uh, football season. I'm cornerback this year. Maybe a shot at a scholarship, which, gotta say, would be a good thing."

I stand there in the heat, squinting into the sun, wondering what to say next, how to make a good exit, or any exit, and why I'm bothering to make one when Mom won't be home for hours. I take a step backward, land on a plastic shovel, stumble.

Jase's hand shoots out. "Easy there."

"Uh. Right. Oopsie. Well. Good-bye." After giving a quick, agitated wave, I hurry home.

Oopsie?

God, Samantha.

Chapter Six

Flip and Tracy come home, sunburned and rumpled, with fried clams and Birch beer and foot-long hot dogs from the Clam Shack. They lay it all out on the kitchen island, stopping to grab each other around the waist, pinch each other's asses, kiss each other's ears.

I wish I'd stayed longer at the Garretts'. *Why didn't I?*

Tim must still have custody of Nan's cell, because this is what I get when I call:

"Listen, Heidi, it's really not a good idea to for us to hang out together again."

"It's Samantha. Where's Nan?"

"Oh, for Christ's sake. You do know we're not *Siamese* twins, right? Why do you keep asking *me* this shit?"

"Oh, I don't know. Maybe because you keep answering her cell. Is she home?"

"I think so. Probably. Or not," Tim says.

I hang up. The landline is busy and the Masons don't have call waiting ("Just an electronic way to be rude," according to Mrs. Mason), so I decide to bike to Nan's house.

Tracy and Flip have moved to the living room couch, and there's much giggling and murmuring. As I get to the hallway, I hear Flip whisper, all urgent, "Oh baby, what you do to me." *Gag*.

"You make me feel so good *insiiiiide*," I sing back.

"Beat it," calls Tracy.

It's high tide, and hot, which means the salty smell of the sound is especially strong, nearly overcoming the marshy scent of the river. The two sides of town. I love them both. I love how you can tell the season and the time of day just by closing your eyes and taking a deep breath. I shut my eyes now, inhaling the thick warm air, then hear a startled screech and look just in time to swerve around a woman wearing a pink visor and socks under her sandals. Stony Bay's on a little peninsula at the mouth of the Connecticut River. We have a wide harbor, so tourists like our town. It's three times as crowded in the summer, so I guess I should know better than to bike with my eyes closed.

Nan opens the door when I knock, house phone to her ear. She smiles, then puts her index finger to her lips, jerking her chin toward the living room as she says into the phone, "Well, you *are* my first choice, so I really want to get a jump on the application."

I always have the same feeling when I walk through the Masons' front door. There are happy-faced Hummel figurines all over the place, and little wall plaques with Irish blessings on them, and doilies sprinkled on top of all the armchairs and even the television. When you go to the bathroom, the toilet paper is hidden underneath the puffy pink crocheted hoop-skirt of a blank-eyed doll.

No books in the bookshelves, just more figurines and photographs of Nan and Tim, very twinnish, in their early years. I study them for the millionth time as Nan spells out her address. Baby Nan and Tim dressed as Santa and Mrs. Claus. Toddler Nan and Tim, fluffy-haired and round-eyed, as chicks for Easter. Preschool Nan and Tim in a dirndl and lederhosen. The pictures stop abruptly when they turn about eight. If I remember correctly, they were dressed as Uncle Sam and Betsy Ross for the Fourth of July that year, and Tim bit the photographer.

In the pictures they look much more alike than they do now. They're both redheaded and freckled. But, because life is unfair, Nan's hair is a pale, washed-out strawberry blond, and she has freckles everywhere and blond eyelashes. Tim's got only a few stipples of freckles across his nose, and his brows and lashes are dark, while his hair is a deep russet. He'd be a knockout, if he weren't always so out of it.

"I'm on hold with Columbia—getting my application," Nan whispers. "I'm glad you came by. I've been totally sidetracked."

"I called your cell but got Tim, and he wouldn't look for you."

"That's where it is! God. He's used up all his minutes and now he's after mine. I'm going to kill him."

"Couldn't you just go to Columbia's website and order the application?" I whisper, even though I know the answer. Nan's hopeless with her computer—she keeps so many windows open at the same time and never shuts them—her laptop's constantly crashing.

"My laptop's in surgery with Macho Mitch again." Mitch is the incredibly good-looking, if vaguely sinister, computer repair guy who makes house calls on Nan's PC. Nan thinks he looks like Steve McQueen, her idol. I think he looks sulky and annoyed because he's constantly fixing the same problems.

"Thanks—yes, and when will this be sent out?" Nan says into the phone just as Tim wanders into the room, hair sticking up in all directions, wearing a ratty pair of tartan flannel pj bottoms and an Ellery Prep Lacrosse T-shirt. He doesn't look at us, just roams over to the Hummel Noah's Ark display on the window seat and rearranges the figures in obscene combinations.

He's just finished putting Mrs. Noah and a camel into a compromising and anatomically difficult position when Nan hangs up.

"I kept meaning to call you," she says. "When do you start lifeguarding? I'll be at the gift shop starting next week."

"Me too."

Tim yawns loudly, scratches his chest, and places a couple of monkeys and a rhino in an unlikely threesome. I can smell him from where I sit—weed and beer.

"You could at least say hi to Samantha, Timmy."

"Heyyyyy kid. I feel as if we spoke only a few brief moments ago. Oh, *that's* right. We did. Sorry. Don't know where the fuck my manners are. They haven't been the same since they shrunk at the dry cleaner. Want some?" He pulls a vial of Visine from his back pocket and offers it to me.

"Thanks, no, I'm trying to cut down," I say. Tim's gray eyes are in need of the Visine. I hate it, watching someone smart and perceptive spend all their time getting blurry and stupid. He collapses on his back on the couch with a groan, draping one hand over his eyes. It's hard to remember what he was like before he started auditioning for Betty Ford.

When we were little, our families spent a lot of summer

weekends together at Stony Bay Beach. Back then, I was actually closer to Tim than Nan. Nan and Tracy would read and sunbathe, dabble their toes in the water, but Tim was never afraid to wade out and pull me with him into the biggest waves. He was also the one who discovered the riptide in the creek, the one that zoomed you down and whipped you out to sea.

"So, babe—gettin' any these days?" He wiggles his eyebrows at me from his supine position. "Charley was going nuts because you wouldn't go for *his* nuts, if ya know what I mean."

"Hilarious, Timmy. You can stop talking now," Nan says.

"No, really—it's a good thing you broke up with Charley, Samantha. He was an asshole. I'm not friends with him anymore either because, strangely enough, he thought *I* was the asshole."

"Hard to imagine," Nan says. "Timmy—just go to bed. Mommy will be home soon and she's not going to keep buying that you took too much Benadryl because of your allergies. She knows you don't have allergies."

"I do so," Tim says loudly, all out-of-proportion indignant. He pulls a joint out of the front pocket of his shirt and waves it at her triumphantly. "I'm allergic to *weeds*." Then he bursts out laughing. Nan and I exchange a look. Tim is usually stoned and drunk. But there's a nervous, jacked-up energy about him now that hints at harder stuff.

"Let's get out of here," I say. "Walk downtown."

She nods. "How about Doane's? I need some chocolate malt ice cream." She grabs her purse from a puffy flowered chair and leans over, giving Tim, who is still chuckling, a shake. "Go upstairs," she says. "Now. Before you fall asleep."

"I'm not gonna fall asleep, sis. I'm just restin' my eyes," Tim mumbles.

Nan nudges his shoulder again. As she moves away, he grabs her purse so she jerks to a stop.

"Nano. Sis. Nan, kid, I need something," he says urgently, his face all desperate.

She raises a pale eyebrow at him.

"A shitload of jelly beans from Doane's, okay? But no green ones. They scare me."

Chapter Seven

On the porch, I grab Nan's hand, squeeze it.

"I know!" she says. "It's so much worse since he got kicked out of Ellery. He spends all day like this, and God knows what he does at night. My parents are completely and totally without a clue. Mommy buys all his lies—'Oh, that's catnip in that bag, Ma. Oh, *those* pills? Aspirin. That white stuff? Just salt.' Then she busts him for swearing—by making him put money in the swear box. He just swipes more from my purse. And Daddy? Well." She shrugs.

Mrs. Mason is the most relentlessly cheerful person I've ever met. All her sentences begin with exclamations: So! My! Well! Goodness! By contrast, Mr. Mason rarely says anything at all. When we were little, I had this windup toy, a plastic chick from an Easter basket—and I thought of him sort of like that. He remained virtually unmoving in a plaid armchair from the moment he got home till dinner, then resumed his position after dinner until bedtime, wound up only long enough to get to and from work and to and from the table.

"He's even got Tim's pot plant in with his own plants, giving it Miracle-Gro. What kind of man was young in the

46

eighties and doesn't recognize marijuana?" She's laughing, but her voice has a hysterical note. "It's like Tim's drowning and they're worried about the color of his swimsuit."

"And you can't tell them?" I ask, not for the first or second or hundredth time. Although who am I to talk? I didn't exactly 'fess up to Mom about Tim either.

Nan laughs but doesn't really answer. "This morning when I came down to breakfast, Daddy was saying maybe Tim needed military school to make a man out of him. Or a stint in the army. Can you imagine? You just know he'd be that soldier who got his superior officers so angry they'd stick him in some horrible underground cave and forget he existed. Or ticked off the campus bully and got himself beaten to death. Or got into trouble with some drill sergeant's wife and then shot in the back by her enraged husband."

"Good thing you haven't spent much time worrying about the possibilities," I say.

Nan loops an arm around my shoulder. "I've missed you, Samantha. I'm sorry. I've been all caught up in Daniel—going to his graduation parties—just staying away from home, really."

"What's going on there?" I can tell she's dying to get into it, get away from the Tim drama.

"Daniel. . . ." She sighs. "Maybe I should stick to crushing on Macho Mitch and Steve McQueen. I can't figure out what's going on with him. He's all tense and wigged out about going to MIT, but you know how brilliant he is—and school doesn't start for three months anyway. I mean, it's June. Can't he just relax?"

"Right." I nudge her with my shoulder. "Because you know

47

all about that, girl who orders college catalogs the millisecond after junior year ends."

"That's why he and I are a perfect match, right?" she says with a little grimace. A breeze comes up as we turn down Main Street, shaking the leaves in the maples that line the road so they make a soft, sighing sound. The air smells lush and green, briny from the sound. As we near the Dark and Stormy, the local dive bar/hamburger joint, two figures emerge from the door, blinking a little in the bright sun. Clay. And a very pretty brunette woman in a designer suit. I stop, my attention caught, as he gives her a big smile, then leans forward to kiss her. On the lips. With a little back-rubbing thrown in.

I'd expected to see more of Clay Tucker, but not like this.

"What is it, Samantha?" Nan asks, pulling at my arm.

What's going on? It wasn't a French kiss, but it was definitely not a she's-my-sister kiss.

"That's my mom's new boyfriend." Now Clay squeezes the woman's shoulder and winks, still smiling.

"Your mom has a boyfriend? You're kidding. When did *that* happen?"

The woman laughs and brushes Clay's sleeve.

Nan glances at me, wincing.

"I don't know when they met. It seems sort of serious. I mean, it looked like it. On my mom's end."

Now the brunette, whom I notice is at least a decade younger than Mom, opens up a briefcase and hands Clay a manila folder. He tilts his head at her in a you're-the-best way.

"Is he married, do you know?" Nan asks in a hushed voice. It suddenly occurs to me that we're standing still on the side-

48

walk, quite obviously staring. Just then, Clay looks over and sights us. He waves at me, seemingly unabashed. *If you cheat on my mother,* I think, then let the thought trail off, because, in all honesty, what'll I do?

"She's probably just a friend," Nan offers, unconvincingly. "C'mon, let's get that ice cream." I give Clay one last look, hopefully conveying imminent harm to treasured body parts if he's cheating on my mom. Then I follow Nan. What else can I do?

I try to erase Clay from my mind, at least until I can get home and think. Nan doesn't bring it up again, thank God.

I'm relieved when we get to Doane's. It's in this little salt-box building near the pier, which divides the mouth of the river from the ocean. Doane's was the penny candy store back when there was such a thing as penny candy. Now its big draw is Vargas, the candy-corn-pecking chicken—a moth-eaten fake chicken with real feathers for which you have to pay a quarter to activate his frantic OCD pecking of ancient candy corn. For some reason, this is a big tourist draw, along with Doane's soft ice cream, taffy, and good view of the lighthouse.

Nan scrounges through her wallet. "Samantha! I had twenty dollars. Now I've got nothing! I'm going to kill my brother."

"Doesn't matter," I tell her, leafing a few bills from my pocket.

"I'll pay you back," Nan tells me, taking the cash.

"It's no problem, Nanny. So, you want the ice cream?"

"Eventually. So anyway, Daniel took me to New Haven to see a movie last night. I thought we had a great time, but he's only texted once today and all he said was 'LVYA' instead of spelling it all the way out. What do you think that means?"

Daniel's always been inscrutable to me. He's the kind of smart that makes you feel stupid.

"Maybe he was in a hurry?"

"With me? If you're going to take time, shouldn't it be with your girlfriend?" Nan's filling her plastic bag with root beer barrels and gummy bears and chocolate-covered malt balls. Sugar rush retail therapy.

I don't know quite what to say. Finally, without looking at her, I just blurt out what I've thought for a while. "Daniel seems like he always makes you nervous. Is that okay?"

Nan's now contemplating Vargas, who seems to be in the midst of an epileptic fit. He's no longer pecking the candy corn, just kind of throbbing back and forth. "I wouldn't know," she says finally. "Daniel's my first real boyfriend. You had Charley and Michael. And even Taylor Oliveira back in eighth grade."

"Taylor doesn't count. We kissed once."

"And he told everyone you'd gone all the way!" Nan says, as if this proves her point.

"Right, I'd forgotten that. What a prince. He was the love of my life, it's true. How was the movie with Daniel?"

Vargas twitches more and more slowly, then shudders to a stop. "The movie?" Nan says vaguely. "Oh, right—*The Sorrow and the Pity*. Well, it was fine—for a three-hour black-and-white movie about Nazis, but then afterward we went to this coffeehouse and there were some Yale grad students there. Daniel suddenly got completely pretentious and started using words like 'tautological' and 'subtext.'"

I laugh. Although it was Daniel's brains that drew Nan, his pompous streak is a recurring theme.

"I finally had to haul him out to the car and get him kissing me so he'd stop talking."

Before the word "kissing" is out of her mouth, I'm picturing Jase Garrett's lips. Nice lips. Full lower lip, but not pouty or sulky. I turn to look at Nan. She's bent over the jelly beans, her fine strawberry hair tucked behind one ear, a ragged fingernail in her mouth. Her nose is a little sunburned, peeling, her freckles darker than they were last week. I open my mouth to tell her *I met this boy* but can't quite say the words. Even Nan never knew I watched the Garretts. It isn't exactly that I kept it from her. I just never brought it up. Besides . . . *I met this boy?* That story could go anywhere. Or nowhere at all. I turn back to the candy.

"What do you think?" Nan asks. "Do we get Tim his jelly beans? You're the one with the cash."

"Yes, let's get 'em. But only the scary green ones."

Nan closes the top of her bag with a loud crumple. "Samantha? What are we going to do about him?"

I scoop a clattering cascade of green apple Jelly Bellys into the white paper bag and remember when we were seven. I got stung by a jellyfish. Tim cried because his mother, and mine, wouldn't let him pee on my leg, which he'd heard was an antidote to the sting. "But Ma, I have the power to save her!" he'd sobbed. That was a joke between us for years: *Don't forget I have the power to save you!* Now he can't even seem to save himself.

"Beyond hoping these are magic beans," I say, "I have no idea."

Chapter Eight

The next afternoon, I'm kicking off my work shoes on our porch, preparing to go in to change, when I hear Mrs. Garrett. "Samantha! Samantha, could you come here for a second?"

She's standing at the end of our driveway, holding Patsy. George is next to her, in only boxers. Farther up the driveway, Harry's lurking behind a wagon with one of those nozzles that attach to a garden hose in his hand, evidently playing sniper.

As I get up close, I see that she's again breast-feeding Patsy. She gives me her wide-open smile, and says, "Oh Samantha . . . I was just wondering. Jase was telling me how great you were with George . . . and I wondered if you ever—" She stops suddenly, looking more closely at me, her eyes widening.

I look down. *Oh. The uniform.* "It's my work outfit. My boss designed it." I don't know why I always add this, except to establish that otherwise there's no way in hell I'd be caught dead in a blue miniskirt and a middy shirt.

"A man, I assume," Mrs. Garrett says dryly.

I nod.

"Naturally. Anyway . . ." She begins talking in a rush. "I wondered if you might ever be interested in doing some babysitting? Jase didn't want me to ask you. He was afraid you'd think that he lured unsuspecting girls into our house so that I could exploit them for my own needs. Like some desperate mom version of white slavery."

I laugh. "I didn't think that."

"Of course you wouldn't." She grins at me again. "I know everyone must believe I do that, ask every girl I see if they babysit, but I don't. Very few people are good with George straight off, and Jase said you *got* him right away. I can use the older children, of course, but I hate making them feel as though I expect it. Alice, for example, always acts as though it's a huge burden." She's talking fast, as though she's nervous. "Jase never minds, but his job at the hardware store and his training take most of his time, so he's gone a lot, except one afternoon a week, and of course part of the weekend. Anyway, I only need a few hours here and there."

"It would be fine," I say. "I don't have much experience, but I learn fast, and I'd be happy to babysit." *As long as you don't tell my mother.*

Mrs. Garrett gives me a grateful look, then pulls Patsy off one breast and, after reaching up to unsnap something, moves her to the other. Patsy wails in protest. Mrs. Garrett rolls her eyes. "She only likes one side," she confides. "Very uncomfortable."

I nod again, though I have no idea why that would be. Thanks to my mother's comprehensive "your body is changing" talk, I'm clear on sex and pregnancy, but still hazy on the nursing end. *Thank God.*

At this point, George interjects. "Did you know that if you drop a penny off the top of the Empire State Building, you could kill someone?"

"I did know. But that never happens," I say quickly. "Because people on the observation deck are really, really careful. And there's a big plastic wall."

Mrs. Garrett shakes her head. "Jase is right. You're a natural."

I feel a glow of pleasure that Jase thought I did anything well.

"Anyway," she continues. "Could you do one or maybe two times a week—in the afternoon, if that works with your summer job?"

I agree, tell her my schedule, even before she offers me more than I make at Breakfast Ahoy. Then she asks, again looking a little self-conscious, if I would mind starting today.

"Of course not. Just let me change."

"Don't change." George reaches out to touch my skirt with a grubby finger. "I like that. You look like Sailor Supergirl."

"More like Sailor Barbie, I'm afraid, George. I have to change because I worked in this all morning and it smells like eggs and bacon."

"I like eggs and bacon," George tells me. "But"—his face clouds—"do you know that bacon is"—tears leap to his eyes—"Wilbur?"

Mrs. Garrett sits down next to him immediately. "George, we've been through this. Remember? Wilbur did *not* get made into bacon."

"That's right." I bend down too as wetness overflows George's lashes. "Charlotte the spider saved him. He lived a

54

long and happy life—with Charlotte's daughters, um, Nelly and Urania and—"

"Joy," Mrs. Garrett concludes. "You, Samantha, are a keeper. I hope you don't shoplift."

I start to cough. "No. Never."

"Then is bacon Babe, Mom? Is it Babe?"

"No, no, Babe's still herding sheep. Bacon is not Babe. Bacon is only made from really mean pigs, George." Mrs. Garrett strokes his hair, then brushes his tears away.

"Bad pigs," I clarify.

"There are bad pigs?" George looks nervous. *Oops.*

"Well, pigs with, um, no soul." That doesn't sound good either. I cast around for a good explanation. "Like the animals that don't talk in Narnia." *Dumb. George is four. Would he know Narnia yet? He's still at Curious George. Edited.*

But understanding lights his face. "Oh. That's okay then. 'Cause I really like bacon."

When I return, George is already standing in the inflatable pool while Harry sprays water into it. Mrs. Garrett efficiently removes Patsy's diaper, pulling on some sort of puffy plastic pants with little suns all over them.

"You haven't really met Harry. Harry, this is Jase's friend Samantha, who's going to be watching you for a while."

How did I get to be Jase's friend? I've talked to him twice. Wow, is Mrs. Garrett ever different from my mother.

Harry, who's got green eyes but fairly straight dark brown hair and lots of freckles, looks at me challengingly. "Can you do a back dive?"

"Um. Yes."

"Will you teach me? Right now?"

Mrs. Garrett interrupts. "Harry, we discussed this. Samantha can't take you in the big pool because she has to keep her eye on the little ones."

Harry's lower lip juts out. "She could put Patsy in the Baby-Björn like you do and go in the water. She could hold George's hand. He can swim pretty good with his swimmies."

Mrs. Garrett glances at me apologetically. "My children expect everyone to multitask to an extreme degree. Harry, no. It's this pool or nothing."

"But I can swim now. I can swim really good. And she knows how to back dive. She could teach me to back dive." *While wearing the baby and holding George's hand? I'd need to be Sailor Supergirl.*

"No," Mrs. Garrett repeats firmly. Then, to me: "A will of iron. Just keep saying no. Eventually he'll move on." She takes me back into the house, shows me where the diapers are, tells me to help myself to anything in the refrigerator, gives me her cell phone number, points out the list of emergency numbers, cautions me not to bring up the subject of tornadoes in front of George, hops into her van, and drives off.

Leaving me with Patsy, who's trying to pull up my shirt, George, who wants me to know that you should never touch a blue-ringed octopus, and Harry, who looks like he wants to kill me.

Actually, it doesn't go that badly.

I've mostly avoided babysitting. It's not that I don't like kids, but I hate the uncertain hours of it. I've never wanted to deal with parents arriving late and apologetic, or that awkward drive home with some dad trying to make small talk. But the Garrett kids are pretty easy. I take them over to our house so I can get our garden sprinkler, which is this complicated standing copper twirling thing. Harry, fortunately, thinks it's amazing, and he and George spend an hour and a half playing in it, then jumping back into the baby pool while Patsy sits in my lap, gnawing my thumb with her gums and drooling on my hand.

I've finished doing the snack thing and am herding the kids back out to the pool when the motorcycle pulls in.

I turn with a tingle of anticipation, but it's not Jase. It's Joel who gets off the motorcycle, leans against it, and does that whole slow-appreciative-scan-of-your-entire-body thing. Which I get quite enough of at Breakfast Ahoy. "George. Harry. Who've you brought home?" Joel says. He is good-looking, but a little too much on the and-well-he-knows-it end of the scale.

"This is Sailor Supergirl," George says. "She knows all about black holes."

"And back dives," Harry adds.

"But you can't have her because she's going to marry Jase," George concludes.

Wonderful.

Joel looks surprised, as well he might. "You're a friend of Jase's?"

"Well, not really, I mean, we just met. I'm here to babysit."

"But she went to his room," George adds.

Joel raises an eyebrow at me.

Again with the full-body blush. All too apparent in a bikini. "I'm just the babysitter."

George grabs me around the waist, kissing my belly button. "No. You're Sailor Supergirl."

"So where *did* you come from?" Joel folds his arms, slanting back against the motorcycle.

George and Harry run back into the copper sprinkler. I'm holding Patsy on one hip, but she keeps trying to pull off my bikini top.

"Move her to the other side," Joel suggests, without batting an eyelash.

"Oh. Right." *Patsy, the baby with the one-breast preference.*

"You were saying?" Joel's still leaning lazily back against the motorcycle.

"Next door. I came from next door."

"You're Tracy Reed's sister?

Of course. Naturally he would not have overlooked Tracy. While I'm blond, Tracy is A Blonde. That is, I'm straw and sort of honey-colored with freckles from Dad, while Tracy's tow-headed with pale skin. She, unfairly, looks like she's never seen the sun, although she spends most of her summers on the beach.

"Yup." Then, suddenly, I wonder if my sister too has secretly interacted with the Garretts. But Joel isn't blond, Tracy's chief boyfriend requirement, right up there with a good backhand, so probably not. Just to be sure, I ask, "Do you play tennis?"

Joel looks unfazed by this non sequitur, no doubt used to flustered girls making no sense.

"Badly." He reaches out for Patsy, who's apparently decided

at this point that any breast will do. Her little fingers keep returning determinedly to my top.

"Yeah, the leather jacket probably slows down your return volley." I hand him the baby.

He gives a mock salute. "Sailor Supergirl *and* smartass. Nice."

Just then a Jeep pulls into the driveway, very fast. Alice slams out, reaching back to disentangle her purse strap from the gearshift and yank the purse to her. Her hair at the moment is electric blue, pulled into a side ponytail. She's wearing a black halter top and very short shorts.

"You knew the score, Cleve," she snaps at the driver of the car. "You knew where you stood." She straightens, stalking over to the kitchen door and slamming it behind her. Unlike her brothers, she's small, but that does nothing to deflect from her unmistakable air of authority.

Cleve, a mild-looking guy in a Hawaiian-print bathing suit and a PacSun shirt, does not look as though he'd known the score. He slumps behind the wheel.

Joel hands Patsy back to me and goes over to the car. "Bummer, man," he says to Cleve, who tips his head in acknowledgment but says nothing.

I return to the sprinkler and sit down. George plunks down next to me. "Did you know that a bird-eating tarantula is as big as your hand?"

"Jase doesn't have one of those, does he?"

George gives me his sunniest smile. "No. He useta have a reg'lar tarantula named Agnes, but she"—his voice drops mournfully—"died."

"I'm sure she's in tarantula heaven now," I assure him hastily, shuddering to think what that might look like.

Mrs. Garrett's van pulls in behind the motorcycle, disgorging what I assume are Duff and Andy, both red-faced and windblown. Judging by their life jackets, they've been at sailing camp.

George and Harry, my loyal fans, rave to their mother about my accomplishments, while Patsy immediately bursts into tears, points an accusing finger at her mother, and wails, "Boob."

"It was her first word." Mrs. Garrett takes her from me, heedless of Patsy's damp swimsuit. "There's one for the baby book."

Chapter Nine

With Mom and Tracy both out, the house is so quiet at night that I can count the sounds. The *whir-clunk* of ice dropping from the ice machine into the freezer bin. The shift of the central air from one speed to another. Then a noise I don't expect as I'm lying in my room at about ten o'clock that night, wondering if I should say anything to Mom about that woman with Clay. It's this rhythmic *bang, bang, bang* sound outside, below my window. I open it, climb out, looking down to find Jase, hammer in hand, nailing something to the trellis. He looks up, nail between his teeth, and waves.

I'm happy to see him, but this is a bit odd.

"Whatcha doing?"

"You have a loose board here." He takes the nail out of his mouth, positions it on the trellis, and begins hammering again. "It didn't seem safe."

"For me or you?"

"You tell me." He gives a final knock to the nail, puts the hammer down on the grass, and, in seconds, has climbed up the trellis and is sitting next to me. "I hear you've been engulfed by my family. Sorry about that."

"It's fine." I sidle back a little. I'm again in my nightgown, which seems a disadvantage.

"They're the best thing I've got, but they can be a little"—he pauses, as though searching for a definition—"overwhelming."

"I'm not easily overwhelmed."

Jase gazes at me, those green eyes searching my face. "No. You wouldn't be, would you?" It strikes me, sitting there, that I can be anyone I want to be with him. Then I notice something move on his shoulder.

"What's that?"

Jase turns his head to the side. "Oh, you mean Herbie?" He reaches up and pulls a squirrel—a rabbit—something furry—off his shoulder.

"Herbie?"

"Sugar glider." He extends his hand, now containing a fuzzy thing that looks like a flying squirrel, with a big black stripe down its back and black-shadowed eyes.

I stroke its head uncertainly.

"He loves that. Very tactile." Jase moves his other hand over so Herbie's cradled in between two palms. His hands are rough and capable. So much about Jase Garrett seems like a man, not a boy.

"Are you . . . like . . . Dr. Doolittle or something?"

"I just like animals. Do you?"

"Well, yeah. But I don't have a zoo in my room."

He peers over my shoulder, in my window, then nods. "No, you sure don't. What a clean room. Is it always like that?"

I feel defensive, and then defensive about feeling defensive. "Generally. Sometimes I—"

"Go a little crazy and don't hang up your bathrobe?" he suggests.

"It's been known to happen." He's sitting so close, I can feel his breath on my cheek. My stomach flip-flops again.

"I hear you're a superhero."

"Yup. A few hours with your family and now I have supernatural powers."

"And you'll need 'em." He leans back, resting Herbie on his stomach, then slanting onto his elbows. "Plus, you do back dives."

"I do. Swim team."

Jase nods slowly, looking at me. Everything he does seems so thought-out and purposeful. I'm used to boys just sort of hurling themselves through life, I guess. Charley, who was basically all about hoping for sex, and Michael, at the mercy of his moods, either elated or in deep despair. "Want to go for a swim?" Jase finally asks.

"Now?"

"Now. In our pool. It's *so* hot."

The air is muggy and earthy, almost thick. *Let's see. Swimming. At night. With a boy. Who's virtually a stranger. And a Garrett.* It's dizzying how many of my mother's rules this is breaking.

Seventeen years of lectures and discussions and reminders: "Think about how it looks, Samantha. Not just how it feels. Make smart choices. Always consider consequences."

Less than seventeen seconds to say:

"I'll get my suit."

Five minutes later, I'm standing in our yard beneath my bedroom window, waiting nervously for Jase to return after

63

changing into his trunks. I keep peering toward our driveway, afraid I'll see a sweep of headlights and it'll be Clay driving my mother home, finding me standing here in my black tankini, so not where she expects me to be.

But instead, I hear Jase's quiet voice. "Hey," he says, walking up my driveway in the dark.

"You don't still have Herbie, do you?"

"Nah, he's not a water fan. Come on." He leads me back down and around my mother's six-foot barricade, up the Garretts' driveway to their backyard, and over to the tall green chain-link fence that encircles their pool. "Okay," he says, "are you a good climber?"

"Why are we climbing over? It's *your* pool. Why don't we just go through the gate?"

Jase folds his arms, leaning back against the fence, smiling at me, a flash of white in the dark. "More fun this way. If you're breaking the rules, it might as well feel like it."

I look suspiciously at him. "You wouldn't be one of those thrill-seeking-get-the-girl-in-trouble-just-for-kicks types, would you?"

"I would not. Climb over. Need a boost?"

I could use one, but would not admit that. I stick my toes in a hole of the chain link and climb up and over, clinging to the other side before dropping down. Jase is beside me almost immediately. A good climber. *Naturally,* I think, remembering the trellis.

He snaps on the underwater pool lights. The pool contains several inflatable toys, something Mom's always lamenting. "Don't they know you're supposed to put those away every night or the filter doesn't work? God knows how unsanitary that pool is."

But it doesn't look unsanitary. It's beautiful, glowing sapphire in the night. I dive right in, swim to the end, come up for air.

"You're fast," Jase calls from the middle of the pool. "Race?"

"Are you one of those competitive beat-the-girl-in-a-race-just-to-prove-a-macho-point types?"

"You seem," Jase observes, "to know a lot of annoying people. I'm just me, Samantha. Race?"

"You're on."

I haven't been on the swim team for a year. Practices started to take too much time away from my homework, and Mom put her foot down. I still swim when I can, though. And I'm still fast. He still wins. Twice. Then I do, at least once. After that we just paddle around.

Eventually, Jase climbs out, pulls two towels from a big wooden bin, and spreads them on the grass. I collapse onto one, staring up at the night sky. It's so hot, the humidity pressing down on me like fingers.

He lies down next to me.

To be honest, I keep expecting him to make a pass. Charley Tyler would have been reaching for the top of my swimsuit faster than Patsy. But Jase just folds one arm behind his head, looking up at the sky. "What's that one?" he asks, pointing.

"What?"

"You said you were into stargazing. Tell me what that one is?"

I squint where his finger is pointing. "Draco."

"And that?"

"Corona Borealis."

"And over there?"

"Scorpius."

"You really are an astrophysicist. What about that one over there?"

"Norma."

A bark of laughter. "Honestly?"

"You're the one who had a tarantula named Agnes. Yes, truly."

He rolls onto his side to look at me. "How'd you find out about Agnes?"

"George."

"Of course. George tells all."

"I love George," I say.

Okay, now his face is close to mine. If I were to raise my head and tilt over just a bit . . . But I will not, because there's no way *I'm* going to be the one who does that. I never have been, and I'm not starting now. Instead I just look at Jase, wondering if he'll lean any nearer. Then I see the sweep of headlights pulling into our circular drive.

I jump up. "I've got to get home. I've got to get home *now.*" My voice is high, panicky. My mother always checks my room before she goes to sleep. I run over to the chain fence, bang through the gate, then feel Jase's hands at my waist, lifting me up so I'm nearly to the top of our tall slippery one, close enough to throw one leg over.

"Easy. You'll make it. Don't worry." His voice is low, soothing. Probably his calm-the-nervous-animal voice.

I drop down on the other side and am running for the trellis.

"Samantha!"

I turn, though I can only see the top of his head over the fence.

"Watch out for the hammer. It's still on the grass. Thanks for the race."

I nod, give a quick wave, and run.

Chapter Ten

"Samantha! Samantha." Tracy comes hurtling into my bedroom. "Where's your navy blue halter top?"

"In my drawer, Trace. Whyever do you ask?" I respond sweetly. Tracy's packing to leave for Martha's Vineyard—half an hour before Flip's picking her up. Typical. She regards it as the right of the first born to co-opt any articles of my clothing she fancies, as long as they're not actually on my back at the time.

"I'm taking it, okay? Just for the summer—you can have it back in the fall, promise." She yanks open my bureau drawer, scrabbling through clothes, pulling out not only the blue top but a few white ones.

"Right, because fall is when I'll really need the halter tops. Put those back."

"Come on! I need more white shirts—we'll be playing tons of tennis."

"I hear they may even have stores on the Vineyard these days."

Tracy rolls her eyes and shoves the shirts back in, whirling to return to her room. Last year she taught tennis at the B&T, and I'm suddenly conscious that it will be weird without her there too, not just at home. My sister is, for all intents and purposes, already gone.

"I'll miss you," I say as she whips dresses off hangers, shoving them helter-skelter into a suitcase of Mom's, not at all bothered by the prominent GCR monogram.

"I'll send you postcards." She opens up a pillowcase, striding into the bathroom. I watch as she sweeps the hair straightener, curling iron, and electric toothbrush off the counter into the sack. "I hope you won't really miss me, Samantha. It's the summer before your senior year. Forget Mom. Bust loose. Enjoy life." She waves her birth control compact at me for emphasis.

Ugh. I so don't need a visual aid for my sister's sex life.

Shoving the compact into the pillowcase, she knots the end. Then her shoulders sag, her face suddenly vulnerable. "I'm afraid I'm getting in too deep with Flip. Spending the whole summer with him . . . Maybe not smart."

"I like Flip," I say.

"Yeah, I like Flip too," she says shortly, "but I only want to like Flip till the end of August. He's going to college in Florida. I'm headed to Vermont."

"Planes, trains, automobiles . . ." I suggest.

"I hate that messy long-distance stuff, Samantha. Plus, then you wonder whether he's got some girl on campus that you don't know about and you're making a fool of yourself."

"Have some trust, Trace. Flip seems pretty devoted."

She sighs. "I know. He brought me a magazine and a Froz-Fruit at the beach the other day. It was so sweet. That was when I realized I might be getting in too deep."

Ooops.

"Can't you just see how it all goes?"

Tracy's smile is rueful. "I seem to remember that when you were dating Charley you had some sort of timetable for every move you'd let him make."

"Charley needed a timetable or he'd have tried for sex in his dad's Prius in our driveway before our first date."

She chuckles. "He *was* a total hound. But great dimples. Did you ever actually sleep with him?"

"No. Never." How can she forget? I'm kind of hurt. I remember every detail of Tracy's love life, including that traumatic summer two years ago when she dated three brothers, breaking two of their hearts and getting hers thoroughly broken by the third.

Flip honks from the driveway, something Mom would generally deplore but somehow puts up with from him.

"Help! I'm late—gotta go! Love you!" Tracy tramples down the stairs, loud as a herd of elephants in tap shoes. I've never understood how my petite, slender sister can make so much noise on the stairs. She throws her arms around Mom, squeezes her a second, dashes to the door, and shouts, "Coming, Flip! I'm worth waiting for, I promise!"

"I know, babydoll!" Flip calls back.

Tracy runs back to me, kisses my cheek noisily, pulls back. "Are you sure about the white shirts?"

"Yes. Go!" I say, and with a twirl of skirt and a slam of the door, she's gone.

"Soooo, there's an SAT test prep at Stony Bay High this August," Nan says as we walk to the B&T. We stopped at Doane's and she's slurping her cookies-and-cream milkshake while I crunch the ice of my lime rickey.

"Be still my heart. It's summer, Nan." I tip my face up to the sun, take a deep breath of the warm air. Low tide. The sun-warm scent of the river.

"I know," she says. "But it's just one morning. I had the stomach flu when we took them last time, and I only got nineteen hundred. That's just not good enough. Not for Columbia."

"Can't you take it online?" I like school and I love Nan, but I'd just as soon not think about GPAs and test scores until after Labor Day.

"It's not the same. This is proctored and everything. The conditions are exactly like the actual test. We could do it together. It would be fun."

I smile at her, reaching over to snag her milkshake for a taste. "This is your idea of fun? Couldn't we just swim in shark-infested waters instead?"

"Please. You know I get totally freaked out about these things. It would help to practice under real circumstances. And I always feel better knowing you're there. I'll even pay your fee. Pleeease, Samantha?"

I mutter that I'll think about it. We've reached the B&T, where we have to fill out paperwork before we start work. And there's another thing I want to do too.

I'm sweating slightly as I knock on the door of Mr. Lennox's office, peering around guiltily.

"Do come in!" Mr. Lennox calls. He looks surprised when I poke my head in.

"Well, hello, Ms. Reed. You do know your first day isn't until next week."

I enter the office and think, as always, that they should get Mr. Lennox a smaller desk. He's not a tall man, and it looks as if the massive slab of carved oak is swallowing him whole.

"I know," I say, sitting down. "Just filling out the paperwork. And I was wondering . . . I need to . . . I'm hoping to get back on the swim team this year. So I want to train. I wondered if maybe I could come in an hour early, before the pool opens, and swim in the Olympic pool?" Mr. Lennox leans back in his chair, impassive. "I mean, I can use the ocean and the river, but I need to get my timing down, and it's easier if I'm sure how far I'm going and how fast."

He tents his fingers under his nose. "The pool opens at ten a.m."

I try not to let my shoulders slump. Swimming with Jase the other night, competing, even in a casual way, felt so good. I hated giving up swim team. My grades in math and science dipped to B's midway through fall semester, and so Mom insisted. But maybe if I up my time and try really hard . . .

Mr. Lennox continues: "On the other hand, your mother is a valuable member of our board of directors . . ." He moves his fingers away from his face enough to show a tiny smile. "And you yourself have always been a Most Satisfactory Employee. You may make use of the pool—as long as you follow the *other* rules—shower first, use a bathing cap, and Do Not Let Another soul Know of our Arrangement."

I jump up. "Thank you, Mr. Lennox. I won't, I promise. I mean, I'll do everything you say. Thank you."

Nan's waiting outside when I emerge. When she sees my smile, she says, "You do realize that this is probably the only time in his entire existence that Lennox has colored outside the lines? I don't know whether to congratulate him or keep pitying him."

"I really want this," I tell her.

"You were always happier when you were swimming," Nan agrees. "And a little out of shape now, maybe?" she adds casually. "It'll be good for you."

I turn to look at her, but she's already a few steps away, heading back down the hall.

I have the late shift at Breakfast Ahoy the next day, nine to one instead of six to eleven. So I decide to make myself a smoothie while Mom frowns at her phone messages. This is the first time I've really seen her in days, and I wonder if now's the time to tell her about Clay. I decide I will just as she snaps her phone shut and opens the refrigerator door, tapping her open-toed sandal on the floor. Mom always does this in front of the fridge, as though she's expecting the bowl of strawberries to shout "Eat ME" or the orange juice to jump out and pour itself into a glass.

Tap. Tap. Tap.

This is a favorite technique too, silence so loud someone has to start talking to fill it. I open my mouth again, but to my surprise, it's Mom who speaks first.

"Sweetheart. I've been thinking about you."

73

And the way she says it, I just can't help myself. "About my summer schedule?" I ask, and instantly feel guilty for the sarcasm under my words.

Mom takes a carton of eggs out, stares at it, returns it to the refrigerator.

"That, certainly. This election won't be easy. It's not like the first time I ran, when my only opposition was that crazy Libertarian man. I could lose my seat if I don't work hard. That's why I'm so grateful for Clay. I need to concentrate, and know you girls are taken care of. Tracy . . ." More foot tapping. "Clay thinks I shouldn't worry. Let her go. She'll be off to college in the fall, after all. But you . . . How can I explain this in a way you'll understand?"

"I'm seventeen. I understand everything." I have another flash of Clay and that woman. How do I bring it up? I lean past her for the strawberries.

Mom reaches out to flick my cheek with a finger. "It's when you say things like that that I remember how very young you are." Then her face softens. "I know it'll be hard for you to get used to Tracy being gone. Me too. It'll be quiet around here. You understand that I'm going to have to be working hard all summer, don't you, sweetie?"

I nod. The house already seems still without Tracy's off-key singing in the shower or her heels hammering down the stairs.

Mom pulls the filtered water out of the refrigerator and pours it into the teakettle. "Clay says I'm bigger than this position. I could be important. I could be something more than the woman with the trust fund who bought her way into power."

There were a lot of editorials that said exactly that when

she won the first time. I read them, winced, and hid the paper, hoping Mom never saw them. But of course she did.

"It's been so long since anyone has looked at me and really *seen* me," she adds suddenly, standing there holding the filtered water. "Your father . . . well, I thought he did. But then . . . after him . . . you get busy and you get older . . . and nobody really looks your way anymore. You and Tracy . . . She's off to college in the fall. That'll be you in another year. And I think . . . It's their turn now? Where did my chance go? It only took Clay a little while to come to terms with the fact that I had teen-aged daughters. He sees me, Samantha. I can't tell you how good that feels." She turns and looks at me, and I've never seen her . . . *glow* like this.

How can I say "Uh—Mom—I think he might be seeing someone else too"?

I think of Jase Garrett, how he seems to understand without me having to explain things. Does Mom feel that way with Clay? *Please don't let him be some skeevy womanizer.*

"I'm glad, Mom," I say. I hit BLEND and the kitchen fills with the sound of pulverizing strawberries and ice.

She brushes the hair off my forehead, then sets the filtered water down and hovers near my elbow until I turn off the blender. Then silence.

"You two, you and Tracy," she finally says to my back, "are the best things that ever happened to me. Personally. But there's more to life than personal things. I don't want you to be the only things that ever happen to me. I want . . ." Her voice trails off and I turn around to find her looking away, off somewhere I can't see. Suddenly, I feel afraid for her. As she stands there, her

75

expression dreamy, she seems like a woman—not my mother, the vacuum cleaner queen, who rolls her eyes at the Garretts, at any uncertainty at all. I've only met Clay twice, really. He has charm, I guess, but apparently my dad did too. Mom's always said that bitterly—"Your father had *charm*"—as though charm were some illicit substance he'd used on her that made her lose her mind.

I clear my throat. "So," I say, in what I hope is a casual, making-conversation tone, not a probing-for-info one, "how much do you know about Clay Tucker?"

Mom's eyes snap to me. "Why do you ask, Samantha? How is that your business?"

This is why I don't say things. I stick my spoon into my smoothie, squishing a slice of strawberry against the side. "I just wondered. He seems . . ."

Like a potential disaster? *Younger?* Probably not a tactful way to put it. *Is* there a tactful way to put it?

So I don't finish my sentence—usually Mom's technique for getting us to tell all. Incredibly, it works in reverse.

"Well, one thing I do know is that he's gone a long way for a relatively young man. He advised the RNC during the last campaign, he's visited G. W. Bush at his Crawford ranch . . ."

Well, ew. Tracy used to tease Mom about the reverent tone she used whenever she spoke the name of our former president: "Mo-om has a cru-ush on the Commander in Chiiee-eef." I was always too creeped out by it to tease.

"Clay Tucker is a real mover and shaker," she says now. "I can't believe he's taking time for my little campaign."

I return the strawberries to the fridge, then root around my smoothie with my spoon, looking for more pieces of fruit that escaped the blender. "How'd he wind up in Stony Bay?" *Did he bring a wife with him? A hometown honey?*

"He bought his parents a summer house on Seashell Island." Mom opens the refrigerator and moves the strawberries from the second shelf, where I had put them, to the third shelf. "That little island downriver? He's been burning himself out, so he came here for a little R and R." She smiles. "Then he read about my race and couldn't help wanting to get involved."

With the campaign? Or with Mom? Maybe he's some kind of secret agent, looking for ways to discredit her. But that would never work. She hasn't got any skeletons in the closet.

"Is that okay?" I scoop out a strawberry and gobble it down. "That you're sort of—dating—and he's, um, advising you? I thought that was a no-no."

Mom's always been incredibly strict about the line between the political and the personal. A few years ago, Tracy forgot to bring money to pay for skates at McKinskey Rink and the guy who ran it, a supporter of Mom's, said not to worry. Mom marched Tracy right in there the next day and paid full price, even though Trace was skating in off-hours.

Her eyebrows draw together. "We're consenting adults, Samantha. Unmarried. There are no rules being broken here." She lifts her chin, folding her arms. "I resent your tone."

"I—" But she's already gone to the closet door and pulled out the vacuum cleaner, cranking it up to the soothing roar of a 747.

I occupy myself with my smoothie, wondering how I could have handled that better. Mom practically ran background checks on Charley and Michael, not to mention some of Tracy's more dubious choices. But when it's her . . .

The vacuum suddenly gives a guttural choking sound and stops dead. Mom shakes it, turns it off, unplugs it, tries again, but nothing.

"Samantha!" she calls. "Do you know anything about this?" which I know from long experience means "Are you responsible for this?"

"No, Mom. You know I never touch it."

She shakes it again, accusingly. "It was working fine last night."

"I didn't use it, Mom."

Suddenly she's yelling. "Then what is *wrong* with this thing? Of all the times for it to break! Clay's coming for dinner with some potential campaign donors and the room's only half-done." She slams the vacuum cleaner down.

As usual, the living room is pristine. You can't even tell which side is the one she's just vacuumed. "Mom. It'll be fine. They won't even notice."

She kicks the vacuum cleaner, glaring at me. "*I'll* notice."

Okay.

"Mom." I'm used to her temper, but this seems over the top.

Suddenly, abruptly, she unplugs the vacuum cleaner, gathers it up, walks across the room, and throws it out the front door. It lands with a crash on the driveway. I stare at her.

"Don't you have to be at work, Samantha?"

Chapter Eleven

Then, of course, work is particularly annoying because Charley Tyler and a bunch of the boys from school come in. Charley and I broke up amiably, but this still means lots of leering and "Avast, what do I see through my spyglass?" and jokes of the wanna-climb-my-mainmast variety. Naturally, they're at one of my tables, table eight, and they keep me running back and forth for water and extra butter and more ketchup, just because they can.

Finally, they get ready to leave. Thank God they overtip. Charley winks at me as they go, working the dimples. "The mainmast offer stands, Sammy-Sam."

"Get lost, Charley."

I'm cleaning up their completely trashed table when someone tugs at the waistband of my skirt.

"Kid."

Tim's unshaven, his rusty hair rumpled, still wearing the clothes he had on the last time I saw him, flannel pajama bottoms incongruous in the summer heat. Clearly, they haven't paid a visit to the washing machine.

"Yo, I need some cash, rich girl."

This stings. Tim knows, or used to know, how much I hate

that label, which got tossed at me by the kids on opposing swim teams.

"I'm not going to give you money, Tim."

"'Cause I'll 'just spend it on booze,' right?" he asks in a high, sarcastic voice, imitating Mom when we passed homeless people on visits to New Haven. "You know that ain't necessarily so. I *might* spend it on weed. Or, if you're generous and I'm lucky, blow. C'mon. Just gimme fifty."

He leans back against the counter, folding his hands and cocking his chin at me.

I stare back. Face-off? Then, unexpected, he lunges for the pocket of my skirt, where I stash my tips. "This is nothing to you. Don't know why the fuck you even work, Samantha. Just give me a few bucks."

I pull back, jerking away so abruptly I'm afraid the cheapo fabric of the skirt will tear. "Tim! Come on. You know I'm not going to."

He shakes his head at me. "You used to be cool. When did you turn into such a bitch?"

"When you turned into such an asshole." I brush past him with my tray full of dirty dishes. Tears spring to my eyes. *Don't*, I think. But Tim used to know me as well as anyone could.

"Trouble?" Ernesto the cook asks, looking up from the six frying pans he's got going simultaneously. Breakfast Ahoy is not a health food restaurant.

"Just some jerk." I dump the dishes into the bussing bin with a clatter.

"Nothing new there. Damn town full of damn folks with silver spoons up their damn . . ."

Oops. Inadvertently activated Ernesto's "favorite rant" button. I tune him out, paste on a fierce smile, and go back to deal with Tim, but the flash of a dirty plaid pajama cuff and the slam of the door is the only sign of him. There's a skim of coins on the table by the door, and a few more on the ground. The rest of my tip is gone.

There was this day a few weeks into seventh grade at Hodges, before Tim got kicked out, when I'd forgotten my lunch money and was looking for Tracy or Nan. Instead I ran into Tim, sitting in the bushes with the worst of the worst of Hodges' stoner crowd—Tim, who, as far as I knew till then, was as innocent of all that stuff as me and Nan. The hub of the crowd was Drake Marcos, this senior druggie guy who always hung with an equally well-baked posse. Quite the achievement for the college essay.

"Oh, it's Tracy Reed's sister. Take a load off, Tracy Reed's sister. You look tense. You need to re-laaax," Drake said. The other kids laughed as though he was hysterically funny. I glanced at Tim, who was staring at his feet.

"Walk on the wild side, Tracy Reed's sister." Drake waved a bag of—I didn't even know what—at me.

I made some lame comment about how I had to get to class, which Drake enjoyed riffing on for several seconds with lots of sycophantic chortles from his loyal groupies.

I started to leave, then turned back and called "Come on" to Tim, who was still staring at his loafers.

That was when he finally looked at me. "Fuck off, Samantha."

Chapter Twelve

It takes me a while to shake off Tim's visit, but things at Breakfast Ahoy come at you fast, and that helps.

Today, however, it's all bad.

The morning also features a woman who becomes extremely indignant when we can't allow her cockapoo to sit at the table with her and a man with two extremely cranky toddlers who throw the jam and sugar packets at me, and squirt mustard and ketchup into their napkin dispenser. As I walk home, I check my cell messages, finding one from Mom, still sounding peeved, telling me to clean the house: *"Make it immaculate,"* she emphasizes. And then *"Make yourself scarce, as Clay's bringing those donors over."*

My mother has never asked me to make myself scarce. Is it because I asked about Clay? I walk up the driveway, pondering this, then see the vacuum cleaner, still sprawled like a vagrant.

"Samantha!" Jase calls from around our fence. "You okay? Looks like life was tough today on the bounding main."

"No sailor jokes, please. Believe me, I've heard 'em all."

He walks closer, smiling, shaking his head. Today he's wearing a white T-shirt that makes him look even tanner. "I bet you have. Seriously, are you all right? You look, uh, disheveled, and that's rare for you."

I explain about cleaning the house and making myself scarce. "And," I say as I kick it, "the vacuum cleaner is broken."

"I can fix that. Let me get my kit." He jogs off before I can say anything. I go inside, ditch the sailor garb, and pull on a light blue sundress. I'm pouring lemonade when Jase knocks.

"In the kitchen!"

He comes in, carrying the vacuum cleaner in both arms like an accident victim, his tool kit dangling from one thumb. "Which is the part of your house that isn't clean?"

"My mother's kind of particular."

Jase nods, raises an eyebrow, but doesn't say anything. He sets the vacuum cleaner down on the tile, opens the toolbox, and cocks his head at it, searching for the right utensil, evidently. I stare at the muscles in his arms and suddenly have such a strong urge to reach out and run my fingers down them that it scares me. Instead, I spray the countertop with disinfectant and attack it with a paper towel. *Out damned spot.*

He's got the vacuum cleaner fixed in less than five minutes. The culprit was apparently one of Clay's cufflinks. I suppress the image of Mom wrestling it off in a frenzy of cougar lust. Then Jase helps me reclean the immaculate downstairs.

"Hard to feel I'm making progress when it was already so perfect," he says, vacuuming under an armchair cushion as I adjust the already symmetrically aligned throw pillows. "Maybe we should get George and Patsy over here, use some

83

Play-Doh and finger paints and then make brownies, so there's actually something to clean."

When we're done Jase asks, "Do you have a curfew?"

"Eleven o'clock," I say, confused since it's just early afternoon.

"Get a jacket and your bathing suit, then."

"What are we doing?"

"You're supposed to make yourself scarce, right? Come get lost in the crowd at my house, then we'll figure something else out."

As always, the contrast between the Garretts' yard and ours is extreme—Dorothy walking out of black and white and into Technicolor. Alice is playing Frisbee with some guy. Little shrieks and screams are coming from the pool. Harry's whacking away at a T-ball stand, but with a tennis racket. Alice wings the Frisbee at Jase, who catches it easily and throws it to the guy—not Cleve-who-knew-the-score, but a hulking football-player type. I hear Mrs. Garrett saying loudly from the pool area, "George! What did I tell you about peeing in here?"

Then the screen door bursts open and Andy charges out, carrying about five different bathing suits. "Alice! You *have* to help me."

Alice rolls her eyes. "Just pick one, Andy. It'll be fine. It's only a date."

Andy, a pretty fourteen-year-old with braces, shakes her head, looking near tears. "A date with Kyle. Kyle! Alice. I've never even been asked on a date and now I have. And you won't even help."

"What's up, Ands?" Jase walks over to her.

84

"Kyle Comstock. From sailing camp? I've practically cap-sized the boat looking at him for three whole summers now? He asked me to go to the beach and then the Clam Shack. Alice is completely and totally no help whatsoever. All Mom says is to wear sunscreen."

Alice shakes her head impatiently. "C'mon Brad, let's get wet." She and the football-player type march off toward the pool.

Jase introduces me to Andy, who turns anxious hazel eyes on me. "Can *you* help? No one should have to have a first date in a bathing suit. It's unfair."

"You're right," I say. "Show me what you've got."

Andy spreads the bathing suits out on the ground. "Three one pieces, two bikinis. Mom says the bikinis are out. What do you think, Jase?"

"No bikinis on a first date." He nods. "I'm sure that's a rule. Or should be. For my sisters anyway."

"What's he like?" I ask, surveying the other suits.

"Kyle? Oh, well, you know. Perfect?" She waves her hands.

"You need to be more specific, Ands," Jase says dryly.

"Funny. Sporty. Popular. Cute but doesn't act like he knows it? The kind who makes everybody laugh without trying too hard."

"That one." I point to the red Speedo.

"Thank you. What about after we swim? Do I change into a dress? Do I put on makeup? How do I even talk to him? Why did I agree to do this? I hate clams!"

"Get a hot dog," Jase advises. "They're cheaper. He'll appre-ciate it."

"No makeup. You don't need it," I add. "Especially after the beach. Throw some conditioner in your hair so it keeps the wet look. A dress is good. Ask lots of questions about him."

"You have saved my very life. I shall be indebted to you for all eternity," Andy says fervently, and streaks back into the house.

"I'm fascinated," Jase observes in an undertone. "How did you decide which suit?"

"She said sporty," I respond. The skin at the back of my neck gives this little twitch at the sound of his voice so close to my ear. "Plus her dark hair and tan skin with red. I'm probably jealous. My mom says blondes can't wear red."

"Here I thought Sailor Supergirl could do anything." Jase opens the door to the kitchen, motioning me in.

"Sadly, my powers are limited."

"Can you make sure this Kyle Comstock is a good guy? That would be a useful power."

"You're telling me," I say. "I could use that one with my mom's boyfriend. But no."

Without saying anything further Jase heads for the stairs, and, snake-charmed again, I follow him up toward his room, to be met in the hallway by a very wide-eyed Duff. He has the family chestnut hair, slightly long, and round green eyes. He's huskier than Jase, and a lot shorter.

"Voldemort has escaped," he announces.

"Hell." Jase sounds upset, which, considering that info about Harry Potter is old news, seems odd. "Did you take him out of his cage?" Jase is at the door of his room in two strides.

"Just for a minute. To see if he was gonna shed his skin soon."

"Duff, you know better." Jase is on his knees, peering under the bed and the bureau.

"Voldemort is—?" I ask Duff.

"Jase's corn snake. I named him."

It takes all my self-control not to leap onto the bureau. Jase is rummaging in the closet now. "He likes shoes," he explains over his shoulder.

Voldemort the corn snake with the shoe fetish. Wonderful.

"Should I get Mom?" Duff is poised in the doorway.

"Nope. Got him." Jase emerges from the closet with the orange, white, and black snake twined around his arm. I back up several paces.

"He's very shy, Samantha. Don't worry. Completely harmless. Right, Duff?"

"It's true." Duff regards me seriously. "Corn snakes are really underrated as pets. They're actually very gentle and intelligent. They just have a bad reputation. Like rats and wolves."

"I'll take your word for it," I mutter, watching Jase uncoil the snake and slip it into its cage, where it lies curled like a big, deadly-looking bracelet.

"I can print out something on it from the Internet, if you like," Duff assures me. "The one thing you have to be careful with about corn snakes is that sometimes they defecate when they are stressed."

"Duff. Please. Go," Jase says.

Duff, face downcast, leaves. Then Joel stalks into the room, wearing a tight black T-shirt, tighter black jeans, and an irritated expression.

"I thought you got it working. I have to pick up Giselle in ten minutes."

"It *was* working," Jase says.

"Not now, bro. Take a look."

Jase looks at me apologetically. "The motorcycle. Come with me while I check it."

Once again, it takes only a few minutes of Jase jiggling something and unscrewing and rescrewing something else for the motorcycle to purr to life. Joel hops on, says something that might be thanks but is impossible to hear over the motor, and speeds off.

"How did you get so good at everything?" I ask Jase as he wipes his greasy hands on a rag from his tool kit.

"At everything," he repeats thoughtfully.

"Fixing things—" I gesture at the motorcycle, then at my house, implying the vacuum cleaner.

"My dad runs a hardware store. It gives me an unfair advantage."

"He's Joel's dad too," I point out. "But you're the one fixing the motorcycle. And taking care of all those pets."

Jase's green eyes meet mine, then his lashes lower. "I guess I like things that take time and attention. More worthwhile that way."

I don't know what it is about this that makes me blush, but something does.

Just then Harry comes charging up, saying, "Now you'll teach me to back dive, right, Sailor Supergirl? Right now. Right?"

"Harry, Samantha doesn't have to—"

"I don't mind," I say quickly, happy to have something to do besides melt into a puddle on the driveway. "I'll get my suit."

Harry's an enthusiastic student, although his front dives are still at the making-a-steeple-of-his-hands-and-belly-flopping-into-the-water stage. He keeps insisting I show him and show him again and again how to back dive, while Mrs. Garrett splashes in the shallow end with George and Patsy. Jase swims a few laps, then treads water, watching us. Alice and her Brad have evidently gone elsewhere.

"Did you know that killer whales don't usually kill people?" George calls from the pool steps.

"I'd heard that, yes."

"They don't like the way we taste. And did you know that the deadliest sharks to people are great white, tiger, hammerheads, and bull sharks?"

"I did, George," I say, holding my hand in the small of Harry's back to get him at the proper angle.

"But there are none of those in this pool," adds Jase.

"Jase, do you think we should all go to the Clam Shack for dinner, just to check on Andy?" Mrs. Garrett asks.

"She'd be completely humiliated, Mom." Jase leans back against the side of the pool, elbows on the concrete surrounding it.

"I know, but honestly, fourteen and dating! Even Alice was fifteen."

He shuts his eyes. "Mom. You said no more babysitting for me this week. And Samantha's not on the clock either."

Mrs. Garrett wrinkles her forehead. "I know. But Andy's

just . . . very young for fourteen. I don't know this Comstock boy at all."

Jase sighs, shooting a glance at me.

"We could drop by the Clam Shack and check him out," I offer. "Subtly. Would that work?"

Mrs. Garrett beams at me.

"An espionage date?" Jase asks doubtfully. "I guess that could work. Do you have a uniform for that one, Samantha?"

I flick water at him, with a jolt of happiness that he's calling it a date. Inside, I am no more suave than Andy.

"No Lara Croft look, if that's what you're after."

"Too bad," he says, and splashes back at me.

Chapter Thirteen

Kyle Comstock's father, a tall handsome man with a long-suffering expression, pulls up in a black BMW soon after this. Kyle gets out and walks into the backyard, looking for Andy. He's cute, with brownish-blond curly hair and an infectious smile, undiluted by the braces.

Andy, in the red bathing suit with a navy terry cloth cover-up over it, hops into the car, after giving Jase and me a quick isn't-he-something look.

When we get to the Clam Shack an hour later, it is, as usual, completely packed. The shack is a small, shabby building on Stony Bay Beach, approximately the size of my mom's walk-in closet, and all summer long there's a line outside. It's the only eatery on the beach and Stony Bay is the biggest and best public one, wide and sandy. When we finally get in, we see Andy and Kyle over at a corner table. He's talking earnestly, and she's toying with her French fries, blushing as red as her bathing suit. Jase closes his eyes at the sight.

"Painful to watch when it's your sister?" I ask.

"I don't worry about Alice. She's like one of those spiders that bites the guy's head off when she's done with him. But Andy's different. Teenage heartbreak waiting to happen."

He looks around to see if there are any available seats, then asks, "Samantha, do you know that guy?"

I look over to find Michael sitting alone at the counter, glaring moodily at us. *Both ex-boyfriends in one day. Lucky me.*

"He's, um . . . we . . . um, went out for a little while."

"I guess." Jase seems amused. "He looks like he's going to come up and challenge me to a duel."

"No. But he will definitely write a hostile poem about you tonight," I say.

There's no place to sit, so we end up carrying Jase's hamburger and my chowder outside and over to the breakwater. The sun's still high and hot in the sky, but there's a cool breeze. I pull on my jacket.

"So what happened with emo dude? Bad breakup?"

"In a way. High drama. That was Michael. It's not like he was madly in love with me. At all. That was the thing with Michael." I chew an oyster cracker, staring out at the water, the waves blue-black. "I was just sort of the girl in the poem, not myself. First I was the unattainable object, and then I was some golden girl who was supposed to save him from sorrow forever, or the siren who was luring him into having sex when he didn't want to—"

Jase chokes on a French fry. "Um. Really?"

I can feel myself flush. "Not like that. He was just very Catholic. So he'd make a move and suffer over it for days."

"Fun guy. We should hook him up with my ex Lindy."

"Lindy the shoplifter?" I reach for one of his French fries, then snatch my hand back. He hands me the container.

"That's the one. No conscience at all. Maybe they'd balance each other out."

"Did you actually get arrested?" I ask.

"Escorted to the station in a police car, which was quite enough for me. I got a warning, but as it turned out, it was not Lindy's first offense when we were caught, so she got a big fine, which she wanted me to pay half of, and community service."

"Did you pay half?" I gobble another of Jase's fries. I'm trying not to look at him. In the honeyed evening light, the green eyes and tan skin and the amused curl of his smile are all just a little much.

"I almost did because I felt like an ass. My dad talked me out of it, since I had no idea what Lindy was doing. She could sweep a dozen things into her purse without blinking an eye. She'd practically cleaned out the makeup counter when the security guard came over." He shakes his head.

"Michael wrote angry breakup poems, a few a day for three months, then mailed them to me, postage due."

"Let's definitely set them up. They deserve each other." He stands up, crumpling the waxed paper from the hamburger and stuffing it into his pocket. "Want to walk out to the lighthouse?"

I'm chilly, but I want to go anyway. The breakwater that leads to the lighthouse is strange—the rocks are perfectly flat and even until about halfway, then get jagged and off-kilter, so walking all the way out involves a certain amount of climbing and clinging. By the time we reach the lighthouse, the evening light has turned from golden to pinkly golden with the sunset. Jase folds his arms on the black pipe-metal railing and looks out at the ocean, still studded in the distance with tiny triangles of white sailboats headed home. It's so picturesque that I half expect orchestral chords to swell in the background.

Tracy's a pro at these things. She'd stumble and bump up against the boy, looking at him through her lashes. Or she'd shiver and press herself a little closer, as if unconsciously. She'd know exactly what to do to get someone to kiss her just when—and how—she wanted him to.

But I don't have those skills. So I just stand next to Jase, leaning on the rail, watching the sailboats, feeling the heat of his arm resting next to mine. After a few minutes, he turns to look at me. That look of his, unhurried, thoughtful, scanning my face slowly. *Are his eyes lingering on my eyes, my lips?* I'm not sure. I want them to. Then he says, "Let's get home. We'll take the Bug and go somewhere. Alice owes me."

As we clamber back over the rocks, I can't stop wondering what just happened there. I could swear he was looking at me like he wanted to kiss me. *What's stopping him? Maybe he isn't attracted to me at all. Maybe he just wants to be friends?* I'm not sure I can pull off being just friends with someone whose clothes I want to rip off.

Oh God. Did I actually just think that? I steal another look at Jase in his jeans. *Yes. Yes, I did.*

We look in again at Andy and Kyle. Now she's talking, and he's taken one of her hands in his and is just looking at her. That seems promising.

⌐∾

When we get to the Garretts' house, their van's gone. We walk into the living room to find Alice and her Brad sprawled on the brown sectional couch, Brad rubbing Alice's feet. George is fast asleep, naked, facedown, on the floor. Patsy is wandering around in purple terry cloth footie pajamas, plaintively saying, "Boob."

"Alice, Patsy should be in bed." Jase scoops her up, her little purple bottom so small in his broad hand. Alice seems surprised to find the baby still there, as though Patsy should have tucked herself in long ago. Jase goes to the kitchen to get a bottle, and Alice sits up, looking at me through narrowed eyes, as though trying to place me. Her hair is now dark red, with some sort of shiny gel making it stick up every which way.

After eyeing me for several minutes she says, "You're Tracy Reed's sister, aren't you? I know Tracy." Her tone implies that, in this particular case, to know Tracy is not to love her.

"Yup, from next door."

"You and Jase seeing each other?"

"Friends."

"Don't hurt him. He's the nicest guy on the planet."

Jase comes back into the room in time to hear this, and rolls his eyes at me privately. Then he scoops the sleeping George easily into his arms, looking around the room.

"Where's Happy?"

Alice, who's settled back into Brad's lap, shrugs.

"Alice, if George wakes up and there's no Happy, he's gonna totally lose it."

"Is Happy the plastic dinosaur?" Brad asks. "'Cause that's in the bathtub."

"No, Happy is the stuffed beagle." Jase rummages around under the couch for a minute, emerging with Happy, who has evidently led a long and eventful life. "I'll just be a sec." He walks by me, letting one palm rest for a moment in the small of my back.

"I mean it," Alice says flatly once he's gone. "You screw with him, you deal with me."

She sounds fully capable of hiring a hit man if I make a wrong move. *Yikes*.

Opening the door to Alice's car, an aged white VW Bug, Jase scoops up about fifty CDs from the passenger seat, then flips open the glove compartment to try to store them there. A lacy red bra falls out. "Jesus," he says, shoving it hastily back in and burying it in CDs.

"Not yours, I take it," I say.

"I really need to get my own car," he says. "Want to go to the lake?"

Just as we start to pull out of the driveway, Mr. and Mrs. Garrett peel in and park, kissing like teenagers, her arms looped around his neck, his hands in her hair. Jase shakes his head as though a little embarrassed, but I stare at them.

"What's it like?" I ask.

He's backing up, his arm resting along the back of my seat. "It?"

"Having happy parents. Together parents. Two parents."

"You never had that?"

"Nope. I've never met my dad. I'm not even sure where he lives anymore."

Jase frowns at me. "No child support?"

"Nope. My mom has a trust fund. I think he tried to get some sort of settlement, but ditching her when she was pregnant counted against him."

"I'd hope," Jase mutters. "I'm sorry, Samantha. Having together parents is all I know. It's like home base. I can't imagine not having that."

I shrug, wondering why I do this with Jase. I've never had a problem keeping stuff private. Something about Jase's quiet watchfulness just makes me talk.

It takes about fifteen minutes to get to the lake, which is on the far side of town. I haven't been here often. I know it's sort of a public school hangout—there's some rite of passage where a lot of the seniors jump in fully clothed on the last day of school. I expect the lake to be crowded with parked cars with steamy windows, but no one else is in the lot when we pull in. Jase reaches into the back of the VW, pulls out a towel, then takes my hand and we walk through the trees to the shore. It's much warmer than it was at the beach, no ocean breeze.

"Race you to the float?" he says, pointing to a shape dimly visible in the gathering dark. I shake off my jacket and yank off my sundress, my bathing suit still underneath, then start to run for the water.

The lake is cool and silky, the water softer than ocean water. The eel grass beneath my feet stops me for a moment, as I try not to think of trout and snapping turtles lurking below. Jase is already swimming fast and I hurry to catch up.

He beats me anyway and is standing on the float to pull me up when I get there.

I look around at the quiet water, the distant shore, and I shiver as his hand closes on mine.

"What am I doing here with you?" I ask.

"What?"

"I hardly know you. You could be some serial killer, luring me out to a deserted lake."

Jase laughs and lies down on the dock on his back, folding his arms behind his head. "Nah, I'm not. And you can tell."

"How can I tell?" I smile at him, lying down beside him, our hips nearly touching. "The whole happy-family-Mr.-Nice-Guy bit could be a cover."

"No, because of instinct. You can tell who to trust. People can, just like animals. We don't listen as well as they do, always, but it's still there. That prickling feeling when something's not right. That calm feeling when it is." His voice is low and husky in the darkness.

"Jase?"

"Mmm-hmm?" He lifts up on one elbow, his face barely visible in the twilight.

"You have to kiss me," I find myself saying.

"Yeah." He leans closer. "I do."

His lips, warm and soft, touch my forehead, then slide down my cheek, moving sideways to my mouth. His hand comes up to press the nape of my neck beneath my wet hair, just as mine slips to his back. His skin's warm beneath the cool sheen of water, his muscles tight as he lies there, still balanced on one elbow. I curl in closer.

I'm not new to kissing. Or I thought I wasn't, but it's never been anything like this. I can't get close enough. When Jase gently deepens the kiss, it feels right, no moment of startled hesitation like I've had before.

After a long time, we swim back to shore and stretch out for a while on our towels, kissing again. Jase's lips smiling under mine as I kiss all over his face. My hands tightening on his shoulders as he nuzzles my neck and softly nibbles my collarbone. It is as if everything else in the world stops as we lie here in the summer night.

"We should go home," Jase whispers, his hands stroking my waist.

"No. Not yet. Not yet," I say back, sliding my lips along the willing curve of his.

Chapter Fourteen

Punctual to a fault, I've never understood the expression "I lost track of time." I've never lost track of anything, not my cell phone, not my homework, not my work schedule, certainly not time. But this night, I do. When we climb into the car it's five of eleven. I try to quell the panic in my tone as I remind Jase of my curfew. He speeds up a little, but stays within the limit, reaching out a calming hand to touch my knee.

"I'll come in with you," he offers as we pull into the circular drive. "Explain that it was my fault."

"No." The headlights of the VW illuminate a Lexus parked in our driveway. Clay? One of those donors? As I fumble with the door latch, my hand is sticky with sweat. I'm scrambling for a plan, a Mom-acceptable excuse. She was not in the best of moods this morning. Unless the donors showered her with money, and probably even if they did, I'm in big trouble. I have to just go in the front door, because chances are my mother has already checked my bed.

"Good night, Jase," I call hurriedly, and run without looking back. I start to open the door, but then it opens swiftly from inside and I practically fall in. Mom's standing there, her face taut with fury.

"Samantha Christina Reed!" she begins. "Do you know what time it is?"

"After curfew. I know. I—"

She shakes the wineglass in her hand at me as if it's a wand that will render me mute. "I'm not going through this with you too—do you hear me? I've done all the troubled-teenager parenting I have time for with your sister. I don't need this, do you understand?"

"Mom, I'm only ten minutes late."

"That's not the point." Her voice rises. "The point is that you don't get to do it! I expect better from you. This summer, especially. You *know* I'm under a lot of pressure. This is not the time for your adolescent drama."

I cannot help but wonder if any parents ever actually schedule in *adolescent drama* on their day planners. *Looks like a slow week, Sarah. I guess I can pencil in your eating disorder.*

"This isn't drama," I tell her, which rings so true to my ears. Mom is drama. Tim is drama. Sometimes even Nan is drama. Jase and the Garretts . . . they're whatever the opposite of drama is. The tidal pool warm in the summer sun, full of exotic life, but no danger.

"Don't contradict me, Samantha," Mom snaps. "You're grounded."

"Mom!"

"What's goin' on, Grace?" asks a softly accented Southern voice, and Clay wanders out of the living room, sleeves rolled up, tie loose around his neck.

"I'm handling it," Mom tells him sharply.

I half expect him to pull back as though she's slapped him,

which I want to do when she gets that tone, but his posture relaxes even more. He leans back against the doorway, flicks something off his shoulder, and says simply, "Seems like you could use my help."

Mom's so tightly wound, she's practically vibrating. She's always been private—would never yell at Tracy and me if we were even remotely in public—then we'd just get a terse whisper—"We will discuss this *later*." But it's Clay, and her hand shoots up to pat her hair in that silly, coy gesture I've only seen her use with him.

"Samantha's late for curfew. She has no excuse for that."

Well, she hasn't exactly given me a chance to offer one, but, true, I don't know what I'd say in my own defense.

Clay looks at his Rolex. "Curfew's when, Gracie?"

"Eleven," Mom says, her voice smaller now.

Clay lets out a rich, low laugh. "Eleven o'clock on a summer night? And she's seventeen? Honey, that's when we *all* miss curfew." He walks over, reaches to squeeze the back of her neck lightly. "I know I did. I'm sure you did." His hand moves to her chin, edging it so she's looking right at him. "Give a little here, sugar."

Mom stares at his face. I'm holding my breath. I shoot a glance at my unlikely rescuer. He winks at me, giving Mom's chin a nudge with his knuckles. In his eyes, there's not a trace of guilt or—and I'm surprised at how relieved I feel—complicity about what he knows I saw.

"Maybe I overreacted," she says finally, to him, not to me.

But I'm beginning to wonder the same thing. Maybe there's an easy explanation for the brunette?

"We all do it, Gracie. Why don't I get you some more wine?"

102

He scoops the glass out of her unresisting fingers and heads off to the kitchen as though it's his own.

Mom and I both stand there.

"Your hair's wet," she says at last. "You'd better shower with conditioner or it'll dry tangly."

I nod, and turn to go up the stairs. Before I've gone far, I hear her behind me. But I act as though I don't, proceeding into my room and flopping facedown on my bed, still wearing my wet bathing suit and damp sundress. The mattress dips as Mom sits down.

"Samantha . . . why would you provoke me like this?"

"I didn't— It's not about—"

She starts rubbing my back the way she did when I had nightmares when I was little. "Sweetie, you just don't understand how hard it is to be a parent, much less a single one. I've been working without a map since you both were born. Never knowing if I'm making the right call. Look at Tracy and that shoplifting incident. And you and that Michael, who might have been doing drugs for all I know."

"Mom. He didn't do drugs. I've told you that before. He was just weird."

"Be that as it may. This is the sort of thing I just can't have going on during the campaign. I need to focus. I can't have you distracting me with these antics."

Antics? Like I've returned stark naked in the wee hours of the morning, reeking of alcohol and pot.

She strokes my back a few more minutes, then frowns. "Why *is* your hair wet?"

The lie slips out easily, though I've never lied to Mom before.

"I took a shower at Nan's. We were trying on makeup and doing a conditioning treatment."

"Ah." Then, her voice low: "I'm keeping an eye on you, Samantha. You've always been my good girl. Just . . . act like it, okay?"

I always have. And this is where I've wound up. Still, I whisper, "Okay," and lie very still beneath her fingers. Finally she stands up, says good night, and leaves.

After about ten minutes, I hear a tapping at my window. I freeze, listening for evidence that Mom heard too. But all's quiet downstairs. I open the window to find Jase crouching on my balcony.

"I wanted to make sure you were okay." Then, looking closely at my face: "Are you?"

"Wait a minute," I tell him, practically shutting the window on his fingers. I hurry to my door, to the top of the stairs, and shout down, "I'm taking that shower now, Mom."

"Use conditioner!" she calls back, sounding much more relaxed. I duck into the bathroom, turn the water on full blast, and return to open the window.

Jase seems perplexed. "Everything all right?"

"Mom's a little protective." I fling one leg, then the other out the window, and sit down next to Jase, who's folded himself comfortably against the gable. The night breeze is sighing past us, and the stars are so bright.

"This was my fault. I was driving. Let me talk to your mom. I'll tell her . . ."

I imagine Jase being confronted by Mom. That I missed curfew for the first time while in the company of "One of Those

Garretts" would confirm, for her, everything she's ever said about them. I just know it.

"It wouldn't help."

He reaches out, folding my cold hand in his warm one. Apparently feeling the chill, his other palm closes on it too. "You sure you're okay?"

I would be if I didn't keep picturing Mom coming up to make sure I was using enough conditioner and finding me out here. I swallow. "I'm fine. See you tomorrow?"

He leans forward, my hand still enclosed in his, moving his lips from the bridge of my nose down to my mouth, coaxing it open. I start to relax into him, then think I hear a knock.

"I've got to go. I—good night?"

He gives my hand a squeeze, then me a grin so dazzling it squeezes my heart even harder. "Yeah. See you tomorrow."

Despite those kisses, I can't relax. *Ten minutes late in a lifetime and I'm an issue for the campaign? Maybe Mom and the Masons can get a discount on military school if they ship me and Tim off together.*

I stop the shower, slamming the frosted glass door loudly. In my room, I pick up my pillow, punching it into shape. I don't know how I'll sleep. My body's tight. In this moment, if Charley Tyler made a pass at me, I'd go all the way, even knowing it meant nothing to him. If Michael actually *were* a drug addict and offered me instant oblivion, I'd take it, even though I hesitate before taking an aspirin. If Jase knocked on the window again and told me we were going to take a motorcycle trip to California right now, I'd go.

What's the use of being the me I've always been when my mother is hardly recognizable?

Chapter Fifteen

The next time I babysit, Mrs. Garrett takes me grocery shopping, so I can entertain the kids and wrestle junk food out of their hands while she scans her stack of her coupons and expertly fields commentary.

"You certainly have your hands full." She hears that one a lot.

"With good things," she responds calmly, removing Count Chocula cereal from George's eager grasp.

"You must be Catholic," is another she gets time and time again.

"No, just fertile." She peels Harry's hands away from the latest Transformer action hero.

"That baby needs a hat," lectures a severe-looking elderly woman in the freezer aisle.

"Thank you, but not really, she has several nice ones at home." Mrs. Garrett picks up an economy-size box of frozen waffles and adds it to the cart.

I hand Patsy a bottle of juice, prompting a crunchy-granola-looking woman in Birkenstocks to say, "That baby is much too old for a bottle. She should be on a sippy cup by now."

Who are these people, and why do they think their own opinions are the only right ones?

"Don't you ever just want to kill them, or at least swear at them?" I ask in an undertone, steering the cart away from the crabby sippy-cup woman, with Harry and George clinging to either side like spider monkeys.

"Of course." Mrs. Garrett shrugs. "But what kind of example would that be?"

I've lost track of how many laps I've done, but I know it's less than I used to be able to do, and I'm winded but invigorated when I climb the ladder, squeezing water from my hair. I've loved swimming ever since I can remember, ever since I was brave enough to follow Tim out of the safe shallows into the bigger waves. *I'm going to get back on that team.* I dash the towel across my face, check the clock—fifteen minutes till the pool opens, which is usually accompanied by a surge of people through the gates. My cell phone buzzes on my chair.

Take a break, Aqua girl! Nan's texted me, from the B&T gift shop. Come C me.

Stony Bay is very proud of Stony Bay. The B&T's gift shop, By the Bay Buys, is chockablock full of items advertising various town landmarks. As I walk in, Nan is already open for business, saying sweetly to a gentleman in pink plaid shorts, "As you can see, you could get this mouse pad of Main Street, and then these placemats with the aerial view of the river mouth, this little lamp that looks like our lighthouse, *and* these coasters with the view of the dock—and you wouldn't need to go outside at all. You could see the whole town from your dining room."

The man appears nonplussed, either by Nan's soft-spoken sarcasm or by the idea of spending so much money. "I really only wanted these," he says, holding up some napkins that say *One martini, two martini, three martini, floor*. "Can you put them on my club tab?"

After Nan rings him up and he leaves, she crosses her eyes at me. "My first day on the job and I'm already regretting this. If all the Sanctification of Stony Bay stuff brainwashes me, and I tell you I need to join the Garden Club, you'll get me deprogrammed, right?"

"I'll be there for you, sister. Have you seen Tim? He was supposed to get here ten minutes early so I can show him his uniform and all that."

Nan checks her watch. "He's not officially late yet. Two more minutes. How did I get the most boring job with the longest hours in town? I only took it because Mrs. Gritzmocker, who does the buying, is married to Mr. Gritzmocker, the bio teacher who I want to write a recommendation for me."

"This is the price of your ruthless ambition," I say. "It's not too late to repent and work for the greater good—like at Breakfast Ahoy."

Nan grins at me, her hundreds of freckles already darkening with the summer sun. "Yeah, well, I'm saving my Naughty Sailorette costume for Halloween." She glances out the window behind me. "Besides, it's gonna take both of us to babysit my brother if he can get himself fired from a hot dog stand."

"How exactly *did* he do that?" I ask, opening one of the

sample lip glosses on the checkout counter, rubbing it on my finger and smelling it. *Ick. Piña colada. I hate coconut.*

"Asked people how hot they wanted their wiener," Nan says absently. "He's out there now. By the concession stand. Go make sure he's not a disaster."

Given our last encounter, I approach warily. Tim's leaning against my lifeguard chair, wearing dark glasses even though it's cloudy. Not a good sign. I edge closer to him. He used to be so easygoing, Nan's opposite. Now he's a time bomb who might detonate in your hands.

"So," I say hesitantly. "You okay?"

"Fine." His voice is abrupt. Either he hasn't forgiven me for not being his ATM or he's got a headache. Probably both.

"Seriously? Because this job is, well, serious."

"Yup, the fate of the world depends on what goes down at the Lagoon pool at the B and T. I get it. I'm your man." He salutes without looking at me, then squirts sunscreen into his palm to rub on his pale chest.

"Honestly. You can't mess around here, Tim. There are little kids and—"

His hand on my arm silences me. "Yeah, yeah. Screw the lecture, Princess Buttercup. I *know*." Taking off his sunglasses, he jabs them at his heart for emphasis with a phony smile. "I'm hungover but I'm straight. I'll save the partying for after hours. Now get off my back and do *your* job."

"You're part of my job. I'm supposed to show you where the uniforms are. Hang on."

I position the Lifeguard Off Duty sign more prominently on my chair, walk through the bushes to the Lagoon pool, and set that one up too. A bunch of moms standing outside the gate with their children and their arms full of floaties look annoyed. "Just five more minutes," I call, adding in an authoritative tone, "Need to resolve a safety issue."

Tim's sweaty and preoccupied as he follows me through the labyrinthine course to the room where uniforms are kept. We pass the bathrooms, with their heavy oak doors, thick iron latches, and signs that say "Salty Dogs" and "Gulls," then spell it out in nautical flags.

"I'm gonna throw up," he says.

"Yeah, It's ludicrous, but—"

He grabs my sleeve. "I mean really. Wait." He vanishes into the men's room.

Not good. I move away from the door so I don't have to hear. After about five minutes, he comes back out.

"What?" he asks belligerently.

"Nothing."

"Right," he mutters. We get to the uniform room.

"So, here's your suit—and stuff," I shove the towel, hat, jacket, and whistle that come with the job, along with the gold-crest embossed navy blue board shorts, into his hands.

"You gotta be kidding. I can't wear my own suit?"

"Nope—you need to display the B and T crest," I say, attempting a straight face.

"Fuck me, Samantha. I can't wear these. How'm I supposed to pick up hot girls and get laid?"

"You're supposed to be saving lives, not scamming on girls."

"Shut up, Samantha."

Seems as though all our conversations run into the same dead end.

I reach over and scoop up the hat with its jaunty insignia, plopping it on his head.

It's removed even faster than Tim can say: "That will be an extra helping of *hell no* with the hat. Do you wear one of those?"

"No—for some reason, only the male lifeguards get that. I get the little jacket with the crest."

"Well, not this guy. I'd just as soon go in drag."

I can't worry about Tim. It's pointless. Besides, this isn't a job that allows for downtime. At the far end of the Olympic pool, a group of elderly women are taking a water aerobics class. Despite the rope blocking off that section, kids keep cannonballing into the class, splashing the ladies and upsetting their fragile balance. There's always a baby who doesn't have a swim diaper, despite the many signs saying this is a must, and I have to talk to the mother, who usually gets antagonistic—"Peyton was toilet trained at eleven months. She doesn't need a diaper!"

At two o'clock, the pool's nearly empty and I can relax a little. The moms have taken little kids home for naps. No one here but tanners and loungers. I'm overheated and sticky from sitting so long in the high plastic chair. Clambering down, I blow my whistle and hoist the Lifeguard Off Duty sign, thinking I'll get a soda at the snack bar to cool off.

"I'm taking a break. Can I get you something to drink?" I call over to Tim.

"Only if it's eighty proof," he calls back through the bushes and granite stones that separate the Olympic pool from the Lagoon one.

The back door buzzer sounds behind me. Weird. All B&T guests have to sign in at the gatehouse. Back door is for deliveries, and Nan didn't say anything about more Stony Bay paraphernalia coming.

I buzz the door open and there's Mr. Garrett, a stack of two-by-fours on his shoulder, so out of place I actually do a double take. He's wandered in from the wrong movie, all bronzed and full of energy against the pale ivory gate. His face breaks into a big smile at the sight of me. "Samantha! Jase said you worked here, but we weren't sure of your hours. He'll be pleased."

My dinky insignia jacket and silly gold-crested suit are so lame, but Mr. Garrett doesn't appear to notice. "This is just the first of the load," he tells me. "They tell you where these're supposed to go?"

Lumber? No, I'm blank, which obviously shows.

"No worries. I'll give the building manager a ring before we get going carrying the rest."

I didn't know Garrett's Hardware even did lumber. I know nothing about the Garretts' business, and I feel shamed by this suddenly, like I should know.

As he's calling, I peer over his shoulder down to the curb, where I can see Jase's distinctive form bent into the back of a faded green pickup truck. My pulse picks up. How is it that my world and the Garretts' had such sharp boundaries until this summer and now they keep interlocking?

"Yup"—Mr. Garrett snaps the phone shut—"they want it

right here between the two pools. I guess they're building a tiki bar."

Right. A tiki bar will blend in great with the whole Henry VIII vibe going on at the B&T. *Bring me a scorpion bowl, wench.* I glance through the bushes in search of Tim, but see only a drift of cigarette smoke.

"Sam!" Jase balances a stack of wood on his shoulder, sweaty in the summer heat. He's wearing jeans and has a pair of thick work gloves on. The wood drops onto the pool deck with a clatter and he comes right up for a kiss, salty warm. His gloves are rough on my arms and he tastes like cinnamon gum. I pull back, suddenly very aware of Mr. Lennox's window overlooking the pool and Tim not twenty feet away. And Nan. Not to mention Mrs. Henderson tanning nearby. She's in the Garden Club with Mom.

Jase stands back to survey me, raising his eyebrows slightly.

"You're an admiral now?" This is not what I expect him to say. He touches the gold braid on the shoulders of my jacket. "Big promotion from Breakfast Ahoy." He smiles. "Do I have to salute you?"

"Please don't."

Jase bends in for another kiss. I stiffen. Out of the corner of my eye, I see Mrs. Henderson sit up, cell phone to her ear. Surely she hasn't got my mom on speed dial . . . ?

The expression in Jase's eyes—it's surprise and a little hurt. He scans my face.

"Sorry!" I say. "Have to keep up appearances while in uniform." I flap my hand at him. *Keep up appearances?* "I mean—keep my eyes on the pool. Not get distracted. The management gets all uptight about 'fraternizing on the job,'" I say, gesturing toward Mr. Lennox's window.

Shooting the Lifeguard Off Duty sign a puzzled glance, Jase falls back and nods. I cringe inwardly. "Okay," he says slowly. "Is this acceptable then?" He ducks to give my forehead a chaste smack.

Mr. Garrett calls, "Hey, J, I need four hands for this one and I've only got the two."

I flush, but Jase just smiles at me and turns to help his dad. *Maybe Mr. Garrett is used to Jase kissing girls in front of him? Maybe this is all easy and expected for both of them. Why is it so weird and hard for me?*

At this point, Mr. Lennox hurries out, looking flustered. I brace myself. "They didn't say *when* you were coming," he says. "Nothing but 'between noon and five'!" I exhale, feeling silly.

"Bad time?" Mr. Garrett asks, easing the latest stack of wood onto the last.

"I just like to have Notice," Mr. Lennox protests. "Did you sign in at the gatehouse? All service people need to sign in with Precise time of Delivery and Departure."

"We just pulled up to the curb. I've delivered here before. I didn't think it would be a problem."

"It's Club Protocol." Mr. Lennox's tone is urgent.

"I'll sign on the way out," Mr. Garrett says. "Do you want the rest in a pile here? When does construction start?"

Apparently another sore point for the flustered Mr. Lennox. "They haven't told me that either."

"Don't worry about it," Mr. Garrett tells him. "We've got a tarp to leave in case it takes a while and there's rain."

He and Jase go back and forth to the truck, alternately carrying single loads and hauling them together, a team. Mr. Lennox hovers, possibly needing CPR soon.

"That's the lot," Mr. Garrett says finally. "I just need this signed." He holds out a clipboard to Mr. Lennox, then stands back, clenching and unclenching his left hand, wincing.

I glance over at Jase. He's stripped off the gloves and is wiping his brow. Though it's cloudy, the temperature's over eighty and it's humid as usual.

"Can I get you guys something to drink?" I ask.

"S'okay. We've got a thermos in the car. Restroom, though?" Jase tips his head at me. "Or do I have to sign in for that one at the gatehouse?"

I don't say anything to this, just direct him to the bathroom and then stand there uncertainly. Mr. Garrett bends to the pool, dips his hands and tosses water on his face, running it through his wavy brown hair, so much like his son's. Though Mr. Lennox has faded away muttering, I feel apologetic. "Sorry about—" I gesture toward the club.

Mr. Garrett laughs. "You're certainly not responsible if they love their rules, Samantha. I've dealt with these guys before. Nothing new."

Jase returns from the bathroom, smiling. "There are, like, griffins overlooking the stalls in there." He jerks his thumb over his shoulder.

"Take a second," Mr. Garrett tells Jase, clapping him on the shoulder. "I have to do some more paperwork in the car."

"Thanks, Dad," Jase murmurs before turning to me.

"So . . . will I see you tonight?" I ask.

"Absolutely. When do you get off work? Aw . . . I forgot. Not till later. Tonight's Thursday, so Dad's training me again. At the beach."

"At the beach for football? How does that work?"

"He's got me doing his old workout. He had Division Two colleges looking at him until he blew out his knee, so I need to bulk up. It means running in the water knee-deep, and that's still a killer for me."

"Jason—all set?" Mr. Garrett calls.

"Coming." He drops his gloves to the ground, sliding his bare palms up my arms, then edging me into the shade of one of the bushes. I want to lean into him, but I'm still tense. Beyond his head, I see Tim, sorting coins in his hand, headed for the snack bar. He looks over at us, takes in the scene, smirks, then wags an index finger at us. *Tsk-tsk*.

"I'll respect the uniform and hold off on the fraternizing," Jase says, kissing my cheek. "But I'll see you tonight."

"Uniform-free," I add, then clap my hand over my mouth.

He grins, but says only: "Works for me."

Chapter Sixteen

Jase holds his hand against the windowpane, bumping it only gently, but I'm so alert for the sound that I hear it, throw the window open, and climb out all in under twenty seconds.

He indicates the blanket spread out on the roof.

"Prepared!" I comment, sliding down next to him.

He reaches for me, slipping an arm around my neck. "I try to think ahead. Plus, I needed incentive to finish the last bit of training, so I thought about meeting you up here."

"I was incentive?"

"You were." His arm is warm behind me. I curl my toes at the bottom of the blanket, brushing against the still-warm roof tiles. It's nearly nine o'clock and the last bit of day is losing the battle against the dark. Another starry night.

"The stars are different around the world, did you know? If we were in Australia, we'd see a whole new sky."

"Not just backward?" Jase pulls me closer, pillowing my head on his chest. I take a deep breath of warm skin and clean shirt. "Or upside down? Completely different?"

"Mostly different," I tell him. "It's winter in Australia, so they see the Summer Cross . . . and Orion's belt. And this orangey red star, Aldebaran, which is part of the eye of Taurus. You know, the bull."

"So how is it, exactly," he asks, tracing his finger idly around the collar of my shirt, a mesmerizing motion, "that you became an astrophysicist?"

"Kind of a roundabout way." I close my eyes, breathe in the smell of cut grass, Mom's rosebushes, Jase's clean skin.

"Go on," he says, sliding the finger up my throat to follow the line of my jaw, then back down along the collar. I feel almost hypnotized by that simple motion and find myself telling a story I've never told.

"You know how my dad left my mom before I was born?"

He nods, his brow furrowing, but doesn't say anything.

"Well, I don't really know how it happened—she doesn't talk about it. Whether she kicked him out or he just left or they had some big fight or . . . what. But he left behind some stuff—in this big box that my mom was supposed to mail to him. I guess. But she was about to have me, and Trace was really little too, only just over a year old. So she didn't send it, she just stuck it in the back of the front hall closet."

I've always thought this was so unlike Mom, not to sweep up every bit.

"Tracy and I found the box when we were about five and six. We thought it was a Christmas present or something. So we opened it, all excited. But it was just full of random things— old T-shirts with band names on them, cassette tapes, pictures of these big gatherings of people we didn't know, sports gear. One sneaker. Stuff. Not what we were hoping for, once we realized what it was."

"What were you hoping for?" Jase's voice is quiet.

"Treasure. Old diaries or something. His Barbie collection."

"Er . . . your dad collected Barbies?"

I laugh. "Not that I know of. But we were little girls. We would have preferred that to some smelly shoes and old R.E.M. and Blind Melon T-shirts."

"Yeah, I guess so." Now Jase's finger has edged down my shorts, tracing the same slow line along the waistband. I take a hard-to-catch breath.

"Anyway, at the very bottom there was this telescope. A fancy one, but still all wrapped up, like he'd gotten it but never opened it. Or someone had given it to him and he didn't want it. So I took it and hid it in my closet."

"Then you used it? On the roof?" Jase shifts, propping himself up on an elbow now, looking at my face.

"Not on the roof, just from my window. I couldn't figure out the directions for a few years. But after that, yeah, I used it. Looking for aliens, finding the Big Dipper, that kind of thing." I shrug

"Wondering where your dad was, at all?"

"Oh, maybe. Probably. At first. After that I just got hooked by the idea of all those planets far away, all those other stories."

Jase nods, as though this makes sense to him.

I find myself feeling a little shaky. "Now it's your turn."

"Hmm?" He circles my belly button with that light finger. Oh my God.

"Tell me a story." I turn my head, bury my lips in the worn cotton of his shirt. "Tell me things I don't know."

So, with nothing to be distracted by, no brothers and sisters bursting in, no crowd of friends, no awkward on-the-job moment, just me and Jase, I learn things about the Garretts I couldn't by watching. I learn that Alice is in nursing school. Jase raises his eyebrow at me when I laugh at this. "What, you don't see my big sister as a ministering angel? I'm shocked." Duff's allergic to strawberries. Andy was born two months early. All the Garretts are musical. Jase plays the guitar, Alice the piccolo, Duff the cello, Andy the violin. "And Joel?" I ask.

"Oh, the drums, of course," Jase says. "It *was* the clarinet, but then he realized that was just not a turn-on."

The soft air smells sweet and leafy. Feeling the slow beat of Jase's heart beneath my cheek, I close my eyes and relax. "How was the training?"

"I'm a little sore," Jase admits. "But Dad knows what he's doing. It worked for Joel, anyway. He got a full ride at State U for football."

"So where are you applying, to college—do you know yet?"

Jase, who's again leaning on one elbow, lies back, rubbing the side of his nose with his thumb. His face, usually so alight and open, clouds.

"I don't know. Not sure I can apply."

"What?"

He tunnels his fingers through his hair. "My parents—my dad—they've always been really good about debt. But then, last year, that new Lowe's started digging ground. Dad figured it would be a good time to take a loan and lay in inventory. Specialty items, things Lowe's wouldn't have. But, uh, people aren't building. The store's barely breaking even. It's tight. Alice has a partial and some money from my great-aunt Alice. She's got a private duty nurse's aid job this summer too. But I . . . well . . . the football thing may work out, but I'm not my brother."

I twist to face him. "There's got to be something, Jase. Some other kind of scholarship . . . student loan. There's something out there, I'm sure."

I think of Mrs. Garrett trying to limit how much juice the kids pour. "Duff, you'll never drink that whole glass. Pour a little, then refill if you're really thirsty." Then of Mom, who makes gourmet dishes on a whim after watching the Food Network, food she won't be home long enough to eat, and that Tracy, and now just me, will never be able to finish.

"There's a way, Jase. We'll find it."

He shrugs, looking slightly less bleak as his eyes rest on me. "Sailor Supergirl to *my* rescue now?"

I salute him. "At your service."

"Yeah?" He leans over, ducking his head so our noses touch. "Could I get a list of those services?"

"I'll show you mine," I breathe, "if . . ."

"Deal," Jase murmurs, then his mouth shifts to mine, warm and sure as his hands pull me close.

Later, he leans up one last time to kiss me as he descends the trellis, then waits while I fold the blanket and toss it down to him. "G'night!"

"Good night!" I whisper, then hear Mom's voice, behind me.

"Sweetheart?"

Oh God. I leap back in through the window, so fast I smack the top of my forehead on the frame. "Ow!"

"Were you talking to someone out there?" Mom, looking

chic in a sleeveless black shirt and fitted white pants, has her arms folded, frowning. "I thought I heard voices."

I try to keep the flush from flooding my face. Unsuccessfully. I'm blushing, and my lips are swollen. I could not *possibly* look more guilty.

"Just calling hello to Mrs. Schmidt across the street," I say. "She was getting her mail."

Incredibly, Mom buys this. She's already distracted.

"I've told you a hundred times not to leave that window open. It lets out the central air and it lets in the bugs!" She slams the window shut, flipping the lock, then looking out. I pray she won't see the incriminating figure of Jase heading home, with, *God*, a blanket! Not that Mom would necessarily put two and two together, but that was *so close* and she's not stupid and . . .

I feel as though my heart might pound its way out of my chest.

"Why don't those people ever put away the clutter in their yard?" she mutters to herself, pulling down the shade.

"Was there something you wanted, Mommy?" I ask, then grimace. I haven't called her *Mommy* for at least six years.

But the word seems to take the edge off and she comes over, to brush my hair from my face, almost as Jase did, except that she pulls it back, gathering it into a ponytail, then shifts to study the effect, giving me that smile that reaches her eyes. "Yes, I need your help, Samantha. I have a few events tomorrow and I'm stuck. Come help me? We can have tea."

A few minutes later, my adrenaline levels gradually easing back to normal, I sip chamomile tea, watching Mom spread linen pantsuits and summer sweaters on her bed. You'd think this would be Tracy's job; she's the one who thinks in terms of outfits and lays out her clothes the night before. But for some reason, it's always been mine.

"Here's what I have," Mom says. "It's a luncheon at the Garden Club, then I need to go to a one-hundredth birthday party, and straight from there to a harbor cruise."

Snuggling back against the satin bolster, I narrow the choices down to basic black dress, casual white linen suit, blue flowered skirt with cornflower-colored wrap.

"The black," I tell her. "Goes with everything."

"Hmmm." Her forehead creases and she scoops up the hanger, draping the black over her body, turning to look in the cheval mirror. "My mother always told me not to wear all black. Too stark, and kind of clichéd." Before I can ask why she bought it, then, she brightens. "But I have the same thing in navy blue."

I pronounce that dress perfect, and it is. Mom vanishes into her walk-in closet to pull out a selection of shoes. I burrow deeper into the pillows. Though she's hardly taller than me, her bed is a California king, one of those outsized deals made for the LA Lakers or whatever. I feel, always, like a little kid when I'm here.

After we sort through the shoes, discarding the wicked highs and torturous Manolos and the "practical but ugly" Naturalizers, Mom sits down on the bed, reaching for her tea. Her shoulders rise and fall with an indrawn breath. "This is relaxing." She smiles at me. "It feels as though we haven't done this in a long time."

It feels like that because it *is* like that. Our tea ritual, choosing clothes, Mom being home at night . . . hard to remember the last time all that came together.

"Tracy e-mailed me the cutest picture of Flip and her at the East Chop Lighthouse."

"I got it too," I say.

"They're a very sweet couple." Mom sips her tea.

"Sweet" would not be the first word I'd use to describe Tracy and Flip, but I've walked in on them at inopportune moments that Mom, against all odds, has never encountered. *What if she'd come to my room five minutes—two minutes—sooner? The open window would have told her where I was. What would I have said? What would Jase have done?*

"Do you miss having a boyfriend, sweetheart?" This catches me totally off guard. She stands up, scooping up the rejected outfits and heading for the closet to rehang them. I say nothing. "I know that's important at your age." She laughs ruefully. "Maybe at my age too. I'd forgotten. . . ." She goes far away for a moment, then seems to catch herself, returning to the subject at hand. "What about Thorpe, Samantha? Flip's younger brother? He's such a nice boy."

She's suggesting dates for me now? This is new, and bizarre, behavior for Mom.

"Uh, Thorpe plays for the other team," I tell her.

"Well, I hardly think his sports allegiances matter," she says. "He's always had lovely manners."

"He's been out of the closet since middle school, Mom."

She blinks rapidly, absorbing this. "Oh. *Oh.* Well, then."

Her cell phone rings, loud in the quiet air. "Hi, honey."

Mom tucks the phone to her shoulder, fluffing her hair even though Clay's not present.

"When? Okay, I'll turn it on right now. Call you back after!"

She reaches for the clicker, neatly contained in a wicker basket on her bedside table. "Channel Seven covered my speech at the Tapping Reeve House. Tell me what you think, Samantha."

I wonder if the children of movie stars get this weird sense of disconnect I have now. The person on-screen *looks* like the woman who makes lemonade in our kitchen, but the words coming out of her mouth are alien. She's never had a problem with immigrants before. Or gay marriage. She's always been conservative in a moderate way. I listen to her, I look at her excited face next to me, and I don't know what to say. Is this Clay? Whatever it is, it makes me squirm.

Chapter Seventeen

When Mom isn't out campaigning, busier than ever, Clay's at our house. This takes getting used to. As I saw from the start, Clay's different. He spreads himself out, taking off his tie and tossing his jacket down on the sofa, kicking his shoes any which way, thinking nothing of opening the refrigerator, taking out leftovers and eating them straight from the Tupperware. Things Mom would never allow Tracy or me to do. But Clay gets a free pass. I walk into the kitchen some mornings to find him cooking breakfast for Mom, mysterious breakfasts full of things she's never eaten, like grits and home fries. While Mom studies the schedule of the day, Clay fills up her coffee cup, her plate, planting a kiss on her head as he does so.

The morning after we choose clothes, he's in the kitchen in an apron (!) when I come downstairs. "Your mama's just gone out to get the papers, Samantha. Would you like some biscuits with sausage gravy?"

Yuck, no. He is wielding the frying pan with the same easy confidence he seems to bring to everything. It's odd to have a man feeling comfortable in our house.

Then I realize, this is the first time I've seen him alone since

I ran into him on Main Street. It's my chance to ask him what's up with that woman, but I have no idea how to begin.

"Here. Try this," he says, setting a plate in front of me. It looks like someone's thrown up on a biscuit, but it actually smells really good.

"C'mon," he says. "Don't be one of those girls who's afraid to put a little meat on her bones."

His hair is flopping boyishly on his forehead and his eyes smile. I want to like him. He makes Mom so happy. And he did stand up for me about curfew. I shift uncomfortably.

"Thanks, by the way. For helping me out the other night," I finally say, poking at the lumpy gravy with my fork.

Clay chuckles. "I was young once too, honey."

You still are, I think, wondering suddenly if he's closer to my own age than Mom's.

"C'mon, Samantha. You're no coward. Take a bite."

All right, I think. I won't be a coward. I look him in the eyes.

"So who was that woman I saw you with?"

I expect him to tell me it's none of my business. Or say he has no clue what I'm talking about. But he doesn't miss a beat.

"Downtown? Have you been fussin' about that?"

I shrug. "I've been wondering. If I should say something to my mom."

He plants his hands on the counter, looking me in the eye. "Because you saw me having lunch with an old friend?"

The air has shifted a little. He's smiling, but I'm not sure he means it now. "You did seem pretty friendly," I say.

Clay studies me, still leaning casually against the counter. I meet his eyes. After a moment, he suddenly seems to relax.

"She's just a pal, Samantha. She was a girlfriend, a while back, but that's history. I'm with your mama now."

I make little indentations in the gravy with my fork. "So Mom knows about her?"

"We haven't sat down and talked about our pasts much. Too much goin' on right here and now. But your mama has no call to be concerned about Marcie. Any more than I would fret about your daddy. Want some OJ?" He pours me a glass before I can answer. "We're grown-ups, sugar. We all have pasts. I bet even you do. But those don't much matter compared to the present, right?"

Well . . . right, I guess. I mean, I can barely remember what I saw in Michael or Charley.

"We all have presents too," he adds, "that we don't tell even the people we love every little thing about."

I look at him sharply. But no, that's crazy. He's here even less often than Mom. He couldn't possibly know about Jase. But wait, does that mean . . .

"Like I said, Marcie's the past. She's not my present, Samantha. And you know me well enough to know I'm a heckuva lot more concerned with the future than the past."

I'm polishing off the surprisingly good biscuit when Mom comes in, flushed from the heat, with a large stack of newspapers. Clay scoops them out of her hands, gives her a big kiss, pulls out a stool for her.

"I've been working on making a Southerner out of your daughter, Gracie. Hope you've got no objection to that."

"Of course not, sweetie." She slides onto the stool next to me. "That looks delicious. I'm famished!"

Clay gives her two biscuits and ladles on the gravy, and Mom tucks into it like a lumberjack. So much for her usual breakfast of cantaloupe and rye toast.

And so it goes. He's in our lives, in our house, everywhere now.

That feels like the last I see of Mom for a while. She dashes out the door every morning with her change of clothes for the evening hanging off the backseat hook in her car. The longest conversations I have with her are by text, as she lets me know she's at a cookout, clam broil, ribbon cutting, fund-raising harbor cruise, union meeting . . . whatever. She even falls behind on vacuuming, leaving Post-it notes directing me to pick up the slack. When she *is* home for dinner, Clay's there too, and halfway into the meal he shoves aside his plate, pulling out a pad to scribble notes on, absently reaching for his fork from time to time, fishing a piece of meat or a bite of tomato off whatever plate he lands on—his own, mine, Mom's.

You hear that phrase "he lives and breathes" about people's enthusiasms, but I've never seen it in action quite like this. Clay Tucker lives and breathes politics. He makes Mom, with her relentless schedule, seem like a casual dabbler. He's turning her into someone new, someone like him. Maybe that's a good thing . . . But the fact is, I miss my mom.

Chapter Eighteen

"Ms. Reed! Ms. Reed? Could you please come here?" Mr. Lennox's voice slices through the air, practically vibrating with rage. "This instant!"

I blow my whistle, put the Lifeguard Off Duty sign on my chair after making sure there are no small kids without parents in the water, and head for the Lagoon pool. Mr. Lennox is standing there with Tim. Once again Mr. Lennox looks a few breaths from an apoplexy. Tim, amused and a little wasted, is squinting in the midday sun.

"This"—Mr. Lennox points to me—"is a lifeguard."

"Ohhhhhh," Tim says. "I get it now."

"No, you do not *get it,* young man. Do you call yourself a lifeguard? Is that what you call yourself?"

Tim's expression is familiar, struggling to decide whether to be a smart ass. Finally he says, "My friends are allowed to call me Tim."

"That is not what I mean!" Mr. Lennox whirls on me. "Do you know how many demerits this young man has accrued?"

He's only worked at the B&T for a week, so I make a conservative guess. "Um . . . five?"

"Eight! Eight!" I'm almost expecting Mr. Lennox to burst

into a ball of flame. "Eight demerits. You've worked here two summers. How many demerits do you have?"

Tim folds his arms and looks at me. "Fraternizing" on the job is worth four demerits, but he's never said a word—to me or, apparently, Nan—about seeing me and Jase.

"I'm not sure," I say. None.

"None!" Mr. Lennox says. "In his brief stint on the job, this young man has"—he holds up one hand, bending down finger by finger—"taken food from the snack bar—twice—without paying. Not worn his hat—three times. Allowed someone else to sit in the lifeguard chair—"

"It was just this little kid," Tim interjects. "He wanted to see the view. He was, like, four."

"That chair is not a toy. You have also left your post without posting the off duty or on break sign—twice."

"I was right there by the pool," Tim objects. "I was just talking to some girls. I would have stopped if someone was drowning. They weren't *that* hot," he adds this last to me, as though he owes me an explanation for this unaccountable sense of responsibility.

"You didn't even notice me when I stood behind you clearing my throat! I cleared it *three times*."

"Is not noticing the throat-clearing a separate offense from not putting up that sign? Or is it three different demerits because of the three times, because—"

Mr. Lennox's face seems to contract and freeze. He straightens up as tall as a very short man can. "You"—finger jabbed at Tim's chest—"do not have the Bath and Tennis spirit." He punctuates each word with another jab.

131

Tim's lip twitches, another bad move.

"Now," Mr. Lennox thunders, "you do not have a *job*."

I hear a sigh from behind me and turn to find Nan.

"A week," she whispers. "A new record, Timmy."

Mr. Lennox turns on his heel, calling, "Please return all items of your wardrobe that are club property to the office."

"Aw, shit," Tim says, reaching into the pocket of the hoodie draped over the lifeguard chair and pulling out a pack of Marlboros. "I was so hoping I'd get to keep the cute hat."

"That's it?" Nan's voice rises unexpectedly in both pitch and volume. "That's all you have to say? This is the fourth job you've lost since you got kicked out of school! Your third school in three years! Your fourth job in three months! How is it even *possible* to get fired that often?"

"Well, that movie theater gig was boring as all fuck, for one thing," Tim offers, lighting up.

"Who cares! All you had to do was take tickets!" Nan shouts. Tim's kept his voice low, but Mr. Lennox was loud and Nan, who hates a scene, doesn't seem to care that she's making one now. A group of small kids are staring, round-eyed. Mrs. Henderson has her cell phone out once again. "And you screwed that up by letting everyone you know in for free!"

"They charge crazy-ass prices for popcorn and candy—the management was hardly losing money."

Nan puts her hands in her hair, sweat-damp with either heat or frustration. "Then the senior center. Giving joints out to senior citizens, Timmy? What was *that*?" Mrs. Henderson has now moved in closer, under the pretext of heading toward the snack bar.

"Hey, Nano, if my ass were in a wheelchair in a place like that, I'd only *hope* you'd show up with some weed. Those poor bastards *needed* their reality blurred. It was like a public service. They had them square dancing. They had fake *American Idol* contests. They had frickin' funny hat day. It was like Torture the Elderly Fest. They—"

"You're such a goddamn loser," Nan, who never swears, says. "It's not possible we're really related."

Then a surprising thing happens. Hurt slices across Tim's face. He shuts his eyes, pops them open again to glare at her.

"Sorry, sis. Same gene pool. I could resent you for swimming to the deep end with all the perfect genes, but since they make you so fucking miserable, I don't. You can have 'em."

"Okay stop it, you two," I say, the way I used to when they clashed as kids, rolling around on the grass, pinching, scratching, punching, no holds barred. It always scared me, afraid they'd really get hurt. Somehow the potential seems so much bigger now that words are the weapons of choice.

"Samantha," Nan says. "Let's get back to work. We need to do those jobs *we* still have."

"Right," Tim calls after her retreating back. "'Cause then you get to keep the great outfits! Priorities, right, Nano?" He picks up his hat, puts it on the lifeguard chair, and stubs out his cigarette in it.

Chapter Nineteen

"I've got a surprise." Jase opens the door of the van for me a couple days later. I haven't seen Tim or Nan since the incident at the B&T, and I'm secretly glad for a break from the drama.

I slide into the van, my sneakers crunching into a crumpled pile of magazines, an empty Dunkin' Donuts coffee cup, various Poland Spring and Gatorade bottles, and lots of unidentifiable snack wrappers. Alice and her Bug are evidently still at work.

"A surprise, for me?" I ask, intrigued.

"Well, it's for me, but you too, kind of. I mean, it's something I want you to see."

This sounds a little unnerving. "Is it a body part?" I ask.

Jase rolls his eyes. "No. Jeez. I hope I'd be smoother than that."

I laugh. "Okay. Just checking. Show me."

We drive to Maplewood, two towns over, more run-down than Stony Bay. Jase pulls the van into a parking lot with a huge red, white, and blue sign that says "French Bob's Used Cars."

"French Bob?"

"Bob unfortunately thinks that adding 'French' makes him sound classier."

"Got it. So, you'd be French Jase?"

"*Oui, oui.* Come on. I want you to tell me what you think of her."

Her?

He takes my hand after we climb out of the car, pulling me into the back lot. There are lots and lots of extremely aged vehicles in various states of disrepair, with big white painted lettering on their windshields. I peer at them, noticing that they all say things like "A STEAL AT $3,999!" or "THEY DON'T MAKE 'EM LIKE THIS ANYMORE" or "PURRS LIKE A TIGER CUB."

We come to a stop in front of a grayish white car with a huge hood and tiny cockpit. The windshield says "THIS SWEET BABY COULD BE YOURS FOR MERE PENNIES."

"*Mere pennies* meaning, of course, fifteen hundred bucks," Jase says. "But isn't she beautiful?"

I'm no car connoisseur, but his eyes are shining, so I say enthusiastically, "Gorgeous."

He laughs at me. "I know, not now. But she's a '73 Mustang. Picture her with paint instead of primer. Picture her with new seat covers and a leather steering wheel and—"

"Fuzzy dice?" I ask dubiously. "Candy apple–red paint? Leopard-print seat covers?"

Jase shakes his head. "Just who do you think I am today, Samantha? No way. British racing green, of course. And no dice. And, before you ask, no dancing hula girl figurines either."

"In that case, I love it."

He grins. "Good. Because I know I can get her working again, and she's a convertible and I just wanted to make sure you . . . liked her because . . . I just wanted to be sure you did."

He pats the hood, ducking his head slightly. "I've been saving for this now for four years. I should put it toward college, I *know*," he says, as though expecting me to give him a lecture on fiscal responsibility. "But Alice, like, *always* has the Bug these days. Apparently Brad is a lousy driver. And you and I can't have all our dates on your roof. Besides, this is such a deal."

My attention has been caught by one thing. "You've been saving for a car since you were thirteen?"

"What? You think that's weird?"

His smile's so infectious that I'm returning it before I even begin to answer. "I don't know. I just thought thirteen-year-olds went for the Xbox first."

"Joel taught me to drive when I was thirteen—in the beach parking lot in the fall. I just got hooked. That's why I started learning how to fix things on cars . . . since I couldn't legally drive 'em yet. You still think I'm nuts, huh? I can tell."

"In a good way," I assure him.

"I can live with that. Now come on, *ma chérie*, and let's pay French Bob."

Bob agrees to have the Mustang towed to the Garretts' house by Friday. As we climb back into the van, I ask, "Where are you going to work on her?" Already, I too am referring to this car as if it has a gender.

"I'll just do it in the driveway. Joel takes the cycle to work these days, so that space will be clear. Besides, there's no room in the garage until my mom has that yard sale she's been talking about for five years."

I can already see my mother, hands on hips, glaring through the window at the disabled car and huffing out an impatient breath. "A rusty old wreck now! What next? Plastic flamingos?" I squeeze Jase's knee, and he instantly covers my fingers with his own, giving me his slow, intoxicating smile. I feel a pang, as though I'm handing over a part of myself I've never offered before. And I suddenly remember Tracy worrying about getting in too deep with Flip. It's only been a few weeks and somehow I seem to have gotten far from shore.

Jase's schedule is as busy as Mom's. The hardware store, training, some odd jobs fixing things at the bike shop, delivering lumber . . . One afternoon after lifeguarding, I'm hesitating on our porch, wondering about calling him, when I hear a whistle and he's walking up our driveway.

He gives my jacket with its epaulets and stupid crested suit the once-over. I'd been so eager to get out of the B&T that I hadn't bothered to change. "Admiral Samantha, once again."

"I *know*," I say. "Lucky you, getting to wear anything you want." I wave my hand at his faded shorts and his untucked forest green oxford shirt.

"But you still look better than me. When does your mom get home today?"

"Late. She's at some fund raiser at the Bay Harbor Grille." I roll my eyes.

"Want to come to my house? You allowed to fraternize off-site?"

I tell him to wait two minutes while I ditch the uniform.

When we get to the Garretts', it is, as usual, a hive of activity. Mrs. Garrett's breast-feeding Patsy at the kitchen table, quizzing Harry on the names of various rope knots for sailing camp. Duff's on the computer. George, shirtless, is eating chocolate chip cookies, dreamily dipping them in milk and leafing through *National Geographic Kids*. Alice and Andy are in an intense discussion over by the sink.

"How do I get him to do it? It's just killing me. I'm gonna die." Andy scrunches her eyes shut.

"What are you dying of, dear?" Mrs. Garrett asks. "I missed it."

"Kyle Comstock still hasn't kissed me. It's killing me."

"It shouldn't take this long," Alice observes. "Maybe he's gay."

"Alice," Jase objects. "He's fourteen. Jesus."

"What's gay?" George asks, his mouth full of cookie.

"Gay is like those penguins we read about at Central Park Zoo," explains Duff, still typing away on the computer. "Remember, sometimes the boy ones mate with other boy ones?"

"Oh. I rem'ber. What's mate, I forget that part?" responds George, still chewing.

"Try this one," Alice suggests. She walks up to Jase, shakes back her hair, casts her eyes down, walks her fingers up his chest, and then toys with the buttons of his shirt, swaying slightly toward him. "That one always works."

"Not on your brother." Jase backs up, rebuttoning.

"I guess I could try that." Andy sounds doubtful. "But what if he sticks his tongue in my mouth right away? I'm not sure I'm ready for that."

"Eeeew," squeals Harry. "Barf. That's rank."

Feeling my face warm, I shift my eyes to Jase. He's blushing too. But he quirks a little smile at me.

Mrs. Garrett sighs. "I think you should just take this at a slow pace, Andy."

"Does it feel really gross, or nice?" Andy turns to me. "It's so hard to imagine, even though I do try. All the time."

"Samantha and I are going upstairs to, uh, feed the animals." Jase grabs my hand.

"Is *that* what they call it now?" asks Alice languidly.

"Alice," Mrs. Garrett begins as we hurry upstairs to the relative quiet of Jase's room.

"Sorry," he says, the tips of his ears still pink.

"No problem." I pull the elastic out of my hair, toss it back, flutter my eyelashes and, reaching out, walk my fingers dramatically up his chest to unbutton his shirt.

"Oh my God," Jase whispers. "It's like I've just gotta . . . I can't help myself . . . I—" He hooks his index finger into the waistband of my shorts, moving me closer. His lips descend on mine, familiar now, but more and more exciting. In the past few weeks, we've spent hours kissing, but only kissing, only touching each other's faces and backs and waists. Jase, who takes his time.

Not like Charley, who was incapable of meeting my lips without reaching for more, or Michael, whose patented move was to thrust his hands up under my shirt, unclasp my bra, then groan and say, "Why do you do this to me?" Now it's my hands that slide up under Jase's shirt, up his chest, while I lower my head to his shoulder and breathe in deeply. All our other kisses have been slow and careful, by the lake, on the roof, potentially not so alone. Now we're in his bedroom, and that feels both tempting and wicked. I move my hands to the hem of his shirt, tugging up, while part of me is completely shocked that I'm doing this.

Jase steps backward, looks at me, intent green eyes. Then he raises his arms so I can slip the shirt off.

I do.

I've seen him without a shirt. I've seen him in a bathing suit. But the only times I got to touch his chest it was dark. Now the afternoon sun slants into the room, which smells earthy and warm with all the plants, quiet except for our breathing.

"Samantha."

"Mmmm," I say, trailing my hand over his stomach, feeling the firm muscles tighten.

His hand reaches out. I close my eyes, thinking how embarrassed I'll be if he stops me. Instead, his fingers close lightly on the hem of my shirt, sliding it up, while the other hand curves around my waist, then moves, touching my cheek, asking a silent question. I nod, and he eases the shirt entirely off.

Then he pulls me close and we're kissing again, which feels much more intimate when so much of his skin is touching mine. I can feel the thud of his heartbeat and the rise and fall of his breathing. I bury my hands in the waves of his curls and press closer.

The door opens and in comes George. "Mommy said to bring these."

We move hastily apart to find him extending a plate of chocolate chip cookies, several of which have large bites out of them. George thrusts the plate at us guiltily. "I had to make sure they were still good." Then, "Hey, you guys have nothing on top!"

"Um, George——" Jase runs his hands through the hair at the back of his head.

"Me neither." George jabs a finger at his own bare chest. "We match."

"G-man." Jase leads him to the door, handing him three cookies. "Buddy. Go back downstairs." He gives his brother a little shove between his skinny shoulder blades, then shuts the door firmly behind him.

"What're the chances he won't mention the no-shirt thing to your mom?" I ask.

"Slim." Jase leans back against the door, closing his eyes.

"George tells all." I hastily tug on mine, yanking my arms into the sleeves.

"Let's just, uh . . . ." Assured Jase is at a loss.

"Feed the animals?" I suggest.

"Right. Yeah. Uh, here." He crosses to some low drawers under his bed. "I have it all separated by . . ."

We sort food and dump out water bottles, refilling them, edge straw into cages. After about five minutes I say, "Put this back on now." I thrust his shirt at him.

"Okay. Why?"

"Just do it."

"Unbelievably distracted by my body, Samantha?"

"Yes."

He laughs. "Good. We're on the same page, then." There's a pause. Then he says, "I said that wrong. Like it was all about how you look, and that's not it. It's just that you're so different than I thought you were."

"Than you thought I was, when?"

"When I saw you. Sitting on your roof. For years."

"You saw me. For years?" I feel myself flush again. "You didn't tell me that."

"For years. Course I didn't tell you. I knew you watched us. Couldn't figure out why you didn't just come over. I thought . . . maybe you were shy . . . or a snob . . . I didn't know. I didn't know you then, Sam. Couldn't help watching back, though."

"Because I'm just so compelling and fascinating?" I roll my eyes.

"I used to see you, out the kitchen window, during dinner or when I was swimming in the pool at night, wonder what you were thinking. You always looked cool and poised and perfect—but that's . . ."

He trails off, ruffling his hair again.

"You're less . . . more . . . I like you better now."

"What do you mean?"

"I like you here—real and just you and coping with all this insanity—George and Andy and Harry, me, I guess—in that calm way you have. I like who you really are."

He regards me contemplatively for a long moment, then turns away, carefully fitting the water bottle into the ferret's cage.

Underneath the flare of pleasure at his words, there's a niggling prickle of unease. Am I calm? Am I somebody who takes things in stride? Jase is so sure he sees me.

A knock on the door. This time, it's Duff wanting help with his sailing knots. Then Alice, who is having a CPR test tomorrow and needs a willing victim.

"No way," Jase says. "Use Brad."

I think it's good we have all these interruptions. Because right now I don't feel the least bit calm, totally unsettled by what happened as we stood there, bare skin to bare skin, with this growing feeling that what happens between us is not on my schedule, in my control. Not me choosing to move away or back off or step apart, but a desire less easily managed. Before, I've always felt curious, not . . . not *compelled*. How much experience has Jase had? He's a fantastic kisser; but then, he's good at everything he does, so that's no guide. The only girlfriend I know about is Shoplifting Lindy, and she certainly seems as though she had no hesitation about taking what she wanted out of life.

When Mrs. Garrett comes up to ask if I want to stay for dinner, I say no, my quiet empty house with its leftovers in Tupperware, somehow, for the first time, a refuge from the steamy silence of Jase's room.

Chapter Twenty

"Here ya go, Grace. Senior Center Pig Roast. Daughters of St. Damien Shad Fest. Sons of Almighty Michael Feast of the Blessed Shad. You need to go to all of these."

Clay has a highlighter and the local newspaper. Mom has a third cup of morning coffee.

"Shad festivals?" she says faintly. "I've never done those before."

"You never had a real opponent before, Grace. Yup, all of them. Look here, they're opening an old boxcar as a diner in Bay Crest. You need to be there."

Mom takes a slow sip. Her hair is as untidy as it ever gets, a platinum tangle where her bun should be as she tips her head back on the sofa.

Clay skids the highlighter over a few more articles, then looks at Mom. "You're tuckered," he says, "I know. But you got what it takes, Gracie, and you need to take that where it's meant to go."

Mom straightens up as though Clay's yanked on her strings. Now she walks over and sits next to him, examining the paper and tucking her hair behind her ears.

The way she is around Clay makes me uneasy. Was she this way with Dad? There's balance between Tracy and Flip, I see that now, but Mom seems to be under a spell sometimes. I think of those moments in Jase's room. If Mom feels that way around Clay, it's not like I don't understand. But . . . but the shivers I feel around Jase are nothing like the prickle of anxiety I get now, watching their blond heads duck closer together.

"Was there something you needed, sugar?" Clay asks, noticing me hovering.

I open my mouth, then shut it again. Maybe Tracy's right and I'm just not used to Mom "having a man." Maybe, despite everything, I'm protective of my invisible father. Maybe I'm just hormonal. I look at the clock—an hour and a half till the B&T. I picture the cool water, sunlight on its surface, that calm underwater world, broken only by my even steady strokes. I grab my gear and go.

"Sailor Supergirl! You're on TV!" Harry hurtles himself at me as I come in the kitchen door. "It's you! Right in the middle of *Mammal Mysteries*. Come see!"

In the Garretts' living room, George, Duff, and Andy are sitting mesmerized in front of one of Mom's political commercials. Right now, it's a shot of her face, in front of the Capitol building. *As women, as parents, we all know family comes first,* she says as the camera shows still photos of me and Tracy in matching dresses with our Easter egg baskets, on the beach, sitting on the lap of the B&T Santa Claus, all with Mom in the background. I didn't think they'd ever snapped a picture of me with Santa without me crying, but I look relatively calm in this one. The B&T Santa always smelled like beer and had a drooping, palpably fake beard. *My family has always been my focus.*

"Your mommy's pretty but she doesn't look like a mommy," George says.

"That's a rude thing to say," Andy tells him as there's another montage of pictures—Tracy accepting a gymnastics award, me winning a prize at a science fair for my model of a cell. "Oh look—you had braces too, Samantha. I didn't think you'd have had to have those."

"I just meant she looked fancy," George says as Mom smiles and says, *When I was elected to be your state senator, I kept my focus. My family just got a lot bigger.*

Next are pictures of Mom standing with a crowd of high school students in caps and gowns, bending next to an old woman in a wheelchair waving a flag, accepting flowers from a little boy.

"Are those people really your family?" Harry asks suspiciously. "I've never seen any of them next door."

Now the camera pulls back to show Mom at a dinner table, with a horde of ethnically diverse people, all smiling and nodding, evidently talking to her about their values and their lives over . . . a banquet of popular Connecticut foods. I spy a clambake, ingredients for New England boiled dinner, pizza from New Haven, things we've never had on our table.

To me my constituents are my family. I will be honored to sit at your table. I will go to the table for you, this November, and beyond. I'm Grace Reed, and I approved this message, Mom concludes firmly.

"Are you okay, Sailor Supergirl?" George pulls on my arm.

"You look sad. I didn't mean anything bad about your mommy."

I snap myself away from the screen to find him next to me, breathing heavily in that small-boy way, holding out the battered stuffed dog, Happy.

"If you're sad," he says, "Happy's magic, so he helps."

I take the dog, then put my arms around George. More noisy breathing. Happy's mushed between us, smelling like peanut butter, Play-Doh, and dirt.

"Come on, guys. It's a beautiful day and you're indoors watching *Mammal Mysteries*. That's for rainy days." I usher the Garretts outside, but not before flicking a glance back at the TV. Despite all the posters and leaflets, the newspaper photos, it's still surreal to see Mom on television. Even stranger to see myself, and how much I look like I belong right there with her.

Chapter Twenty-one

Following Tim's B&T firing, the Masons, still researching scared-straight boot camps, are trying to keep him busy. Tonight they've given him money to take me and Nan to the movies.

"Please," Nan urges over the phone. "It's a movie. How bad can that be? He won't even care—or even notice—if we pick a chick flick."

But the moment I slide into the backseat of Tim's Jetta, I know this plan is not going to work. I should get out of the car, but I don't. I can't leave Nan in the lurch.

"Tim. This isn't the way to the movies!" Nan leans forward in the passenger seat.

"So right, sis. Screw Showcase. This is the way to New Hampshire and tax-free cases of Bacardi."

The speedometer edges past seventy-five. Tim takes his eyes off the road to scroll through his iPod or punch in the lighter or fumble around in his shirt pocket for another Marlboro. I keep feeling the car drift, then lurch back into its lane as Tim yanks the wheel. I look at Nan's profile. Without turning, she reaches back a hand, grabbing on to mine.

After about twenty minutes of speeding and weaving, Tim

pulls over at a McDonald's, slamming the brakes so hard that Nan and I pitch forward and back. Still, I'm grateful. My fingers are stiff from clutching the door handle. Tim returns to the car looking even less reliable, his pupils nearly overtaking his gray irises, his dark red hair sticking straight up in front.

"We have to get out of this," I whisper to Nan. "You should drive."

"I only have my learner's permit," Nan says. "I could get in big trouble."

Hard to imagine how much bigger trouble could get. I, of course, can't drive at all, because Mom has put off my driver's ed classes time after time, claiming that I'm too young and most of the drivers on the road are incompetent. It never really seemed like a battle worth fighting when I could catch rides with Tracy. Now I wish I'd forged Mom's name on the parental consent forms. I wonder if I could just figure it out. I think of those six-year-olds you occasionally hear about in news stories who drive their stricken grandparent to the hospital. I check the front of the Jetta. It's a stick shift. There's no way.

"We need to think of something, fast, Nanny."

"I *know*," she murmurs back. Leaning forward, she puts her hand on Tim's shoulder as he tries, unsuccessfully, to maneuver the key into the ignition.

"Timmy. This doesn't make sense. We're going to eat up all the tax-free savings in gas just getting to New Hampshire."

"It's a fucking *adventure*, sis." Tim finally gets the key in, presses the accelerator down to the ground, and burns rubber out of the parking lot. "Don't you ever crave one?"

The car surges faster and faster. The urgent hum of the engine vibrates through the seats. Tim's passing other cars on the right. We've shot past Middletown and are closing in on Hartford. I check my watch. It's eight fifty . . . My curfew is eleven. We won't be anywhere near New Hampshire by then. Assuming we aren't wrapped around a tree somewhere. My fingers ache from holding so tightly to the door handle. I feel a prickle of sweat across my forehead.

"Tim, you have to stop. You have to stop and let us out," I say loudly. "We don't want to do this with you."

"Lighten up, Samantha."

"You're going to get us all killed!" Nan pleads.

"Betcha you'll both die virgins. Kinda makes you wonder what the fuck you were saving it for, huh?"

"Timmy. Will you please stop saying that word?"

Of course, this request is all Tim needs. "What word? Ohhhh. *That* word!" He makes a little song out of the word, says it loud, quietly, all strung together. On and on and on with the F-bomb for the next few minutes. Then he puts it to the tune of "Colonel Bogey's March," on and on and on again. A bubble of hysterical laughter fights its way to my lips. Then I see that the speedometer has leaped into the 100s. And I'm more terrified than I've ever been in my life.

"Shit. Cops." Tim pulls a wide unsteady turn into a truck stop. I pray that the police car will follow us, but it speeds on by, siren blaring. Nan's face is parchment. The Jetta squeals sideways to a halt. Tim staggers out of the driver's seat, saying, "Damn, I gotta pee," and wanders off in the direction of a gigantic blue Dumpster.

I yank the keys out of the ignition, climb out, and hurl them into the bushes at the side of the parking lot.

"What are you *doing*?" Nan screams, following me, palms outstretched at her sides.

"Making sure we get out of this alive."

She shakes her head. "Samantha, what were you thinking? Tim had his . . . bike lock keys on that."

I'm bending over, resting my hands on my knees, breathing deeply. I turn to look at her. Seeing the expression on my face, she starts to laugh.

"Okay. That's crazy," she allows. "But how are we gonna get out of this?"

Just then, Tim weaves back toward us. He slides into the front seat, then drops his forehead onto the steering wheel. "I don't feel good." He sucks in a deep breath, wrapping his arms around his ducked head, making the horn honk. "You're nice girls. You really are. I don't know what the hell's the matter with me."

Clearly, neither Nan nor I have an answer. We close the side door of the car, and lean against it. Traffic streaks past on our left. So many people. All oblivious. We might as well be stranded in the desert. "Now what?" Nan asks.

Mom's given me a thousand lectures on what to do in a situation with an unreliable driver. So I call her. I call home. I call her cell. Ugh, Clay's cell. Tracy's—not that she could help me from the Vineyard, but . . . No answer anywhere. I try to remember where Mom said she was going tonight but come up blank. Lately, it's all a big blur of "economic roundtable" and "town hall meeting" and "staffing support information event."

So, I call Jase. He answers on the third ring. "Samantha! Hey, I—"

I interrupt to tell him what's happening.

Nan, who's checking on Tim, calls, "He's passed out! I think. He's all sweaty. Oh my God. Samantha!"

"Where exactly are you?" Jase asks. "Alice, I need help," he shouts into the background. "Are there any highway signs? What's the nearest exit?"

I peer around but can't see anything. I call to Nan, asking what town we last passed, but she shakes her head and says, "I had my eyes closed."

"Just hang on," he tells me. "Get in, lock the doors, and hit the hazard lights. We'll find you."

They do. Forty-five minutes later, there's a tap on the car window and I look up to see Jase, Alice behind him. I open the door. My muscles are cramping and my legs are about to give way. Jase wraps his arms around me, warm and solid and calm. I sink into him. Nan, scrambling out after me, raises her head, sees us, stops dead. Her mouth drops open.

After a minute, he lets go and helps Alice, surprisingly silent and forbearing, shove the unconscious Tim into the backseat of the Bug. Tim lets out a loud snore, clearly down for the count.

"What did he take?" Alice asks.

"I—I don't know," Nan stammers.

Alice bends, fingers on his wrist, smells his breath, shakes her head. "I think he's fine. Just passed out. I'll take these guys home, if she"—Alice gestures to Nan—"tells me where to go, then you swing by and pick me up, okay, J?" She flings herself into the driver's seat, jerking it closer to the wheel to accommodate her small frame.

Nan, piling into the Bug next to Alice, frowns at me and mouths, "What's going *on*?" then mimes putting a phone to her ear. I nod, then take a long, shaky breath. I wait for Jase to ask what the hell I was thinking, going anywhere with someone in that condition, but instead he says, "You did exactly the right thing."

I scramble to be that girl Jase thinks I am. That calm unruffled girl who doesn't let things faze her. She's nowhere to be found. Instead, I burst into tears, those embarrassing noisy ones where you can't catch your breath.

Of course, he rolls with that. We stand there until I get hold of myself. Then he reaches into the pocket of his jacket and hands me a Hershey's bar. "Good for shock, Alice tells me. She is, after all, a medical professional in training."

"I threw the car keys in the bushes."

"Smart move." He heads into the thicket, ducking to sweep his hands on the ground. I follow, doing the same.

"You must have some arm," he says finally, when we've searched for about ten minutes.

"Hodges Heroines softball through eighth grade," I offer. "Now what do we do?"

Instead of answering, Jase walks back to the Jetta and opens the passenger door, gesturing for me to climb in. I do, watching in fascination as he yanks off this plastic piece from the steering column, then pulls off some of the coating on two red pieces of wire and twists them together. Then he hauls out this brown wire and touches it to the red ones.

Sparks fly. "You're hot-wiring the car?" I've only seen that in the movies.

"Just to take it home."

"How'd you learn this?"

Jase glances at me as the engine revs into high gear. "I love cars," he says simply. "I've learned all about them."

After we've driven for ten minutes in silence, Jase says musingly, "Timothy Mason. I might have known."

"You've met him before?" I'm surprised. First Flip, now Tim. Somehow, because I didn't know the Garretts, I imagined them in a world completely separate from my own.

"Cub Scouts." Jase holds out his hand, two fingers up in the traditional salute.

I chuckle. "Boy Scout" is not exactly what comes to mind when I think of Tim.

"Even then he was a disaster waiting to happen. Or already in progress." Jase bites his bottom lip reflectively.

"Cocaine at the campouts?" I ask.

"No, mostly just trying to start fires with magnifying glasses and stealing other people's badges . . . a good enough guy, really, but it was as if he just *had* to get in trouble. So his sister's your best friend? What's she like?"

"The opposite. Compelled to be perfect." Thinking of Nan, I look at the clock on the dash for the first time. It's 10:46. My rational mind—which so recently deserted me—tells me there's no way on earth my mother can blame me for breaking curfew under these circumstances. Still, I can feel my body tense up. Mom can find a way—I know she can—to make this all my fault. And, worse, Jase's.

"I'm sorry I got you into this."

"It's nothing, Samantha. I'm glad you're all okay. Nothing else is important." He looks at me for a moment. "Not even curfew." His voice is low, gentle, and I feel the tears gathering in my eyes again. What's wrong with me?

For the rest of the drive, Jase keeps me distracted. He gives an exhaustive and totally incomprehensible list of the things he needs to do to get the Mustang working ("So I've got about three hundred hp with my trick flow aluminum heads and exhaust, and the clutch is slipping at about two-sixty horse-power in third gear, and I want the center-force aftermarket unit, but that's a big five hundred bucks, but the way the Mustang slips every time I floor it in third gear is killing me") and looking "how it's meant to." Then he tells me that he was working on it earlier this evening in the driveway while Kyle Comstock and Andy sat together on the front steps.

"I was trying not to listen, or look, but oh, man, it was so painful. He kept trying to do the smooth-guy move—that knee bump maneuver or the yawn arm stretch deal and he'd lose his nerve at the last minute. Or he'd reach out a hand and then pull it back. Andy licked her lips and tossed her hair until I thought her head was going to snap off. And the whole time they were having this conversation about how last year they had to dissect a fetal pig in biology lab."

"Not exactly an aphrodisiac."

"Nope. Biology lab *might* have promise, but dissection and a dead pig are definitely going down the wrong road."

"So hard to find that right road." I shake my head. "Espe-cially when you're fourteen."

"Or even seventeen." Jase flips the signal switch to ease off the interstate.

"Or even seventeen," I concur. Not for the first time, I wonder how much experience Jase has had.

When we pull up outside the Masons' house, Alice and Nan have evidently just pulled in themselves. They're standing outside the Bug, debating. Most of the lights in the Masons' house are dark, just a faint orange glow coming from the bowed living room windows, and two porch lights flickering.

"Can't we please get him in without anyone seeing?" Nan's begging, her thin fingers clutching Alice's arm.

"The real question is whether we *should* get him in without anyone seeing. This is not the sort of thing your parents shouldn't know about." Alice's tone is deliberately patient, as though she's already been through this several times.

"Alice's right," Jase interjects. "If he doesn't get caught, well, maybe if I hadn't that time with Lindy, I'd have discovered a taste for shoplifting. This is more than just that . . . If nobody knows how bad it's gotten, Tim could find himself in this situation again, with a different outcome. So could you. So could Samantha."

Alice nods, looking at Nan but addressing her brother. "Remember River Fillipi, Jase? His parents let him get away with anything, turned a blind eye to everything. He ended up blindsiding three cars before he hit the median on 1-95."

"But you don't understand. Tim's in so much trouble already. My parents want him to go away to some awful military camp. That's the last thing that's going to help. The very last thing. I

156

know he's an idiot and sort of a loser, but he's my brother—" Nan cuts off abruptly. Her voice is shaking, along with the rest of her. I go over and take her hand. I think of those awkward dinners I've had at their house, Mr. Mason's unseeing gaze at the table, Mrs. Mason prattling on about how she stuffs her artichokes. I feel as though I'm on a seesaw swaying back and forth between what I know is right and true, and every past moment and reason I know has led to this. Jase and Alice are right, but Tim's such a mess, and I keep remembering him saying, so lost, *I don't know what the hell's the matter with me.*

"Can you sneak in and open the bulkhead door?" I ask Nan. "Maybe we could get Tim down to the basement and he can crash in the rec room. He'll be in better shape to face it all in the morning anyway."

Nan takes a deep breath. "I can do that." We look at Alice and Jase.

Alice shrugs, frowning. "If that's what you want, but it seems all wrong to me."

"They know the situation better than we do," Jase points out. "Okay, Nan. Go open the cellar door. We'll get this guy in there."

Naturally, as we're carrying him in, Tim wakes up, disoriented, and throws up all over Alice. I pinch my nose. The smell's enough to make anyone gag. Surprisingly, Alice doesn't get angry, just rolls her eyes and, without any self-consciousness at all, whips off her ruined shirt. We sling Tim, who, despite being thin, is tall and not easily portable, onto the couch. Jase fetches a bucket from beside the washing machine and puts it next to him. Nan sets out a glass of water and some aspirin.

Tim lies on his back, looking pale, pale, pale. He opens red-dened eyes, focuses hazily on Alice in her black lace bra, says, "Whoa." Then passes out again.

I got in big trouble for being ten minutes late for curfew last time. But tonight, when I actually was involved in a life-threatening incident, one in which I definitely could have used better, swifter judgment—*why on earth didn't I call 911 on my cell and report a drunk driver?*—on this night when the VW pulls into our driveway, the house lights are dark. Mom isn't even home yet.

"Dodged more than one bullet tonight, Samantha." Jase hops out to open my door.

I go around to the driver's side. "Thanks," I tell Alice. "You were great to do this. Sorry about your shirt."

Alice fixes me with a stare. "No sweat. If the only thing that idiot comes out of this with is a horrible hangover and a dry-cleaning bill, he's way luckier than he has any right to be. Jase deserves better than trauma over some girl who made dumb choices and wound up dead."

"Yes, he does." I look right back at her. "I know that."

She turns to Jase. "I'll go home now, J. You can say good night to your damsel in distress."

That one stings. Blood rushes to my face. We get to the front door and I lean back against it. "Thank you," I repeat.

"You'd have done the same for me." Jase puts his thumb under my chin and tips it up. "It's nothing."

"Well, except that I can't drive, and you never would have gotten yourself into that situation and—"

"Shhh." He pulls on my lower lip gently with his teeth, then fits his mouth to mine. First so careful, and then so deep and deliberate, that I can't think of anything at all but his smooth back under my hands. My fingers travel to the springy-soft texture of his hair, and I lose myself in the movement of his lips and his tongue. I'm so glad I'm still alive to feel all those things.

Chapter Twenty-two

When I get to the B&T—an hour early—the next day, I head straight for the pool. I breathe in the chlorine scent, then focus on the steady back and forth motion of my strokes. The routine is coming back. *Swim no rest, kick no rest, stroke drill, rest, breath to right, breath to left, breath every third stroke.* And so is the timing. Everything else falls away. Forty-five minutes later, I shake out my hair, cupping my hands to my ears to get out the water, then head into Buys by the Bay to find Nan.

Who hasn't answered any of my texts. I'm imagining the worst. Her parents heard us, came down, and Tim's already en route to some hard-core camp in the Midwest where he's going to have to chip granite and eventually get shot by an angry counselor.

But then Nan wouldn't be calmly sorting aprons in the corner of the store, would she? Maybe she would. Like my mother, my best friend sometimes puts order over the physical world first.

"What's up with Tim?"

Nan turns around, leans her elbows back against the counter, and looks at me. "He's fine. Let's talk about what really matters. Which wasn't important enough to tell me. Why?"

"What wasn't important . . . ?"

Nan pales under her freckles. Angry at *me*? Why? And then I get it. I duck my head and feel a flush creeping up my neck.

"You didn't think to *mention* that you have a boyfriend? Or that he's, like, incredibly hot? Samantha, I'm your best friend. You know everything about me and Daniel. *Everything*."

My stomach twists. I haven't said anything to Nan about Jase. Nothing. *Why not?* I shut my eyes and for a second feel his arms surround me. Such a good thing. Why wouldn't I tell Nan? She scrunch-folds an apron that says *Life's a beach and then you swim* and piles it carelessly on top of the others.

"You're my best friend. You obviously didn't meet this guy yesterday. What's going on?"

"It hasn't been that long. A month. Maybe even a little less." Heat rises to my face. "I just . . . felt . . . didn't want to . . . Mom's always so down on the Garretts . . . I just got in the habit of keeping it a secret."

"Your mom's down on everyone. That never stopped you from telling me about Charley and Michael. Why is this any different? Wait . . . the Garretts? You mean the they-multiply-like-rabbits family next door?" When I nod, she says, "Wow. How'd you finally meet one of them?"

So I tell Nan the story. All about Jase, this summer, nearly getting grounded and him climbing up to my room. And all the stars.

"He climbs up to your window?" Nan puts her fingers over her mouth. "Your mother would have a cow over this! You do know that, don't you? She'd have a herd of buffalo if she knew this was going on." Now she sounds less angry, more admiring.

"She would," I say as the bells over the door jangle, heralding the arrival of a woman in a fuchsia beach tunic with a very large straw hat and a determined expression.

"When I was here the other day," she says in those slightly-too-loud tones some people use when speaking to salespeople, "there were some darling T-shirts. I've come back for them."

Nan straightens, schooling her face to blankness. "We have many lovely T-shirts."

"These had sayings," the woman tells her challengingly.

"We have a lot of those," Nan rejoins, straightening her shoulders.

"*Stony Bay . . . not just another sailing town,*" the woman quotes. "But in place of the 'not' there was a—"

"Drawing of a rope knot," Nan interjects. "Those are over in the corner near the window seat." She jerks her thumb in that direction and turns more toward me. The woman pauses, then makes her way to the stack of shirts.

"How big *is* this relationship I know nothing about, Samantha? He looks—I don't know—older than us. Like he knows what he's doing. Have you and he . . . ?"

"No! No, I would have told you that," I say. *Would I?*

"Is there a discount if I buy one for each crew member on our cruiser?" calls the woman.

"No," Nan says tersely. She leans in closer to me. "Daniel and I are talking about it. A lot lately."

I have to admit this surprises me. Daniel's so controlled, it's hard to remember he's also an eighteen-year-old boy. Of course he and Nan are discussing having sex after all this time. I get a flash of Daniel in his school uniform leading the debate team at Hodges, calling out in his measured way, "Cons go first, then the pros will have an equal amount of time."

"Tim thinks I'm an idiot." Nan presses her index finger into the wax of a candle shaped like Stony Bay Lighthouse. "He says Daniel's a putz and will suck in bed anyway."

Tim! "What happened with him? Did your parents catch on?"

Nan shakes her head. "No. He got lucky. Or rather, he survived to mess up another day thanks to your surprise boyfriend and his scary sister. Mommy and Daddy didn't hear a thing. I went down to the basement before I left and dumped the bucket o' vomit out. I just told Mommy he'd stayed up late and was tired."

"Nans, Alice may be right about not pretending about this now. Last night was—"

She nods, a quick inhale of breath, nibbling on her thumbnail. "I know. I know. A disaster. But packing him off to some boot camp? I don't see how that's going to help him."

The woman has come up to the register, her arms full of shirts, all pink.

Nan turns to her with a bright, professional smile. "I can ring those up for you. Would you like to put them directly on your club tab, or pay separately?"

I hover nearby until the clock tells me I've got to report for duty. Nan doesn't say anything else, though, until I'm getting ready to leave, when she pauses in changing the paper for the cash register to say, "Samantha. You have what every girl wants."

"You have Daniel," I say.

"Sure. But you have everything. How do you always do that?" Her voice is ever so slightly bitter. I think of the Nan who just *has* to do the optional extra credit work for every school project. Who has to point out to me whenever I have a minus next to my grade while she has a plus. Who has to comment that pants that fit me would be "way too big" for her. I've never wanted to compete with her, only be her friend, the one person she doesn't have to best. But sometimes—like now—I wonder if, for Nan, there's any such thing.

"I don't do anything special, Nanny." The bell jingles as another customer walks in.

"Maybe you don't." Her voice is weary. "Maybe you're not even trying. But it all works out for you anyway, doesn't it?" She turns away before I can offer an answer. Assuming I even had one.

Chapter Twenty-three

I pour myself a lemonade after work and am climbing out of my stupid crested bathing suit right in the kitchen when the doorbell rings. Even our doorbell chime has changed since summer began. Now we have this one that can chime the first few notes of about twenty different tunes, all the way from "Take Me Out to the Ball Game" to "Zip-a-Dee-Doo-Dah." In the last two weeks, Mom's programmed it to chime the opening of "It's a Grand Old Flag." I kid you not.

I grab a tank top and shorts from the laundry room and pull them on hastily, then peer through the frosted glass. It's Nan and Tim. Odd. Thursday and Friday are Daniel nights for Nan. And my house is not exactly Tim's preferred hangout. It's not even *my* preferred hangout.

"Are you interested in a closer relationship with the Lord?" Tim asks when I open the door. "'Cause I've been saved, and I want to pass on the Good News to you—for only a thousand dollars and three hours of your time. Kidding. Can we come in, Samantha?"

As soon as they get into the kitchen, Nan heads for the fridge to get some of my mother's lemonade. After all these years, she knows exactly where to locate the special ice cubes with mint and lemon peel. She pours a glass for Tim and he takes it, frowning at the little ice cubes with their flecks of yellow and green frozen inside.

"Got any tequila? Just kidding, once again. Ha-ha."

He's uncomfortable. It's been a long time since I've really seen anything from Tim but bored indifference, stoned apathy, or jacked-up contempt.

"Tim wanted to say he was sorry about last night," Nan offers, crunching an ice cube.

"Ac-tu-ally, *Nan* wanted me to say I'm sorry," Tim clarifies, but he looks directly at me. "I wanted to say I'm *fucking* sorry. That was wicked stupid, and I would have thought anyone else who did that with my sister—or you—was a complete and unredeemable asshole, which of course, leads to the inescapable conclusion that that is, in fact, indubitably what I am." He shakes his head, takes a gulp of lemonade. "Note my use of impressive SAT words, though. Too bad I got my ass booted out of boarding school, huh?"

How long has it been since I've heard Tim apologize for anything? He's got his head hunched down, sandwiched between his folded arms, taking deep breaths as though he's been running miles, or this all takes more oxygen than just breathing. Even his hair is damp, like he's sweating. He seems so unmoored that just looking at him hurts. I glance at Nan, but she's polishing off her lemonade, her face impassive.

"Thanks, Tim. We all survived. But you're really scaring me. How are you?"

"Well, aside from being the same idiot I was yesterday—only not quite as trashed—I'm fine. And you? S'up with ole

Jase Garrett and you? Is he gettin' any further than my buddy Charley did? 'Cause Charley was pretty damn frustrated. More importantly, what's doin' with Jase's hot sister?"

"His hot sister has a boyfriend who's a football player and weighs about two hundred and fifty pounds," I answer, dodging the Jase question.

"Course she does," Tim says with a smirk. "He probably teaches Sunday school too."

"No. But I think he might be a Mormon." I smile back. "Cheer up, though. They've been together for about a month, and from what Jase tells me, that's pretty much Alice's limit."

"I'll live in hope, then." Tim drains his glass and plunks it down. "Do you have anything like plain carrots or celery or apples? Everything in our fridge has some kind of crap in it."

"It's true," Nan says. "I bit into a perfectly ordinary-looking plum this afternoon and it had some weird blue-cheese filling. It's that thing Mommy got from QVC."

"The Pumper. It injects tasty filling deep into the heart of all your favorite foods," Tim quotes in a Moviefone voice.

Just then the doorbell rings again. It's Jase this time. He's wearing a faded gray T-shirt and jeans—must have come straight from work.

"Hi!" Nan says brightly. "In case you didn't figure this out last night, I'm Nan, Samantha's best friend. I'd love to say I've heard all about you, but actually, she hasn't said a word. My brother says he knows you, though." She extends her hand to Jase. After a beat, he takes it, shakes it, looking over at me with a slightly nonplussed expression.

"Hullo Nan. Mason." His voice gets an edge as he greets

Tim, and I see Tim's jaw muscles clench. Then Jase moves to my side and slips an arm tight around my waist.

We wind up in the backyard, because everything inside my house is so hard and formal, no comfortable place to sit and lounge. Jase lies on his back in the grass on our sloping lawn, and I lie, crossways, with my head on his stomach, ignoring the occasional flick of Nan's eyes.

We don't talk much for a while. Jase and Tim idly discuss people they knew from soccer in middle school. I find myself studying the boys together, wondering what my mother would see. There's Jase with his olive skin and broad shoulders, his air of being older than seventeen, nearly a man. Then there's Tim, so pale, dark circles under his eyes, freckles standing out in strong relief, rangy skinny legs cross-legged, his face handsome but pale and angular. Jase's jeans are stained with grease, and his T-shirt is frayed at the collar, stretched out of shape. Tim's in crisp khakis, with a blue-striped oxford shirt rolled up at the sleeves. If Mom was asked who was "dangerous," she would immediately point to Jase, who fixes things, and saves animals, and saves me. Not Tim, who, as I watch, is casually crushing a daddy longlegs.

Wiping his hand on the grass, Tim says, "I need to get my GED, or I'll either be shipped to the foreign legion by my parents, or spend the rest of my life—which will then be very short—living in their basement."

"My dad did that—got a GED," Jase offers, playing with my hair. "You could talk to him."

"Your sister Alice didn't do it too, by any chance?"

Jase's lips twitch. "Nope."

"Bummer. I also need a job so I don't have to spend my days at home with Ma, watching her figure out new uses for the Pumper."

"There's an opening at Mom's campaign," I say. "She needs all the help she can get now that she's totally distracted by Clay Tucker."

"Who the hell's Clay Tucker?"

"The . . ." Nan lowers her voice, even though all she says is: ". . . younger man Samantha's mother's dating."

"Your ma's dating?" Tim looks shocked. "I thought she pretty much confined herself to a vibrator and the shower nozzle since your dad screwed her over."

"Timmy." Nan turns scarlet.

"There's always a job to do at my dad's store." Jase stretches and yawns, unfazed. "Restocking, placing orders. Nothing too exciting, but—"

"Right." Tim's eyes are cast down as he tears at a hangnail on his thumb. "I'm sure that's just what your pop needs—a plastered dropout stock boy with a jones for illegal substances."

Jase props himself up on one elbow, looking squarely at him. "Well, provided that stock boy isn't still drinking, et cetera, taking *my* girlfriend on a joyride when he's hammered. Ever again." His voice is flat. He watches Tim for another moment, then lies back down.

Tim turns, if possible, slightly paler, then flushes. "Uh . . . Well . . . I . . . uh . . ." He glances at me, at Nan, then returns his attention to the hangnail. Silence.

"Well, restocking and stuff might not be thrilling, but that's probably a good thing," Nan says after a minute or two. "What do you think, Timmy?"

Tim's still focusing on his thumb. Finally, he looks up. "Unless Alice does restocking too, preferably spending most of her time on a ladder in those little short-shorts, I'm thinking I'll talk to gorgeous Grace about politics. I like politics. You get to manipulate people and lie and cheat and it's all good."

"From what I read, Samantha's mom prefers to think of it as working for the common weal." Jase stretches his arms over his head, yawning. I sit up, surprised to hear Jase recite Mom's last campaign slogan, the one Clay Tucker mocked so mercilessly. Jase and I never mention politics. But he must have been paying attention to hers all along.

"Cool. Sign me up. I'll be a cog in the common weal. With my track record, I'll probably be able to screw up all three branches of government in about a week and a half," Tim says. "Does hot Alice have any interest in politics?"

Mom gets back early, luckily after Nan and Tim have trudged home and Jase is again training. She has a meet-and-greet in East Stonehill tonight and wants me to come along. "Clay says that since I'm focusing on family, we really need to see more of mine." I stand next to her at Moose Hall for approximately eight thousand years, repeating "Yes, I'm so proud of my mother. Please vote for her," while she shakes hand after hand after hand.

When she first got elected, this was kind of fun and exciting. All these people I'd never met who seemed to know me, happy to meet us. Now it just seems surreal. I listen hard to Mom's speech, trying to analyze how things have changed. She's much more assured, with all these new hand gestures—chopping the air, arms outspread in appeal, hands crossed over her heart . . . but it's more than that. Last time, it was mostly local issues Mom talked about, and mildly. But now she's taking on federal spending and the size of government, and the unfair taxation of the wealthy, who create all the jobs . . . "You're not smiling," Clay Tucker says, bumping up next to me. "So I figured you were hungry. These hors d'oeuvres are amazing. I'll take over while you eat a few." He hands me a plate of shrimp cocktail and stuffed clams.

"How much longer does this go on?" I ask, dunking a shrimp.

"Till the last handshake, whenever that is, Samantha." He gestures at my mom with a toothpick. "Look at Grace. You'd never know she'd been doing this for two hours and her shoes probably hurt and she might need to visit the little girls' room. She's a pro, your mama."

Mom does indeed look fresh and calm and cool. She's bending her head to listen to an old man as though he's the most important thing in her world. Somehow I've never seen her ability to fake it as a strength but right now, I guess it is.

"You gonna eat that?" Clay asks, spearing a scallop before I can answer.

Chapter Twenty-four

Late that night, I'm lying on my bed, staring at the ceiling, fresh out of the shower, wearing a white nightgown I've had since I was eight. It used to be romantically long; now it clings to my thighs.

Mom's finally admitted exhaustion and has gone to bed in her suite. For the first time I find myself wondering if Clay's ever spent the night here. I wouldn't even know if he had—her rooms are on the other side of the house and there are stairs from the yard. *Ugh, don't think about that.*

There's a tap at my window, and I look over to find a hand splayed on the glass. Jase. Seeing him is like that feeling you get when you've gotten the wind knocked out of you and then can, at last, draw a deep, full breath. I go over, put my hand against his, then push up the window.

"Hey. Can I come in?"

He does, gracefully, legs planting themselves firmly, while ducking carefully under the transom, as though he's done this a thousand times before. Then he looks around the room and smiles at me. "It's so tidy, Sam. I've gotta do this."

He takes off one of his sneakers and tosses it toward my desk, then the other, carefully and quietly, toward the door.

Then one sock, hurled to the top of my bureau, and the other, into the bookcase.

"Don't hold back." I catch hold of his shirt, yank it off, and throw it across the room, where it hooks onto my desk chair.

As I'm reaching for him, he puts his hand on my arm. "Sam."

"Hmmm," I say, distracted by the thin line of hair that circles his belly button and edges lower.

"Should I be worried?"

I look up at him, my thoughts scattered. "About what?"

"The fact that you're apparently the one girl on the planet who doesn't tell her best friend everything the moment it happens. I have sisters, Sam. I thought that was a rule—the best friend knows all. Yours didn't even know I existed."

"Nan?" I ask quickly, then realize I don't know what else to say. "It's kind of complicated with her. She's got a lot going on . . . I just thought I'd . . ." I shrug.

"You're being considerate?" Jase asks, moving away from me and sitting down on the bed. "Not ashamed?"

I feel the breath whoosh out of my lungs and can't seem to take the next breath. "Of you? No. *No*. Never. I just . . ." I bite my lip.

His eyes assess my face. "I'm not trying to put you on the spot. Just figuring out what's what. You're . . . I don't know . . . the 'State Senator's Daughter.' I'm . . . well . . . 'one of those Garretts'—as Lindy's dad used to say."

He says the phrase as though it's in quotes, and I can't stand it. I sit down on the bed next to him, put one hand on his cheek.

"I'm just me," I tell him. "I'm glad you're here."

Jase studies my face, then takes my hand, pulling me down. He carefully curls around me, so my head is resting on his arm, and his head's resting on my shoulder. His fingers move slowly through my hair. The paradox of Jase is that at the same time I'm so conscious of the heat of his chest against my back, and the muscles under the shorts on the legs twined around mine, I feel so safe and comfortable that I fall, almost immediately, asleep.

I wake to Jase shaking my shoulder. "I should go," he whispers. "It's morning."

"Can't be." I tug him closer. "That was too short."

"Is." Jase kisses my cheek. "I've gotta go. It's five twenty-seven."

I grab his wrist, squinting at his digital watch. "Can't be."

"Honest," Jase says. "Listen. Mourning doves."

I tilt my head, discern a series of owl-like sounds. Sliding out of bed, Jase hauls on his shirt and socks and shoes, comes back over to me, leans forward, kisses my forehead, then moves his lips slowly to the corner of my mouth.

"Do you *have* to go?"

"Yeah. Samantha, I—" He stops talking. I put my arms around his neck and tug him down. He resists for a moment, then slides in next to me. He has his hands in my hair, which came out of its braid during the night, and our kisses get deeper and a little wilder. I slip one arm under him and pull, moving him on top of me, looking into those green eyes, which widen a fraction. Then he leans on his elbows and those careful, competent hands undo the front buttons of my nightgown.

Strangely, I'm not embarrassed at all. I'm impatient. When his lips descend, my sigh of pleasure feels like it is traveling through every inch of my body.

"Jase . . ."

"Mmmm." He nudges his lips against one breast and slowly skims his fingertips over the other, so lightly, giving me goose bumps all the same.

"Jase, I want—I want . . . please."

He looks up at my face, his eyes drowsy and dazzled. "I know. I know. I want too. But not like this. Not with no time. Not with nothing—" He swallows. "Not like this. But Jesus, Samantha. Look at you."

And the way he does look at me makes me feel absolutely beautiful.

"I can't look away," he whispers huskily. "But I have to go." Taking a deep breath, he buttons my nightgown back up, then presses a kiss to my throat.

"Jase, are you—have you—"

I feel his head shake once, then he moves so he's looking me in the face. "No. I haven't. Almost. With Lindy. But then, no. I just didn't . . . I never felt with her the way I feel whenever I even catch sight of you. So, no . . . I haven't."

I lay my palm against the stubbly skin at the side of his face. "Me neither."

His lips curve and he turns his head to touch them to my palm.

"Then we do need time. So we can—" He swallows again and shuts his eyes. "Sometimes when I look at you, I can't think. We need time so we can figure it out together."

"Okay," I say, suddenly shy for some reason. "Um . . ."

"I love the way your whole body turns pink when you're embarrassed," he murmurs. "Everywhere. Your ears blush. Even your knees blush. I bet your toes blush. "

"That's not the way to get them to stop." I flush even more.

"I know." He slides slowly off me and off the bed. "But I don't want them to stop. I love it. I *have* to go now. When will you be home today?"

I fumble to think about something other than yanking Jase back down onto me. "Um. . . . I have a double shift at Breakfast Ahoy. So just till three."

"Okay," Jase says. "Too bad the store's open late tonight. I'll be back around seven. I'll miss you all day until then."

He slides the window open and slips out. I close my eyes, lift my hand to touch my throat where he kissed me.

I'm a virgin. Apparently Jase is too. I've heard the Sexual Congress lecture in health class. Seen R-rated movies. Listened to Tracy brag about how many times a day she and Flip can do it. Read books with steamy scenes. But there's so much I still don't know. Does instinct just take over? Is it good right away or do you have to acquire a taste for it, the way people say you do for wine or cigarettes? Does it hurt like anything that first time? Or barely at all? Does this mean I have to buy condoms? Or will he? The Pill takes forever to be safe, right? I mean, you have to take it for a month or more first, right? And I'd have to go to my doctor to get it—my doctor who's in his early eighties and has a handlebar mustache and nostril hair and was my mother's pediatrician too.

I wish I could ask my mother these questions, but imagining her face if I tried is scarier than not knowing the answers. I wish I could ask Mrs. Garrett. But . . . he's her son after all, and she's only human. It would be weird. *Very* weird. Even though this is something I know I want, I start to panic a little, until I remember the person I trust more than anyone else in the world. Jase. And I decide he's right. We'll figure it out together.

Chapter Twenty-five

When I get home from Breakfast Ahoy, with sore feet and smelling like bacon and maple syrup, the only sign of Mom is a Post-it note: *Vacuum living room*. A task I blow off. The lines from the last vacuuming are still visible. The phone rings, but it's not Mom. It's Andy.

"Samantha? Can you come over? Mom's sick and Daddy isn't home yet and I have, well, I'm going to see Kyle and . . . would it be okay if you babysat until Jase gets back? Duff isn't good with diapers and Patsy has this major rash? You know, the kind you need a prescription cream for? It's all over her bottom and down her legs."

I, of course, know nothing about diaper rash, but say I'll be right over.

The Garretts' house is unusually hectic. "Mom's upstairs, sleeping? She really doesn't feel good." Andy fills me in while trying to apply eyeliner and put on her shoes at the same time. I redo the eyeliner for her and French-braid her hair.

"Has everyone eaten?"

"Patsy. But the other guys are really hungry? Even though I gave them all Lucky Charms. Alice's out with Brad or something? I can't remember. Anyway"—Andy peers out the door—"Mr. Comstock's here. Bye." She dashes out, leaving me to Harry and Duff and George, who are practically brandishing forks, and Patsy, who smiles confidingly up at me and says, "Poooooooooop."

I start to laugh. "This is what comes after *boob*?"

Duff opens the refrigerator. Discouraged, he sighs. "Guess so. Mom's really gonna have to get creative with the baby book. We got nothin' here, Samantha. What're you making for us?"

In the end, the Garretts' dinner that night consists of English muffin toaster pizzas, boxed macaroni and cheese, and my mom's lemonade and broccoli/sun-dried tomato and pecan pasta salad (less than a success), which I send Duff over to my house to get, explaining about the special ice cubes.

While I'm giving Patsy and George a bath, there's a commotion from down the hall. Voldemort the corn snake has escaped again. I hear Duff's footsteps thundering around, and Harry shouting excitedly, and then see this slim shape squiggling into the room, trying to coil itself into George's dirty Transformer sneaker. I'm so proud of the way I reach out, scoop up Voldemort, and calmly hand him over to Duff. Without even screaming when Voldemort, evidently stressed, does what corn snakes will do, and defecates all over my hand. "Pooooooop!" Patsy shouts delightedly as I go over to the sink to wash it off.

Half an hour later, Patsy's asleep in her crib, with the five pacifiers she insists on holding in her hands—she never puts them in her mouth. George stretches out drowsily on the couch, nodding over Animal Planet's *Ten Most Startling Animal Metamorphoses*. Duff's on the computer, and Harry's building what looks like the Pentagon out of Magna-Tiles when the door slams. In comes Alice, whose hair is now a deep auburn with an inexplicable blond streak in front, and Jase, evidently fresh from delivering lumber, sweaty and rumpled. He lifts his chin when he sees me, his face breaking into a broad smile. He heads toward me but Alice blocks him.

"Shower before you smooch, J," Alice says. "I rode in the Bug with you and you're officially disgusting."

While he's upstairs, I fill Alice in. "Mom's *asleep?*" She's incredulous. "Why?"

I shrug. "Andy said she felt lousy."

"Crap, I hope it's not the flu. I've got three tests coming up and no time to play stand-in mom." Alice starts taking the dinner dishes off the table and dumping leftovers into the disposal.

"Samantha's done here now." Jase, returning to the room, picks up a yellow plastic backscratcher that is on the kitchen counter, along with a pair of dirty socks, an empty Chips Ahoy! box, five Matchbox cars, Andy's eyeliner, and a half-eaten banana. He taps the backscratcher on each of Alice's shoulders. "You're now officially Mom until Dad gets home. Samantha and I are going upstairs." And he takes my hand, dragging me after him.

But all that urgency is apparently more about getting away from the chaos downstairs than about luring me to his bed, because once we get up to the room, he just loops his arms around my waist and leans in for a leisurely kiss. Then he tilts back, surveying me.

"What?" I ask, reaching back out for him, wanting more.

"Here's what I was wondering, Samantha. Do you want to—"

"Yes," I respond immediately.

He laughs. "Here's where you need to hear the actual question. I was thinking, a lot, about what we talked about this morning. How do you . . . ? Do you . . . want to plan it all out or—"

"You mean like the date and the time and the place? I think that would make me too tense. Like some sort of countdown. I don't want to plan you. Not that way."

He looks relieved. "That's how I feel. So I was thinking we should just make sure we're . . . well, uh, prepared. Always. Then see when things move there so we're both . . ."

"Ready?" I ask.

"Comfortable," Jase suggests. "Prepared."

I give his shoulder a little shove. "Boy Scout."

"Well, they didn't exactly have a badge for this." Jase laughs. "Though that one would've been popular. Not to mention useful. I was in the pharmacy today and there are *way* too many options just in, uh, condoms."

"I know." I smile at him. "I was there too."

"We should probably go together next time," he says, picking up my hand, turning it over to kiss the inside of my wrist. My pulse jumps, just at that brush of his lips. *Wow.*

In the end, we go to CVS later that night, because Mrs. Garrett wakes up and comes out of her room, rumpled in a sapphire bathrobe, to ask Jase to pick up some Gatorade. So here we are, in the family planning aisle with a cart full of sports drinks and our hands full of . . . "Trojans, Ramses, Magnum . . . Jeez, these are worse than names for muscle cars," Jase observes, sliding his finger along the display.

"They do sound sorta, well, forceful." I flip over the box I'm holding to read the instructions.

Jase glances up to smile at me. "Don't worry, Sam. It's just us."

"I don't get what half these descriptions mean . . . What's a vibrating ring?"

"Sounds like the part that breaks on the washing machine. What's extra-sensitive? *That* sounds like how we describe George."

I'm giggling. "Okay, would that be better or worse than 'ultimate feeling'—and look—there's 'shared pleasure' condoms *and* 'her pleasure' condoms. But there's no 'his pleasure.'"

"I'm pretty sure that comes with the territory," Jase says dryly. "Put down those Technicolor ones. No freaking way."

"But blue's my favorite color," I say, batting my eyelashes at him.

"Put them down. The glow-in-the-dark ones too. Jesus. Why do they even *make* those?"

"For the visually impaired?" I ask, reshelving the boxes.

We move to the checkout line. "Enjoy the rest of your evening," the clerk calls as we leave.

"Do you think he knew?" I ask.

"You're blushing again," Jase mutters absently. "Did who know what?"

"The sales guy. Why we were buying these?"

A smile pulls the corners of his mouth. "Of course not. I'm sure it never occurred to him that we were actually buying birth control for ourselves. I bet he thought it was . . . a . . . housewarming gift."

Okay, I'm ridiculous.

"Or party favors," I laugh.

"Or"—he scrutinizes the receipt—"supplies for a really expensive water balloon fight."

"Visual aids for health class?" I slip my hand into the back pocket of Jase's jeans.

"Or little raincoats for . . ." He pauses, stumped.

"Barbie dolls," I suggest.

"G.I. Joes," he corrects, and slips his free hand into the back pocket of my jeans, bumping his hip against mine as we head back to the car.

Brushing my teeth that night, listening to the sound of a summer rain battering against the windows, I marvel at how quickly things can completely change. A month ago, I was someone who had to put twenty-five unnecessary items— Q-tips and nail polish remover and *Seventeen* magazine and mascara and hand lotion—on the counter at CVS to distract the clerk from the box of tampons, the one embarrassing item I needed. Tonight I bought condoms, and almost nothing else, with the boy I'm planning to use them with.

Jase took them all home, since my mom still periodically goes through my dresser drawers to align my clothes in order of color. I'm pretty sure she wouldn't buy the "supplies for a really expensive water balloon fight" excuse. When I asked if Mrs. Garrett would do the same and find them, Jase looked at me in complete mystification.

"I do my own laundry, Sam."

I've never had a nickname. My mother's always insisted on the full *Samantha*. Charley occasionally called me "Sammy-Sam" just because he knew it bugged me. But I like being Sam. I like being Jase's Sam. It sounds relaxed, easygoing, competent. I want to be that person.

I spit out toothpaste, staring at my face in the mirror. Someday, someday not too far away, Jase and I will use those condoms. Will I look different then? How different will I feel? How will we know when to say when?

Chapter Twenty-six

Two days later, Tim's following my directions to Mom's campaign office for an interview. He looks like a completely different person than the one at the wheel for the Bacardi run to New Hampshire, neatly clad in a khaki suit with a red and yellow striped tie. He drums his fingers on the steering wheel, lights a cigarette, smokes it, firing up another the moment he's done.

"You feeling okay?" I ask, indicating that he should turn left at the four-way intersection.

"Like shit." Tim tosses the latest cigarette butt out the window, punching the lighter down again. "I haven't had a drink or a joint or anything in days. That's the longest that's happened since I was, like, eleven. I feel like shit."

"You sure you want this job? Campaigning—it's all show— it makes *me* feel that way and I'm not even drying out."

Tim snorts. "*Drying out?* Who the hell says that? You talk like my frickin' grandpa."

I roll my eyes. "Sorry I'm not all down with the current slang. You get my point anyway."

"I can't stay home all day with Ma. She drives me up the frigging wall. And if I don't prove that I'm doing 'something valuable with my time,' it's off to do hard time at Camp Toma-hawk."

"You're joking. *That's* the name of the place your parents want to send you?"

"Somethin' like that. Maybe it's Camp Guillotine. Camp Castration? Whatever the hell it is, it doesn't sound like anyplace I'll survive. No way I'm gonna have some epiphany about how I need to apply myself to life while living on roots and berries and learning how to build a compass out of spiderwebs or whatever the hell they have you do when they drop you in the wilderness by yourself. That shit is just not me."

"I think you should go for the job with Jase's dad." I point to the right as we come to another intersection. "He's a lot more relaxed than Mom. Plus, you'd have your evenings free."

"Jase's dad runs a goddamn hardware store, Samantha. I don't know the difference between a screwdriver and a wrench. I'm not Mr. Handyman like lover boy."

"I don't think you'd have to fix anything, just sell the tools. It's this building, right here."

Tim skids into the driveway of campaign headquarters, where the lawn is plastered with huge red, white, and blue *GRACE REED: OUR TOWNS, OUR FAMILIES, OUR FUTURE* posters. In some of them she's wearing a yellow Windbreaker and shaking hands with fisherman or other heroic, salt-of-the-earth types. In others she's the mom I know, hair coiled high, in a suit, talking to other "movers and shakers."

Tim hops out and walks up the sidewalk, yanking his tie straight. His fingers are trembling.

"You going to be all right?"

"Will ya quit asking that? It's not like my answer's gonna change. I feel like I'm about an eight point nine on the Richter scale."

"So don't do this."

"I gotta do something or I'll lose what's left of my mind," he snaps. Then, glancing at me, his voice softens. "Relax, kid. When not too blasted to pull it off, I'm the master of fakin' it."

I'm sitting in the lobby flipping through *People* magazine and wondering how long this interview will run when I get a call on my cell from Jase.

"Hey, baby."

"Hey yourself. I'm still at Tim's interview."

"Dad said to swing by when you're done if he wants to interview here. Bonus, the guy on staff kinda has a thing for you."

"That so? And how is this guy on staff—is he running the four-minute mile in army boots on the shore yet?"

"Actually, no. Still coming up short. I think he was kind of distracted by the girl timing him, last few times he ran."

"That so? He should probably work on his focus, then, shouldn't he?"

"No way. He likes his focus right where it is, thanks. See you when you get here."

I'm smiling into the phone when Tim stomps back out and shakes his head at me. "You two are fuckin' nauseating."

"How'd you know it was Jase?"

"Gimme a break, Samantha. I could see you quivering from across the room."

I change the subject. "So how'd you go over with Mom's campaign manager?"

"Who *is* that officious little dude? He definitely gives the words 'pompous dickhead' a new dimension. But I'm hired."

Mom emerges from the back office and puts her hand on Tim's shoulder, clenching tight.

"Our Timothy is an up-and-comer, Samantha. I'm so proud! You should spend more time with him. He really knows where he's going."

I nod icily while Tim smirks.

Once we're out on the sidewalk I ask, "What exactly did you do to deserve that?"

Tim snorts. "Hell, Samantha. I would've been kicked out of Ellery years ago if I hadn't learned how to suck up to the powers that be. I wrote a paper on the Reagan years last winter. In there"—he indicates the building behind us—"I just plagiarized a bunch of phrases from the Gipper. The little dude and your mom practically had orgasms—"

I hold up my hand. "I get the picture. "

"What's *with* you and Nan? Damn, you two are uptight," Tim says. He drives—too fast—for a few minutes, then says, "Sorry! I feel like I'm gonna jump out of my skin. All I really want to do is get spun."

Hoping, ridiculously, that this will distract him, I tell him about Mr. Garrett's offer.

"I'm desperate enough to fill my time to try this. But if I have to wear a frickin' apron, there's no way I'm taking this job."

"No apron. And Alice drops in a lot."

"Sold." Tim lights up once again.

When we get to the store, Mr. Garrett and Jase are behind the counter. Jase has his back to us as we walk in the door. The way Mr. Garrett is leaning forward, resting his elbows on the countertop, is the same way Jase relaxes against the kitchen table at his house. He's huskier than Jase, more like Joel. Will Jase look like him when he's in his forties? Will I know him then?

Mr. Garrett glances up, spotting us. He smiles. "Tim Mason—from Cub Scouts. I was your troop leader, remember?"

Tim looks alarmed. "You fu—er—remember me and you're willing to interview me anyhow?"

"Sure. Let's go in the back office. You can take off the jacket and tie, though. No point being uncomfortable."

Tim follows him down the corridor, looking uncomfortable anyway, sensing that plagiarizing Ronald Reagan won't help in this situation.

"So, was your dad always a hard-ass?" Tim asks, driving us home an hour later.

I'm automatically defensive, but Jase seems unperturbed. "I thought you'd think so."

I watch Jase's profile in the passenger seat of the car, his hair flipping in the wind. I'm in the back. Tim's again working his way through way too many cigarettes. I wave my hand in front of my face and open my window a little further.

"Helluva condition for employment." Tim tips the sunshade down so the packet of Marlboros falls into his lap. "Not sure it's worth it."

"No skin off my back." Jase shrugs. "But is it any worse than now? Can't see how, really."

"It's not that it's worse, asshole. It's that it's not a choice."

"Like you've got so many," Jase says. "Worth a try, I'd say, man."

I feel as though they're speaking in code. I have no idea what is going on. When I lean forward to look at his profile, he seems elusive, not that boy who kisses me good night so sweetly.

"Here you two are," Tim says, pulling into the Garretts' driveway. "Home again, home again, jiggety jig. Good night, young lovers."

After we say bye to Tim, we're left standing on the Garretts' lawn. I glance over at my house to find, as expected, all the lights out. Mom's not home yet. I pull at Jase's wrist and check the time. 7:10. Must be another motivational meeting/civic function/town hall arena . . . or whatever.

"What's going on with Tim?" I ask, flipping over his wrist to trace the faint blue lines of his veins with my index finger.

"Dad made ninety meetings in ninety days a condition of employment," Jase says. "That's what he says people need to not drink. I kinda knew he'd do that." His mouth brushes gently against my collarbone.

"Ninety meetings with him?"

"Ninety AA meetings. Alcoholics Anonymous. Tim Mason isn't the only one who ever screwed up. My dad was a major partier, a very heavy drinker, in his teens. I've never seen him have a drink, but I know the stories he tells. I had a hunch he'd figure Tim out."

I raise my hand, touch Jase's lips, tracing the full curve of the lower one. "So what if Tim can't handle it? What if he just messes up?"

"We all deserve a chance not to, right?" Jase says, and then he slips his hands up under the back of my T-shirt, closing his eyes.

"Jase . . ." I say. Or sigh.

"Get a room, you two," suggests a voice. We look up to see Alice striding toward us, Brad trailing after her.

Jase takes a step back from me, running his hands through his hair, leaving it rumpled and even more appealing.

Alice shakes her head and walks past us.

Chapter Twenty-seven

Our house is buzzing with this strange energy on the Fourth of July.

The Fourth, you must understand, is *the* town holiday for Stony Bay. Early in the Revolutionary War, the British burned some ships in our harbor as a quick gesture on their way somewhere more significant, so Stony Bay has always felt personally invested in Independence Day. The parade starts at the cemetery behind town hall, goes up the hill to the Olde Baptist Church, where the veterans lay a wreath at the grave of the unknown soldier, then wends down the hill, running into tree-lined Main Street, past the houses painted regulation white and yellow and barn-red, neat and tidy as the boxes in a watercolor set, and finally to the harbor. Bands from all the local schools play patriotic songs. And since her election, Mom always gives the opening and closing speeches. The valedictorian of the middle school recites the Preamble to the Constitution, and another star student reads a paper about life, liberty, and the pursuit of justice.

This year, that student is Nan.

"I can't believe it," she says over and over again. "Can you? Last year it was Daniel and now me. I didn't even think this

Four Freedoms one was my best paper! I thought the one for English on Huckleberry Finn's and Holden Caulfield's rebellion against life was much better."

"But not exactly apt for the Fourth of July," I point out. To be honest, I'm surprised too. Nan hates creative writing. She's always been happier with memorizing than theorizing. And that's not the only weird thing today.

Mom, Clay, Nan, and I are in the living room. Mom's been listening to Nan practice her speech while Clay goes over the usual Fourth of July proceedings, trying to figure out how Mom, in his words, "can put some extra zing in this year."

He's lying on his stomach in front of the fireplace, press clippings and pieces of yellow-lined paper spread out in front of him, a highlighter in one hand. "Seems as though you've got your standard stump speech goin' on here, Gracie. The curse of the 'common weal.'" He looks up and winks at her, then at Nan and me. "This year we're going to need fireworks."

"We have them," Mom says. "Every year Donati's Dry Goods donates some— we get the permit lined up months in advance."

Clay ducks his head. "Grace. Sugar. I mean figurative fire-works." He slaps the press clippings with the back of his knuckles. "This is fine for the expected line from the local pol. But you can do better. And darlin', if you're going to win this year, you'll *have* to."

Pink washes across Mom's cheekbones, the unmistakable flag of blond chagrin. She comes over next to him, rests a hand on his shoulder, bending to see what he's highlighting. "Tell me how," she says then, clicking her pen open and flipping to an empty page on her pad, Nan and me forgotten.

"Wow," Nan says as we get on our bikes to ride to her house. "That was freaky. That Clay's really pulling the strings with your mom, huh?"

"I guess," I say. "It's like that all the time lately. I can't figure out . . . I mean . . . she's obviously really into him, but . . ."

"Do you think it's"—Nan lowers her voice—"the sex?"

"Yuck, Nan. I have no idea. I don't want to think about either of them in that context."

"Well, it's either that or she's had a frontal lobotomy," Nan murmurs. "So what do you think I should wear? Do you think it has to be red, white, and blue?" She slips off the sidewalk onto the road so she can ride parallel with me. "Please say no. Maybe just blue. Or white? Is that too virginal?" She rolls her eyes. "Not that that's not appropriate. Should I have Daniel film me reading the essay and sub that with my college application? Or would that be dorky?"

She keeps asking questions I don't have answers to because I'm completely distracted. *What's happening to my mother? When did Mom ever listen to anybody but Mom?*

Tracy comes home for the Fourth of July command performance. She's okay with that because, she tells me, "The Vineyard is *jammed* with tourists over this weekend." There's no point in asking her how a month or so of waiting tables at a Vineyard restaurant has separated her from the tourists. Tracy is Tracy.

Flip's home too. He's given Trace a tennis bracelet with a tiny gold racket dangling from it that has spawned lots of new Tracy hand-and-wrist flicking gestures designed to show it off. "The note that came with it said *I live to serve you*," she whispers to me the night she gets home. "Can you stand it?"

To me it sounds like one of the T-shirts Nan would sell at the B&T, but my sister's eyes are shining.

"What happened to the long-distance love thing and how that wasn't going to work?" I ask. *Call me Killjoy*.

"That's September!" Tracy laughs. "Jeez, Samantha. Months away." She pats me on the shoulder. "You'd understand if you'd ever been in love."

Part of me so much wants to say, "Well, Trace, actually . . ."

But I'm so used to saying nothing now, so used to being the audience while Mom and Tracy are the ones with the stories. I just listen as she tells me about the Vineyard and the Harbor Fest and the Summer Solstice Celebration. What Flip Did and What Flip Said and what Tracy did then.

By the time the school bands assemble at eight in the morning on the Fourth, it's already eighty-five degrees, and the sky is that searing summer slate-blue-gray that tells you it's only going to get steamier. Despite this, Mom looks cool and poised in her white linen suit topped by a big blue straw hat with a red ribbon. Tracy, under protest, is wearing a navy sundress adorned with a white sash. I'm in a smocked white silk dress Mom loves, in which I feel about ten, tops.

Standing with Mom and Tracy as the parade marchers assemble, I can see Duff balancing his tuba, red in the face before the marching even begins, and Andy, squinting her eyes shut, tightening one of the strings on her violin. She looks up as she perches it on her shoulder, spots me, and gives me a broad grin, braces twinkling.

Garrett's Hardware isn't open today, but Jase and Mr. Garrett are selling little flags and bunting and streamers for bike wheels outside the store, with Harry next to them hawking lemonade in an aggressive fashion: "Hey you! Mister! You look thirsty. Twenty-five cents! Hey you! Lady!" Mrs. Garrett is somewhere lost in the throng with George and Patsy. I don't think I ever realized before how everyone in town really does come to this parade.

The first song the band plays is "America the Beautiful." At least I think that's what it is. The band's pretty bad. Then Mr. McAuliffe, who leads the Stony Bay Middle School band, is off and marching, the parade dragging behind him.

The drummers roll as Mom stands behind the podium. Tracy and I sit on the bleachers right behind her, with Marissa Levy, the middle school valedictorian, and Nan in their assigned seats. From where we are, I can finally locate Mrs. Garrett, on the sidelines with a huge fluff of cotton candy in her hand, doling it out sparingly to George while Patsy reaches for it. The Masons are front row, center, Mr. Mason with his arm around his wife and Tim next to them in a . . . tuxedo? I know Mrs. Mason told him to dress up. Trust Tim to take that to the extreme. He must be boiling.

Mom gives her speech, all about how two hundred and thirty years of pride have brought Stony Bay to this point, two hundred and thirty years of excellence, etc. I'm not sure how it's any different from what she usually says, but I see Clay over near the NewsCenter9 camera, nodding and smiling, bending in close to the photographer, like he's making sure they got the key footage.

After Mom, it's quiet, and Nan walks quickly to the podium. Like so much in their twin-DNA exchange, the height genes were measured inequitably. Nanny tops me by two inches, at the most five four, while Tim shot over six feet years ago. She has to climb a few steps to peek over the lectern. She sets the paper down, brushing it flat and swallowing visibly, her freckles vivid against her pale face.

Long silence, and I start to worry. Then her eyes meet mine, she quickly crosses hers, and begins. "We are accustomed now, in this country, in this time, to celebrate what we have. Or what we want. Not what we lack. On this day that celebrates what our forefathers dreamed and hoped for us, I would like to celebrate the four freedoms . . . and to note that . . . while two, freedom of speech and freedom of worship, celebrate what we have, an equal number celebrate what we are missing . . . freedom from want . . . freedom from fear."

The microphone is a little squeaky, periodically sounding out a high-pitched whine. Mom has her head tilted to the side, taking the speech in intently, as though she didn't hear Nan rehearse it half a dozen times. Tracy and Flip are knocking their feet together, hands intertwined, but both their faces are somber. I look into the crowd to find Mrs. Mason, her hands clasped under her chin, and Mr. Mason, his eyes fixed on Nan, shoulder tipped toward his wife. I search for Tim, only to find him with his head ducked, his fists over his eyes.

When Nan winds to a close, the applause is thunderous. She turns the shade of her hair, bobs a quick curtsy, and backs up to sit in the bleachers next to Mom.

"Could that have been more beautifully stated?" Mom calls.

"The Fourth of July is a day to celebrate what our forefathers chose—and what they refused—what they dreamed for us, and what we made reality from the power of their dreams."

There's a lot more in that vein, but what I see is Nan being hugged by her parents, her mom and dad finally celebrating Nan's accomplishments, not focusing on Tim's disasters, her face so joyous above their interlocked arms. I look around for Tim, expecting to see him close the circle, but he's gone.

Mom goes on with her speech, freedom and choice and how we stand strong. Clay, now planted back in one of the last rows, flashes her a smile and a thumbs-up.

The wreath to commemorate soldiers lost is dropped after the slow march down the hill to the harbor, and Winnie Teixeira from the elementary school plays Taps. Then everyone recites the Pledge of Allegiance, and the formal part of the Fourth of July disbands into getting cotton candy, frozen lemonade, and Italian ices from carts set up by Doane's.

I look for Nan, but she's in the crowd with her parents. Tracy and Flip are rapidly moving away from Mom, Tracy calling something over her shoulder and waving. Mom's in a swarm of people, shaking hands and signing things and . . . erk . . . kissing babies. Mom doesn't even like babies, but you would never know it as she exclaims over a series of tiny, bald, drooling citizens. I stand there irresolutely, wondering if I'm supposed to stay by her all day, wanting only to get rid of my itchy childish dress and go someplace cool.

Arms come around my waist from behind me then and Jase's lips nuzzle my neck. "What, Sam? No uniform? I was trying to guess whether you'd be the Statue of Liberty or Martha Washington."

I turn in his arms. "Sorry to disappoint you."

More kissing. *I've turned into someone who kisses on a public street.* I open my eyes, pull back, glancing around for my mom.

"You hunting for Tim too?"

"Tim? No—"

"He came by the stand," Jase says, "looking kinda grim. We should find him."

We stay by the turnstile at the top of Main Street for a while, me perching on the white brick stand, Jase using his height to scan around, but there's no sign of Tim. Then I see him, stark in his black tuxedo with all the festive summer colors, talking to Troy Rhodes, our ever-dedicated local drug dealer.

"He's over there." I nudge Jase.

"Great." Jase bites his lip. "In good company." *Guess Troy makes the rounds at the public school too.*

Jase and I wade through the crowd, but by the time we reach Troy, Tim's vanished again. Jase squeezes my hand. "We'll get him," he says.

He's back with his parents. We reach the Masons just in time to hear old Mr. Erlicher, who runs the volunteer league at the Stony Bay Library, say, "And here's our shining star," kissing Nan. He turns to Tim, who's thrown himself into a slouch in the seat next to Nan. "And your mother tells me *you're* having a bit of trouble finding your feet, young man."

"That's me," Tim tells him without looking up, "the guy with lost feet."

Mr. Erlicher prods him on the shoulder. "I was a late bloomer myself, you know. Heh-heh-heh. Look at me now."

He means well, but since the biggest achievement we know of his is being nearly impossible to escape from once he starts talking, Tim looks anything but consoled. His eyes search the throng of people, lock on me and Jase, and skip away as though that's no help at all.

"Hey," Jase says neutrally. "It's hot. Let's get out of here."

Daniel has found his way to Nan, looming behind her as she accepts more congratulations. Nan's beaming so much, the sun pales.

"C'mon, Tim," Jase repeats. "I've got the Bug over by the store. Let's hit the beach."

Tim looks back and forth between us, then into the crowd again. Finally, he shrugs and slogs after us, hands stuffed in the pockets of his tux. When we get to the Bug, he insists on crawling into the back, even though the length of his legs makes this ludicrous.

"I'm cool," he says curtly, waving away my repeated offers of the front seat. "Sit next to lover boy. It's a crime to keep you guys apart anyway, and I've got enough of those on my conscience. I'll just sit back here and perform a few of the more acrobatic positions in the Kama Sutra. By myself. Sadly."

The sun's so hot and high that you'd expect everyone in town to lemming to the beach, but it's still deserted when Jase, Tim, and I get there.

"Whew," Jase says. "I'm swimming in my shorts." He pulls

his shirt off and tosses it through the window of the Bug, bending to pull off his sneakers.

I'm about to say I'm going to walk home for my suit when I see Tim fall back into the sand, tuxedo and all, and I'm not going anywhere. Did he buy anything from Troy? Even if he did, when would he have had time to smoke it or take it or whatever?

Jase straightens. "Wanna race?" he calls to Tim.

Tim moves his forearm away from his eyes.

"Hell, yeah. Race. 'Cause you're an athlete in peak training condition and I'm an out-of-shape fuckup. Let's definitely race. On the beach. With me in a tux." He holds up a finger. "No. Second thought, let's not. I have too many unfair advantages. Wouldn't want to make you look bad in front of Samantha here."

Jase kicks at the sand. "Don't be an ass. I just thought it might help get you out of your head. I run when I'm trying not to think about stuff."

"No shit?" Tim's voice is at its most sarcastic. "That works for you? Does running keep your mind off Samantha's hot body and—"

"If you want me to hit you, man," Jase interrupts, "you don't have to be more of a dick than usual. You don't need to bring Samantha into it."

Tim drags his arm across his eyes again. I look out at the blue waves. I want to get my suit, but what if Mom's already there and I get sucked into some political event?

"Alice always keeps suits in the trunk of the car," Jase tells me, just as my cell phone rings.

"Samantha Reed! Where are you?"

"Um, hi Mom, I—"

Luckily the question is rhetorical because Mom charges ahead. "I looked around at the end of the parade and you were nowhere to be found. Nowhere. I expect this from Tracy, not you—"

"I—"

"Clay and I are taking the Steamboat train upriver. I'm making a speech in Riverhampton, then we're taking the riverboat back down to the sound to see the fireworks. I wanted you to come along. Where are you?"

Tim's methodically taking off his cummerbund and bow tie. Jase leans against the Bug, bending one ankle, then the other, to his thighs, stretching out. I scrunch my eyes shut. "With Nan," I say, leaping off a precipice of hope that Nan's not standing right there next to Mom.

Thank God, her voice softens. "She was wonderful today, wasn't she? A perfect lead-in to my speech. What?" she calls, muffled, to someone in the background. "The train's leaving, honey. I'll be home about ten. Check in with Tracy. I'm coming, Clay! Be good, sweetheart. See you later."

"Everything good?" Jase asks.

"Just Mom," I tell him, frowning. "I can find a suit where?"

He flips open the front hatch of the Bug. "I don't know whether they'll—well, Alice kind of . . ." He looks chagrined, and I'm wondering why, but then my cell beeps again.

"Samantha! Samantha!" Nan shouts. "Can you hear me?"

"Gotcha."

She continues yelling, as though that will help. "I'm on my

cell, but I have to talk fast. Tim's used all my minutes again!
Daniel's taking me out on his parents' boat. Can you hear me?
My reception stinks!"

I bellow that I can, hoping it'll go through.

"TELL MY PARENTS I'M WITH YOU," she hollers. "OKAY?"

"IF YOU TELL MY MOM I'M WITH YOU! OKAY?"

"WHAT?" she shrieks

"WHAT?" I shout back.

"WE MAY STAY ON THE BOAT TONIGHT. SAY IT'S A
SLEEPOVER AT YOUR HOUSE!" She's loud enough to make
my cell into a speakerphone. Tim sits up, alert.

"I want to talk to her," he tells me urgently.

"TIM WANTS TO TALK TO YOU." He grabs the phone out
of my hand.

"I'LL TELL YOU ALL ABOUT IT," Nan roars. "JUST DO THIS
ONE THING."

"OF COURSE!" Tim hollers into the phone. "ANYTHING
FOR YOU, MY PRIZE-WINNING SISTER!"

He hands the phone back to me.

"Is Tim okay?" Nan asks, in a quiet voice.

"I don't—" I start, then the phone gives that depressed-
sounding *doo-dle* that signals the end of the battery, and shuts
down altogether.

"You're not in trouble, are you, Sam?" Jase asks.

"I note you don't ask me," Tim calls, taking off his pants to
reveal boxer shorts with little crests on them. He notices me
looking.

"Ellery Prep sells boxers. I got these for Christmas from
Mom. They don't confiscate them when you're kicked out."

Jase is still looking at me quizzically. I scrounge in the back of the Bug.

"We'll meet you at the shore after you change," Jase says. "C'mon Tim."

Rustling through the available suits in the trunk, buried under lacrosse sticks and soccer balls, Gatorade bottles and sports bar wrappers, I get what Jase means. The only matching pieces are these two tiny bits of black fake leather. Other than that, there's nothing but a few pairs of Jase's Stony Bay soccer team shorts and what looks like a one-piece bathing suit for Patsy. That's probably Alice's too.

So I put on the black leatherish stuff, grab a towel, and try to march nonchalantly onto the beach.

Not exactly possible.

Jase looks at me, blushes, looks again, and backs into deeper water. Tim looks at me and says, "Holy fuckin' Catgirl!"

"It's Alice's suit," I say. "Let's swim."

The rest of the day is just lazy. Jase, Tim, and I lie on the beach, get hot dogs at the Clam Shack, and lie around some more. Finally, we go back to the Garretts' and hang out by the pool.

George snuggles up next to me. "I like your bathing suit, Samantha. But you kind of look like a vampire. Have you ever seen a vampire bat? Did you know that they don't really get tangled in your hair? That's just a myth. They're really very nice. They only drink from cows and stuff. But blood, not milk."

"Nope, I've never seen one," I answer. "I'm in no hurry to, actually, however nice they may be."

The back door slams and Andy drifts out onto the pool

deck, beaming. She collapses against the fence, closing her eyes dramatically. "It finally happened."

"Kyle Comstock?" I ask.

"Yes! He finally kissed me. And it was"—she pauses—"actually kind of painful? He's got braces too. But it was still wonderful. He did it right in front of everyone too. After the parade? I'm going to remember it for all eternity. It'll be my last thought as my eyes close for the final time. Then he kissed me again after we got ice cream and then when—"

"We get the picture," Jase interrupts. "I'm happy for you, Andy."

"Now what, though?" she asks, looking anxious. "Do you think he'll use his tongue next time?"

"He didn't *this* time?" Tim's incredulous. "Christ."

"Well, no. Was he supposed to? Did we do it wrong?"

"Ands, there aren't any rules about this sort of thing." Jase stretches out on his back on the towel next to me and George.

"There really should be," Andy argues. "'Cause how on earth are you supposed to figure it all out? That was nothing like kissing my bedpost. Or the bathroom mirror."

Both Jase and Tim burst out laughing.

"No tongue there," Jase mutters.

"Or only your own. And solo's never as good," laughs Tim.

"Why would you kiss your bedpost, Andy? That's kinda yuck." George wrinkles his nose. Andy gives all three boys an annoyed look and floats back into the house.

Tim reaches for his jacket, taking his cigarettes out of the inside pocket and tapping one into his palm. George's eyes get round.

"Is that a cigarette? Are those cigarettes?"

Tim looks a bit nonplussed. "Sure. D'you mind?"

"You'll die if you smoke those. Your lungs get black and shrivel up. Then you die." George is suddenly near tears. "Don't die. I don't wanna see you die. I saw Jase's hamster die and it got all stiff and its eyes stayed open but they weren't shiny anymore."

Tim's face goes blank. He glances over at Jase as if for instruction. Jase just gazes back at him.

"Hell," Tim says, and shoves the cigarette back in. He stands up, stalks to the pool, and dives in deep.

George turns to me. "What's that mean? Does that mean no or yes?"

Mrs. Garrett sticks her head out the back door. "Jase—the garbage disposal broke again. Can you help me out?"

The Garretts have fireworks, thanks, Mrs. Garrett tells me, to her brother Hank, who lives down south and ships them up illegally every year. So we're all on the Garretts' lawn as the summer sky darkens.

"Jack!" Mrs. Garrett calls. "Please don't burn off your hand! Why do I need to say this? I tell you this every year."

"If I do," Mr. Garrett says, placing some fireworks in a circle of stones, "I'm suing your brother. He never sends instructions. Light up, Jase!"

Jase strikes a long match and hands it to his dad. Mrs. Garrett encircles George and Patsy in her arms. "You wouldn't read them anyway!" she calls out as the match flares blue and the fireworks shoot into the night sky.

As the last firework fizzles down, I roll onto my side, following the lines of Jase's face with my index finger.

"You've never played for me," I say.

"Mmm?" he sounds sleepy.

"I've seen Andy and Duff play their instruments. You *claim* you can play the guitar. But I've never seen evidence. When are you going to play me a ballad?"

"Uh, never?"

"Why not?" I ask, tracing the arch of one of his dark eyebrows.

"Because that would be incredibly lame, not to mention goofy. And I try to steer clear of lame. Not to mention goofy."

He shifts to his back, pointing into the night sky. "Okay, what's that star? And that one?"

"The Summer Triangle. That's Vega, and Deneb and Altair. Over there is . . . Lyra, Sagittarius . . ." I follow the path of the flickering stars with my index finger.

"I love that you know this," Jase says softly. "Hey, is that a shooting star? You can wish on those, right?"

"An airplane, Jase. See the little red taillight?"

"Jesus. Okay. So much for not being lame and goofy."

I laugh, lean over to kiss his neck. "You can wish on the airplane anyway, though, if you want."

"Somehow the thrill is gone," he says, pulling me close. "Besides, what else would I wish for?"

Chapter Twenty-eight

"Hello sweetheart." The voice is cool as water. "Have anything to say to me?"

I freeze in the act of silently closing the front door. *Oh God. Oh God. How did I not see Mom's car? I thought the fireworks and steam train would take longer. How could I have stayed out so late?*

"I never thought I'd be doing this for *you*." The voice is amused now, and I look up to see Tracy sitting on the couch, shaking her head at me.

I'd forgotten her pitch-perfect imitation of Mom, which, combined with her impressive forgery skills, got her out of field trips she didn't want to go on, school days with tests she hadn't studied for, and health classes she was bored by.

I laugh and take a deep breath. "Jeez, Trace. You almost gave me a heart attack."

She's smirking. "Mom called right at curfew to make sure you were safe and sound. I told her you'd been tucked up in your little bed for hours, dreaming sweet innocent dreams. Good thing she can't see you now." She stands up and walks behind me, turning me to face the mirror in the hallway. "So who's the guy?"

"There isn't—" I begin.

"Samantha, please. Your hair's a mess, your lips are all puffy, and you'll be needing that stupid Breakfast Ahoy scarf to cover that hickey right there. I repeat: Who's the guy?"

I do indeed look flushed and rumpled, a look I've seen on Tracy many a time but am still getting used to on myself. "You don't know him," I say, attempting to straighten my hair. "Please don't say anything to Mom."

"Little Miss Perfection has a secret lov-ah!" Tracy's giggling now.

"We're not . . . We haven't—"

"Huh," Tracy says, unimpressed. "Judging by the expression on your face, it's just a matter of time. I covered for you. Now, spill. If I don't know him, there's got to be a reason why. Please tell me it's someone Mom won't have a fit about."

"She would not be happy," I admit.

"Why? Is he a druggie? A drinker?"

"A Garrett," I say. "From next door."

"Holy heck, Samantha. You're really pushing the limits, aren't you? Who knew *you'd* turn out to be the big rebel? Is he the one with the leather jacket and the motorcycle? If so, you are doomed. Mom'll ground you till you're thirty-five."

I blow out an impatient breath. "Not him—his younger brother. Jase. Who's probably the best person I've ever met . . . kind and smart and . . . good. He . . . I . . ." I run out of words, rub my lips with my fingers.

"You're a goner," Tracy groans. "I can tell by listening to you that he's totally got the upper hand. You can't let that happen no matter how amazing you think the dude is. If you are going to be knocking boots, make sure he thinks you're doing *him* the favor. Otherwise you're just asking to be done and dumped."

My sister, the hopeless romantic.

Well? I text Nan the next morning.

???? she replies.

R U still on the boat? What happened?

No. Daniel had 2 get it back b4 parents knew he'd had it all night. I'm home.

And???

Where R U?

I'm at the beach before work at the B&T, watching Mr. Garrett train Jase. At the moment, Jase is slogging through the water knee-deep, emerging to do some push-ups and wading back in. If you'd told me I'd find this riveting a few weeks ago, I'd have laughed. My fingers hover, still hesitant to reveal too much to Nan, but finally I type: At SB beach.

Give me 10, she texts back.

Nan shows up fifteen minutes later, just as Jase flops onto the sand for another round of push-ups.

"Oh, I get it now," she says with a knowing smile. "I thought you were swimming, or catching some early sun. But it's all about the boyfriend, huh, Samantha?"

I ignore her. "What happened with Daniel?"

Nan flops on her back, wrist over her eyes—almost exactly what Tim did yesterday. Even after all these years, I'm fascinated by the way they sometimes unconsciously echo each other. She squints in the sun, then rolls onto her stomach, turning to look at me with serious gray eyes.

"On the boat? Well, we went upriver to Rocky Park, and anchored there and had a picnic. Then we went out in the sound. Daniel swam, but I was freaked that there might be great white sharks. He said it was too cold for them but—"

"Nan! You know that's not what I mean."

"I do?" she asks innocently, then relents. "Do you mean did Daniel and I 'Take Our Relationship to the Next Level'?"

"Um, no. Because who calls it that?" I flick a toenail shell at her.

"Daniel calls it that." Nan sits up, looking out at the water now, shielding her eyes from the sun. "We did not."

"Because . . . ? You decided you weren't ready? Or it wasn't what Daniel had in mind?"

Jase slogs back into the water, massaging his thigh as though he has a cramp.

"Why's he doing this?" Nan asks. "It seems like torture. I keep expecting his dad to get out a hose and spray him in the face with cold water. Or make him sing one of those macho rhyming songs *Navy Wings are made of lead, hup, two, three . . .*"

"Training for football season," I say, flicking another orange-pink shell at her. "You're evading the question."

"It was what Daniel had in mind. What I had in mind. But at the last minute . . . I just couldn't." Nan sits up now, pulling her knees to her chest, ducking her chin down. "He overtalked it. First he got me wine, which would have been okay, but he had to explain that it was 'to loosen my inhibitions.' Then he went on and on about how this was a big step and it was irrevocable, and it would Change Our Relationship Permanently. I kept waiting for him to pull out a release form."

"Sexy, baybee," I say.

"I know! I mean . . . I know life isn't like *Love With the Proper Stranger*." This is Nan's favorite movie, with her beloved Steve McQueen and Natalie Wood. "I don't expect . . . bells and banjos. Well . . . not from Daniel." She ducks her head. "Maybe not ever."

I watch Jase, and, as though sensing it, he turns, flashing his incandescent smile.

"Why not, Nanny?" I ask gently.

"I think these things through." Nan's biting her already too-short thumbnail, a habit she's had since kindergarten. I reach out, pull it away from her mouth, a habit *I've* had since kindergarten. "There's not going to be mad passion here. We've been dating for two years . . . We're compatible. It wouldn't be awkward."

Mr. Garrett gives Jase a thumbs-up, calling, "You're good, son."

"Joel," Jase replies, in between deep, ragged breaths, "could do it faster. I think."

"And I couldn't," Mr. Garrett calls. "Still had colleges looking. You're doing fine." He claps Jase on the shoulder.

"Shouldn't it be better than 'not awkward,' Nanny?"

Nan pulls her hand away from mine, starting on her pinkie nail. "In the real world? The only advice Mommy's given me about sex is: 'I was a virgin when I got married. Don't do that.'"

I pull her hand away again and she swats at me playfully. Jase has thrown himself down for another round of push-ups. I can see his arms trembling.

"Mom told me the mechanics when I got my period, then told me never to have sex."

"That approach worked so well with Tracy." Nan giggles, then her brows pull together, following my gaze.

"Daniel's going places." She traces a finger in the sand. "Clearly. He was valedictorian, he got in early-decision to MIT. We're alike that way . . . All I want is to get out of here." She sweeps her hand across the horizon as though she could erase it with that one gesture. "I'll apply ED to Columbia in the fall, I'll get away from Tim and Mommy and Daddy and . . . everything."

"Nan . . ." I say, then don't know how to continue.

"Who's he going to be, this Garrett guy?" Nan asks. "I mean, he's gorgeous now, God knows. But in five years, ten . . . Just like his dad. Running some hardware store in this podunk Connecticut town. Having too many kids . . . Daniel and I may not stay together, but . . . at least . . . he's not going to drag me down."

I feel my face prickle. "Nan, you don't even know Jase," I start, but then he jogs up to us at exactly this moment, bends, his hands splayed on his outspread thighs, gasping for air.

"Hey Sam, Nan. Sorry, have to catch my breath. I gotta stop, Dad."

"One more run," Mr. Garrett says. "Just pull it out. You can do it."

Jase shakes his head, shrugs at us, but wades into the water anyway.

Chapter Twenty-nine

Much to everyone's surprise, and probably his own, Tim thrives at Mom's campaign office. He makes voter registration calls in twenty different accents. He convinces ordinary folks who believe in Mom to write in to local papers about how their lives have been changed because Senator Grace Reed cares. Within two weeks, he's even writing short speeches for Mom. She and Clay can't stop talking about him.

"That kid really has it all going on," Clay marvels as we drive to yet another meet-and-greet, where I stand next to Mom, trying to look wholesome and supportive. "He's got smarts and he's wily. Always thinking on his feet."

"Yeah, well. Turns out it's all about manipulating things— and people," Tim allows when I repeat this to him. We're hanging out in the driveway of the Garretts' house while Jase works on the Mustang. I'm sitting on the hood, on a blanket, which Jase sheepishly insisted on, saying he didn't want any of the primer scratched off. He's wrestling with some sort of wiring issue. "Who knew that years of lying and bullshitting would be so useful?"

"You're cool with this?" Jase asks. "Hey, Sam, can you hand me the wrench? God knows what the guy who owned this before me did. Drag races? The clutch is completely burned out . . . and the five-speed's making this whining noise even though it's still operable. Plus all the u-joints are loose."

"English, dude?" Tim requests as I hand Jase the wrench. He's under the car, working hard, and I feel this urge to kiss the line of sweat trailing from his throat. I'm out of control.

"Somebody didn't take care of this car," Jase responds. "But you—sorry Sam—you don't believe in anything Grace Reed is supporting, Tim. You aren't even a Republican. Don't you feel wrong helping her out?"

"Sure," Tim answers easily. "But when haven't I felt wrong? Nothin' new there."

Jase ducks out from below the Mustang, slowly straightening up. "That feels okay? 'Cause I can't see how."

Tim shrugs.

Jase ruffles his hair, the way he always does when he's confused or hesitant.

"So Nan went to New York with the boyfriend this weekend," Tim mutters.

I start. I didn't know Nan was going somewhere with Daniel.

"From what I can see, he's a conceited douche bag who's only going to wind up hurting Nan. But did I stop her? Nope. I've made a million mistakes. Time for ol' Nano to catch up."

Jase's fingers close on something in his tool kit. He slides under the car again. "You'll feel so much better when she's unhappy?"

"Maybe." Tim reaches for the Mountain Dew he's been nursing for the last half hour. "At least I won't be alone."

"Samantha, you're slouching. Stand up straight and smile," Mom whispers to me. I'm standing next to her at a Daughters of the American Revolution gathering, shaking hands. We've been here for an hour and a half and I've said "Please support my mother. She cares deeply about the State of Connecticut" approximately fifteen million times. And she does care. That much is true. I just find myself feeling worse, more guilty, at each event, about *what* she cares about.

I'm no political animal. I know about current events from the newspaper and discussions at school, but it's not like I go to rallies or picket for causes. Still, the space between what I believe and what my mom believes seems to be widening by the day. I've heard Clay talking to her, telling her it's great strategy, that Ben Christopher's big weakness is that he's too liberal, so the more Mom talks up the other side, the better for her. But . . . last time she ran, I was eleven. And she ran against this maniac who didn't believe in public education.

But this time . . . I wonder how many children of politicians have thought the way I'm thinking right now, shook all those hands and said "Support my mom," while thinking, "Just not what she stands for. 'Cause I don't."

"Smile," Mom hisses through her teeth, bending to listen to a small, white-haired lady who is angry about some new construction on Main Street. "Things should have a certain look, and this does not! I am up in arms, Senator Reed, up in arms!"

Mom murmurs something soothing about making sure it complies with the bylaws, and having her staff look into it.

"How much longer?" I whisper.

"Until it ends, young lady. When you're working on behalf of the people, you don't have regular hours."

I look off in the distance at one of Mom's posters propped on a tripod—*GRACE REED, FIGHTING FOR OUR FOREBEARS, OUR FAMILIES, OUR FUTURE*—and try not to notice, just outside the French windows, the turquoise shimmer of a pool. I wish I could lunge into it. I'm hot and uncomfortable in the navy blue empire-waist dress Mom insisted I wear. *"These are very conservative women, Samantha. You need to show as little skin as possible."*

I have a mad desire to rip off my dress. If everyone here screamed and fainted, we could all go home. Why didn't I just tell Mom no? What am I, a mouse? A puppet? Clay rules Mom, Mom rules me.

"You didn't need to be so unpleasant the entire time," she says crossly as we're driving home. "Some daughters would be thrilled to be involved in this. The Bush twins were everywhere when W ran."

I have nothing to say to this. I pick at a pulled thread in the seam of my dress. Mom reaches over, closing her hand on mine to stop me. Her grip is firm. Then it relaxes. She takes my hand, squeezes.

"All that sighing and shuffling your feet." She sighs. "It was embarrassing."

I turn and stare at her. "Maybe you shouldn't bring me along next time, Mom."

She shoots me a sharp look, seeing right through that one.

There's steel in her eyes again, and she shakes her head. "I don't know *what* Clay's going to say about your little performance."

Clay left a little early, to go back to the office and get more paraphernalia for the next event, a clambake in Linden Park, where I fortunately am not required.

"I don't think Clay was paying attention to me. He only has eyes for you," I tell her.

A flush crosses her cheekbones and she says softly, "You may be right. He's very . . . dedicated."

Mom spends several minutes expounding on Clay's expertise and dedication, while I pass them hoping she's only speaking professionally. Though she's not. He leaves clothes and keys and things around our house all the time now, has a favorite chair in the living room, has tuned the radio in the kitchen to the station he likes. Mom buys his favorite brand of soda, some weird Southern cherry drink called Cheerwine. I think she's actually having it sent up from below the Mason-Dixon Line.

When we're finally home, climbing out of the car in silence, I hear a rumble, and Joel's motorcycle heads down the street. But it's not Joel riding it. It's Jase.

I say a quick prayer that he'll wheel into his own driveway, but he sees us, circles into ours, stops. Pulling off his helmet, he wipes his forehead with the back of his hand, giving me his warmest smile. "Hey, Samantha."

Mom looks at me sharply. "Do you know this boy?" she asks under her breath.

"Yes," I say emphatically. "This is Jase."

Ever polite, he's already extending his hand. I pray he won't mention his last name.

"Jase Garrett, from next door. Hi."

Mom gives his hand a perfunctory shake, shooting an unreadable glance at me.

Jase looks back and forth between us, pauses, then pops the helmet back on. "Just going for a ride. Wanna come, Sam?"

I wonder exactly how much trouble I'll get in if I do. Grounded till I'm thirty? Who knows? Who cares. I find, suddenly, that I don't. I've been stuffed inside a crowded room for hours, pretending, badly, to be the daughter my mom wants. Now the sky overhead is dazzling blue, the horizon wide. I feel a sudden rush—like the wind, but instead it's the blood whooshing in my ears, like when Tim and I were little and would go plunging headlong into the huge waves at the beach. I fling my leg over the back of the motorcycle and reach for the spare helmet.

We rocket off. I bury my head in Jase's shoulder, determinedly not looking back at my mother, but still somehow expecting sirens or helicopters with SWAT teams to overtake us. Soon, sheer sensation carries me away from all that. The wind flips my hair and my hands tighten around Jase's waist. He drives along the sandy, sea grass–lined Shore Road for a while, then through town, such a contrast with its neat red and white saltbox houses and evenly spaced maples. Then back to Shore Road near the beach. He cuts the engine in McGuire Park, near a playground I haven't been to for years. It used to be the stop on the way home from half-day kindergarten.

"So, Samantha." Jase takes off his helmet, hanging it on a handlebar, and reaches out a hand to help me off the seat. "Guess I'm from the wrong side of the tracks." He turns away, knocking down the motorcycle kickstand with the side of his sneaker.

"I'm sorry," I say reflexively.

He still doesn't look at me, kicking at the pebbles. "First time I've met your mom. Thought she was just strict. About you. I didn't realize this was actually about me. Or my family."

"It's not. Not really." My sentences are coming out short and choppy. I can't seem to catch my breath. "It's her. She's . . . I'm sorry . . . She is—she can be one of those people who make comments at the supermarket. But I'm not."

Jase lifts his chin, looks at me for a long moment. I stare back, willing him to believe me.

His face is a handsome, indecipherable mask he's never offered me before. Suddenly, I get angry. "Stop that. Stop judging *me* by what my mom did. That's not me. If you're going to decide what *I'm* like because of how *she* acts, you're as bad as she is."

Jase doesn't say anything, nudging at the ground with his sneaker. "I don't know," he says at last. "I can't help but notice that . . . well, you're in my life . . . at our house, with my family, in my world. But am I really in yours? Things got pretty awkward when I saw you at your club. You never even told your best friend about me. I've never . . ." He runs both hands through his hair, shaking his head. "Had dinner at your house. Or . . . I don't know, met your sister."

"She's away for the summer," I point out in a small voice.

"You know what I mean. I mean—you're all over the place with me. In my room and at the store and helping me train and just . . . there. Where am I with you? I'm not sure I know."

I get that thick feeling at the back of my throat. "You're everywhere with me too."

"Am I?" He stops kicking the dirt and advances, heat radiating from his body, hurt from his eyes. "You sure about that? Seems as though the closest I get is your roof—or your room. Sure you're not just . . . I don't know . . . slumming?"

"Slumming? By seeing my next-door neighbor?"

Jase looks at me as though he wants to smile, but can't. "You've got to admit, Sam, your mom wasn't exactly looking at me in a neighborly way. Not like she wanted to send over a casserole or something. More like a restraining order."

Relieved that he's joking, I take off my helmet. "It's my mother, Jase. Nobody's good enough for me. In her mind. My first boyfriend, Charley, was a deviant sex fiend who wanted to use me and discard me. Then Michael, that emo guy you saw, he was a druggie loner who was probably going to lure me into addiction and then go assassinate a president."

"You'd think I'd look good by comparison. But I guess not." He winces.

"It was the motorcycle."

"Oh yeah?" Jase reaches out to take my hand. "Remind me to wear Joel's leather jacket next time."

He gestures toward the bushes at the end of the cul-de-sac, away from the seesaw and the monkey bars and rusty swings. McGuire's a town park all neatly laid out, nothing left to chance, but once you leave the playground behind, the grassy hill slowly dips low through the cluster of low wild-raspberry bushes into a long labyrinth of stones that lead into the river. You can leap from one to another and wind up sitting on a large flat granite rock, well out in the water.

"You know about the Secret Hideaway?" I ask.

"I thought it was just mine." He grins at me, a little reserved, but still a grin. I smile back, thinking of Mom. *Smile, Samantha.* No one needs to prompt me now. We brush through the tangle of bushes, swatting the tiny thorns away from our faces, then jump, stone by stone, out to the raft-like rock in the river. Once there, Jase sits, knees up, arms around them, and I land next to him. I shiver, remembering how much cooler it always is with the breeze blowing up river. Without a word, he takes off his hooded sweatshirt and hands it to me. Afternoon light pours down, the river smell surrounds us, warm and brackish. Familiar and safe.

"Jase?"

"Uh-huh?" He picks up a stick lying on the rock and hurls it far out into the water.

"I should have told her sooner. I'm sorry. Are we good?"

For a moment he doesn't say anything, watching the ripples eddy wider and wider. But then: "We're good, Sam."

I lean back, flat on the rock, looking up at the deep azure sky. Jase lies down next to me, points.

"Red-tailed hawk."

We watch the hawk circling for a few minutes, then he reaches over and takes my hand, squeezes it, and holds on. The river sighs around us, and the little gears in my body that were spinning at breakneck speed all day slow to the lazy speed of the hawk, and the slow beat of my heart.

Chapter Thirty

It's good we have those moments, because the second I walk into the house I can feel fury rolling off Mom like fog from the sound. I could hear the vacuum cleaner growling before I even opened the door, and when I do, she's chasing it around the house, jaw set.

The door closes and she jerks the plug out of the wall, turning to me, expectant.

I'm not going to apologize as though she's right and I've done something unforgiveable. That would make what I said to Jase a lie. I'm not lying to him anymore, even by not telling the whole truth. Instead I stride to the fridge and pull out the lemonade.

"That's *it*?" Mom says.

"Want some?" I offer.

"So you're just going to be nonchalant about this? As though I didn't see my underage daughter get on a *motorcycle* with a *stranger*."

"He's not a stranger. That's Jase. From next door."

"I'm well aware where he's from, Samantha. I've spent the last ten years putting up with that unkempt yard and that loud, enormous family. How long have you known this boy? Do you often ride off on his motorcycle to God knows where?"

I swallow, take a slug of lemonade, and clear my throat. "Nope, that was a first. It's not his motorcycle, it's his brother's. Jase is the one who fixed your vacuum cleaner when you threw—when it broke."

"Will I be getting a bill for this?" Mom asks.

My mouth falls open. "Are you kidding? He did that to be nice. Because he's a good person and I asked him. He doesn't want your money."

Mom tilts her head, studying me. "Are you seeing this boy?"

The words that spill out are braver than I am, but not quite brave enough. "We're friends, Mom," I say. "I'm seventeen. I get to pick my own friends." This is the kind of argument Tracy, not me, has with Mom. When I used to listen to them fight, all I wanted was for my sister to be quiet. Now I understand why she couldn't be.

"I don't believe this." Mom reaches under the kitchen sink, pulling out a can of Ajax and sprinkling it on the spotless countertop. "You're *friends*? Exactly what does that mean?"

Well, we've bought some condoms, Mom, and sometime soon . . . For a moment I want to say it so badly, I'm afraid it'll just tumble out.

"It means I like him. He likes me. We like spending time together."

"Doing what?" Mom lifts the carafe of lemonade and wipes away the circle of condensation beneath it.

"You never ask Tracy that about Flip."

I've always assumed that was because she didn't want to

know the answer, but now she says, in the same tone in which one would say "we hold these truths to be self-evident," "Flip's from a good, responsible family."

"So's Jase."

Mom sighs and walks over to the side window that overlooks the Garretts' lawn. "Look."

Duff and Harry are evidently fighting. Duff's waving a toy light saber menacingly at his younger brother, who, as we watch, picks up a plastic bucket and throws it at him. George is sitting on the steps sucking on a Popsicle, without pants. Mrs. Garrett's feeding Patsy, holding out a book she must be reading aloud.

Jase has the hood of the Mustang up, tinkering away.

"So what?" I say. "He has a big family. Why is that such an issue for you? What does it matter to you?"

Mom is shaking her head slowly, watching them the way she always does.

"Your father came from a family just like that. Did you know that?"

He did. That's right. I think of the pictures, crowded with people, in that box Tracy and I opened so long ago. Were those his family? I'm torn between grabbing on to this scrap of information with both hands and concentrating on what's happening now.

"Just like that," Mom repeats. "Big and messy and completely irresponsible. And look how your father turned out."

I want to point out that I don't actually know how my father turned out. But then . . . he left us. So I guess I do.

"That's Dad's family. Not Jase's."

225

"Same thing," she says. "We're talking about a sense of accountability here."

Are we? That doesn't feel like what we're talking about. "What's your point, Mom?"

Her face freezes, only her lashes fluttering, as I've seen happen during difficult debates. I can sense her struggling to contain her temper, summon tactful words. "Samantha. One thing you've always been good at is making choices. Your sister would jump in with her eyes shut, but you would think. Even when you were very little. Smart choices. Smart friends. You had Nan. Tracy had that awful Emma with the nose ring, and Darby. Remember Darby? With the boyfriend and the hair? I know that's why Tracy got into all that trouble in middle school. The wrong people can lead you to make the wrong decisions."

"Did Dad—" I start, but she cuts in.

"I don't want you seeing this Garrett boy."

I won't let her do this—take away Jase like he's an obstacle in her path, or mine, like the way she'll sometimes just throw out clothes I've bought if she doesn't like them, like the way she made me quit swim team.

"Mom. You can't just say that. We haven't done anything wrong. I rode on a motorcycle with him. We're friends. I'm seventeen."

She pinches the bridge of her nose. "I'm not comfortable with this, Samantha."

"What if I'm not comfortable with Clay Tucker? Because I'm not. Are you going to stop seeing *him*, stop having him"— I make air quotes, something I despise—"*advise* you on the campaign?"

"It's a completely different and a separate situation," Mom says stiffly. "We're adults who know how to be answerable for consequences. You're a child. Involved with someone I don't know and have no reason to trust."

"*I* trust him." My voice is rising. "Shouldn't that be enough? Me being the responsible one who makes smart choices and all?"

Mom pours soap into the blender I'd left in the sink, sprays water into it, then scrubs furiously. "I don't like your tone, Samantha. When you talk like this I don't know who you are."

This makes me furious. And then in the next second, exhausted. Whoever I am scares me a little. I've never talked to my mother like this, and it's not the chill of the central air-conditioning that prickles the skin of my arms. But as I see Mom cast yet another of a decade's worth of critical looks over at the Garretts in their yard, I know where I'm going.

I walk to the side door and bend to put on my flip-flops.

Mom's right behind me.

"You're walking away? We haven't resolved this! You can't leave."

"I'll be right back," I toss over my shoulder. Then I march across the porch, around the fence, and up the driveway to put my hand on the warm skin of Jase's back, bent over the innards of the Mustang.

He turns his head to smile at me, quickly wiping his forehead with his wrist. "Sam!"

"You look hot," I say.

He shoots a quick glance over at his mother, still reading to George and feeding Patsy. Duff and Harry have evidently taken their fight elsewhere.

"Um, thanks." He sounds bemused.

"Come with me. To my house."

"I'm kind of—I should probably take a shower. Or get a shirt."

I'm pulling at his hand now, slippery with sweat and grease. "You're fine the way you are. Come on."

Jase looks at me for a moment, then follows. "Should I have gotten my tool kit?" he asks mildly as I tow him up the steps.

"Nothing needs fixing. Not like that."

I can hear from outside that Mom's got the vacuum cleaner back on. I open the door and gesture inside. Jase, eyebrows raised, steps in.

"Mom!" I call.

She straightens up from vacuuming one of the sofa cushions, then just stands there, looking back and forth between us. I walk over and flip the vacuum off.

"This is Jase Garrett, Mom. One of your constituents. He's thirsty and he'd love some of your lemonade."

Chapter Thirty-one

"So now you've met my mother," I say to Jase that night, leaning back on the roof.

"I sure have. That was awesome. And completely uncomfortable."

"The lemonade made it all worthwhile, though, right?"

"The lemonade was fine," Jase says. "It was the girl who made it awesome."

I sit up, edge over close to my window, and push it open, slipping one leg in, then the next, turning back to Jase. "Come on."

His smile flashes in the gathering dark as his eyebrows lift, but he climbs carefully in as I lock my bedroom door.

"Be still," I tell him. "Now I'm going to learn all about you."

A while later, Jase is lying on his back on my bed, wearing shorts but nothing else, and I'm kneeling beside him.

"I think you already know me pretty well." He reaches out to tug the elastic out of my hair so it falls free, draping over his chest.

"Nope. Lots to learn. Do you have freckles? A birthmark?

Scars? I'm gonna find 'em all." I lean down to touch my lips to his belly button. "There, you have an innie. I'm filing this information away."

Jase sucks in a breath. "I'm not sure I *can* be still. Jesus, Samantha."

"Look, and over here . . ." I lick in a line down from his navel. "You *do* have a scar. Do you remember where you got this one?"

"Samantha. I can't even remember my name when you're doing this. But don't stop. I love the way your hair feels like that."

I shake my head, making my hair fan out more. I am wondering where this take-charge confidence is coming from, but at the moment, who cares? Watching what it does to him takes away any hesitation, any embarrassment.

"I don't think I'm going to get the whole picture with these here." I reach for the top of his shorts.

His lashes flutter closed as he takes another deep rough breath. I slowly slide them down, tugging over his lean hips.

"Boxers. Plain. No cartoon characters. I figured."

"Samantha. Let me look at you too. Please."

"What is it you want to see?" I'm preoccupied by edging the shorts all the way off. And a little bit using this as an excuse because my bravado has wavered after seeing Jase in only boxers. And not exactly immune to me.

Okay, I know about arousal, I do. It was pretty much Charley's perpetual state. Michael suffered over his, but that never stopped him from pulling my hand to his crotch. But this is Jase, and that I can do that to him, with him, makes my mouth go dry, and other parts of me ache in a completely unaccustomed way.

He reaches up, brushing my hair away from the back of my dress so he can find the zipper. His eyes are still closed but, as the zipper slides down, he opens them and they're brilliant green, like leaves when they first show up in the spring. He smoothes the tips of his fingers around my shoulders and then eases the dress down, taking my hands to pull them out of the armholes. I shiver. I'm not cold, though.

I wish I had some exotic underwear. It's an ordinary tan bra I'm wearing, the kind with that little meaningless bow in the center. But just as I find Jase's plain boxers perfectly compelling, he seems mesmerized by my utilitarian bra. His thumbs brush over the front of it, tracing the outline, circling. My turn to take a deep breath now. Except that I can't seem to, as his hands return to my back, searching for the clasp.

I look down. "Ah. You *do* have a birthmark." I touch his thigh. "Right up here. It looks like a fingerprint, almost." The tip of my index finger covers it completely.

Jase slides my bra off, whispering, "You have the softest skin. Come close."

I lie on top of him, skin to skin. He's tall, I'm not, but when we lie like this, we fit together. All the curves of my body relax into the strength of his.

When people talk about sex, it sounds so technical . . . or scarily out of control. Nothing like this sense of rightness, of being made to fit together.

But we don't carry it any further than lying together. I can feel Jase's heart thudding beneath me, and the way he curves away a little, embarrassed, probably, that his need shows more clearly than mine. So I just stroke his cheek and say—yes *I* say, the girl who has always guarded her heart—I say, for the first time, "I love you. It's okay."

Jase looks straight into my eyes. "Yeah," he whispers. "It is, isn't it? I love you too, my Sam."

For the next few days after our blowup over Jase, Mom works her way through a) the silent treatment, with its accompaniment of sighs, frosty glances, and hostile muttering under her breath; then b) interrogating me about my plans for every hour of the day; and c) laying down rules: "That boy is not to be coming in here while I'm at work, young lady. I know what happens when two teenagers are alone, and that's not happening under my roof."

I manage not to snap back that, in that case, we'll find a handy backseat or a cheap motel. Jase and I are getting closer and closer. I'm hooked on the smell of his skin. I'm interested in every detail of his day, the way he analyzes customers and suppliers, summing them up so concisely, but empathetically. I'm captivated by the way he looks at me with a bemused smile while I talk, as though he's both listening to my voice and absorbing the rest of me. I'm pleased by all the parts of him I know, and each new part I discover is like a present.

Is this how Mom feels? Does every bit of Clay feel like it was designed specifically to make her happy? The idea kind of grosses me out. But if she feels that way, what kind of person am I that I just don't like him being around?

"You're gonna have to handle this one for me, kid," Tim says, coming into the kitchen, where I am easing warmed focaccia squares out of the oven, sprinkling them with pre-grated Parmesan. "They need more wine out there and it's not a real great idea to ask me to be the sommelier. Gracie said two bottles of the pinot grigio." His voice is teasing, but he's sweating a little, and probably not from the heat.

"Why did they ask you? I thought you were here to be office support, not waitstaff." Mom is having twelve donors over for dinner. It's catered, but she's concealing the fact from the donors, having me carry out the precooked, reheated food.

"The lines get kinda blurred sometimes. You have no idea how many coffee and donut runs I've made since I signed on to your ma's campaign. Do you know how to open those?" He nods at the two bottles I've extracted from the lower rack of the fridge.

"I think I can figure it out."

"I hate wine," Tim says meditatively. "Never liked the smell of it, if you can believe that. Now I could just chug both of those in two seconds flat." He shuts his eyes.

I've peeled off the metal coating on top and am inserting the corkscrew, a fancy new one that looks more like a pepper grinder. "Sorry, Tim. If you want to go back out there, I'll bring these out."

"Nah. The pretentiousness is getting a little thick. Not to mention the bigotry. That Lamont guy is a supersized douche bag."

I agree. Steve Lamont is a tax attorney from town and the poster child for political incorrectness. Mom's never liked him, since he's also sexist and fond of joking about wearing black every year on the anniversary of the day when women got the vote.

"I don't understand why he's even here," I say. "Clay's from the South but he's not a bigot, I don't think. But Mr. Lamont . . ."

"Is fuckin' rich, babe. Or as Clay would put it, 'He's so loaded he buys a new boat every time the old one gets wet.' That's all that matters. They'd put up with a hell of a lot worse to get some of that."

I shudder, jerking the cork, which breaks. "Oh, damn."

Tim reaches for the bottle, but I move it away from him. "It's okay, I'll just try to get the broken bit."

"Timothy? What's taking so long?" Mom marches through the swinging kitchen door, glancing between us.

I hold out the bottle. "Oh, honestly!" she says. "That's going to ruin the whole bottle if any cork gets in." She pulls it from my hands, frowns at it, then drops it into the trash and opens the refrigerator to get another. I start to take it from her hands, but she picks up the opener and twists it herself, deftly. Then does the same to the second bottle.

Then she hands one to Tim. "Just go around the table and top off people's glasses."

He sighs. "Okay, Gracie."

She removes a wineglass from the dish rack and fills it, then takes a deep swallow. "Remember that you are not to call me that in public, Tim."

"Right. Senator." Tim's holding the bottle out in front of him, as though it might explode.

Mom takes another sip. "This is very good," she tells us

234

absently. "I think it's going really well out there, don't you?" She directs this question at Tim, who nods.

"You can practically hear the purse strings loosening," he says. If his voice is slightly sardonic, Mom doesn't pick up on that.

"Well, we won't know until the checks come in." She finishes the glass of wine in one last swallow, then looks over at me. "Do I have any lipstick left?"

"Just a rim," I say. Most of it is on the glass.

She blows an impatient breath. "I'll run upstairs and reapply. Tim, get out there and fill 'em up. Samantha, the foccacia's getting cold. Bring it out with some more olive oil for dipping."

Whirling, she heads up the stairs. I take the wine out of Tim's hand, replacing it with the bottle of oil.

"Thanks, kid. This isn't nearly as tempting."

I look over at the glass with its blush-pink stain. "She kind of knocked that back."

He shrugs. "Your ma doesn't like asking folks for shit. Not really her style. Dutch courage, I guess."

Chapter Thirty-two

"You're not gonna *believe* what just happened to me," Jase says the minute I flip my cell open, taking advantage of break at the B&T. I turn away from the picture window just in case Mr. Lennox, disregarding the break sign, will come dashing out to slap me with my first-ever demerit.

"Try me."

His voice lowers. "You know how I put that lock on the door of my room? Well, Dad noticed it. Apparently. So today, I'm stocking the lawn section and he comes up and asks why it's there."

"Uh-oh." I catch the attention of a kid sneaking into the hot tub (there's a strict no-one-under-sixteen policy) and shake my head sternly. He slinks away. Must be my impressive uniform.

"So I say I need privacy sometimes and sometimes you and I are hanging out and we don't want to be interrupted ten million times."

"Good answer."

"Right. I think this is going to be the end of it. But then he tells me he needs me in the back room to have a 'talk.'"

"Uh-oh again."

Jase starts to laugh. "I follow him back and he sits me down and asks if I'm being responsible. Um. With you."

Moving back into the shade of the bushes, I turn even further away from the possible gaze of Mr. Lennox. "Oh God."

"I say yeah, we've got it handled, it's fine. But, seriously? I can't believe he's asking me this. I mean, Samantha, Jesus. *My* parents? Hard not to know the facts of life and all in *this* house. So I tell him that we're moving slowly and—"

"You *told* him that?" *God, Jase! How am I ever going to look Mr. Garrett in the eye again? Help.*

"He's my dad, Samantha. Yeah. Not that I didn't want to exit the conversation right away, but still . . ."

"So what happened then?"

"Well, I reminded him they'd covered that really thoroughly in school, not to mention at home, and we weren't irresponsible people."

I close my eyes, trying to imagine having this conversation with my mother. Inconceivable. No pun intended.

"So then . . . he goes on about"—Jase's voice drops even lower—"um . . . being considerate and um . . . mutual pleasure."

"Oh my God! I would've died. What did you say?" I ask, wanting to know even while I'm completely distracted by the thought. *Mutual pleasure, huh? What do I know about giving that? What if Shoplifting Lindy had tricks up her sleeve I know nothing about? It's not like I can ask Mom. "State senator suffers heart attack during conversation with daughter."*

"I said 'Yes sir' a lot. And he went on and on and all I could think was that any minute Tim was gonna come in and hear my dad saying things like, 'Your mom and I find that . . . blah blah blah.' "

I can't stop laughing. "He didn't. He did *not* mention your mother."

"I *know*!" Jase is laughing too. "I mean . . . you know how close I am to my parents, but . . . Jesus."

"So, what do you think?" Jase asks, picking up two cans of paint from the floor and setting them on the counter. He pops one lid open, then the other, dipping in the flat wooden stirrer, swirling the paint around. "For the Mustang? We've got your plain racing green." He slides the stick along a piece of newspaper. "Then your slightly sparkly one." Another slide. "Which would you choose?"

They're barely different. Still, I scrutinize both sticks carefully. "What was the original paint job on the Mustang?" I ask.

"The plain green. Which kind of seems right. But then—"

My cell phone sings out.

"Hey kid—I need your help." It's Tim. "I'm at headquarters and I left my laptop at the store. I wrote this speech, intro thing, for your ma to use tonight. I need you to forward the copy to her e-mail. It's in the supply room—on Mr. Garrett's desk."

I locate the laptop easily. "Okay, what now?"

"Just go on in, I can't remember what it's called—there aren't that many files. Work or something like that."

"What's your password?" My fingers hover over the keyboard.

"Alice," Tim says. "But I *will* deny that if you tell anyone."

"In Wonderland, right?"

"Absolutely. Gotta go—that tight-assed Malcolm dude is

having a fit about something. Call me back if you can't find it."

I enter the password and look for documents. There's nothing labeled WORK. I scroll through, searching, and finally come upon a folder labeled CRAP. Close enough, knowing Tim. I click on that, and up pops a series of documents. *Give that Girl an A: A Study of Hawthorne's Hester Prynne. A Comparison of Huckleberry Finn and Holden Caulfield. Danger in Dickens. The Four Freedoms.*

I click on *The Four Freedoms* . . . and there it all is. Nan's prize-winning Fourth of July speech. Dated last fall.

But she wrote it for American government. This spring.

Daniel took American government last year. I remember him going on and on about John Adams at our lunch table. So Nan must have gotten the syllabus from him. She's always prepared like that. But still . . . writing the paper before the class even started? Extreme. Even for Nan.

And why would it be on Tim's computer? Okay. Nan did borrow his laptop a lot when hers was a mess.

I shift the mouse, edging it to *Holden Caulfield and Huckleberry Finn*, Nan's essay to be published in the literary journal. Here it is, the Lazlo-winning essay, word for word.

I know she covered for him. We both have, let's face it. But this is so much further than I thought she'd go.

I can't believe it. Tim's been using Nan's work.

I continue to stare at the screen, feeling like someone siphoned all the blood out of my head.

"Samantha, I need you! Can you un-Velcro yourself from The Boyfriend for a while?" Nan's voice crackles over my cell, high and shaking.

"Of course. Where are you?"

"Meet me at Doane's. I need ice cream."

Nan's going for sugar-rush therapy again. *Bad sign. Did she go to New York with Daniel? It's only Saturday. I thought Tim said she'd told her parents he was taking her to some Model UN and they were staying at his very strict uncle's house.*

I don't even know if Daniel *has* an uncle who lives in NYC, although if he did, that the uncle would be strict is a safe bet.

The Masons' house is much closer to town than mine, so I'm not surprised to find her sitting at the counter at Doane's when I get there. I *am* surprised to find her already plowing into a banana split.

"Sorry," she says through a mouthful of whipped cream. "Couldn't wait. I almost jumped the counter and dug into the buckets with my fingers. I definitely need some chocolate malt salvation now. Just like Tim. Since he stopped drinking he's like a maniac with the sweet stuff."

"But you're not kicking a habit," I say. "Or are you? What's up with Daniel?"

She turns bright red and tears come to her eyes, spill down her flushed, freckled cheeks.

"Aw, Nan." I start to put my arms around her, but she shakes her head.

"Order yours and let's sit at the picnic table outside. I don't want everyone in Doane's to hear this."

The only other people in Doane's at the moment are a mother with a toddler who is screaming because she won't let him buy a foot-long Tootsie Roll. "BAD MOMMY. I'M GOING TO KILL YOU WITH A SWORD!"

"Yeah, we'd better get out of here before we're material witnesses to a homicide," I say. "I'll get ice cream later. Lead the way."

She sets her bowl in front of her on the table, scoops up the cherry, and dunks it in a pool of chocolate sauce. "This is how many million calories, you think?"

"Nan. Tell me. What happened? Tim said you were spending the whole weekend."

"I'm sorry I didn't tell you. Daniel didn't want anyone to know. I only told Tim the truth because I thought he could help me come up with a better cover story, but he said the Model UN and the strict uncle were inspired. Although he said it would have been even better if I'd said we were staying with his aunt at a convent."

"You could have told me. I would never tell on you." Does she know about Tim stealing her essays? Should I tell her?

Her eyes fill again and she dashes the tears away impatiently, taking another mountainous scoop of ice cream. "I know. I'm sorry. I was . . . I felt like you were too busy with the Hometown Hottie to care. I thought I'd just go and come back a Sophisticated Woman Who Took Her Relationship to the Next Level in the Big Apple."

I wince. There's no way I'm bringing up Tim right now. "Did Daniel use that phrase again? Maybe if we made him a little dictionary? We could translate his words into something remotely sexy. Take Our Relationship to the Next Level could be Come on, Baby, Light My Fire."

She gulps another scoop of ice cream, swallows, then says, "What would It's Time to Push Our Comfort Zone be?"

241

"Oh Nan. Really?"

She nods. "He can't really be our age. Maybe it's like *Freaky Friday* and some middle-aged insurance salesman has taken over Daniel's body." She scoops up another enormous spoonful.

"What comes after pushing the comfort zone, Nan?" I probe.

"Well, we were at his uncle's town house—that part was true. But his uncle was away in Pound Ridge for the weekend, so . . . we'd had dinner and walked in the park—not for very long, because Daniel kept thinking someone was going to mug us. Then we walked back, and he put on music."

"Please tell me it wasn't Ravel's *Boléro*."

"Actually, he couldn't get the station he wanted, so we wound up with all these rap songs. But he thought that was sort of funny too. I noticed that he got less starchy when we, well, when I got more—um—"

"Confident?"

"Right. I kind of knew that was Daniel's Kryptonite. So I was wearing my green dress with all the little buttons down the front and I just ripped it open. Buttons everywhere. You should have seen his face!"

"Wow." I can't imagine Nan doing this. She still changes in her closet when I spend the night.

"Then I said, 'Stop talking, Professor.' And I ripped open *his* shirt." She's smiling a little now.

"Nan, you shameless hussy." The smile fades away and she puts her head down on the table next to her melting sundae and sobs. "I'm sorry, I was kidding. What then? He didn't make you go right out to Madison Avenue and buy him a new one, did he?"

"No. He was totally into it. He told me this was a new side of me and he wasn't threatened by confident women." She digs out a chunk of banana dribbling with syrup but then drops the spoon back down and blows her nose on the hem of her T-shirt. "That I was beautiful and there was nothing better than brains and beauty together, and then he stopped talking and started kissing me like crazy. We were lying on the floor in front of the fireplace and—" Another sob.

My hand is stroking the back of Nan's head, my mind racing with every possible scenario. *Daniel announced he's gay. Daniel has Erectile Dysfunction. Daniel confessed to being a vampire and not being able to have sex with her because he might kill her.*

"His uncle came in. Right into the library. He wasn't even away. That was supposed to be next weekend. He'd been at work when we dropped off our suitcases and now he was upstairs taking a bath and he heard noises and he came in with a cane ready to kill us."

Oh poor Nanny.

"He's shouting at Daniel and calling me a slut and all this stuff and Daniel can't find his pants so he's just standing there naked, and then he shoves me in front of himself."

Damn Daniel. Couldn't he even be gallant and shield her? Tim was right. He's a putz.

"What a coward." *Oops*, will that make Nan mad? I brace myself. But she just nods her head and says, "I know, right? Steve McQueen would never have done that. He would have beaten him up like he does to the bad doctor in *Love With the Proper Stranger*."

"So then what?"

243

"So then the uncle and Daniel start fighting. Daniel's begging him not to tell his parents and his uncle keeps screaming at him. Finally, he agreed not to tell if we 'Left the Premises at Once.'"

I can see where Daniel gets his diction. "So you came home then?"

"No, it was really late. We used my emergency American Express card to stay at the Doubletree Midtown. Daniel tried to pick up where we left off, but the mood was gone. We just watched a *Star Trek* marathon and fell asleep."

I reach out my arms and this time she slides into them, her drooping head on my shoulder, her own shoulders shaking.

"Why can't things ever work for me? I just wanted to be irresistible and adventurous. Now I'm a Scarlet Woman and I didn't even *get* the sex. I'm a Faux Scarlet Woman." Her hot tears soak my collarbone.

"I think you were awesome. Ripping off his shirt, taking charge. You're a Scarlet Woman in all the best ways, Nan Mason."

"It was really hard to rip off, actually." She wipes her eyes with the back of her hand. "Brooks Brothers must sew those buttons on with wire."

"He said you were beautiful and brave," I tell her. "And you were."

"Don't tell anybody what happened. I didn't even tell Tim. I told him Daniel rocked my world. Ugh."

Seems to me Tim would understand things not turning out as planned.

I rub her back gently and say, "Pinkie swear."

She sits up suddenly. "No matter what you do, don't tell that Garrett boy. I can't stand the thought of you guys laughing at us."

I wince. Knowing how protective Jase is of his sisters, how he tried to nudge Tim into having more compassion for Nan, I know he would never laugh. That Nan would think he would hurts, almost as much as it hurts that she thinks I would. But all I say is, "I won't tell anybody."

"I need more ice cream." She says. Her face is so red and swollen that her eyes are squinted. "Want to split that Doane's Dynamo thing that has ten scoops and comes in a Frisbee?"

Chapter Thirty-three

"Wish me luck at Chuck E. Cheese." Mrs. Garrett sighs as she drops Jase and me off at the hardware store. "Hell on earth, with pizza and a giant talking mouse."

It's Jase and Tim's shift today. Except that Tim didn't show up to give us a ride. Mrs. Garrett, saying she didn't need me to babysit because of a birthday party George is invited to at Chuck E. Cheese, drove us. My early afternoon free from Breakfast Ahoy, I'm thumbing idly through the SAT test prep guide Nan gave me.

Jase begins unpacking a shipment of nails. We say nothing about Tim's absence, but I notice Jase's eyes, under their thick dark lashes, flicking to the clock over the door, just as mine do. I don't want Tim to screw up. But ten minutes go by, then twenty, then half an hour.

Mr. Garrett comes out of the back room to say hello. He claps Jase on the back and kisses me on the cheek, telling us there's plenty of coffee in his office. He's holed up back there, he says, doing the quarterly books. Jase whistles under his breath, sorting nails, scribbling amounts down on a pad. I hear a little repetitive sound coming from Mr. Garrett's office. I flip pages in the prep guide, trying to identify the sound.

Click-click-click-click-click.

I look over at Jase inquiringly.

"Pen cap," he explains. "My dad says clicking it always helps him add—or, in our case, subtract." He opens a bag of bullet-head nails, letting them clatter into the clear plastic drawer in front of him.

"No better—the finances?" I come up to stretch my arms around his back, resting my cheek against his shoulder blade. He's wearing a gray sweatshirt today and I inhale the Jase smell.

"But no worse," he responds with a grin, turning to face me, cupping the heel of his hand to the back of my neck, smiling as he pulls me closer.

"You look beat." I trace the dark bluish shadow under his eye with a slow finger.

"Yup. I am. That feels good, Sam."

"Are you burning the midnight oil? Doing what?"

"I guess I'm burning the daylight oil, but it sure doesn't feel like daylight at four in the morning."

His eyes are still shut. I smooth my finger down his cheek, then slide it back up to the other eye.

"You're getting up at four in the morning? Why?"

"Don't laugh."

Why does that phrase always bring out a smile? He opens his eyes and grins back at me.

I school my face into a somber expression. "I won't."

"I'm a paperboy now."

"What?"

"I'm delivering papers for the *Stony Bay Sentinel*. Starting at four, six days a week."

"How long have you been doing this?"

"Two weeks. I didn't think it would be quite this bad. You never see paperboys in movies chugging down Red Bull and No-Doz."

"Probably because they're usually ten. Couldn't Duff do it?" His hand slides up to tangle in my hair, to pull out my elastic, because that's what he always does.

"Duff doesn't hope to go to college next year. I do. Even though it's damn unlikely, the way things are going. Hell, I shouldn't have bought that car. I just wanted it . . . so badly. And it's nearly running now. With more money poured in, that is." I bite my lip. I never have to worry about money. "Don't look so sad, Sam. It'll be okay. I shouldn't have brought it up."

"I brought it up," I remind him. "I'm your girlfriend. You're supposed to be able to talk about this stuff with me. It's not just about me making free with your hot body, you know."

"Though that completely works for me," Jase says, twisting his fingers in my hair and pulling me closer.

"Oh hell. Not more of this PDA crap."

We turn toward the door as Tim stalks in, wearing his gray Impress Grace Reed suit and looking crumpled and extremely pissed off.

"Mason," Jase greets, not letting go of me. "You okay?" He indicates the clock with a hitch of his shoulder.

"That would depend on what 'okay' is." Tim yanks off his jacket and shoves it onto a coat hook. He untwines his tie as though it's a boa constrictor with a chokehold around his neck. "Which I wouldn't frickin' know, would I?" Stalking over, he takes his place beside Jase, who surreptitiously checks his pupils and sniffs his breath. I can't smell anything. I hope Jase doesn't. Tim doesn't look high . . . just furious.

"What's up?" Jase hands him his time card.

Tim bends over to scribble the time in black marker. "Samantha? How the fuck much do you know about that Clay Tucker?"

"Tim, come on. Stop swearing." I put a hand on his arm. He's been easing up on the four-letter words lately, sometimes getting through an entire conversation without one.

"Why, Samantha? Why the fuck should I?" He gives me his fake-charming smile. "I get to say it. You guys get to *do* it. The way I figure it, you come out ahead."

"Knock it off, Tim. This isn't Samantha's fault. What's going on with Clay Tucker?" Jase leans his hip against the side of the counter, crossing his arms.

"I dunno. I mean, I'm not one to criticize manipulative bas-tards, being one myself and all. But this guy . . . new levels. And your mom, Samantha . . . right there with him." Tim rubs his forehead.

"What do you mean?" I say at the same time Mr. Garrett asks, "You going back there to work tonight?" He must have come into the room without any of us hearing.

Tim shakes his head, but a flush climbs up his neck. He's never been late before, not here.

"Good, then. You'll stay on after closing and finish that inventory of the stockroom you started the other day."

Tim nods, swallowing. Mr. Garrett puts a hand on his shoul-der. "Never again, Timothy. Ya hear?" He walks off down the hall to his office, his broad shoulders looking a little slumped.

Jase pulls a package of Trident gum out of his jeans pocket and offers it to Tim. "So go on."

"So old Clay . . ." Tim takes six sticks of gum, half the package. Jase raises his eyebrows but says nothing. "He's freaking everywhere. You lift a rock in this campaign and he crawls out from under it. Grace has this entire staff and Clay's in charge of fuckin' all of it. He says something and everybody jumps. Even me. The guy never sleeps. Even that little dude, your mom's suck-up campaign manager, Malcolm, is looking bushed, but Clay's going along like the friggin' Energizer Bunny of Connecticut politics. He's even got this babe . . . this hot brunette from Ben Christopher's office . . . being like a double agent for him. She shows up every morning to give him the goods on what Christopher's doing. So Grace can get a jump on it, show it up, look better."

Realization smacks me hard, but I barely have time to process because Tim keeps going.

"He's all about the photo ops too. Yesterday it was some poor bastard who lost both legs in Afghanistan coming stateside. Clay was on the spot, makin' sure Gracie got a half-page spread in the *Stony Bay Bugle* kissing him hello." Tim jams his hands into his pockets, pacing around the room as he talks. "Then we go to some day-care center where he gets Grace's photo taken with six cute blond kids piled around her. He practically shoved this girl with one of those big red birthmarks on her face outta the way. I mean, he's good at what he does. It's amazing watching him work. But somehow, frickin' scary too. And your Mom . . . she just says nothin', Samantha. She snaps to attention like *she's* working for *him*. What the fuck's up with that?"

It's not as though I haven't thought all these things. But when Tim says them, I feel defensive. Besides, who is Tim to talk?

"Look," I say. "It may seem like he's the boss, but Mom would never back off completely like that. She loves this job and she's totally committed to winning and this is a tough race . . ." I trail off. *I sound like her.*

"Yeah, and she's ahead in all our internal polling. Even with the margin of error. Close, but ahead. But of course, that's not enough for Clay. Clay has to hedge his bets. Clay has to have his little November surprise in the works, so he makes abso-friggin'-lutely sure that not only does she win, but her opponent fucking loses. Big. Not just the race. His whole career."

Jase is absently sliding the palm of his left hand up and down my side, while still pulling plastic packs of nails out of the cardboard box. "And he's doing this by . . . ?"

"Digging up dirt that doesn't matter. Making sure it matters. And sticks."

We both stare at Tim.

"Ben Christopher, who's running against Grace? He has two DUIs," he says. "The first was from thirty years ago, high school. The second was twenty-six years ago. He did his service, paid his fines. I see the dude in meetings. He's *seriously* decent. He's done everything he can to make up for it. But old Clay's already got it lined up to make sure you can never keep your past in the past. He knows from his little pet spy that the

Christopher campaign is shitting bricks about it coming out. And he's gonna have old Gracie do a rally with some asshole there who's going to let it all slip. Three days before the election."

"Where are you in all this?" Jase asks.

Tim looks at us pleadingly. "I don't *know*. Clay Tucker thinks I walk on water. For some reason, every damn thing I do impresses this jerk-off. Today he complimented me on how I collated papers, for Christ's sake. No one has *ever* been this impressed with me. Not even when I was faking my ass off. I'm not now. I'm actually good at this crap. Plus, I need the recommendation." His voice rises a few octaves. " 'The hardware store is all very well, Timothy, but it's your campaign experience, and what the state senator says about you that'll go a long way toward repairing the damage you've done yourself.' "

"Your mom?" I ask.

"Natch. There's not a person on the planet who would say as many nice things about me as Clay Tucker. And of course, my luck, he has to ruin a good man along the way."

At this point the store gets a sudden run of customers. A hassled-looking woman with her teenage daughter chooses paint chips. An elderly woman wants a leaf blower that doesn't take any muscle to run. A clueless-looking bearded guy tells Tim he wants "One of those things you fix stuff with, like on TV." After five minutes of Tim offering him everything from spackle to a DustBuster to a Ginzu knife, Jase finally figures out it's a tool kit. The guy trots off, looking satisfied.

"So, what are you going to do?" I ask.

"Hell, hell, hell," Tim responds, reaching for his shirt pocket where his cigarettes still reside, then letting his hand drop away, empty. No smoking in the building. He closes his eyes, looking as though someone's pounding a nail through his temple, then opens them and looks no better. He smacks his fist against the counter, sending a plastic container of pens jumping. "I just can't make myself quit. I've screwed up so much already. This will look like more of the same . . . even though it's not." He bends forward over the cash register, digging the heels of his hands into his eyes. Is he *crying*?

"You could tell him what you think of his tactics," Jase points out. "Tell him they're wrong."

"Like he'll care. I hate this. I hate knowing the right thing to do and not having the balls to do it. This sucks. This is payback, isn't it? You wouldn't believe the things I've done, the tests I've cheated on, the rules I've broken, the times I've fucked up, the people I've screwed over."

"Oh knock it off already, man, with the 'nobody knows the horrors I've seen' routine. It's getting really old," Jase snaps.

I take a deep breath like I'm going to say something—what, I have no idea—but he continues before I can. "It's not like you murdered newborns and drank their blood. You screwed up at prep school. Don't overrate yourself."

Tim's eyebrows have shot to his hairline. Neither Tim nor I have ever seen Jase lose his temper.

"It's not the moral dilemma of the century." Jase runs his fingers through his hair. "It's not whether to develop the atom bomb. It's just whether you're going to do a decent thing or keep doing shitty things. So choose. Just stop *whining* about it."

Tim gives a little nod, an upward jerk of his chin, then turns his attention to the register as though the numbers and symbols on it are the most fascinating thing he's ever seen. His face has been so much more expressive lately than usual, but now he's assumed that bland mask that I had come to think of as his real face. "I should go to the stockroom," he mutters, and heads down the hallway.

Jase pours the last plastic bag full of nails into the plastic container. The clatter breaks the silence.

"That didn't sound like you," I offer quietly, still standing beside him.

Jase looks embarrassed. "Kinda just came out. It's . . . it makes me feel . . . I get tired of . . ." His hand rubs the back of his neck, then slides all the way across his face to cover his eyes. "I like Tim. He's a good guy . . ." He pulls his hand down to smile at me. "But I can't say I wouldn't appreciate a crack at all those choices—chances—Tim had. And when he acts like he's under this curse or something . . ." He shakes his head, as though brushing the thought off, turns and looks at me, then nods at the clock. "I told Dad I'd stay late tonight and make out some reorder forms." He reaches for a few strands of my hair, twining them around his finger. "You busy later?"

"I was supposed to go to a meet-and-greet in Fairport with Mom, but I told her I needed to study for SATs."

"She believed this? It's summer, Sam."

"Nan's got me signed up for this crazy prep simulation. And . . . I *might* have told Mom when she was a little distracted."

"But not intentionally, of course."

"Of course not," I say.

"So if I were to come see you after eight, you'd be studying."

"Absolutely. But I might want a . . . study buddy. Because I might be grappling with some really tough problems."

"Grappling, huh?"

"Tussling with," I say. "Wrestling. Handling."

"Gotcha. Sounds like I should bring protective gear to study with you." Jase grins at me.

"You're pretty tough. You'll be fine."

Chapter Thirty-four

I've just gotten in the door when my cell phone starts up.

"So, because we have to get such an early start in the morning . . . The factory opens at five, can you imagine . . . really makes more sense . . . see you when you get back from school." My cell gets perfect reception, but the tinny voice spilling out of it seems to come and go, as though I'm having problems tuning in to a certain radio frequency. Because this voice saying she'll be gone all night because she has an early-morning meet-and-greet at a factory way up in the western corner of the state . . . this just can't be Station Grace Reed. I must have tuned in to an alternative program. Or universe. But she concludes, "We're halfway there already and it doesn't make sense to drive all the way home. Clay's found us a gorgeous hotel room. You'll be fine, right?"

I'm so taken aback that I nod before remembering she can't see me. "No problem, Mom. I'll be fine. Enjoy the hotel." I almost add that she could stay another night if she wanted before deciding that might sound suspiciously overeager.

She'll be gone. All night. With Clay—and his confusing agenda—in a gorgeous hotel room. But I won't think about that. What I do think about, what I immediately think about, is the *all night* part. Which is why I'm hitting Jase's number on my cell instantly.

"Sam." I can hear the smile in his voice. I just left the store ten minutes ago. "You having a study crisis already?"

"My mom won't be home tonight. At all."

There's a pause, during which I feel flustered. *Do I have to spell things out more? How do I even do that? "Want to have a sleepover?" We're not six.*

"Your mom won't be home at all?" he repeats.

"That's right."

"So maybe you'd like company, since you're grappling with all those study problems."

"That's what I'd like."

"Door or window?" he asks.

"I'm unlocking the window right now."

I pull my hair out of its braid, brush it loose. I've really got to cut it one of these days. It's down to the small of my back now, takes forever to dry after a swim. Why am I even thinking about this now? I guess I'm a little nervous. I didn't want to overthink, but unless we just pounce on each other in the heat of the moment—hard to do, logistically speaking, there has to be a little planning. A little time for overthinking. I hear a tapping and go over to the window to fit my hand against Jase's before I nudge the glass open.

He's brought a sleeping bag, one of those big green bulky L.L. Bean ones. I look at it questioningly.

Following my gaze, he turns red. "I told my parents I was going to help you study, then we might watch a movie, and if it got late enough, I'd crash on your living room floor."

"And they said?"

"Mom said, 'Have a nice time, dear.' Dad just looked at me."

"Embarrassing much?"

"Worth it."

He walks slowly over, his eyes locked on mine, then puts his hands around my waist.

"Um. So . . . are we going to study?" My tone's deliberately casual.

Jase slides his thumbs behind my ears, rubbing the hollow at their base. He's only inches from my face, still looking into my eyes. "You bet. I'm studying you." He scans over me, slowly, then returns to my eyes. "You have little flecks of gold in the middle of the blue." He bends forward and touches his lips to one eyelid, then the other, then moves back. "And your eyelashes aren't blond at all, they're brown. And . . ." He steps back a little, smiling slowly at me. "You're already blushing—here"—his lips touch the pulse at the hollow of my throat—"and probably here . . ." The thumb that brushes against my breast feels warm even through my T-shirt.

In the movies, clothes just melt away when the couple is ready to make love. They're all golden and backlit with the soundtrack soaring. In real life, it just isn't like that. Jase has to take off his shirt and fumbles with his belt buckle and I hop around the room pulling off my socks, wondering just how unsexy that is. People in movies don't even *have* socks. When Jase pulls off his jeans, change he has in his pocket slips out and clatters and rolls across the floor.

"Sorry!" he says, and we both freeze, even though no one's home to hear the sound.

In movies, no one ever gets self-conscious at this point, thinking they should have brushed their teeth. In movies, it's all beautifully choreographed, set to an increasingly dramatic soundtrack.

In movies, when the boy pulls the girl to him when they are both finally undressed, they never bump their teeth together and get embarrassed and have to laugh and try again.

But here's the truth: In movies, it's never half so lovely as it is here and now with Jase.

I take a deep breath as his hand skims down, down, to the back of my thigh. The feeling of his skin, all his skin, against mine gives me goose bumps. Then he pulls me closer and we plunge into a kiss that is like deep, deep water. When we finally stop for air, I wrap both legs around his hips. The corners of his eyes crinkle. His hands tighten on my bottom as he walks over to the bed. I slide off and am lying on my side, looking up at him. Jase bends down, crouching beside the bed, and stretches out his hand to put it on my heart. I do the same, feel his heart pounding, fast, fast.

"Are you nervous?" I whisper. "You don't seem it."

"I'm worried it'll hurt for you, at first. I'm thinking it's not fair that it's like that."

"It's okay. I'm not worried about that. Come closer."

Jase straightens up, slowly, then goes over to his jeans to pull out one of the condoms we bought together. He holds his palm out, flat. "Not nervous at all." He ducks his head to indicate his fingers, which are trembling, slightly.

"What's that one called?" I ask.

"I don't even know. I just grabbed a bunch before I came over." We lean over the little square of foil. "Ramses."

"What's *with* these names?" I inquire as Jase gently begins to open the packet. "I mean, were the Egyptians known for their effective birth control or what? And why Trojans? Aren't they mostly remembered as the guys who lost? You'd think they'd use Macedonians, weren't they the winners? I mean, I know it doesn't sound as manly, but—"

Jase puts two fingers on my lips. "Samantha? It's okay. Shhh. We don't have to . . . We can just . . ."

"But I want to," I whisper. "I want to." I take a deep breath and reach out for the condom. "Do you want me to help, um, put it on?"

Jase blushes. "Yeah, okay."

When we're both lying on the bed, entirely naked, for the first time, just looking at him in the moonlight makes my throat ache. "Wow," I say.

"I think that's my line," Jase whispers back. He puts his hand against my cheek and looks at me intently. My hand moves to cover his and I nod. Then his body is moving over me, and mine is opening to welcome him.

Okay. It does, after all, hurt a bit. I thought it might not, just because it's Jase. There's pain, but not wrenching or stabbing, more like a sting as something gives way, then aches a little as he fills me.

I bite down hard on my lower lip, opening my eyes to find Jase biting his, looking at me so anxiously that something in my heart yields even more completely.

"You okay? This okay?"

I nod, pulling his hips more tightly to my own.

"Now we'll make it better," Jase vows, and begins to kiss me again as he starts to move in a rhythm. My body follows, unwilling to let him go, already glad to have him come back.

Chapter Thirty-five

As you might imagine, I'm useless at Breakfast Ahoy the next day. Thank God I'm not lifeguarding. If I can't remember how some people who come in every single day like their eggs, if I stare aimlessly at the coffeemaker, unable to stop smiling, at least no one's life is threatened.

When Jase climbed out my window at four this morning, he got halfway down the trellis, then came back up. "Stop by the store after work," he whispered after one last kiss.

So that's where I head the minute I clock out, fast enough that I'm almost running. When I get to Main Street I try to slow down, but can't. I fling the store door open, forgetting that the hinges are broken and it slams loudly against the wall.

Mr. Garrett glances up from his post behind the register, reading glasses perched on nose, pile of papers in lap. "Well. Hullo, Samantha."

I didn't even change out of my uniform, which no one could call empowering and confidence-building. I feel completely embarrassed and remember the lock on the door and think: *He knows, he knows, it shows, shows completely.*

"He's out back," Mr. Garrett tells me mildly, "unpacking shipments." Then he returns to the papers.

I feel compelled to explain myself. "I just thought I'd come by. Before babysitting. You, know, at your house. Just to say hi. So . . . I'm going to do that now. Jase's in back, then? I'll just say hi."

I'm so suave.

I can hear the ripping sound of the box cutter before I even open the rear door to find Jase with a huge stack of cardboard boxes. His back's to me and suddenly I'm as shy with him as I was with his father.

This is silly.

Brushing through my embarrassment, I walk up, put my hand on his shoulder.

He straightens up with a wide grin. "Am I glad to see you!"

"Oh, really?"

"Really. I thought you were Dad telling me I was messing up again. I've been a disaster all day. Kept knocking things over. Paint cans, our garden display. He finally sent me out here when I knocked over a ladder. I think I'm a little preoccupied."

"Maybe you should have gotten more sleep," I offer.

"No way," he says. Then we just gaze at each other for a long moment.

For some reason, I expect him to look different, the way I expected I would myself in the mirror this morning . . . I thought I would come across richer, fuller, as happy outside as I was inside, but the only thing that showed was my lips puffy from kisses. Jase is the same as ever also.

"That was the best study session I ever had," I tell him.

"Locked in my memory too," he says, then glances away as though embarrassed, bending to tear open another box. "Even though thinking about it made me hit my thumb with a hammer putting up a wall display."

"This thumb?" I reach for one of his callused hands, kiss the thumb.

"It was the left one." Jase's face creases into a smile as I pick up his other hand.

"I broke my collarbone once," he tells me, indicating which side. I kiss that. "Also some ribs during a scrimmage freshman year."

I do not pull his shirt up to where his finger points now. I am not that bold. But I do lean in to kiss him through the soft material of his shirt.

"Feeling better?"

His eyes twinkle. "In eighth grade, I got into a fight with this kid who was picking on Duff and he gave me a black eye."

My mouth moves to his right eye, then the left. He cups the back of my neck in his warm hands, settling me into the V of his legs, whispering into my ear, "I think there was a split lip involved too."

Then we are just kissing and everything else drops away. Mr. Garrett could come out at any moment, a truck full of supplies could drive right on up, a fleet of alien spaceships could darken the sky, I'm not sure I'd notice.

We stand there, leaning back against the door, until a large truck really does pull in and Jase has to unload more things. It's only 11:30 and I'm not due at the Garretts' till three, so I don't want to leave, which means I busy myself doing unnecessary things like rearranging the order of the sample chips in the paint section, listening to the *click-click-click* of Mr. Garrett's pen cap, and reliving everything in my happy heart.

Later, I struggle to concentrate and help Duff build a "humane zoo habitat for arctic animals out of recyclable materials" for his science camp exhibit. The task is complicated by the fact that George and Harry keep eating the sugar cubes we're trying to use as building material. Also by the fact that Duff is unbelievably anal about what "recyclable" means.

"I'm not sure sugar counts as recyclable. And definitely not pipe cleaners!" he says, glaring at me as I slap white paint on egg cartons, transforming them into icebergs, which are going to float in our fake aluminum-foil arctic waters.

The kitchen door bursts open and Andy storms through, without explanation, in floods of tears, her wails echoing down the stairs.

"I can't get these cubes to stay together. They keep melting when I put the glue on them," Duff says crossly, swirling his paintbrush in the puddle of Elmer's, which has just dissolved another sugar cube.

"Maybe if we put clear fingernail polish on them?" I suggest.

"That'll melt too," Duff says gloomily.

"We could just try," I offer.

George, crunching, suggests we build the walls out of marshmallows instead. "I'm sort of sick of sugar cubes."

Duff reacts with a rage out of all proportion. "George. I'm not building this as a *snack* for you. Marshmallows don't look

anything like glass bricks in a wall. I need to do well on this—
if I do, I get a ribbon and next month's camp costs half off."

"Let's ask Dad," Harry suggests. "Maybe boat shellac? Or
something?"

"My *life* is *over*," Andy sobs from upstairs.

"I think I should go talk to her," I tell the boys. "You call
your father—or Jase."

I head up the stairs toward the echoing wails, grabbing a
box of Kleenex from the bathroom before I go into Andy and
Alice's room.

She's lying facedown on her bed, in her soggy bathing suit,
having cried so hard that there's a big damp circle on her pillow. I sit down next to her, handing her a wad of Kleenex.

"It's over. Everything's over."

"Kyle?" I ask, grimacing, because I know that's what it has
to be.

"He . . . he broke up with me!" Andy raises her head, her
hazel eyes swimming with tears. "By . . . *Post-it note*. He stuck it
on my lifejacket while I was practicing rigging the jib."

"You're kidding," I say, which I know is the wrong thing to
say, but honestly.

Andy reaches under the pillow and pulls out a neon orange
square that reads: *Andrea. It's been fun, but now I want 2 go with
Jade Whelan. See ya, Kyle.*

"Suave."

"I *know*!" Andy bursts into a fresh round of tears. "I've loved
him for three years, ever since he taught me how to make a slip
knot on the first day of sailing camp . . . and he can't even say
this to my face! 'See ya'?! Jade Whelan? She used to take boys

266

behind the piano in fourth-grade assembly and show them her bra! She didn't even need one! I hate her. I hate him."

"You should," I say. "I'm sorry."

I rub Andy's back in little circles much the way I did Nan's. "The first boy I kissed was this guy Taylor Oliveira. He told everyone at school I didn't know what to do with my tongue."

Andy gives a faint watery giggle. "Did you?"

"I had no clue. But neither did Taylor. He used his like a toothbrush. Yuck. Maybe because his dad was a dentist."

Andy giggles again, then looks down and sees the Post-it note. The tears resume.

"He was my first kiss. I waited for somebody I really cared about . . . and now it turns out he was a jerk. Now I can't take it back. I wasted my first kiss on a jerk!" She curls into a ball on the bed, sobbing even louder.

"Shut up, Andy, I can't concentrate on my project!" Duff calls up the stairs.

"My world is coming to an end," she retorts loudly, "so I don't particularly care!"

At this point Patsy wanders in, having recently learned both to climb out of her crib and to remove her diaper, in whatever state it may be. In this case, fully loaded. She waves it triumphantly at me. "Pooooooooooop."

"Ugh," Andy moans. "I'm gonna throw up."

"I'll get it." I reflect on the fact that two months ago I had never come in contact with a diaper. Now I could practically teach a Learning Annex course on the many ways of dealing with any potential toileting disaster.

Patsy watches me with detached curiosity as I clean up

her wall (*ew*), change her sheets (*again, ew*), plunk her into a short bath, and re-diaper and clothe her in something sanitary. "Where poop?" she asks mournfully, craning her neck to examine her bottom.

"Gee-ooorge!" a furious voice bellows from the kitchen. I go down to find that George has used the hammer from his Bob the Builder tool kit to smash the remaining sugar cubes while Duff was on the phone with his father. Now George, spindly legs flying, is running out the door, wearing nothing but Superman underpants, with Duff, angrily brandishing the phone as though it's a weapon, careening after him.

I chase them up the driveway just as the Bug pulls in and Jase climbs out, all loose-limbed grace.

"Hey now." He reaches out to me. We stand in the driveway with Jase kissing me as though the fact that Harry is making vomiting noises and Duff is about to kill George doesn't matter at all. Then he loops his arm around my neck, turns to his brothers, and says, "Okay, what's going on?"

In no time he has it all sorted out. Duff is painting Popsicle sticks white to replace the crumbling sugar walls. Andy's eating a Milky Way and watching *Ella Enchanted* on the big bed in her parents' room. Pizza Palace is on its way. Harry's making a gigantic pillow house cage for Patsy and George, who're pretending to be baby tigers.

"Now," Jase observes, "before some or all of that falls apart again, come here." He leans back against the counter, pulling me between his thighs and smoothing his hands up and down my back.

It's all so good. My body is singing-happy, my days are full of good moments, my life feels more right than it ever has been before. And that can be, I learn, how it happens. You're walking along on this path, dazzled by how perfect it is, how great you feel, and then just a few forks in the road and you are lost in a place so bad you never could have imagined it.

Chapter Thirty-six

When I clock out from the B&T the next day, I'm surprised to see the Jetta pulling into the parking lot, and Tim beckoning to me from inside. "I need you," he calls, pulling up—illegally—in the fire zone.

"What for?" I ask, nonetheless climbing into the car, awkwardly pulling down my short skirt.

"I bagged out on your mom. Well, mostly on Clay. I called and quit. Now I need to get my shit from the office and I need a shield. A—how much do you weigh?—one-hundred-ten-pound shield."

"One twelve," I correct. "I don't even think Clay's there. He and my mom were doing some factory thing."

Tim knocks a Marlboro out of the pack stored in the sun visor, sticking it into the corner of his mouth. "I know. I know his schedule." He taps a finger against his temple. "Maybe I just need you along so I'll actually do this and not turn chickenshit at the last minute. Maybe I need you to give me a shove in—and out—the door. You gonna help me out?"

I nod. "Sure. But if you're looking for a shield, Jase is a lot bigger than I am."

"Yeah, yeah. But lover boy's busy today, as I'm sure you know."

I'm not about to admit that I do. Instead I tug my hair out of its braid.

"Man, you're such a babe." Tim shakes his head. "Why do all the hot girls want the jocks and the good boys? We losers are the ones who need you."

I check his expression warily. I've never before had any impression Tim was attracted to me. *Maybe my new non-virgin state shows. Maybe I radiate smokin' sex now.* Somehow I doubt this, especially in my fetching crested lifeguard jacket and navy spandex skirt.

"Don't stress." Tim finally lights the dangling cigarette. "I don't wanna be that lame guy who comes on to the girl he can't have. I'm just sayin'." He makes a wide—and illegal— U-turn to go more quickly in the direction of Mom's local office. "Wanna smoke?" He drops the Marlboros in my lap.

"I don't. You know that, Tim."

"What do you do with your time—with your *hands*— that's the thing I can't figure out." Tim takes one hand off of the wheel and shakes it at me vigorously, as though he has an uncontrollable twitch. "What do you hold on to?"

I feel my face heat.

Tim smirks at me. "Oh, *riiight.* I forgot. Besides lover boy and his—"

I hold up my hand in a *stop* motion, changing the subject before he can finish his sentence. "Is it still hard, Tim, not drinking and stuff? It's been, what, a month?"

"Thirty-three days. Not that I'm counting. And yeah, of course it's frickin' hard. Things only come easy to people like you and Mr. Perfect. For me, it's like every day—a million times a day—I want to get back together with that scorchin' girl, aka the quart of Bacardi or the bag of coke or whatever, even though I know she's only going to screw me over again."

"Tim, you've got to get over this 'everything's easy for everyone else' stuff. It's not true and it makes you boring."

Tim whistles. "Channeling Jase, are you?"

I shake my head. "No, it's just . . . It's just watching you and Nan . . ." I trail off. Is there any point to telling him I know he used her work? What does it matter now? He got expelled. Nan got the awards.

"Watching Nan do what?" Tim asks, picking up on the way my voice wobbles when I say her name. He tosses the butt of the first cigarette out the window, reaching for another.

I hedge. "She's so stressed out, this summer, already, about colleges. . . ."

"Yeah, well, we Masons do obsession and compulsion well." Tim snorts. "I generally stick to compulsion and let Nano handle the obsession, but sometimes we swap. I love my sister, but there's no rest for either of us. I'm always there to provide her with an object lesson of how much it sucks to screw up, and she's always there to remind me how miserable she is looking perfect. And, speaking of miserable, here we are."

He wheels into the parking lot by Mom's office.

Even though Mom's schedule is jam-packed, I'm somehow still surprised to find the office is full of people, in assembly lines, folding pamphlets, putting them in envelopes and putting on labels and stamps. People really believe in her, enough to sit in stuffy offices doing boring tasks during the most beautiful days of Connecticut's all-too-short summer.

As we walk in, two older women at a big central table look up and give Tim broad, motherly smiles.

"We heard a rumor you were quitting on us, but we knew that couldn't be true," the taller, thinner one says. "Grab a chair, Timothy dear."

Tim puts his arm around her bony shoulder. "Sorry, Dottie. The rumor is reality. I'm leaving to spend more time with my family." He says the last in his Moviefone voice.

"And this is . . ." The other woman squints at me. "Ah! The senator's daughter." She cuts her eyes to him. "And your— girlfriend? She's very pretty."

"No, alas, she belongs to another, Dottie. I just pine for her from afar."

He starts cramming papers and—I notice—office supplies into his backpack. I roam around the office, picking up brochures and buttons advertising Mom, then putting them back down. Finally, I wander into her quiet office.

Mom likes her comforts. Her office chair is top-of-the-line ergonomic, fine leather. The desk is no gray metal one from office supply but a rich carved oak antique. There's a vase of red roses and a picture of Mom with me and Tracy in matching satin-and-velvet Christmas outfits.

There's also a big basket of gardening tools, gift-wrapped in shiny green cellophane, with a note saying *We at Riggio's Quality Lawns are Grateful for your support.*

A couple of tickets to a Broadway show thumbtacked to the

corkboard: *Allow us to treat you to some quality entertainment in thanks for all you do,* from some people named Bob and Marge Considine.

A business card saying *Thanks for giving our bid serious consideration,* from Carlyle Contracting.

I don't know campaign rules, but all this doesn't seem right to me. I'm standing there, with a sick feeling in my stomach, when Tim strolls in, backpack hitched onto one shoulder, cardboard box in hand. "C'mon, kid. Let's get ghost before we have to deal with your ma or Clay. Word is they're on their way here now. Being on the side of the Morally Superior is new to me, and I might screw up my lines."

Once we're outside, Tim throws his box of stuff and backpack into the backseat of the Jetta, then flips the passenger seat forward so I can climb in.

"How bad is Clay?" I ask quietly. "I mean, is he a sleaze for real?"

"I did Google him," Tim admits. "Helluva impressive resume for a guy who's only thirty-six."

Thirty-six? Mom's forty-six. *So he's young. That doesn't necessarily mean he's bad.* Mom listens to him like he's the one true frequency, but that doesn't mean he's bad either. But . . . but what's up with the double agent? This is a tiny race in Connecticut, not the Cold War.

"How do you think he got so high up so fast?" I ask Tim. "I mean, really—thirty-six? And if he's this big star in the Republican firmament, why is he taking the time to help out this dinky state senatorial race? That's got to be a blip on the radar."

"I don't know, kid. He sure loves this stuff, though. The other day this commercial ran for some race in Rhode Island, and Clay's all over it, calling the office up there to tell them what's wrong with their message. Maybe it's his idea of a vacation helping out your ma." He shoots a look at me, then smirks. "A vacation with a few extra benefits."

"Would those be from my mom? Or that brunette you talked about?"

Tim folds himself into the driver's seat, turning the ignition and punching in the lighter simultaneously. "I don't know what's up with that. He's flirty with her, but those Southern guys are like that. He certainly *is* all over your ma."

Ick. I know this, but don't want to think about it.

"But luckily it's not my problem anymore."

"It doesn't go away because it's not your problem."

"Yes, Mother. Listen, Clay cuts corners and is all about politics. That's working out just fine for him, Samantha. Why should he change? No incentive. No payback. In my brief shining moments as a political animal, that's one thing I've learned. It's all about incentive, payback, and how it all looks. Being a politician is a lot like being an alcoholic in denial."

Chapter Thirty-seven

The day of the practice SATs, Nan and I bike to Stony Bay High to take the test. It's August, with heat shimmering off the sidewalks and the lazy *whirrrr* of cicadas. But once we walk into the school, it's as though a switch has been flipped. The room is airless and smells like pencil shavings and industrial strength disinfectant, all overlaid with too-fruity perfume and sports deodorant, too many bodies.

Stony Bay High is one of those low, endless, cookie-cutter brick schools, with ugly green shaded windows, peeling gray paint on the doors, and curling red linoleum on the floors. It's a far cry from Hodges, which is built like a fortress, with battlements, stained-glass windows, and portcullises. It even has a drawbridge, because you never know when your prep school might be attacked by the Saxons.

Public or private, there's that same school smell, so out of context today as I shift in my sticky seat, listening to the lazy roar of a lawnmower outside.

"Remind me why I'm doing this again?" I ask Nan as she takes her place in the row in front of me, positioning her backpack at her feet.

"Because practice makes perfect. Or at least close enough

to get in the low two thousands, which will give us a shot at the college of our dreams. And because you're my best friend." She reaches into the pocket of her backpack and pulls out some ChapStick, applying it to her slightly sunburned lips. As she does this, I can't help but notice that she's not only wearing her prized blue-and-white Columbia T-shirt, but also the cross she got for her Communion and a charm bracelet her Irish grandmother gave her which has green-and-white enamel four-leaf clovers hanging from it.

"Where's Buddha?" I ask. "Won't he feel left out? What about Zeus? A rabbit's foot?"

She pretends to glare at me, lining up her seven number 2 pencils in a precise row along the edge of her desk. "This is important. They say SATs aren't as big as they used to be, but you *know* that's not true. Can't be too careful. I'd burn sage, embrace Scientology, and wear one of those Kabbalah bracelets if I thought it would do me any good. I've got to get out of this town."

No matter how often Nan says this, it never fails to give me a prickle of hurt. Ridiculous. It's not about me. The Mason house is nobody's idea of a refuge.

Confirming this, she continues, "It's even worse now that Tim's only working at Garrett's. Mommy starts all her conversations with him like, 'Well, since you've made up your mind to be a loser all your life,' and then just ends up shaking her head and leaving the room."

I sigh. "How's Tim dealing?"

"I think he's up to three packs a day," Nan says. "Cigarettes *and* Pixy Stix. But no sign of anything else . . . yet." Her voice is resigned, clearly expecting to find evidence of worse at any moment. "He——" she starts, then falls silent as the side door of the classroom opens and a small beige woman and a tall sandy-haired man come in, introducing themselves as our proctors for this practice SAT. The woman runs through the procedures in a monotone, while the man wanders through the room, checking our IDs and handing out blue notebooks.

The air-conditioning blasts to a higher level, nearly drowning out the beige woman's monotonous voice. Nan pulls a cardigan out of her backpack and scrabbles around to position a hoodie at the top, just in case. She sits back up, puts her elbows on the desk, leans her chin on her folded hands, and sighs. "I hate writing," she says. "I hate everything about it. Grammar, usage . . . blech." Despite the light tan she always acquires in the late summer, she looks pale under her freckles, only her sunburned nose betraying the season.

"You're the big writing star," I remind her. "You'll coast through this. Lazlo Literary Anthology, remember? The SATs are the minor leagues for you."

The tall blond man points extravagantly at the clock and the beige woman says "Shhh" and begins the countdown as solemnly as if we are blasting off at Cape Canaveral, rather than taking a practice test. "In ten, nine, eight . . ." I glance around the room. Everyone, evidently as driven as Nan, has their blue books and their pencils lined up in perfect symmetry. I look over again at Nan, to see her adjust the sleeve of her sweatshirt in her backpack again, allowing me, from my vantage point to the left and back to see the corner of her electronic dictionary peeking out from the light blue edge of her sweatshirt.

She's staring at the clock, her mouth a grim line, her pencil so tightly held in her fingers it's a wonder it doesn't snap in half. Nan's left-handed. Her right hand rests on her thigh, in quick-draw reach of her backpack.

Suddenly, I get these pictures in my head of the way Nan's sat in test after test I've taken alongside her, always with her backpack leaned to the side, her hoodie or sweater or whatever draping out. Memories click into place, like frames of a film slowly forwarding one after another, and I realize this is no isolated incident. Nanny, my always-head-of-the class best friend, Nan the star student, has been cheating for years.

Good thing for me it's a practice test, because I can barely focus. All I can think about is what I saw, what I know for sure now. Nan doesn't need to cheat. I mean, nobody needs to cheat, but Nan's only ensuring a sure thing anyway. I mean, look at her essays.

Her essays.

Those files on Tim's computer that I looked at, that I . . .

That I blamed Tim for stealing. The realization freezes me in place. Minutes tick by before I finally pick up my pencil and try to concentrate on the exam.

During break, I splash water on my face in the ugly aqua-tiled bathroom and try to figure out what to do. Tell the proctors? Out of the question. She's my best friend. But . . .

As I'm standing there, staring into my own eyes, Nan comes up next to me, squirting antibacterial lotion on her hands and rubbing it up her arms as though scrubbing up for surgery.

"I don't think it washes off," I say, before I can think.

"What?"

"Guilt. Didn't work for Lady Macbeth, did it?"

She turns white, then flushes, freckled translucent skin so quick to show both shades. She glances quickly around the bathroom, making sure we're alone. "I'm thinking about the future," she hisses. "*My* future. You may be happy hanging out at the garage with your handyman, eating Kraft macaroni and cheese, but I'm going to Columbia, Samantha. I'm going to get away from—" Her face crumples. "All of this." She waves her hand. "Everything."

"Nan." I move toward her, arms outstretched.

"You too. You're part of it all." Turning, she stalks out of the bathroom, stopping only to scoop up her backpack, from which the sweatshirt sleeve dangles uselessly.

Did that really just happen? I feel sick. *What just went wrong here? When did I become just another thing Nan wanted to escape?*

Chapter Thirty-eight

The hotel ballroom's stifling and overheated, like someone forgot to flip on the air-conditioning. It would probably make me drowsy even if I hadn't gotten up at five this morning, restless, thinking about Nan, and gone to the ocean to swim. Not to mention that we're in Westfield, the other end of the state, a long, long drive from home, and I'm constricted in my formal blue linen dress. There's a big fountain in the middle of the room, and tables of finger sandwiches and buffet food set up around that. Out-of-season Christmas lights twinkle around statue reproductions of Venus rising from the waves and Michelangelo's David, looking as sulky and out of place as I feel at this fund-raising rally. Mom makes her speech at the podium, flanked by Clay, and I struggle to stay conscious.

"You must be so proud of your mother," people keep telling me, sloshing their fruity champagne cocktails over tiny plastic cups, and I repeat over and over again: "Oh, yes, I am. I am, yes." My seat's next to the podium and as Mom's introduced, I can't help tipping my head against it, until she gives me a sharp jab with her foot and I jerk back upright, willing my eyes open.

Finally she gives some sort of good-night summary speech

and there's lots of cheering and "Go Reed!" Clay rests his hand in the small of her back, propelling her, as we edge out into the night, which isn't even really dark, kind of tea-colored, since we're in the city. "You're a wonder, Gracie. A twelve-hour day and still looking so fine."

Mom gives a pleased laugh, then toys with her earring. "Honey?" She hesitates, then: "I just don't understand why that Marcie woman has to be at just about every event of mine."

"Was she there tonight?" Clay asks. "I didn't notice. And I've told you—they send her the same way we had Tim out counting the cars at Christopher's rallies, or Dorothy checking on his press conferences."

I know this is the brunette woman. But Clay doesn't sound like he's trying to pull one over on Mom. He sounds like he genuinely didn't realize "Marcie" was there.

"Ya gotta ashess"—he pauses, laughs, then repeats carefully—"*assess* your opponent's strengths and weaknesses."

Clay trips a little on the pavement and Mom gives a low laugh. "Easy, honey."

"Sorry—those stones kinda got away from me there." They halt, leaning together in the darkness, swaying slightly. "You'd better drive."

"Of course," Mom says. "Just give me those keys."

Much chuckling while she searches for them in his jacket pockets—oh erk—and I just want to be home.

Mom starts the car with a roar, *VROOM*, and then giggles in surprise as though cars never make that sound.

"Actually, sugar, better give me the keys," Clay tells her.

"I've got it," Mom says. "You had four glasses to my three."

"Maybe," Clay says. "I might could have done."

"I just love your Southern phrases," Mom murmurs.

Time hazes. I slide down in my seat, stretching my legs out over an uncomfortable pile of Grace Reed signs and boxes of campaign flyers, tilting my eyes against the hard leather padding under the window. I watch the highway lights, my eyelids sinking, then the dimmer streetlights as the roads get smaller and smaller, closer to home.

"Take Shore Road," Clay tells her softly. "Less traffic. Nearly there now, Gracie."

The window glass is chilly against my cheek, the only cool thing in the warm car. Other headlights flash by for a while, then fade away. Finally, I see by the glint of the moon on the open water that we're passing McGuire Park. I remember being there with Jase, lying on the sun-warmed rock in the river, then my lids slowly close, the hum of the engine like Mom's vacuum cleaner, a familiar lullaby.

BLAM.

My nose smacks the seat in front of me, so hard that stars dazzle against my eyes, and my ears ring.

"Oh my God!" Mom says in a high panicky voice scarier than the sudden jolt. She slams on the brakes.

"Back up, Grace." Clay's voice is level and firm.

"Mom? Mom! What happened?"

"Oh my God," Mom repeats. She always freaks out about dings in her paint job. There's a sudden whoosh of cool night air as Clay opens the passenger-side door, climbs out. A second later, he's back.

"Grace. Reverse. Now. Nothing happened, Samantha. Go back to sleep."

I catch a flash of his profile, arm around Mom's neck, fingers in her hair, prodding her. "Reverse and pull away now," he repeats.

The car jolts backward, jerks to a halt.

"Grace. Pull it together." The car revs forward and to the left. "Just get us back home."

"Mom?"

"It's nothing, sweetheart. Go to sleep. Hit a little bump in the road. Go back to sleep," Mom calls, her voice sharp.

And I do. She might still be talking, but I'm just so tired. When Tracy and I were younger, Mom sometimes used to drive us down to Florida for winter vacation, instead of flying. She liked to stop in Manhattan, in Washington, in Atlanta, stay in bed-and-breakfasts, poke around antiques stores along the way. I was always so impatient to get to the sand and the dolphins that I tried to sleep every single hour we were in the car. I feel like that now. I sink into soft blackness so absolute, I can barely drag myself out when Mom says, "Samantha. We're home. Go on to bed." She jiggles my arm, roughly enough that it hurts, and I drag myself upstairs, collapse on my mattress, too weary to take off my dress or dive under the covers. I just embrace nothingness.

My cell buzzes insistently. I shoved it under my pillow as usual. Now I hunt for it, half-asleep, my fingers clutching and closing on bunches of the sheets while the buzzing goes on and on and on, relentless. Finally I locate it.

"Sam?" Jase's voice, hoarse, almost unrecognizable. "Sam!"

"Hmm?"

"Samantha!"

His voice is loud, jarring. I jerk the cell away from my ear.

"What? Jase?"

"Sam. We, uh, we need you. Can you come over?"

I crawl across the bed, blearily check my digital clock.

1:16 a.m.

What?

"Now?"

"Now. Please. Can you come now?"

I haul myself out of bed, yank off my dress, pull on shorts and a T-shirt, flip-flops, climb out the window, down the trellis. I glance quickly back at the house, but Mom's bedroom lights are off, so I run through the light rain across the grass, to the Garretts'.

Where all the lights—the driveway, porch, kitchen lights—blaze. So out of the ordinary at this time of night that I stumble to a halt in the driveway.

"Samantha!" Andy's voice calls from the kitchen door. "Is that you? Jase said you'd come."

She's silhouetted in the doorway, surrounded by smaller shadows. Duff, Harry, George, Patsy in Andy's arms? At this hour? *What's going on?*

"Daddy." Andy's holding back tears. "Something happened to Daddy. Mom got a call." Her face crumples. "She went to the hospital with Alice." She throws herself into my arms. "Jase went too. He said you'd be here to take care of us."

"Okay. Okay, let's go inside," I say. Andy's pulled back, taking deep breaths, trying to get hold of herself. The little ones watch, wide-eyed and bewildered. The frozen expression on George's face is one of the hardest things I've ever had to look at. All his imagined disasters, and he never imagined this.

Chapter Thirty-nine

In the light of the kitchen, all the children are blinking, sleepy and disoriented. I try to think what Mrs. Garrett would do to rally everyone, and can only come up with making popcorn. So I do that. And hot chocolate, even though the air, despite the rain, is stifling as an electric blanket. George perches on the counter next to me as I stir chocolate powder into milk. "Mommy puts the chocolate in first," he reproves, squinting at me in the brightness of the overhead light.

This is no doubt a good idea, as I'm stuck with grainy lumps of powder I'm trying to mash against the side of the pot. Mom makes hot cocoa with some fancy chocolate shavings from Ghirardelli's in San Francisco. They melt more easily.

"We don't have any whipped cream." Harry's glum. "There's no point to hot chocolate without whipped cream."

"There's a point if there are marshmallows," George insists.

"Boob?" Patsy calls mournfully from the circle of Andy's arms. "Where boob?"

"What if Daddy's dead and they aren't telling us?" interjects Andy. George begins to cry. When I pick him up, he snuggles his head against my shoulder, warm tears slipping on my bare skin. I'm reminded for a second of Nan crying in my arms, all defenses down. And how she's raised her shields so completely now. What could have happened to fit, strong Mr. Garrett: a heart attack, a stroke, a brain aneurysm—

"He's not dead," Duff says stoutly. "When you're dead, policemen come to your door. I've seen it on TV."

Harry runs over to whip open the porch door. "No policemen," he calls back. "But, uh . . . Hi Tim."

"Hi kiddo." Tim shoulders his way into the room, hair soggy, wetness shining on his Windbreaker. "Jase called me, Samantha. You go to the hospital. I'll hang here." He flips me the keys to the Jetta. "Go," he repeats.

"I can't drive."

"Oh for fuck's sake. Okay." He turns to Andy. "I'll take her to the hospital and then be back to help you . . . uh, do whatever . . . except change diapers." He jabs his index finger at Patsy. "Don't you *dare* poop."

"Poooooop," Patsy says, in a small, subdued voice.

Before we get to the ER, Tim insists on skidding to a halt at a Gas-and-Go to buy cigarettes, scrabbling in his pockets for cash.

"We don't have time for this," I hiss. "Plus, it's bad for your lungs."

"Got ten bucks?" he rejoins. "My lungs are the *least* of our problems at the moment."

I shove a handful of bills at him. Once he's gotten his fix, we head off again toward the hospital.

There's no sign of Mrs. Garrett. Or Alice. But Jase is sitting in one of the ugly orange plastic bucket seats in the waiting room, hunched over, heels of his hands against his forehead. Tim gives me an unnecessarily hard shove and takes off.

I slip into the seat next to Jase. He doesn't move, either not noticing or not caring that there's someone next to him.

I put my hand on his back.

His arms drop and he turns to look at me. His eyes are full of tears.

Then he wraps himself tight around me and I wrap around him. There we are for a long time, not saying a word.

After a while, Jase stands up, goes over to the water fountain, splashes water on his face, comes back over, and puts his cold, wet hands on my cheeks. We still haven't said anything.

A door bangs. Alice.

"Head injury," she tells Jase grimly. "He's still unconscious. Maybe a subdural hematoma. They really can't tell how serious right now, just containing. There's a lot of swelling. Definitely a pelvic fracture—bad break. Some ribs . . . that's not a big deal. It's the brain stuff we won't know about for a while."

"Hell. Hell," Jase says. "Alice. . . ."

"I know," she says. "I don't get it. Why was he walking on Shore Road so late? There aren't any meetings out there. Not usually."

Shore Road.

Shore Road.

It's like some awful fog clears and I can see Mom driving home from Westfield, taking the uncrowded route along the river. *McGuire Park. By the river. Shore Road.*

"I've got to get back in there," Alice tells us. "I'll be out when I know more."

I've never spent any time in hospitals. The waiting room fills up with people who appear desperately sick, and people who seem to be as calm as though they are waiting at a bus stop to travel on to a destination they don't really care about. The small hand of the clock moves from two to three to four. Some of the bus stop people get called in before the people who look as though their time on earth is measured in milliseconds. Jase and I sit there as the monitors murmur. *Doctor Rodriques. Paging Dr. Rodriques. Dr. Wilcox. Code blue. Dr. Wilcox.*

At first I lean on Jase's shoulder, then he bows his head and it dips lower and lower. By the time Alice returns, his head is in my lap and I'm nodding over his curls.

She shakes me forcefully, startling me back from some confused dream about Shore Road to this room with fluorescent lights and the weight of Jase in my lap and the catastrophe of everything.

"Mom says you two should go on home." Alice pauses to swig from the bottle of Coke in her hand, then holds it against her temple. "He's got to open the store. We can't stay shut for a day. So he needs a few hours sleep."

"What?" Jase jolts awake. "Huh?" He usually seems older than me, but now, his hair a mess and his drowsy green eyes hazy, he looks so young. Alice's eyes meet mine, hers imperative, saying *take care of him* without uttering a word.

"Go home. We don't know anything yet." Alice polishes off her Coke in a few long swallows, and arcs it into the blue plastic recycling bin, a perfect basket.

The light rain is still falling when Jase and I go out to the van, droplets of soft mist. Jase tips his head to the sky, which is clouded over, impossible to see the stars.

We don't say anything on the drive home, but he reaches out one hand from the steering wheel, tangling it with mine, holding on so tightly, it almost hurts.

The Garretts' house is still lit like a birthday cake when we pull into the driveway.

"They can't all be awake, still," Jase mutters.

"They were pretty scared," I say, wondering how much chaos there'll be when we get in. Leaving Tim in charge? Perhaps not the best idea.

But the house is silent. The kitchen looks as though an invading army came hungry and left swiftly, cartons of ice cream, bags of chips and cereal boxes and bowls and plates stacked everywhere, but no one's stirring.

"You could have mentioned that this kid never sleeps," Tim calls from the living room. We go in to find him slumped in the easy chair next to the pulled-out sofa bed. Andy's sprawled out on the bed, long tan legs in a V, George gathered in her arms. Duff, still in his clothes, lies across the bottom, Harry curled in a ball on the pillow under Andy's outstretched leg. Safety, as much as could be found, must have lain in numbers.

Patsy's fingering Tim's nose and pulling on his bottom lip, her eyes wide-blue open.

"Sorry, man," Jase says. "She's usually good to go at bedtime."

"Do you have any idea how many times I've read *If You Give a Mouse a Cookie* to this kid? That is one fucked-up story. How is that a book for babies?"

Jase laughs. "I thought it was about babysitting."

"Hell no, it's addiction. That friggin' mouse is never satisfied. You give him one thing, he wants something else, and then he asks for more and on and on and on. Fucked up. Patsy liked it, though. Fifty thousand times." Tim yawns, and Patsy snuggles more comfortably onto his chest, grabbing a handful of shirt. "So what's doin'?"

We tell him what we know—nothing—then put the baby in her crib. She glowers, angry and bewildered for a moment, then grabs her five pacifiers, closes her eyes with a look of fierce concentration, and falls very deeply asleep.

"See you at the store, dude. I'll open up. 'Night Samantha." Tim heads out into the dark.

Jase and I stand in the doorway for a few minutes, watching Tim's headlights light up, the Jetta backing out of the driveway.

Then the silence gapes between us.

"What if Dad's got brain damage, Sam? A head injury? What if he's in a coma? What if he never wakes up?"

"We don't know how serious it is yet," I say. *It can't be bad. Please don't let it be bad.*

Jase bends over, pulling off a sock. "His head, Sam? No way that's good. Mom and Dad don't have health insurance for themselves. Just for us kids."

I shut my eyes, rubbing my forehead as though that'll erase those words.

"They dropped it last spring," Jase tells me softly. "I heard them talking . . . they said only for a few months, they were both healthy, young enough, nothing pre-existing . . . it wasn't a big deal." He drops his second sneaker with a clunk, adding, under his breath, "It is now."

I swallow, shaking my head, nothing to say for consolation, for anything, really.

Straightening, he reaches a hand for me, drawing me toward the stairs.

His room's gently lit by the heat lamp in Voldemort's cage, a faint red glow that barely illuminates the other cages and nests, redolent with the earthy plant smell and the tang of the clean sawdust in the animal cages, scored by the soft whirring noise of the hamster wheel.

He turns on his bedside light, takes his cell phone out of his back pocket, turns up the volume on the ringer, drops it on the bedside table. He moves Mazda the cat, who's sprawled in the middle of the bed with her paws in the air, to the bottom. He goes over to his bureau, pulls out a white T-shirt and hands it to me.

"Sam," he whispers, turning to me, a beautiful, bewildered boy.

I sigh into his neck, dropping the shirt to the floor as Jase's hands slip down the bend of my waist, pulling me close enough that his heartbeat sounds against mine.

What I'm imagining is true cannot possibly, *cannot possibly,* be the truth, so I hold on to Jase and try to pour all my love and any strength I have into him, through my lips and my arms and my body. I push away that whisper of "Shore Road" and Mom saying "Oh my God" and Clay's steady voice and that awful thump. I fold them up, pack them away, wrap them in bubble wrap and duct tape.

We've been urgent together, in a hurry to feel all we can feel, but never like this, never so frantic. He's pulling at my shirt and I'm gliding my palms up his smooth sides, feeling his muscles twitch with tension and response, his lips warm on my throat, my fingers in his hair, a little desperate and somehow a relief, some sense of the strength of life in this still night.

Afterward, Jase ducks his head, bending it heavily against my shoulder, breathing hard. We say nothing for a while.

Then, "Do I need to apologize?" he asks. "I don't know what that . . . I don't know why I . . . It helped, but . . ."

I slide my fingers slowly to his lips. "No, don't. Don't. It helped me too."

We stay there for a long time, our heartbeats edging gradually back to normal, sweat drying on our skin, our breaths intermingling. Finally, without words, we climb into Jase's bed. He urges my head to his chest gently, warm hand against my neck. In no time, his breathing evens out, but I lie awake, staring at the ceiling.

Mom. What did you do?

Chapter Forty

"Jase. Honey? Jase." Mrs. Garrett's voice is loud outside the hushed room. She rattles the doorknob slightly, but he'd locked it, so it doesn't open. He springs up, at the door in a flash, his tall body silhouetted against the light, unlocking, but then opening it as little as possible.

"Is Dad . . . What's happening?" His voice cracks.

"He's stable. They did an emergency procedure—drilled something called a burr hole to relieve pressure in his skull. Alice says that's standard. I just came home to change clothes and pump for Patsy. Joel's there. We really can't tell much until he wakes up." Her voice is strong but full of tears. "Sure you can take care of the store today?"

"I'm on it, Mom."

"Alice is going to stay with me, to interpret the medical-ese. Joel has to go to work, but he'll be back tonight. Can you get Tim to help you out? I know it's not his day, but—" Moving out into the hall, he bends to hug her. I always think of Mrs. Garrett as tall. With a shock, I realize she's as small as me against her lanky son.

"It'll be fine. We'll work it out. Tim already said he'd open up. Tell Dad . . . tell Dad I love him. Bring something to read to him. The *Perfect Storm* book? He's been wanting to read that one forever. It's in his truck."

"Samantha? Can you stay with the kids?" Mrs. Garrett calls.

Even in the dim light, I see him flush. "Sam was just . . ." He trails off. *Poor Jase. What can he say? Dropping by? Helping me feed the animals?*

"It's okay," she says quickly. "Can you stay, Sam?"

"I'll be here," I call.

The day passes in a blur. I do the things I do when baby-sitting for the Garretts, but they don't work the way they're supposed to. I've never had Patsy for more than a few hours, and it's a toss-up which she hates more—the bottle or me. Mrs. Garrett calls in at ten, apologizing: She can't come home to nurse her and there's some breast milk in the freezer. Patsy won't have any of that. She bats the bottle away, wailing. By two in the afternoon, she's a red-faced, sobbing, sweaty mess. I know from the note of hysteria in her cry how tired she is, but she won't nap. When I put her in the crib she throws all the stuffed animals out of it in a clear protest. George doesn't leave my side. He recites facts to me in a hushed, tense tone, clutching my arm to make sure I pay attention, crying easily. Harry systematically works his way through the things he's not supposed to do, hitting George and Duff, throwing an entire roll of toilet paper in the toilet "to see what happens," taking a tube of cookie dough out of the refrigerator and starting to eat it with his fingers. By the time Jase comes in at five, I'm inches away from lying down on the rug next to Patsy and drumming my heels too. But I'm glad I'm busy because it almost . . . not quite, but almost . . . shuts down the line of thoughts that run through my mind like a news crawl at the bottom of a TV screen. *This can't have anything to do with Mom. It can't. There's no way.*

Jase looks so drained, and I pull myself together, ask how sales went, if he's heard more from the hospital.

"More nothing," he says, unlacing one sneaker and tossing it into the mudroom. "He's stable. There's no change. I don't even know what *stable*'s supposed to mean. He's been hit by a car and had a hole drilled in his skull. 'Stable' is what you say when everything is the same. But nothing's the same here." He throws his second sneaker hard against the wall, leaving a black smudge. The noise startles Patsy in my arms and she starts wailing again.

Jase looks at her, then reaches out his arms, cuddles her in, his tan skin stark against her soft pale arms. "I'm guessing your day sucked too, Sam."

"Not the same way." Patsy grabs a fistful of his T-shirt and tries to put it in her mouth.

"Poor baby," Jase says softly into Patsy's neck.

Alice comes home soon after this, bringing pizza and more no news wrapped in medical jargon. "They had to do the burr hole to relieve intracranial pressure, Jase. Swelling of the brain is always a concern when there's a head injury, and it seems as though he landed right on his head. But patients usually recover from that with no long-term sequelae—consequences—as long as there isn't additional trauma we don't know about yet."

Jase shakes his head, biting his lip and turning away as the

297

younger kids tumble into the kitchen, lured by the smell of pizza and the sound of older people who can make sense of everything.

"I biked out to Shore Road this afternoon," Duff offers, "looking for clues. Nothin'."

"This isn't *CSI*, Duff." Alice's voice is sharper than the wheel she's using to slice pizza.

"It's a mystery, though. Someone hit Dad and just drove away. I thought maybe I'd see skid marks and we could ID the tires. Or broken bits of plastic from a headlight or something. Then maybe we could match it to a certain type of car and—"

"Get nowhere," Alice says. "Whoever hit Dad is long gone."

"Most hit-and-run drivers are never identified," admits Duff. "I read that online too."

I shut my eyes as a shameful wave of relief rolls through me.

Jase walks over to the screen door, clenching and unclenching his fists. "Jesus. How could someone do that? What kind of a person *would*? Hit someone—hit another human being with their car and just keep on going?"

I feel sick. "Maybe they didn't know they'd hit someone?"

"Impossible." His voice is harder, tougher than I've ever heard it. "When you're driving, you know when you hit a rough patch of gravel, an old piece of tire, a fast-food container, a dead squirrel. No way could you hit a one-hundred-and-seventy-pound man and not notice."

"Maybe the person who hit him was the person he was meeting up with," Duff speculates "Maybe Dad is involved in some top secret business and—"

"Duff. This is not *Spy Kids*. This is real life. Our life." Alice shoves a paper plate violently toward her younger brother.

Duff's face flushes, tears flooding his eyes. He swallows, looking down at his slice. "I'm just trying to help."

Jase moves behind him, squeezing his shoulder. "We know. Thanks, Duffy. We know."

The little kids dig in, their appetites intact, despite everything.

"Maybe Dad's in the mob," Duff speculates a little while later, eyes dry now, mouth full. "And he was about to blow the whistle on the whole thing and—"

"Shut the heck up, Duff! Daddy's not in the mob! He's not even Italian!" Andy shouts.

"There's a Chinese mob and a—"

"Knock it off! You're just being stupid and annoying on purpose." Now Andy bursts into tears.

"Guys," Jase begins.

"Be. Quiet. *Now*," Alice says in a flat voice so deadly, everyone freezes.

George puts his head down on the table, covering his ears. Patsy points an accusing finger at Alice and says, "Butt!" Duff sticks his tongue out at Andy, who glares back at him. My Garretts are in chaos.

There's a long silence, broken by sobs from George.

"I want Daddy," he howls. "I don't like you, Alice. You're a big meanie. I want Mommy and Daddy. We need to get Daddy out of the hostible. He's not safe there. He could get an air bubble in his IV. He could get bad medicine. He could get a mean nurse who is a murderer."

"Buddy." Jase scoops George up. "That's not gonna happen."

"How do you *know?*" George asks fiercely, his legs dangling. "D'you *promise?*"

Jase shuts his eyes, rubs one hand on George's little pointy-sharp shoulder blade. "Promise."

But I can see that George doesn't believe him.

Worn out, Patsy falls asleep in her high chair, her rosy cheek drooping into a smear of tomato sauce. George and Harry watch a very unlikely movie about a bunch of baby dinosaurs having adventures in the tropics. Alice heads back to the ICU. I call Mom to tell her I won't be home for dinner. She answers from some loud place with lots of laughter in the background. "That's okay, sweetheart, I'm at a meet-and-greet at the Tidewater anyway. So many more people showed up than we expected. It's a huge success!"

Her voice is even and cheerful, no tension there at all. It must be a coincidence, has to be, that bump in the night and Mr. Garrett. There can't be any connection. If I brought it up, I'd sound crazy.

She raised us to be conscientious. The worst thing Tracy and I could do was lie: "What you did was wrong, but lying about it made it a hundred times worse" was a speech so familiar, we could have set it to music.

Chapter Forty-one

Dishes clatter and crash when I call in to Breakfast Ahoy to quit, the next day. I can hear Ernesto swearing about the unusually big morning rush as I tell Felipe that I won't be coming back in. He's incredulous. Yeah, I know, it's completely unlike me to quit without notice. Much less at the height of the summer season. But the Garretts need me.

"No creo que se pueda volver y recuperar su trabajo," Felipe snaps, moved to his native Spanish before he translates. "Don't think you can come marching back in and get your job back, missy. You go out now, and you go out for keeps."

I suppress a stab of sorrow. The relentless pace and energy of Breakfast Ahoy have been an antidote to the long stretches of stillness and tedium at the B&T. But I can't escape the B&T— Mom would hear about that right away.

Jase protests, but I ignore him.

"Getting rid of that uniform? Long overdue," I tell him. More importantly, quitting Breakfast Ahoy frees up three mornings of my week.

"I hate that this changes your life too."

But nothing like the way things are changing for the Garretts. Mrs. Garrett practically lives at the hospital. She comes home to feed Patsy, snatch a few hours of sleep, and have long, ominous-sounding conversations on the phone with the hospital billing department. Alice, Joel, and Jase trade off spending nights with their dad. George wets his bed constantly and Patsy hates the bottle with a mighty passion. Harry starts swearing more often than Tim, and Andy spends all her time on Facebook and reading, rereading *Twilight* again and again.

The night air in my room is warm and close, suffocating, and I wake, gasping for cool air and water. I head downstairs toward to the kitchen, stopping when I hear Mom. "It doesn't feel right, Clay."

"We've gone over this. How many glasses of wine had you had?"

Her voice is high and shaky. "Three—four, maybe? I don't know. Not all of them, anyway, just a few sips here and there."

"Over the legal limit, Grace. This would end your career. Do you understand? No one knows. It's done. Move on."

"Clay, I—"

"Look at what's at stake here. You can do more good to more people if you get reelected. This was a blip—a misstep. Everybody in public life has 'em. You're luckier than most—yours *wasn't* public."

Mom's ringtone sounds. "It's Malcolm from the office," she says. "I'd better take it."

"Hold on," Clay says. "Listen to yourself, sugar. Listen. Your first thought is for your duty. Right in the middle of a personal crisis. You really want to deprive people of that dedication? Think about it. Is that the right thing to do?"

I hear the tap of Mom's heels moving into her office, and I start to edge back up the stairs.

"Samantha," Clay says quietly. "I know you're there."

I freeze. *He can't know. The stairs are carpeted, I'm barefoot.*

"You're reflected in the hall mirror."

"I was just . . . thirsty and I . . ."

"Heard all that," Clay concludes.

"I didn't . . ." My voice trails off.

He comes around the corner of the stairs, leaning against the stairway wall, arms folded, a casual stance, but there's something unnaturally still about him.

"I didn't come here by chance," he tells me softly. He's back-lit by the kitchen light and I can't quite make out his face. "I'd heard about your mother. Your mama . . . she's *good*, Samantha. The party's interested. She's got the whole package. Looks, style, substance . . . she could be big. National. Easy."

"But—" I say. "She hit him, didn't she?" It's the first time I've said it out loud. He turns slightly and now I can see him better. I want so much for surprise or confusion to cross his face. But they aren't there, just that focused, intent look, a little grimmer now.

"An accident."

"Does that matter? Mr. Garrett's still hurt. Badly. And they don't have medical insurance and they're already broke and—"

"That's sad," Clay says. "Really. Good people struggle. Life's not fair. But there are people who can change things, who are important. Your mother's one of them. I know you're close to those Garretts. But think about the big picture here, Samantha."

In my head I see Mr. Garrett patiently training Jase, coming up behind Mrs. Garrett in the kitchen, dropping a kiss on her shoulder, making me feel welcome, reaching out to Tim, scooping up the sleepy George, his face in the shifting light of the fireworks, solid and capable, clicking his pen and rubbing his eyes over accounts at the store. "They *are* the big picture."

"When you're seventeen with your hormones in a riot, maybe." He laughs softly. "I know that seems like the whole world now."

"It's not about that," I argue. "Mom did something wrong. You know it. I know it. Something that hurt someone seriously. And—"

Clay sits down on the steps, tilts his head back against the wall, tolerant, almost amused. "Shouldn't your first concern be for your own mother? You know how hard she works at this job. How much it means to her. Could you really live with yourself if you took that away?"

His voice gets softer. "You and me and your mama. We're the only three people in the whole world who know about this. You start talking, you tell that family and everyone will know. It'll be in the papers, on the news—might even go national. You wouldn't be the privileged princess in her perfect world any-more. You'd be the daughter of a criminal. How would that feel?"

Bile burns the back of my throat. "I'm not a princess," I say.

"Of course you are," Clay responds evenly. He waves his hand, indicating the big living room, elegant furnishings, expensive artwork. "You've always been one, so you think it's normal. But everything you have—everything you are—comes from your mama. From her family money and her hard work. Fine way to pay her back."

"Couldn't she just—explain—I mean—come forward and—"

"You can't talk your way out of leaving the scene of an accident you've caused, Samantha. Especially if you're in public office. Not even Teddy Kennedy managed that, in case you haven't heard. This would ruin your mother's life. And yours. And, just to put it on a level you can understand, I don't think it would do much for your romance either. I'm not sure your fella would really want to be dating the daughter of the woman who crippled his dad."

The words drop from Clay's mouth so easily, and I picture trying to tell Jase what happened, how he'd look at me, remembering his face in the waiting room at the hospital, the lost expression in his eyes. He'd hate me. *What kind of a person could do that?* he'd asked. How can I possibly answer: "My own mother."

Clay's calm face wavers through the tears that have rushed to my eyes. He reaches into his pocket, pulls out a cloth handkerchief and hands it to me.

"This isn't the end of the world," he says gently. "Just one boy, one summer. But I'll tell you something I've learned in my time, Samantha. Family is everything."

Leaving scene of accident: One of most serious felonies in the state of Connecticut. Up to ten years of prison time and 10,000 dollars fine. I stare at the information I've hunted for online until the stark black words mallet against my eyeballs.

What would happen if Mom went to jail for a decade? Tracy'd have college, then she'd be off, somewhere . . . But where would I go? It's not as if I can throw myself on the mercy of my father. Since he didn't stick around for me to be born, I'm guessing he wouldn't be thrilled to have me show up on his doorstep as a teenager.

But Mr. Garrett . . . It was Jase's night at the hospital tonight. He called me to say, "Dad's awake, and that's good, and he recognized us. But now he's got something called 'deep vein thrombosis' and they can't give him drugs for it because of the head thing. They don't want bleeding into his brain. I listen to the medical jargon . . . don't get why they don't just say it in English. Maybe because it's so damn scary."

I can't tell him. I can't. What can I do? *Be there for them* is vague and meaningless. Like a T-shirt slogan or a bumper sticker making a statement that never needs to be backed up with action.

I can babysit. All the time. For free. I can . . .

What? Pay the hospital bills? I pull my savings book from my desk drawer, scanning the numbers I've saved working, and hardly spent, in the last three summers: $4,532.27. That'll probably cover some Band-Aids and aspirin. Even if I could find a way to give it to them without them knowing.

I spend the next few hours coming up with ways. An envelope in the mailbox "from a sympathetic friend." Slipping money into the cash register at the store. Forging documents indicating the Garretts have won the lottery; lost a sick, elderly, unpleasant, unknown relative. . . .

Dawn comes without any brilliant ideas. So I do the least I can do, the only thing I can think of . . . run across the yard, around our fence, flip-flops slapping up the drive, let myself in with the key the Garretts keep under the kiddie pool, sharp and jagged, nearly buried in the too-long grass.

I make coffee. I pull out cereal boxes. I try to make sense of the clutter on the kitchen table. I'm wondering who's here and whether to go up to Jase's room when the screen door slams and he walks in, rubbing his eyes, then starting at the sight of me.

"Training?" I ask, although at a second glance he looks too tidy for that.

"Paper route. Do you know there's actually a guy on Mack Lane who waits to catch the paper every morning when I throw it? He yells if I'm five minutes late. What're you doing here, Sam? Not"—he comes up next to me, dipping his head to my shoulder—"that I'm not glad to see you."

I wave at the table. "Just thought I'd get a head start. Didn't know if your mom was home or . . ."

Jase yawns. "Nope. I stopped on my way back. She was going to stay at the hospital all day today. Alice rented that pump thing." He flushes. "You know, for Patsy. Anyway, so she's taken care of. Mom didn't want to leave Dad since he was finally talking."

"Does he—remember anything?" If he does, he can't have told Jase, whose open, expressive face never holds a thought back.

"Zip." He opens the fridge, pulls out milk, drinks directly from the plastic gallon. "Only being out there, after a meeting, deciding to walk home for some fresh air, thinking it was going to rain, then waking up with tubes everywhere."

Is it the disloyal or the loyal part of me that's so relieved?

Jase lifts his hands over his head, bending from one side to another, stretching, closing his eyes. Very softly, almost under his breath, he says, "Mom's pregnant."

"*What?*"

"I don't know for sure. I mean, not exactly the right timing for the announcement, huh? But I'm pretty sure. She's been sick in the mornings, chugging Gatorade . . . let's just say I know the signs."

"Wow," I say, sitting down hard in one of the kitchen chairs.

"It's a good thing, right? I should be glad. I've always been glad before, but . . ."

"Not exactly the right timing," I echo.

"I feel so damn guilty sometimes, Sam, lately, for the things I find myself thinking."

For some reason, well as we know each other, I've never thought about Jase feeling things like guilt. He just seems too healthy, too balanced for that.

"You know how much those people piss me off," he continues, still in such a low voice, as though he doesn't even want to hear what he's saying. "The ones who come up to Mom in the supermarket or wherever and tell her there's such a thing as birth control. Or this asshole guy who fixed the generator at the store last month. When Dad asked him if he could pay in installments, the guy said, 'Didn't you know you'd be broke all the time if you had so many kids?' I wanted to deck him. But . . . sometimes I think that too. I wonder why my parents didn't ever . . . imagine . . . what having another kid would mean each of us *not* having. I hate myself for it. But I think it."

I take his face in my hands, holding tight. "You can't hate yourself."

"I do. It's just wrong. Like, who would I want to do without? Harry? Patsy? Andy? None of them . . . but . . . but Samantha, I'm only kid number three and there's already no money for college. What's gonna happen when we get to George?"

I think of George's somber face bent over his animal books, of all the facts at his fingertips. "George is like his own college," I say. "Garrett U."

Jase laughs. "Yeah. You're right. But . . . I'm not like that. I want to go to college. I want to be . . . good enough." He pauses. "For you. Not that guy from the quote-unquote wrong side of the tracks, Samantha."

"That's her. It's not me."

"I guess part of it's me, then," he says heavily, "because, Samantha . . . look at you."

"I'm just some girl with an easy life and a trust fund. With no problems. Look at *you*." Then I have a horrible thought. "Do you . . . like . . . resent me for that?"

He snorts. "Don't be ridiculous. Why would I? You don't take it for granted. You work hard all the time." He pauses for a moment. "I don't even resent Tim anymore. I did, for a while, 'cause he seemed so oblivious. But he really isn't. And his parents are the *worst*."

"Aren't they?" There's Mr. Mason, sleeping his way through life in his recliner, ignorant to everything, and Mrs. Mason with her cheery voice and her cheery Hummel figurines and her miserable children. I think of Nan. Will she turn out like her mom?

"Jase," I say slowly. "I've got . . . some money. Saved. It doesn't mean to me what it means to you. I could—"

"No," he says, his voice harsh. "Just stop it. Don't."

The silence between us now is heavy and still, stifling. Different. I hate it. I fuss with gathering enough bowls out of the cabinets, finding spoons, keeping my hands busy.

Jase stretches, locking his fingers behind his head. "I've gotta remember how lucky I am. My parents may be broke, things may be bad now, but they're great. When we were little, Alice used to ask Mom if we were rich. She always said we were rich in all the things that matter. I need to remember she's right."

So like Jase, to pull himself right back to counting blessings.

He comes close, touches my chin with a roughened finger. "Kiss me, Sam, so I can forgive and forget myself."

"You're forgiven, Jase Garrett, for being only human," I say.

He's so easy to forgive. No sins at all. Not like my mom. Not like me. When our lips meet, I don't feel the familiar warmth and ease. I feel like Judas.

Chapter Forty-two

There's a big hole where Nan should be. I could go to her and tell her everything and surely Nan would listen and maybe even help me find my way. Of all people, Nan would understand. She was there the day I got my period, on the tennis court during gym class, in white shorts. She noticed before anyone else did, pulled me to the side and took off her own pants—shy Nan—walking in her underwear to her gym locker to get another pair—and a tampon. I was there the first time we saw Tim really drunk—he was twelve—and hustled him into a cold shower (didn't help) and made him coffee (likewise) before putting him to bed to sleep it off. She was there when Tracy had a huge "day" party at our house while Mom was at work, then left with her boyfriend, leaving us—at fourteen—to kick out forty older teenagers and clean the house before Mom returned.

But now she doesn't answer texts, or return periodic calls. When I come by the gift shop, she busies herself with customers or says, "I'm on my way to inventory the stockroom/have lunch/see my supervisor."

How did our entire friendship, the whole twelve years we've known each other, get canceled out by what I saw? Or what she did. Or what I said about what she did. *I can't let her just walk away like this*, I tell myself, though Nan seems to have no problem doing exactly that. So, at five o'clock, the end of the B&T day, I catch up with her as she's making out an order form.

When I put my hand on her shoulder, she twitches it off, reflexively, like a horse shaking off a troublesome fly.

"Nan. *Nanny*. You're just going to freeze me out? Forever?"

"I don't have anything to say to you."

"Well, I've got things to say to *you*. We've been friends since we were five. That counts for nothing? You hate me now?"

"I don't hate you." For an instant there's a flicker of an emotion I can't identify in Nan's eyes, then she drops her gaze, turning the key on the cash register to lock it. "I don't hate you, but we're just too different. It's too much work to be your friend."

This last is unexpected. "Too much *work*? How?" *Could I be high-maintenance without knowing it*? I scan through my memories. Have I gone on too long about my mother to her? Have I talked too much about Jase? But I know, I know, it's been at least equal. I've listened for hours to the Tim drama-fest. I've heard every twist and turn in her relationship with Daniel. I've sympathized with her over her parents. I've seen her beloved Steve McQueen movies with her even though I've never really gotten the charm. *All that counts for nothing?*

She straightens up, looking me in the eye. Her hands are unsteady, I notice.

"You're rich and beautiful. You have the perfect life, the perfect body, the perfect grade point average, and you never have to work for a thing," she hisses at me. "Nothing comes hard

312

to you, Samantha. It all drops into your lap. Michael Kristoff *still* writes poetry about you. I know that because he was in my fiction class this spring. Charley Tyler tells everyone you're the hottest girl in the school. And lies about having had sex with you. I know *that* because someone told Tim and Tim told me. Now this Jase Garrett, who's definitely too gorgeous to be real, thinks you hung the moon. It makes me sick. You make me sick. Hanging around with you and being your sidekick is way too much work." Her voice drops even lower. "Not to mention the fact that now you know something about me that you could use to ruin my life."

"I'm not going to tell anyone," I say softly, trying to swallow down the hurt. My chest feels so tight, I can't take a deep breath. *Way too much work, Nan? What, because there's no way to cheat at being a friend?* "Don't you know me at all? I would never do that. I just— You don't need to cheat—you're too smart in every way to do that, and I want to be your friend and . . . and I need you. Something happened to Jase's dad and—"

"I heard," she says briefly. "Tim told me about it. And your guy came by the house the other day too, to let me know how fabulously helpful you'd been and that you missed me. Not going to tell anyone, huh? Hometown Hottie obviously knew something was up."

"I didn't tell him everything. Hardly anything." I hate that I sound self-justifying. "Just that we'd fought." Looking down at her hands, I see that her nails, always ragged, are now bitten to the quick, bloody and painful. "I never expected he'd come to your house."

"Well, he did. Mr. Hero to the Rescue again. It's the thing you always get. While I get . . . Daniel."

I want to say *You picked Daniel*, but that wouldn't make anything better. She's red in the face now, with that look I know comes right before tears. "Nan—" I begin, but she cuts me off.

"I don't need your pity. And I don't want your friendship." Picking up her purse and hauling it up onto her thin shoulder, she says, "Come on. I have to lock up." I follow her into the hall. She flips the deadbolt, turns, and walks away. At the last moment, she swings around, looking skinny and stiff. "How does it feel *not* to get what you want, Samantha?"

I've never felt like this before.

I've had that thought again and again since I met Jase. But it's always meant good things, not this pit in my stomach that travels with me everywhere.

Jase picks me up at the B&T, asking if I mind if we swing by the hospital.

I feel a fist grip my insides. I haven't seen Mr. Garrett since what Mom did. "Of course not," I say, the kind of polite lie I've never told him before.

The ICU is on the fourth floor and we need passes to get up there. When we do, Jase braces himself visibly before heading into the hospital room. Invisibly, I do the same.

He looks so shrunken in his hospital gown, tubes sprouting everywhere, his tan skin startlingly pale in the bluish hospital light. This is not the man who carries stacks of wood easily on his shoulders, hoists Harry and George up high, arcs a football effortlessly. Jase pulls the chair closer and sits, then reaches out for his dad's hand with the tape and the tubes. He bends to say something in Mr. Garrett's ear, and I stare at the heart monitor going up and down and up and down.

Driving home, Jase stares straight ahead. He doesn't reach for my hand as usual, but keeps both of his on the wheel, gripping tight enough that his knuckles whiten. I edge down in my seat, propping my heels on the dashboard. We drive past the exit for Main Street.

"Aren't we going home?" I ask.

Jase sighs. "I thought I'd head to French Bob's. See what he could give me for the Mustang if I sold it back. I've put a lot of time into it, not to mention cash."

I grab at his arm. "No. You can't. You can't sell the Mustang."

"Just a car, Sam."

I can't stand it. All the hours Jase has spent on the Mustang, whistling through his teeth, tinkering away. How he pores through *Car Enthusiast* or *Hemmings* magazine, dog-earing the pages. It's not just a car. It's the place he goes to relax, find himself again. The way I used to search the stars. Or watch the Garretts. The way I swim.

"It's not," I say. "Only that."

Instead of continuing on the highway toward French Bob's he pulls off now and loops back on the long road that lines the river, stopping in McGuire Park.

The Bug is old and noisy, but that's probably not why it's so silent when he turns the key and shuts off the ignition. It's the first time I've been here since that night. There are noises—the slow lap of the waves on the rocks, since a speedboat has just hurried by, seagulls calling and plunging, dropping clams on the rocks. Jase climbs out, nudging at a rock on the dirt road with the toe of his sneaker, headed not to the Secret Hideaway, but toward the bend in the road by the playground.

"I keep calling them," he tells me. "The police. They just say there's nothing, really, they can do. Without witnesses." A well-aimed kick sends the rock skittering off the sandy road onto the grass. "Why did it have to be raining that night? It's hardly rained all summer."

"Does it really matter that it was?" I ask.

"If not"—he drops into a crouch, moves his finger in the dirt—"there might have been something. Tire tracks. Something. As it is . . . whoever did this will get completely away and will never know how much harm they did."

Or they'll know and not care.

Shame burns in my chest now, replacing the anger over Nan. More than anything in the world I want to tell him the truth. From the start, it's been easy to tell him that, truths I've never told anyone. He's always listened and understood.

But there's no way to understand this.

How can he, when I don't understand it myself.

Chapter Forty-three

"Hi sweetheart! I'm making up some meals for you to have on hand. I'm gone so often these days that we don't get to have dinners together. I don't want you living on that garbage from Breakfast Ahoy or the snack stand at the club. So I've made up some dinners—that roast chicken one you like with the mushrooms, and some pasta Bolognese." Mom says all this cheerily as I drag myself into the kitchen after coming home from lifeguarding. "I've labeled them all and I'm going to put some in the freezer." And on and on.

Her voice is firm and calm, chatty. She's wearing a watermelon-colored wrap dress and her hair down, looking young enough to be my older sister. Mrs. Garrett has circles under her eyes these days, is gaunt and perpetually distracted. Though I've tried to keep things clean, the Garretts' house gets messier by the day. Patsy's fussy, George clingy, Harry misbehaving, Andy and Duff fighting like bears. Jase is tense and preoccupied, Alice even more acerbic. Everything is different next door. Nothing's changed here.

"Would you like some lemonade?" Mom asks. "They had Meyer lemons at the Gibson's Gourmet the other day, so I made it with those for a change. I think this is the best batch ever."

She pours me a glass, the picture of graceful efficiency and maternal solicitude.

"Stop it, Mom," I say, sliding into the kitchen stool.

"You don't want me to mother you so much, I know. But all the other summers when I've had to work, you've had Tracy to keep you company. Should I post a chart of what's frozen and what's fresh? I don't need to do that. You'll remember, right? I just suddenly realized how alone you are."

"You have no idea."

Something in my tone must get to her because she halts, glances at me nervously, then continues rapidly, "When this election is over, we'll take a good, long vacation. Maybe somewhere in the Caribbean. I've heard great things about Virgin Gorda."

"I can't believe you. Are you, like, a robot now? How can you just act like everything's normal?"

Mom stills in the act of putting Tupperware in the freezer. "I don't know what you're talking about," she says.

"You need to tell the truth about what happened," I say.

She straightens up slowly, looking me in the eye for the first time in days, chewing her bottom lip. "He'll be fine." She snaps a lid tightly. "I've followed it in the news. Jack Garrett's a relatively young man, in good shape. Things might be rough for a while, but he'll be fine. In the end, no real damage done."

I lean forward, hands flat on the counter, my palms sliding across the cool surface of the kitchen island. "How can you even say that? Do you actually believe it? This isn't some, some *nothing*—" I fling one hand out, accidentally hitting the Water-ford crystal fruit bowl full of lemons, sending it flying toward the wall, splintering on the tile floor with a jarring crash, lemons bouncing everywhere.

"That belonged to my grandparents," Mom says tightly. "Don't move. I'll get the vacuum cleaner."

Something about the accustomed sight of her, bent over, moving the vacuum in orderly symmetrical strokes in her dress and her heels, makes me feel as though I'm going to explode. I jump down from the stool and flick the OFF button.

"You can't just tidy it up and forget it, Mom. The Garretts have no health insurance. Did you know that?"

She pulls the trash can out from under the sink, snapping on her rubber gloves, and begins methodically putting the larger chunks of glass into the bag. "That's not my fault."

"It's your fault that it *matters* that they don't. He's going to be in the hospital for months! Then maybe rehab—who knows for how long? The hardware store was already struggling."

"That also has nothing to do with me. Many small businesses are struggling, Samantha. It's unfortunate, and you know I've made speeches about that very issue—"

"Speeches? Are you serious?"

She winces at the volume of my voice, then turns and switches the vacuum on again.

I yank the plug out of the wall.

"What about everything you've ever told me about facing up to your responsibilities? Did you mean any of it?"

"Don't speak to me that way, Samantha. I'm the parent here. I *am* doing the responsible thing, staying where I can do the greater good. How will it help the Garretts if I lose my job, if I have to retire in disgrace? That won't fix anything. What's done is done."

"He could have died. What if he'd died, Mom? The father of eight children. What would you do then?"

"He didn't die. Clay called the police from the pay phone at Gas-and-Go that night. We didn't just ignore the whole thing."

"But you *are* ignoring the whole thing. That's exactly what you're doing. Mrs. Garrett is pregnant. Now they're going to have another baby and Mr. Garrett won't be able to work! What's wrong with you?"

Mom jerks the vacuum cleaner cord out of my hands, winding it into tight coils. "Well, there you go. Who has that many children in this day and age? They shouldn't have had such a large family if they couldn't afford one."

"How is Jase even going to go back to school this fall if he has to replace his dad at the store?"

"There, you see!" Mom says sharply. "It's just like Clay told me. It all comes down to your feelings for this young man. This is all about you, Samantha."

I stand there, incredulous. "It doesn't have anything to do with me!"

She folds her arms and looks at me pityingly. "If I had accidentally hit someone you didn't know, a stranger to you, would you be acting like this? Would you be asking me to give up my entire career because of something that's going to cause some temporary challenges for someone?"

I stare at her. "I hope I would. I think I would. Because that's the right thing to do."

Her exhalation of disgust ruffles a few strands of her tidy hair. "Oh spare me, Samantha. The right thing to do is so easy to see when you are seventeen years old and don't have to make any big decisions. When you know that no matter what you do, someone will take care of you and fix everything. But when you're grown up, the world is not that black and white, and the right thing doesn't have a tidy little arrow pointing to it. Things happen, adults make decisions, and that's the bottom line."

"The bottom line is that you hit a man and drove away—" I start to say, but the shrill of Mom's cell phone interrupts.

She checks it, then says, "Here's Clay now. This conversation is over. What's done is done and we're *all* going to move on." She snaps the phone open. "Hello, sweetie! No, I'm not busy. Sure, just let me go into the office and get that."

Her heels click on the tile down the hallway.

The corner of the kitchen is still covered with lemons and tiny crystal shards.

I slump back onto the stool, resting my cheek on the cool granite of the countertop. I've armed myself for days to talk to my mother, going over things in my head, the clearest arguments I could make. Now I've made them all, but it's like the entire conversation didn't even exist, like it just got swept up and put away.

That night I climb out my window, perching in my old accustomed spot. Despite all the years I sat in this same place alone, now it feels strange and wrong to be without Jase. But he's at the hospital again. Through the Garretts' kitchen window, I can see Alice doing dishes. The rest of the house is dark. As I watch, the van pulls into the driveway. I wait for Mrs.

Garrett to climb out, but she doesn't. She sits there, staring straight ahead until I can't watch anymore and climb back into my room.

Nan said things just come my way without me lifting a finger.

It's never felt like that to me, but I've always been able to get what I really wanted if I worked hard enough.

Not now.

No matter how hard I try, and I've never tried so hard for anything, I can't make things better at the Garretts'. Worst of all, things with Jase are stressful. I offer to be the coach when he trains. "If your dad had the workouts written down, I can read them and call them out to you."

"They were all in his head. So thanks, but I'm all right." Dusty from delivering lumber, Jase turns on the faucet over the cluttered sink and splashes water on his face, then ducks his head to drink, accidentally knocking a half-full glass of milk off the counter. When it crashes onto the floor, instead of picking it up, he gives it a kick that sends it ricocheting across the linoleum, scattering milk.

Alarm grips the back of my throat, metallic-tasting. I go over and put my hand on his shoulder. His head is down and I can see a muscle in his jaw twitch. His arm is unyielding beneath my fingers and he doesn't look at me. The leaden fist around my throat tightens.

"Dude!" Tim calls from the backyard, where he's vacuuming the pool. "The frickin' thing's blowing *out* the dirt into the pool instead of sucking it in. Can you do your thing?"

"Yeah, yeah, I'll fix it," Jase calls back without moving.

"What would anybody do around here without you?" I say, going for a light tone. "*Everything* would be broken."

He snorts without any humor. "Kind of already is, isn't it?"

I move closer, rest my cheek against his shoulder, rubbing his back.

"How can I help?" I ask. "I'll do anything."

"There's nothing you can do, Sam. Just . . ." He turns away, shoves his hands in his pockets. "Maybe . . . just . . . give me a little space."

I back toward the kitchen door. "Right. Sure. I'll head home for a while."

This doesn't feel like us at all. I hover in the doorway, expecting . . . I'm not sure.

Instead he nods without looking at me and bends to mop up the spilled milk.

When I get home, where it's still and clean and hushed, all the outdoor sounds muffled by the central air, I climb upstairs, feeling as though I'm pushing through water or wearing shoes made of lead. I sit down abruptly halfway up, lean my head back against the step above me, shut my eyes.

A thousand times since this happened, I've been about to blurt out the whole story, unable to stop myself, unable to keep something this big inside from Jase. Every time, I've bitten my tongue, stayed silent, with the thought: *If I tell him, I'll lose him.*

Tonight is when I know.

I already have.

Late that night, there's only one dim light shining in the living room. Mom likes the overhead ones, so I know right away it's not her. And I'm right. Clay's sitting in the big armchair by the fireplace, shoes off, this big golden retriever at his feet. Mom is curled up on the couch, fast asleep, her hair tumbling out of her careful bun, draping over her shoulders.

Clay jerks his chin in the direction of the dog. "Courvoisier. I call him Cory. Pure bred from champions. He's old now, though."

Indeed, the muzzle that rests on Clay's bare foot is white with age. Cory raises his head at my entrance, though, thumping a greeting with his tail.

"I didn't know you had a dog. Mom's asleep?" I ask, stating the obvious.

"Long day. Meet-and-greet at five a.m. at General Dynamics. Then we had a speech at Republicans for Change and dinner at the White Horse Tavern. She's a pro, your mama. Just keeps going and going. She's earned her rest." He stands up and pulls the woven beige throw from the top of the couch, covering her.

I start to turn away, but he stops me, hand on my arm. "Have a seat, Samantha. You're burning the candle at both ends too. How're those Garretts doing?"

How can he even ask that question, in his calm way? "Not well," I say.

"Yeah. A tough break." Clay picks up his wineglass and takes a casual sip. "That's the thing about a one-man business . . . all riding on luck."

"Why do you even pretend to be sympathetic about this?" I ask, my voice unexpectedly loud in the quiet room. Mom twitches in her sleep, then snuggles her head into the pillow.

"Like what happened is some sort of act of God, not something you were involved in? Like you even know what they're going through?"

"Y'all don't know much about me, do you?" He takes another swallow of wine, reaching down to stroke Cory's head. "I know better than you ever will what it's like to be poor. My daddy ran a service station. I did the books. Our town was so small, you hardly needed a car to get from one end to the other. And folks in West Virginia are what you might call naturally frugal. A lot of months he didn't make enough to pay his employees and draw a salary himself. I know *all* about being broke and having your back against the wall."

His eyes are suddenly intent on mine. "And I've left that *far* behind. Your mom's the real ticket, with a bright future. I won't let some teenager with a grudge take that away from her. Or me."

Mom stirs again, then curls up, almost in a fetal position.

"You need to distance yourself from that family," Clay adds, his voice almost gentle. "And you need to do that now. Otherwise things are going to come out that shouldn't come out, hormonal teenagers not being known for their discretion."

"I'm not my mother," I say. "I don't have to do whatever you say."

He leans back against the chair, blond hair falling across his forehead. "You're not your mama, but you're not stupid either. Have you taken a good look at the books for the Garretts' store?"

I have, we all have, Tim and me and Jase, working on them. Math-challenged as I am, the numbers don't look good. Mr.

Garrett would be clicking his pen furiously over them.

"Did you happen to notice the contract from Reed Campaigns? Your mom is using Garrett's for all her yard signs, her billboards, her visibility flags. That's a helluva lot of lumber. She wanted to go with Lowe's, but I told her picking a local business looks better. That's steady cash flow for the store, straight on through November. Not only that, but the Bath and Tennis Club is using Garrett's. Your mama's suggestion. They're adding on a new wing for an indoor pool. Cash that goes straight into the store. Cash that could go away with a comment or two. Green wood, sloppy workmanship . . ."

"What are you saying? If I don't break up with Jase you'll, what, pull those contracts?" In the glow of the light, Clay's blond hair shines angel-fair, nearly the same color as Cory's. He looks tidy and innocent in his white shirt with the sleeves rolled up, his eyes big and blue and frank.

He smiles at me. "I'm not saying anything, Samantha. Just stating the facts. You can draw your own conclusions." He pauses. "Your mama's always telling me how smart you are."

Chapter Forty-four

Early in the morning the next day, I cross the short distance from my yard to the Garretts' to find Jase.

As I walk up the driveway, I can hear him whistling. It almost makes me smile.

His tan legs and worn Converse are visible first, sticking out from beneath the Mustang. He's lying on his back, Duff's skateboard under him, working on the underbody. I can't see his face, and I'm glad. I'm not sure I can do this if I can see Jase's face.

He recognizes my step, though. Or my shoes.

"Hey, Sam. Hi, baby." His voice is cheerful, more relaxed than it's been in days. He's at peace, doing something he's good at, getting away from everything else for a while.

I swallow. My throat feels thick, as though the words I have to say have snarled into a choking ball.

"Jase." I don't even sound like myself. Kind of appropriate, since I'd rather not think this is me at all. I clear my throat. "I can't see you."

"I'll be out in a sec. I just have to tighten this up or all the oil will drain right out."

"No. I mean I can't see you anymore."

"What?" I hear the crack of metal against bone as he sits up, forgetting where he is. Then he slips out from under the car. There's a smudge of black oil on his forehead, an angry red spot. It'll bruise.

"I can't see you anymore. I can't . . . do this. I can't babysit George or Patsy or see you. I'm sorry."

"Sam—what is this?"

"Nothing. I just can't do it. You. Us. I can't do it now." He's standing close to me, so tall, so near I can smell him, wintergreen gum, axle grease, Tide-clean clothes.

I take a step back. *I have to do this.* So much has already been ruined. I have no doubt Clay meant what he said. All it takes is remembering the look on his face when he talked about leaving his past behind, his implacable voice telling Mom to back up and drive away. If I don't do this, he'll do whatever it takes to ruin the Garretts. It won't take much. "I can't do this," I repeat.

Jase shakes his head. "You can't do *this.* You have to give me a chance to fix whatever it is I've done. What *have* I done?"

"It isn't you." The oldest, weakest breakup excuse in the world. And, here, the most true.

"This isn't *you*! You don't act like this. What's wrong?" He takes a step toward me, his eyes shadowed with concern. "Tell me so I can fix it."

I fold my arms, stepping farther away. "You can't fix everything, Jase."

"Yeah, well, I didn't even know it was broken. I don't understand. Talk to me." His voice lowers. "Is it the sex . . . did we go too fast? We can slow down. We can just . . . Anything, Sam. Is it your mom? Tell me what you need."

I turn away. "I need to go."

He wraps his fingers tightly around my upper arm to stop me. My whole body seems to shrink, as though I'm folding smaller into my skin.

Jase stares at me incredulously, then drops his hand. "You, like, don't want me to touch you? *Why?*"

"I can't talk anymore. I have to go." I have to get away before I can't do this, before I blurt out everything, no matter what will happen about Mom and Clay and the store. I have to.

"You're just going to walk away—like that? You're leaving it this way? Now? I love you. You can't. . . ."

"I have to." Every word feels like it's strangling me. I turn away and head down the driveway, trying to walk calmly, not to run, not to cry, not to feel anything at all.

I hear quick steps as Jase follows me.

"Leave me *alone*," I toss over my shoulder, picking up my pace, racing to my house as though it's some refuge. Jase, who could easily catch up or outrun me, falls back, leaving me to wrench open the heavy door and stumble into the foyer, and then curl into a ball, pressing my hands to my eyes.

I expect to be called to account for this. Alice ringing my doorbell to beat me up. Mrs. Garrett coming over with Patsy on her hip, angry at me for the first time ever. Or George showing up, big-eyed and bewildered, to ask what's going on with Sailor Supergirl. But none of that happens. It's as though I don't make a ripple as I drop off the face of the earth.

Chapter Forty-five

I'm not the one who was hit by a car. I'm not the one who has eight children and is expecting another. I'm not Jase, trying to hold it all together while thinking of selling the thing that gives me peace.

Waking up every morning and feeling like pulling the covers over my head gives me a kick of self-hatred. *I'm not the one this happened to.* I'm just some girl with an easy life and a trust fund. Just like I told Jase. And yet I can't get out of bed.

Mom is extra-cheerful and solicitous these days, blending my smoothie before I have a chance to, leaving little packages on my bed with cheery Post-it notes. "Saw this cute top and knew it would look great on you." "Bought some sandals for myself and knew you'd love them too!" She doesn't say anything about me sleeping till noon. She ignores my monosyllabic conversation, amping up her own to fill the silences. Over dinner, she and Clay chatter away about getting me an internship in Washington, D.C., next summer, or maybe something in New York, fanning out the possibilities in front of me like paint chips—"How lovely this would look on your future!"—while I poke at my chowder.

No longer caring what Mom will say, I give notice at the B&T. Knowing Nan is just a few yards away, radiating anger and resentment through the walls of the gift shop, makes me feel sick. It's also impossible to concentrate on watching every swimmer at the Olympic pool when I keep finding myself staring fixedly at nothing at all.

Unlike Felipe at Breakfast Ahoy, Mr. Lennox doesn't get belligerent. Instead he argues when I give him my notice and try to hand him my clean, neatly folded suit and jacket and skirt.

"Oh now, Ms. Reed! Surely . . ." He glances out the window, takes a deep breath, then goes over and shuts his office door. "Surely you don't want to make this Precipitous Choice."

I tell him I have to, unexpectedly touched by how flustered he is. He pulls a small paisley silk handkerchief out of his jacket pocket and hands it to me. "You have always been an excellent worker. Your work ethic is unparalleled. I would hate to see you Retire Impulsively. Is there . . . perhaps . . . a Delicate Situation on the job which makes you uncomfortable? The new lifeguard? Is he making Unwelcome Advances on your Person?"

Part of me wants to giggle hysterically. But Mr. Lennox's large brown eyes, magnified by his glasses, radiate sincerity and concern.

"Do I need to Have Words with Someone?" he asks. "Is there something you need to Get off Your Chest?"

If you only knew.

For a moment, the words crowd into my mouth. My mother nearly killed the father of the boy I love and now I've broken his heart and I can't tell anyone. My best friend hates me for something she did and I can't fix it. I don't know who my own mother is anymore and I don't recognize myself and everything is terrible.

I imagine pouring all those words out to Mr. Lennox, who was flustered by not knowing the right hour for a lumber delivery. There's no way.

"It's nothing about the job. I just can't stay here."

He nods. "I accept your resignation with Great Regret."

I thank him. As I turn to go, he calls, "Ms. Reed!"

"Hm?"

"I do hope you will continue to swim. You may keep the key. Our Arrangement for your training stands."

Recognizing this for the gift it is, I say, "Thank you." And leave before I can say more.

With no schedule, no babysitting or breakfast shift or lifeguard gig, days and nights bleed into one another. I can't settle down during nights and spend them roaming the house restlessly or watching Lifetime movies, where everyone is worse off than I am.

Why don't I call my sister?

The answer is, of course, that I do. Of course I do. She knows this situation from the inside out, knows Mom, me. Knows it all. But here's what happens when I call:

Straight to voicemail. My sister's husky voice, her deep-from-the-belly laugh, so familiar and so far away. "Got me. Or not, really. You know what to do. Talk to me! I may even call you back." My imagining: Tracy out on beach, bright blue eyes squinting against the sun, having that carefree summer she told Mom she'd earned, phone in Flip's pocket, or switched to off, because what was the big deal. Their perfect summer. I open my mouth to say something, but snap the phone shut.

The strangest part? Mom used to notice if I had a nearly invisible stain on my shirt, or hadn't conditioned my hair enough, or if my morning routine deviated in some miniscule way: "You always have a smoothie before work, Samantha. Why are you having toast? I've read that a change in a teenager's routine could be a red flag for a drug habit." But now? Clouds of pot smoke could be unfurling under my door and that probably wouldn't stop the blizzard of Post-it notes that are her primary form of communication these days.

Please pick up my silk suit at the dry cleaner. Toile chair in study has stain, apply OxiClean. Will be out very late tonight; turn on alarm when you go to bed.

I've quit all my jobs and become a recluse. And my mother doesn't seem to notice.

"Sweetheart! Good timing," Mom says jovially as I drag myself into the kitchen in response to her *Yoo-hoo, Samantha, I need you.* "I was just showing this nice man how I make my lemonade. Kurt, did you say your name was?" Mom asks the man seated at our kitchen island after waving cheerfully at me with the lemon zester.

"Carl," he responds. I know him. He's Mr. Agnoli, who takes the photographs for the *Stony Bay Bugle.* He always photographed the winning swim teams. Now he's in our kitchen, looking starstruck by Mom.

"We thought a quick piece about the state senator at home would be great along with pictures of her making lemonade. A metaphor for what she can do for the state," Mr. Agnoli tells me.

Mom turns around and checks the sugar/water mixture melting on the stove, enlightening Mr. Agnoli about how it's the added lemon zest that really does the trick.

"I'm going back upstairs," I say, and do so. Maybe if I can just sleep for a hundred years, I'll wake up in a better story.

I'm jolted awake by Mom jerking on my arm. "You can't doze the day away, sweetheart. I've got plans."

Everything about her looks the same as always: her smoothly uptwisted chignon, her faultless makeup, her calm blue eyes. I'm in a backward version of the way I felt after Jase spent the night. When big things happen to you—shouldn't they show on your face? Not on Mom's, though.

"I took the whole day off." She's rubbing my back now. "I've been so busy, neglecting you, I know. I thought maybe we could go get facials, maybe—"

"*Facials?*"

She pulls back a little at the sound of my voice, then continues in the same lulling tone, "Remember how we used to do that, the first day of summer vacation? It was a tradition and I skipped right over it this year. I thought I could make it up to you, we could go out to lunch afterward—"

I sit up abruptly. "Do you really think that's how it works? I'm not the one you need to make it up to."

She walks over to the window overlooking the Garretts' lawn. "Stop this. It's not doing any good."

"Maybe if I could understand why not, Mom." I haul myself out of bed and stand next to her at the window, looking down

on the Garretts' house, the toys in the yard, the inflatables floating in the pool, the Mustang.

Her jaw tightens. "The truth? Fine. I never enjoyed it when
you and Tracy were small. I'm not like that woman over
there—" She gestures out the window in the direction of the
Garretts'. "I'm not some broodmare. I wanted children, sure. I
was an only child growing up, I was always lonely. When I met
your father with his big family, I thought . . . But I hated the
mess and the smells and the constant distractions. As it turned
out, he'd had enough of all that growing up too. So he took
off to be a boy again, and left me two little babies. I could have
afforded ten nannies, and you just had the one, and she only
came in during the weekdays. I got through that time. Now
I've finally found a place for myself." She reaches out, takes
hold of my upper arm again, jogging it, as though she's trying
to wake me up all over again. "You want me to give that up?"

"But—"

"I work so hard, have worked hard for longer than you can
even remember. I'm supposed to pay penance for the rest of
my life for one night where I was able to relax and have a good
time?"

Another arm-shake. Her face is very close to mine.

"Do you really think that's right, Samantha?"

I don't know what's right anymore. My head hurts and my
heart feels nothing but numb blankness. I want to reach into
her argument and pick out the thread that's wrong, but it all
seems like a tangle.

⌒

I still watch the Garretts, relieved when I see signs of normalcy—Alice lying in a lawn chair tanning or Duff and Harry having a squirt-gun fight. But watching doesn't give me the feeling it used to—at once hopeful and calming, that there were worlds other than my own, where extraordinary things could happen. Now it feels like I'm exiled, back in Kansas with all that color bleached to black and white.

I try hard to skirt around memories of Jase, but they're everywhere. I found one of his shirts under my bed yesterday and stood there with it in my hand, frozen in amazed horror that I hadn't noticed it—and Mom hadn't either. I shoved it to the back of my own shirt drawer. Then I pulled it out and slept in it.

Chapter Forty-six

I'm walking up our driveway, one of the few times I've cast my shadow outdoors, when I feel a touch on my shoulder and turn around to see Tim.

"What the fuck are you doing?" he demands, grabbing hold of my hand.

"Leave me alone." I yank it away from him.

"The hell I will. Don't you pull that ice queen bullshit with me, Samantha. You dumped Jase with no explanation. Nan won't say jack shit about you except that you aren't friends anymore. Look at you—you look like hell. You're all skinny and pale. You don't even look like the same girl What the fuck's happening to you?"

I take out my key to unlock the door. Despite the heat of the day, it feels like it's made of stone, so heavy and cold in my hand. "I'm not going to talk to you, Tim. It's none of your business."

"Screw *that* too. He's my friend. *You* were the one who brought him into my life. He's made things better. There's no way I'm going to stand by and watch you crap on him when his world is already messed up. He's got enough to deal with."

I open the door and drop my purse, which also feels as

though it's made of lead. My head hurts. Tim, of course, king of no mercy, follows me right in, letting the door slam shut behind us.

"I can't talk to you."

"Fine. Talk to Jase."

I twist to look at him. Even that movement feels painful. Maybe I'm slowly turning to stone myself. Except that then things wouldn't hurt so much, would they?

Tim looks at my face and the anger in his fades, replaced by concern.

"Please, Samantha. I *know* you. This is not how you act. This is how crazy, messed-up girls into power trips act. This is how assholes like me act. I've known you since you were little, and you were put together *then*. This doesn't make any sense. You and Jase . . . you two were solid. You don't just walk away from that. What the fuck is up with you?"

"I can't talk to you," I repeat.

His cool gray eyes scan slowly over my face, measuring. "You've gotta talk to someone. If not Jase, if not Nan . . . I'm sure not your ma . . . Who're you gonna to talk to?"

Just like that, I start to cry. I haven't cried at all, and now I can't stop. Tim, clearly horrified, glances around the room as though hoping someone, anyone, has come in who can save him from this sobbing girl. I slide slowly down the wall and keep crying.

"Shit, stop it. It can't be that bad. Whatever it is . . . it can be solved." He crosses to the kitchen island, pulling a length of paper towel off the porcelain holder, thrusting it toward me. "Here, wipe your eyes. Anything can be fixed. Even me. Listen,

I enrolled to work toward my GED. I'm gonna move out. My friend Connor from AA has this apartment over his garage, and I'm gonna live there, which means I don't have to deal with my folks anymore, and I can . . . Here, blow your nose."

I take the scratchy paper and blow. I know my face is red and swollen and now that I've started crying, I think it's very possible I won't ever be able to stop.

"That's it." Tim pats me awkwardly on the back, more like he's trying to dislodge something stuck in my throat than comfort me. "Whatever's going on, it'll be okay . . . but I can't believe ditching Jase is gonna help."

I cry harder.

With a resigned expression, Tim shears off more paper towels.

"Can I . . . ?" I'm now doing that hiccupping thing that comes after too much sobbing, making it difficult to catch my breath.

"Can you what? Just spit it out."

"Can I move in with you? To the garage apartment?"

Tim goes still, his hand frozen in the act of wiping my eyes. "Wha-at?"

I don't have enough breath—or maybe courage—to repeat myself.

"Samantha—you can't . . . I'm flattered, but . . . why the hell would you wanna do something like that?"

"I can't stay here. With them next door and with Mom. I can't face Jase and I can't stand to look at her."

"This is about Grace? What'd she do? Tell you she was yanking your trust fund if you didn't ditch Jase?"

I shake my head, not looking at him.

339

Tim skids down against the wall next to me, stretching out his long legs, while I'm crouched in this small hunched circle, knees to chest.

"Spill, kiddo." He looks me in the face, unblinking. "Hit me. I go to meetings now, and you wouldn't believe the shit I've heard."

"I know who hurt Mr. Garrett," I squeeze out.

Tim looks incredulous. "Fuck me. Really? Who?"

"I can't tell you."

"Are you freakin' crazy? You can't keep that a secret. Tell the Garretts. Tell Jase. Maybe they can sue the bastard and get millions. How'd you find out, anyway?"

"I was there. That night. In the car. With my mom."

His face blanches under his freckles, making his hair stand out like flame.

Silence falls between us like a curtain.

Finally Tim says, "I picked the wrong day to give up amphetamines."

I stare at him.

"Sorry. *Airplane* joke. I'm immature. I know what you're saying. I just don't really *want* to know what you're saying."

"Then go."

"Samantha." He grabs at my sleeve. "You can't keep quiet. Gracie committed a fucking crime."

"It would ruin her life."

"So you'll let her ruin theirs?"

"She's my mother, Tim."

"Yeah, and your ma screwed up big-time. Because of that

340

you're trashing Jase's life and Mrs. G's and all those kids'? And your own . . . ? That's just fucked up."

"So what am I supposed to do? Go over there—look Jase in the eye and say, 'Sorry—you know that person you couldn't believe existed, the one who would hit someone and drive away? She's your next-door neighbor. She's my mom.'"

"He deserves to know."

"You don't understand."

"Nope, I sure as hell don't. This is not exactly something I've run into. God, I need a smoke." He pats at his shirt pocket but comes up empty.

"It would destroy her."

"I could really use a drink right now too."

"Yeah, that would help," I say. "That's what happened. She'd had too much wine and she was driving and—" I bury my face in my hands. "I was asleep, and there was this awful thump." I look up at him through my fingers. "I can't get it out of my head."

"Aw, kid. Aaah, shit." *Gingerly,* Tim wraps an arm around my shaking shoulders.

"Clay told her to keep going, to back up and drive off and . . . she *did.*" I hear my voice breaking, still incredulous. "Just like that."

"I *knew* that guy was scum," Tim spits. "I knew it. Worst frickin' type too. Smart scum."

We sit there in silence for a few minutes, our backs against the wall. Then Tim repeats, "You have to tell Jase, tell him all that."

I shove my fists against my cheeks. "She'd have to resign and she might go to jail and it would all be because of me." Now that I'm finally talking, the words are tumbling out of my mouth in a rush.

"No. *No*, kid. Because of *her*. She did the wrong thing. You'd be doing the right one."

"Like you did the right thing with Nan?" I say quietly.

Tim's eyes flick to mine, widening. He tilts his head, staring at me, and then realization crystallizes on his face, and he reddens, looks down at his hands.

"Uh well, hey," he says. "Nan's a pain in the ass and I like to screw with her and generally make her life miserable—but she *is* my sister."

"She *is* my mother."

"It's different," Tim mutters. "See, I already *was* a fuck-up. I didn't cheat on papers, but I did every other shitty thing that occurred to me. Kinda seemed like karma that I'd get cheated from. But you're not like that. You *know* who you are."

"A mess."

He looks at me. "Well . . . kind of. But if you blow your nose again, maybe brush your hair a little . . ."

I can't help but laugh, which makes my nose run more and adds, I'm sure, to my general charming appearance.

Tim rolls his eyes, straightens up, and hands me the entire roll of paper towels. "Have you talked to your mom? Mr. Garrett's got some infection now—this high fever, and things are just all messed up. Maybe if she knew how bad this shit is."

"I tried. Of course I've tried. It's like talking to a wall. It happened, it's over, resigning won't do the Garretts any good, blah blah blah."

"Suing her ass would do them some good," Tim mumbles. "What about the police? What if you gave them an anonymous tip? No, they'd need proof. What if you talked to Mrs. Garrett first? She's cool."

"I can barely stand to look at their house, Tim. I can't talk to Mrs. Garrett."

"Then start with Jase. The guy's wrecked, Sam. Working at the store all the time and going to the hospital and keeping up with that crazy-ass training and trying to keep it together at home . . . all while wondering what the fuck happened to his girl—if you couldn't deal, or if he did something wrong or if you think his family's just a train wreck you don't want to handle."

"That's Mom," I say automatically. "Not me." My theme song still.

But . . . it is me. Staying quiet, pretending. I am doing exactly what Mom has done. I am, after all, just like her.

I stand up. "Do you know where Jase is? At the store?"

"Store's closed, Samantha, it's after five. I don't know where he is now. I locked up. But I have my car and his cell number. I'll get you to him. Not stay or anything. This has to be between you two. But I'll getcha there." He crooks his elbow out, offering his arm, like some courtly nineteenth-century gentleman. Mr. Darcy. In somewhat unusual circumstances.

I take a deep breath, wrap my fingers around his elbow.

"And, for the record," Tim adds, "I'm so fucking sorry, Samantha. I'm fucking, fucking sorry about all this."

343

Chapter Forty-seven

From that first day, I've walked right into the Garretts' without knocking. But now when Tim puts his hand on the screen door handle, I shake my head. There's no doorbell, so I tap loudly on the metal of the doorframe, rattling it. I can hear George's husky voice talking on and on in another room, so I know someone's home.

Alice comes to the door. The smile drops off her face immediately.

"What do *you* want?" she says through the screen.

"Where's Jase?"

She looks over her shoulder, then comes out onto the steps, slamming the screen door behind her. She's wearing a white bikini top and a pair of faded cutoffs. Beside me, I feel Tim's focus disappearing faster than helium from a burst balloon.

"Why?" Folding her arms, Alice settles herself firmly against the door.

"I have something I have to—say to him." My voice is hoarse. I clear my throat. Tim moves a little closer, either in support or to peer down Alice's bikini.

"I'm pretty sure it's all been said," she says flatly. "Why don't you go back where you came from?"

The part of me used to doing what I'm told, toeing the line, my mother's daughter, runs down the driveway in tears. But the rest of me, the real me, doesn't budge. I can't go back where I came from. That Samantha's gone.

"I need to see him, Alice. Is he here?"

She shakes her head. Since Mr. Garrett's accident, she hasn't kept up with her constant hair transformations, and now it's wavy brown with blond highlights growing out badly. "I don't see any reason to let you know where he is. Leave him be."

"It's important, Alice," Tim cuts in, evidently regaining focus.

After fixing him with a withering stare, she turns back to me. "Look, we don't have time or space for your dramas, Samantha. I'd started to think you were different, not just another private school princess, but looks like that's exactly what you are. My brother doesn't need that."

"What your brother doesn't need is you fighting his battles." I wish I were taller and could intimidate her by looming imposingly, but Alice and I are the same height. All the better for her to shoot her death-ray glare straight into my eyes.

"Yeah, well, he's my brother, so his battles are my battles," Alice says.

"Whoa, you two." Tim moves into our midst, towering over both of us. "I can't believe I'm actually breaking up a fight between two hot babes, but this is fucked up. Jase needs to hear what Samantha has to say, Alice. Put away your bullwhip."

Alice ignores him. "Look, I know you want to do that whole make-yourself-feel-better routine, la-la-la, you never meant to hurt him and you'd like to stay friends and all that garbage. But let's just skip all that. Go. You're done here."

"Sailor Supergirl!" says a happy voice, and there's George, pushing his nose into the mesh of the screen. "I had an Eskimo pie for breakfast today. Do you know that it's not really made by Eskimos? Or"—his voice drops—"*out* of Eskimos. Did you know that Eskimos make their ice cream out of seal fat? That's kinda yuck."

I bend down, away from Alice. "George—is Jase home?"

"He's in his room. Want me to take you there? Or go get him?" His face is so alight and alive seeing me, no reproach for my disappearing act. *George of the forgiving heart.* I wonder what the Garretts—Jase—told him—told anyone—about me. As I watch, though, his expression clouds over. "You don't think they make the ice cream out of baby seals, do you? Those little white fluffy ones?"

Alice pushes herself more firmly against the door. "George, Samantha was just leaving. Don't bother Jase."

"They would never make ice cream out of baby seals," I tell George. "They only make ice cream out of . . ." I have no idea how to finish this sentence.

"Terminally ill seals," Tim intervenes. "Suicidal seals."

George looks understandably confused.

"Seals who *want* to be ice cream," Alice tells him briskly. "They volunteer. There's a lottery. It's an honor."

He nods, digesting this. We're all watching his face to see if this explanation flew. Then I hear a voice behind him say, "Sam?"

His hair's sticking out in all directions, shower-damp. The smudges beneath his eyes are deeper and his jaw sharper.

"Hey, dude," Tim says. "Just bringing your girl by, admiring your bodyguard, all that. But," he says, backing down the steps, "goin' now. Catch you later. Feel free to call anytime to set up that mud-wrestling match, Alice."

Alice reluctantly moves aside as Jase pushes open the screen door, then shrugs, heading back into the house.

Jase steps out, face expressionless.

"So," he says. "Why're you here?"

George returns to the screen. "Do you think it has flavors? The ice cream? Like chocolate chip seal or seal with strawberry swirl?"

"Buddy," Jase tells him. "We'll check it out later, okay?"

George backs off.

"Do you have the Bug? Or the motorcycle?" I ask.

"I can get the Bug," he says. "Joel's got the cycle at work." He turns back to the door and shouts, "Al, I'm taking the car."

I can't quite hear Alice's response, but I'm betting all the words have four letters.

"So, where are we going?" he asks, once we get into the car.

I wish I knew.

"McGuire Park," I suggest.

Jase flinches. "Not full of happy memories right now, Sam."

"I know," I say, putting my hand on his knee. "But I want to be private. We can walk out to the lighthouse or something if you want. I just need to be alone with you." Jase looks at my hand. I remove it.

"Let's do McGuire then. The Secret Hideaway is a safe bet." His voice is level, emotionless. He reverses the car, hitting the gas harder than he usually does, turning down Main Street.

It's silent between us, the kind of awkward silence that

never used to happen. The well-trained (Mom's daughter) part of me wants to fill it with babble: *So, lovely weather lately, I'm fine, thank you, and you? Great! How about them Sox?*

But I don't. I just stare at my hands on my lap, stealing glances at his impassive profile from time to time.

He reaches out automatically to help me as we jump from stone to stone to the tilted rock in the river. The clasp of that warm strong hand is so familiar, so safe, that when he lets go as we reach the rock, my own feels incomplete.

"So . . ." he says, sitting down, wrapping his arms around his legs, and looking, not at me, but out at the water.

There may be proper words for this situation. A tactful way to lead up. A convincing explanation. But I don't know them. All that comes out is the unvarnished, awful truth.

"It was my mother who hit your father. She was driving the car."

Jase's head snaps around, eyes wide. I watch the color leach from his face under his tan. His lips part, but he doesn't say anything.

"I was there. Asleep in the backseat. I didn't see it. I wasn't sure what had happened. For days. I didn't realize." I meet his eyes, waiting to see astonishment turn to scorn, scorn to contempt, telling myself I'll survive. But he just keeps staring at me. I wonder if he's gone into shock and I should repeat it. I remember him giving me a Hershey's bar after that ride with Tim because Alice said chocolate was good for shock. I wish I had some. I wait for him to say something, anything, but he just looks as though I've punched him in the gut and he can't breathe.

"Clay was there too," I add uselessly. "He was the one who told her to drive away, not that it matters, because she did it, but—"

"Did they even stop?" Jase's voice rises, harsh. "And make sure he was breathing? Tell him help was coming? Anything?"

I try to pull a full breath of air into my lungs, but can't seem to manage. "They didn't. Mom backed up and drove away. Clay called 911 from a pay phone nearby."

"He was all alone there in the rain, Samantha."

I nod, trying to swallow the barbed wire caught in my throat. "If I had known, if I'd realized," I say, "I would have gotten out of the car. I would have. But I was asleep when it happened, they just backed away—it happened so fast."

He straightens up, turning to stare out at the water. Then says something in a voice so low, the river breeze carries the words away. I move next to him. I want to touch him, to bridge this gap like that, but he's stiff and still, a force field around him, holding me back

"When did you know?" he asks, in that same low tone.

"I had a feeling when you talked about Shore Road, but—"

"That was the next *day*," Jase interrupts, loud now. "The next day when the surgeons were drilling holes in Dad's skull and the police were still acting like they were going to figure this all out." Shoving his hands in his pockets, he walks away from me, away from the flat part of the rock to the jagged side that slopes into the water.

I follow, touch his shoulder. "But I didn't really know. Let myself know. Not until I heard Clay and Mom talking a week later."

Jase doesn't turn toward me, still looking out at the river. But he doesn't jerk away either.

"That's when you decided it was a good time to break up?" No emotion in his always expressive voice.

"That's when I knew I couldn't face you. And Clay had threatened to rescind all these contracts Mom's campaign has with your dad's store, and I . . ."

He swallows, absorbing this. Then his eyes flick to mine. "This is a lot. To take in."

I nod.

"I haven't been able to get that picture out of my head. Dad lying there in the rain. He landed face-first, did you know that? The car bumped him and threw him through the air. Ten feet, probably. He was in a puddle when the EMTs got there. A few more minutes and he would have drowned."

Again, I want to just run. There's nothing to say and no way to fix anything.

"He doesn't remember anything about that," Jase continues. "Only noticing it looked like rain and then fade to black until the hospital. But I keep thinking he must have realized at the time. That he was alone and hurt and there was nobody there who cared." He wrenches his body toward mine. "You would have stayed with him?"

They say you never know what you'd do in a hypothetical situation. We'd all like to think we'd be one of the people who gave up their lifejackets and waved a stoic good-bye from the slanting deck of the *Titanic*, someone who jumped in front of a bullet for a stranger, or turned and raced back up the stairs of one of the Towers, in search of someone who needed help rather than our own security. But you just don't know for sure if, when things fall apart, you'll think *Safety first* or if safety will be the last thing on your mind.

I look into Jase's eyes and tell the only truth I have. "I don't know. I didn't have that choice. But I know what's happening now. And I'm choosing to stay with you."

It's not clear who reaches for whom. Doesn't matter. I have Jase in my arms and mine hold him tight. I've done so much crying that there are no tears. Jase's shoulders shake but gradually still. No words for a long time.

Which is fine, because even the most important ones—*I love you. I'm sorry. Forgive me? I'm here*—are only stand-ins for what you can say better without talking at all.

Chapter Forty-eight

The drive back to the Garretts' is as silent as the drive to the park was, but a whole different kind of silence. Jase's free hand intertwines in mine when he doesn't need to shift gears, and I lean across the space between our seats to rest my head on his shoulder.

We're pulling into the driveway next to the van when he asks, "What now, Sam?"

Telling him was the hardest part. But not the end of the hard parts. Facing Alice. Mrs. Garrett. My mom.

"I only got as far as you."

Jase nods, biting his bottom lip, shifting the clutch into park. His jaw tightens and he looks down at his hands. "How do you want to do this? Are you going to come in with me?"

"I think I have to tell Mom. That you know. She's going to be—" I scrub my hands over my face. "Well, I have no idea what she's going to be. Or do. Clay either. But I've got to tell her."

"Look, I'm gonna take some time to think. How to say it. Whether I start with Mom or . . . I don't know. I'll have my cell. If anything happens, if you need me, call, okay?"

"Okay." I begin climbing out of the car, but Jase catches hold of my hand, stopping me.

"I'm not sure what to think," he says. "You knew this. From the start. I mean, how could you not have?"

Kind of a crucial question.

"How could you not have realized that something terrible had happened?" Jase asks.

"I was asleep," I answer. "Longer than I should have been."

I know Mom's home when I get there because her navy blue sandals are outside the door, her Prada purse slung on the lowboy in the hallway, but she's not in the kitchen or living room. So I head upstairs, to her suite, feeling this sense of trespassing, even though I'm in my own home.

She must be deciding what to wear to some new event, and indecisively, because there are piles of clothes tossed on the bed . . . a rainbow of florals, soft pastels, and rich ocean colors, starkly contrasted by her power-suit whites and navies.

The shower's running.

Mom's bathroom's huge. She's renovated it a bunch of times over the years. Each time it's gotten bigger, more luxurious. It's fully carpeted with a couch and a sunken bathtub, towel warmers and a glass shower with seven nozzles spraying from every direction. It's all done in a color my mother calls oyster, which looks like gray to me. She's got a vanity and a little upholstered bench set up in the corner, with a parade of perfumes and lotions, glass bottles, squat jars, and miles of makeup. When I crack the door open, the room's filled with clouds of steam, so thick I can barely see. "Mom?" I call.

She gives a little shriek. "Don't *do* that, Samantha. Don't walk in when someone's taking a shower! Haven't you seen *Psycho*?"

"I have to talk to you."

"I'm exfoliating."

"When you're done. But soon."

The shower squeaks off abruptly. "Can you hand me a towel? And my robe?"

I unhook her apricot silk robe from the door, where, I cannot help but notice, a navy blue man's robe also hangs. She reaches out around the shower door and clutches at the silk.

Once the robe is knotted neatly around her waist and the plush oyster-colored towel wraps her hair like a turban, she sits down at the vanity, reaching for her skin cream.

"I've been considering a little Restylane between the eyebrows," she says. "Not enough to look 'done,' just to take away that little crinkle here." She indicates a nonexistent wrinkle, then pulls her forehead taut with both hands. "I think it would be a smart career move, because lines in your forehead make it seem like you're fretting. My constituents shouldn't think I'm concerned about anything—that would undermine their confidence, don't you think?" She smiles at me, my mother with her convoluted logic and her towel crown.

I have chosen the Road of No Small Talk. "Jase knows."

She pales beneath her face cream, then her brows snap together. "You didn't."

"I did."

Mom springs up from the upholstered bench so quickly, she knocks it over. "Samantha . . . why?"

"I had to, Mom."

She paces across the room, walks back. And for the first time, I do notice the lines across her forehead, the long grooves parenthesizing her mouth. "We *had* this conversation, agreed that for the good of all, we would put this behind us."

"That was the conversation you had with Clay, Mom. Not the one with me."

She stops, eyes shooting sparks. "You gave me your word."

"I never did. You just didn't hear what I really said."

Mom deflates onto the bench, shoulders slumped, then looks up at me, eyes wide and beseeching. "I'll lose Clay too. If there's a scandal, *when* there's a scandal, and I have to resign— he won't stick around. Clay Tucker plays for the winning team. That's who he is."

How could Mom even want to be with a man she knew that about? *If trouble comes, babe, I'm outta here.* I'm glad I don't know my father. Sad, but true. If he and Clay are how my mother thinks men are, I can only pity her.

Tears glisten in her eyes. Knee-jerk, tired guilt kicks in, but doesn't coil in my stomach the way saying nothing did.

Mom pivots back to the mirror, propping her elbows on the counter and staring at her reflection. "I need time to myself, Samantha."

I put my hand on the door handle. "Mom?"

"What now?"

"Can you look at me?"

She meets my eyes in the mirror. "Why?"

"Face-to-face."

With a gusty sigh, Mom turns around on the bench. "Yes?"

"Tell me to my face that you think I did the wrong thing. You look at me and say that. If that's what you really believe."

Unlike my own eyes, flecked with gold and maybe green

too, Mom's are an undiluted blue. She meets my gaze, holds it for a beat, then looks away.

"I didn't tell anyone yet," Jase says when I open the window to him early that evening, the sun hanging low in the sky.

Worn out from talking with Mom, I'm simply glad I don't have to confess anything to anyone else or deal with anyone's reactions to anything.

But that selfish thought only lingers for a moment. "Why not?"

"Mom came home and went up to take a nap. She'd stayed all night last night because they had to intubate my dad because of this infection thing. I thought I'd let her sleep. But I did think about what to do next. Seems to me the talking stick is the way to go."

"The what?"

"The talking stick. It's this piece of driftwood Joel found and Alice painted when we were really little. Mom had this friend back then—with these *insane* kids—I mean 'climbing the curtains and swinging from the rafters' insane. The friend, Laurie, kinda had no idea how to handle them, so she used to follow the boys around shouting, 'This will be a topic next time we use the talking stick.' I guess they had family meetings and whoever was holding the stick got to talk about something that was 'affecting the family as a whole.' Mom and Dad used to sort of laugh about it, but then they noticed whenever we all tried to discuss something as a family, everyone spoke at once and nobody heard anyone else. So we made a talking stick of our own. We still bring it out when there's some big decision to be made or news to be told." He laughs, looking down at his feet. "Duff once said in show-and-tell that 'every time Dad brings out the big stick, Mommy's having a baby.' They had to have a teacher conference about that one."

It feels good to laugh. "Yikes." I plop down on the bed, pat the space next to me.

Jase doesn't sit. Instead, he shoves his hands in his pockets, tilting his head back against the wall. "There's this one thing I was wondering about."

I feel a shiver of apprehension. There's a note in his voice I don't recognize, something that stains the sheer pleasure of having him this close to me again.

"What?"

He flips up a corner of the rug with the toe of his Converse, then edges it back down "It's probably nothing. It just occurred to me, thinking about you coming over before. Tim knew what you had to say. You told him. First. Before you told me."

Is that unfamiliar note jealousy? Or doubt? I can't tell.

"He basically shook it out of me, wouldn't let up until I did. He's my friend." Staring at Jase's bowed head, I add, "I'm not in love with him, if that's what you think."

He looks at me then. "I think I know that. I *do* know that. But aren't you supposed to be most honest with the people you love? Isn't that the point?"

I come closer, tip my head to scan his clear green eyes.

"Tim's used to things being screwed up," I offer, finally.

"Yeah, well, I'm getting pretty used to that too. Why not tell me from the start, Sam?"

"I thought you would hate me. And Clay was going to ruin

357

the hardware store. I'd already ruined everything else. I thought it was better to leave than to have you hate me."

His forehead crinkles. "I'd hate you because of something your mother did? Or that scumbag threatened? Why? What sense would that make?"

"Nothing made sense. I was stupid and just . . . just lost. Everything was wonderful and then everything was awful. You have this happy family and it all works. I come into it and something from my world messes it all up."

Jase turns to look out the window, out over our ledge to his house.

"It's all the same world, Sam."

"Not entirely, Jase. I've got—meet-and-greets and the griffins at the B and T and pretending everything's okay when it's not and just *junk*. And you've got—"

"Debt and diapers and messy rooms and more junk," he concedes. "Why didn't you think that if it was your world, if you had to deal with it, I might care enough to want it to be mine too?"

I close my eyes, take a deep slow breath, open them to find him looking at me with so much love and trust.

"I lost faith," I say.

"And now?" he asks quietly.

I extend my hand flat, palm open, and Jase's hand closes around it. He gives a little tug, and then I am in his arms, holding on. There is no soaring music, but there is the sound of his heart, and my own.

Then my bedroom door snaps open and my mother is standing there, staring at us.

Chapter Forty-nine

"You're both here," Mom says. "Perfect."

Not what I would have imagined her saying when she caught us together in my bedroom. The astonishment on Jase's face must mirror mine.

"Clay's on his way," she continues breathlessly. "He'll be here in a few minutes. Come down to the kitchen."

Jase glances at me. I shrug. Mom heads downstairs.

Once we reach the kitchen, she turns and smiles, her social we're-all-good-friends-here smile. "Why don't we have something to drink while we're waiting? You hungry, Jase?" Her voice has that tinge of a Southern drawl that has rubbed off from Clay.

"Uh . . . not really." Jase is looking at her warily, like she's an animal whose temperament he's unsure of. She's wearing a bright lemon-yellow dress, her hair neat, her makeup flawless. A far cry from the stunned woman in her robe with the mask of skin cream I left behind just a while ago.

"Well, when Clay gets here, we'll all go in the office. Maybe I should make tea." She surveys Jase. "You don't look like a tea drinker, though. A beer?"

"I'm underage, so no, thanks, Senator Reed." Jase's voice is flat.

"You can call me Grace," Mom says, missing any sarcasm. *Ooo-kay.* Not even Nan and Tim, who have known her nearly a lifetime, are on a first-name basis with Mom. Publically, anyway.

She walks a little closer to Jase, who's standing very still, maybe in case she turns out to be one of those animals who strike without warning. "My, what broad shoulders you have."

My, what a creepy Blanche DuBois vibe you have, Mom

"What's going on here—" I start, but she cuts in.

"It's mighty hot today. Why don't I get you two some lemonade? I think we might even have cookies!"

Has she lost her mind? What's she expecting Jase to say: Are they chocolate chip? With nuts? Because if so, all's forgiven! What's a little hit and run compared to this awesome treat?

I take his hand, squeezing mine, stepping closer as we hear the front door bang open.

"Gracie?"

"In the kitchen, honey," Mom calls warmly. Clay strides in, hands in his pockets, sleeves of his button-down rolled up.

"Hi there, Jason, is it?"

"I go by Jase." Now Jase is dividing his attention between two creatures of unknown temperament. I edge closer to him and he moves forward, blocking me behind his back. I circle around, stand beside him.

"Jase it is, then," Clay says easily. "How tall are you, son?"

What's up with this sudden obsession with Jase's physique? He shoots me a look that asks: *Is he measuring me for a coffin?* But still responds politely, "Six two . . . sir."

"Basketball your game?"

360

"Football. I'm a cornerback."

"Ah—a key position. I was quarterback myself," Clay says. "I remember one time I—"

"That's great," Jase interrupts. "Could you please tell us what's going on here? I know what happened, with my dad. Sam told me."

Clay's calm, genial expression doesn't change. "Yes, so I hear. Why don't we all go into Grace's office. Gracie, sugar, you lead the way."

Mom's home office is more feminine than her work one, with pale blue walls and white linen upholstery on the couch and the chairs. Instead of an office chair, she has an ivory silk brocade armchair. She settles into this, behind the desk, while Clay sprawls back in one of the other chairs, slanting it onto its hind legs the way he always does.

Jase and I move close together on the long couch.

"So, Jase, hoping to keep on playing football in college, are you?"

"I'm not clear on why we're talking about this," Jase says. "My college career doesn't have much to do with the senator and what she did to my dad. Sir."

Clay's expression is still blandly pleasant. "I admire blunt speaking, Jase." He chuckles. "When your career's in politics, you don't hear nearly enough of it." He smiles at Jase, who returns his look stonily.

"All right, then," Clay says. "Let's be honest with one another. Jase, Samantha, Grace . . . What we have here is a situation. Something's happened, and we need to deal with it. Am I right?"

Since this generic summation could cover everything from the dog peeing on the new rug to inadvertently launching nuclear warheads, Jase and I nod.

"A wrong's been done, am I right about that too?"

I glance over at Mom, whose tongue flicks out to lick her upper lip nervously.

"Yes," I say, since Jase has returned to his wary he-could-strike-at-any-moment watching of Clay.

"Now, how many people know about this? Four, right? Or have you told anyone else, Jase?"

"Not yet." Jase's voice is steely.

"But you're planning to, because that would be the right thing to do, am I right, son?"

"I'm not your son. Yes."

Crashing the chair back to its upright position, Clay inclines forward, elbows on his knees, hands outspread as if in supplication. "There's where, with all due respect, I don't think you're thinking clearly."

"Really?" Jase asks acidly. "Where am I confused?"

"By thinking two wrongs will make a right. When you tell other people what happened, Senator Reed will assuredly suffer. She will lose the career she's dedicated her life to, the one where she serves the people of Connecticut so well. I'm not sure you've thought through, though, how much your girlfriend will suffer. If this gets out, she will, as they say, be tarred with the same brush. It's a pity, but that's what happens to the children of felons."

Mom flinches at the word *felons* but Clay continues, "Are you prepared to live with that? Everywhere Samantha goes, people will be speculating about her morals. Thinking she must not have all that many. That could be a dangerous thing for a young woman. There are men who won't hesitate to take advantage of that."

Jase looks down at his hands, which have balled into fists. But on his face there's pain, and worse—confusion.

"I don't care about that," I say. "You're being ridiculous. What are you even saying—that the whole world will assume I'm a tramp because Mom hit someone with her car? Give me a break. They must have handouts with better lines than that at Cheesy Villain School."

Jase laughs and puts his arm around me.

Unexpectedly, Clay laughs too. Mom's impassive.

"In that case, I guess offering you two hush money in unmarked bills isn't going to fly, huh?" Clay stands up, ambles behind Mom and begins massaging her shoulders. "Fine, then, where do we stand? What's your next move, Jase?"

"I'm going to tell my family. I'll let my parents decide what they want to do, once they have all the information."

"You don't need to be so defensive. Hey, I'm from the South. I admire a man who stands up for his family. It's commendable, really. So you're going to tell your folks, and, if your folks want to call a press conference and announce what they know, you're fine with that."

"That's right." Jase's arm tightens around my shoulder.

"And if the accusations don't bear weight because there are no witnesses and people think your parents are just crackpots out to make a buck, that's all good with you too?"

Uncertainty returns to Jase's face. "But . . . ?"

"There's a witness, and it's me," I point out.

Clay tilts his head, looking at me, nods once. "Right. I forgot that you had no problem betraying your mom."

"*That* line's straight out of Cheesy Villain School too," I tell him.

Mom buries her head in her hands, her shoulders shaking. "There's no point," she says. "The Garretts will hear and they'll do what they'll do and there's nothing to be done about it." She lifts her face, teary, to Clay. "Thank you for trying, though, honey."

Reaching into his pocket, he pulls out a handkerchief and gently dabs her lashes dry. "Grace, sugar, there's always a way to play it. Have a little faith. I've been in this game a while."

Mom sniffs, her eyes cast down. Jase and I exchange disbelieving looks. *Game?*

Clay hooks his thumbs in his pockets, coming around in front of the desk again, starting to pace. "Okay, Grace. What if you call the press conference—*with* the Garretts. You speak first. Confess everything. This terrible thing happened. You were wracked by guilt, but because your daughter and the Garrett boy were personally involved"—he pauses to smile at us, as if bestowing his blessing—"you kept quiet. You didn't want to taint your daughter's first true love. Everyone will identify with that—we all had that—and if we didn't, we sure wish we had. So you kept quiet for the sake of your daughter, but . . ." He paces a little more, brow puckered. ". . . you couldn't honorably represent the people with something of this magnitude on your conscience. This way's riskier, but I've seen it work.

Everybody loves a repentant sinner. You'd have your family there—your daughters standing by their mom. The Garretts, salt-of-the-earth types, the young lovers—"

"Wait just a minute here," Jase interrupts. "What Sam and I feel about each other isn't some"—he pauses, searching for words—"*marketing* tool."

Clay tosses him an amused smile. "With all due respect, son, everyone's feelings are a marketing tool. That's what marketing is all about—hitting people in the gut. Here we have the young lovers, the working family struck with an unexpected crisis—" He stops pacing, grins. "Gracie, I've got it. You could also use the moment to introduce some new legislation to help working families. Nothing too radical, just something to say Grace Reed has come through this experience with even more compassion for the people she serves. This all makes perfect sense to me now. We could get Mr. Garrett—the wounded blue-collar man—to say he wouldn't want Senator Reed's good work to be destroyed by this."

I look at Jase. His lips are slightly parted and he's staring at Clay in fascination. Sort of the way you'd look at a striking cobra.

"Then you could appeal to the people, ask them to call or write or send e-mails directly to your office if they still want you as their senator. We in the business call that the 'Send in Your Box Tops' speech. People get all het up and excited because they feel part of the process. Your office gets besieged—you lay low for a few days, then call another conference and humbly thank the citizens of Connecticut for their faith in you and pledge to be worthy of it. It's a killer moment, and at least fifty percent of the time, it makes you a shoo-in at election time," he concludes, grinning at Mom triumphantly.

She too is staring at him with her mouth open. "But . . ." she says.

Jase and I are silent.

"C'mon," Clay urges. "It makes perfect sense. It's the logical way to go."

Jase gets to his feet. I am pleased to notice that he's taller than Clay. "Everything you say makes sense, sir. I guess it's logical. But with all due respect, you're out of your fucking mind. Come on, Sam. Let's go home."

Chapter Fifty

The day has dimmed into twilight by the time we leave the house. Jase's long legs eat up the driveway and I'm nearly jogging to keep up with him. We've almost reached the Garretts' kitchen steps before I come to a standstill. "Wait."

"Sorry. I was practically towing you along. I feel like I need a shower after all that. Holy hell, Sam. What was that?"

"I know," I say. "I'm sorry." How could Clay have said all that, smooth as Kentucky bourbon, and Mom just sitting there as if she'd already drunk the bottle? I rub my forehead. "Sorry," I mutter again.

"It'd be good if you'd stop apologizing right about now," he tells me.

I take a deep breath, looking down at his shoes. "It's about all I've got. To fix things."

Jase has these huge feet. They dwarf mine. He's wearing his usual sneakers, and I'm in flip-flops. We stand toe to toe for a minute, then he edges one big foot in between my smaller ones.

"You were great back there," I say, hanging on to what's true.

He jams his hands in his pockets. "Are you kidding? You were the one who called him on his bullshit every time I

367

started to get hypnotized by his wrong-is-right, up-is-down arguments."

"Only because I'd heard 'em all before. It took me weeks to see through the hypnotism."

Jase shakes his head. "Suddenly the whole thing was a photo op. How'd he even do that? I get why Tim was so mental about that guy."

We're quiet, looking back at my house.

"My mother," I start, then stop. Despite what Clay says, that I'm a casual turncoat daughter, this isn't easy. How can Jase ever know, really understand, all those years when she did teach us well? Or the best she could.

But he waits, patient and thoughtful, until I can say more.

"She's not a monster. I want you to know that. It doesn't really matter because what she did was so wrong. But she's not an evil person. Just"—my voice wobbles—"not all that strong."

Jase reaches out, pulls the elastic band from my hair, letting it slip free over my shoulders. I've missed that gesture so much.

I didn't look over at Mom when we walked out. No point to it. Even before, when I *did* look at her face, I had no idea what to read there. "I'm guessing Mom won't want me showing up for dinner at the B and T tonight. Or when I'll be welcome at home."

"Well, you're welcome in mine." He draws me in close, hipbone to hipbone. "We can just listen to that suggestion of George's. You can move into my room, sleep in my bed. I thought that was a brilliant idea the minute he came up with it."

"George just mentioned the room, not the bed," I say.

"He did tell you I never peed in my bed. That was incentive right there."

"There are those of us who would take clean sheets as a given. We might need *more* incentive."

"I'll see what I can do," Jase says.

"Sailor Supergirl!" George shouts through the screen. "I'm going to have a baby brother! Or a sister, but I want a brother. We have a picture. Come see, come see, come see!"

I turn to Jase. "It's confirmed, then?"

"Alice shook it out of Mom with her ninja nurse tactics. Kind of like Tim with you, I guess."

George returns to the screen, squashing some printout against it. "See. This is my baby brother. He kinda looks like a storm cloud now, but he's gonna change a lot because that's what Mommy says babies do best of anything.."

Jase says, "Stand back, buddy," nudging the door open wide enough for us to pass through.

I haven't seen Joel for a while. Where he once projected all laidback cool, now he's edgy, stalking around the kitchen. Alice churns out pancakes and the younger kids sit at the table, watching as if their older siblings are Nickelodeon.

We walk in just as Joel's asking, "Why does Dad have that thing in his windpipe? He was breathing fine. Are we going backward?"

Alice edges a small, flat, very dark pancake off the pan. "The nurses explained all this."

"Not in English. Please, Al, translate?"

"It's because of the deep vein thrombosis—kind of a clot he got. They put him in those inflatable boots for that, because they didn't want to give him anti-coag drugs—"

"*English,*" Joel reiterates.

"Stuff that makes his blood thinner. Because of the head injury. They put him in the boots, but someone ignored or didn't notice the order that they were to go on and off every two hours."

"Can we sue this someone?" Joel asks angrily. "He was talking, getting better, now he's worse off than ever."

Alice chips four more skinny charcoal briquette-looking pancakes off the pan, then adds some butter. "It's good they caught it, Joey." She looks up, seeming to notice for the first time that I'm standing beside Jase.

"What are *you* doing here?"

"She belongs here," Jase says. "Drop it, Alice."

Andy starts to cry. "He doesn't look like Dad anymore."

"He does so. Look like Dad," George insists stoutly. He hands me the computer printout. "This is our baby."

"He's very cute," I tell George, scrutinizing what does, indeed, look like a hurricane off the Bahamas.

"Dad's all skinny," Andy continues. "He smells like the hospital. Looking at him freaks me out. It's like he's this old man suddenly? I don't want an old man. I want Daddy."

Jase winks at her. "He just needs more of Alice's pancakes, Ands. He'll be fine then."

"Alice makes the worst pancakes known to humankind," Joel observes. "These are like coasters."

"*I'm* cooking," Alice observes sharply. "You're what? Critiquing? Doing a restaurant review? Go get takeout, if you want to be useful. Ass-hat."

Jase glances around at his siblings, then back at me. I understand his hesitation. Though things at the Garretts' are unbalanced—mealtimes off, everyone more cranky, it all still

370

seems normal. Not right to detonate the bomb of some big announcement. Like barging into Mr. and Mrs. Capulet's argument about whether they are overpaying the nurse with *"We now interrupt this ordinary life with an epic tragedy."*

"Yo." The screen door opens, letting in Tim, laden with four pizza boxes, two cartons of ice cream, and the blue-zipped bag in which the Garretts keep the contents of the till from the hardware store balanced on top.

"Hello, hot Alice. Wanna put on your uniform and check my pulse?"

"I never play games with little boys," Alice snaps without turning around from her position at the stove, where she's still doggedly turning out pancakes.

"You should. We're full of energy. And mischief."

Alice doesn't bother to answer.

Taking the boxes, Jase begins piling them on the table, batting away his younger siblings' questing hands. "Wait till I get plates, guys! Jeez. How was the take at the end of the day?"

"Actually, surprisingly good." Tim hauls a wad of paper napkins out of his pocket and fans them out on the table. "We sold a wood chipper—that freaking big one in the back that was taking up all the space."

"No way." Jase pulls a gallon of milk out of the fridge, carefully distributing it into paper cups.

"Two-thousand-dollar way." Tim flips slices of pizza onto plates, shoving them in front of Duff, Harry, Andy, George, and the still-scowling Joel.

"Hey, kid. Good to see you here." Tim smiles at me. "Back where you belong, and all that crap."

"Mines!" Patsy shouts, pointing at Tim. He goes to her, rumples her scanty hair.

"See, hot Alice? Even the very young feel the pull of my magnetism. It's like an irresistible urge, a force like gravity, or—"

"Poop!"

"Or that." Tim removes Patsy's hand, which is now tugging up his shirt. Poor girl. She really hates drinking from bottles.

He grins at Alice. "So, hot Alice. Whaddya think? How about putting on that uniform and checking my reflexes?"

"Stop putting the moves on my sister in our kitchen, Tim. Jesus. Just so you know, Alice's nurse's uniform is a pair of green scrubs. She looks like Gumby," Jase says, returning the gallon of milk to the fridge.

"I'm starving, but I don't want pizza," Duff says heavily. "That's all we ever eat anymore. I'm sick of pizza *and* Cheerios, and those used to be my two favorite things on the planet."

"I used to think it would be fun to watch TV all the time," Harry says. "But it's not, it's boring."

"I stayed up until three last night, watching Jake Gyllenhaal movies, even the R-rated ones," Andy offers. "Nobody even noticed or told me to go to bed."

"Are we all sharing grievances now?" Joel says. "Should I get out the talking stick?"

"Well, actually," Jase begins, and then there's a knock on the door.

"Joel, did you order out even though you *knew* I was making pancakes?" Alice asks angrily.

Joel raises his hands in self-defense. "God knows I wanted to, but I hadn't gotten around to it. I swear."

The knock sounds again, and Duff opens the screen door to let in . . . my mother.

"I wondered if my daughter was here." Her gaze drifts over everyone at the table, Patsy with her hair smeared with butter, syrup, and tomato sauce; George without his shirt, little rivulets of syrup edging down his chest; Harry lunging for more pizza; Duff at his most truculent, the teary Andy. Jase, who freezes in his tracks.

"Hi, Mom."

Her eyes settle on me. "I thought I'd find you here. Hi, sweetheart."

"Yo Gracie." Tim drags an armchair from the living room to the kitchen island. "Take a load off. Let your hair down. Have a slice." He cuts a glance at my face, then Jase's, eyebrows lifting.

Jase is still staring at Mom, that confused look he had in her office returning. My mother regards the boxes of pizza as though they are alien artifacts from Roswell, New Mexico. Her preferred pizza toppings, I know, are pesto, artichoke hearts, and shrimp. Nonetheless, she sinks into the chair. "Thank you."

I look at her. This is neither the broken woman in the silk robe nor the brittle hostess offering Jase a beer. There's something in her face I haven't seen before. I glance over to find Jase still studying her too, his expression impassive.

"So, you're Sailor Supergirl's mommy." George struggles to talk around a mouth full of pizza. "We never saw you up close before. Only on TV."

My mother gives him a tiny smile. "What's your name?"

I rush through introductions. She looks so stiff and uncomfortable, immaculate and out of place in the comfortable chaos of this kitchen. "Should we go home, Mom?"

She shakes her head. "No. I'd like to meet Jase's family. Goodness. Is this all of you?"

"'Cept my daddy, cause he's in the hostible," George says chattily, getting up from the table and circling over to Mom. "And Mommy, cause she's taking a nap. And our new baby, because he's in Mommy's belly drinking her blood."

Mom pales.

Rolling her eyes, Alice says, "George, that's not how it works. I explained when you asked how the new baby ate. Nutrients go through the umbilical cord, along with Mom's blood, so—"

"I know how the baby got in there," announces Harry. "Someone told me at sailing camp. See, the dad puts—"

"Okay, guys, enough," Jase interrupts. "Settle down." He looks over at Mom again, drumming his index finger on the countertop.

Silence.

A little awkward. Not to mention unusual. George, Harry, Duff, and Andy are busy eating. Joel has unzipped the cash register bag and is sorting through the bills, separating by denomination. Tim's opened one of the cartons of ice cream and is eating directly out of it.

Which gets Alice's attention. "Do you have *any* idea how unsanitary that is?"

He drops the spoon guiltily. "Sorry. I didn't think. I just needed sugar. All I do these days is eat sweets. I may be sober, and not smoking much, but morbid obesity is my future."

Alice actually smiles at him. "That's part of the withdrawal process, Tim. Completely normal. Just . . . get yourself a bowl, okay?"

Tim grins back at her and there's this funny stillness there before Alice turns away, reaching into a drawer. "Here."

"I want ice cream. I want ice cream." George bangs his own spoon on the table.

Patsy, getting into the spirit, whacks her high chair with her hands. "Boob," she yells. "Poop."

Mom frowns.

"Her first words," I explain hastily. Then shame prickles my face. Why do I feel as though I have to explain away Patsy?

"Ah."

Jase meets my eyes. His are stormy with bafflement and pain so intense it hits me like a slap.

What is she doing here now? Jase and I were fine, we were connected, and here she is. Why?

He jerks his head toward the door. "We'd better get some more ice cream from the freezer in the garage. Come on, Sam."

There are two full cartons on the table. Alice looks down at them, then at Jase. "But—" she starts.

He shakes his head at her. "Sam?"

I follow him out. I can see a muscle jump in his jawline; feel the tension in the set of his shoulders as though they are part of my own body.

As soon as we've cleared the steps, he wheels on me. "What is this? Why is she here?"

I stumble back. "I don't know," I say. My mom's acting so normal, so calm, the friendly neighbor dropping by. But *nothing* is normal. How can she be calm?

"Is this more of Clay's bullshit?" Jase demands. "Is he having her come over here and act all nicey-nice, before everyone else finds out?"

My eyes prickle, tears so close. "I don't know," I say again.

"Like maybe my family will think that this sweet lady could never do something so bad, and I've just lost it or something and—"

I grab his hand.

"I don't know," I whisper. Could this be yet another part of Clay's game? Of course it could. I'd been thinking, somehow, that Mom was making a gesture in there . . . a peace offering, but maybe it *is* just another political tactic. My stomach coils. I don't know what to think. I don't know what to feel. The tears I've been fending off spill over. I scrub at my cheeks angrily.

"I'm sorry," Jase says, pulling me to him so my cheek rests against his chest. "Of course you don't. I just . . . seeing her sitting there in the kitchen, eating pizza as if everything's all great, it makes me—"

"Sick," I finish for him, shutting my eyes.

"For you too. Not just Dad. For you too, Sam."

I want to argue, repeat again that she's not a bad person. But if she really has come over here at Clay's bidding to show the "softer side of Grace," then . . .

"Got that ice cream?" Alice calls out the door. "I didn't think it was possible, but we'll actually be needing it."

"Uh . . . just a sec," Jase calls back, hastily lifting the garage door. He reaches into the Garretts' freezer case, always loaded from Costco, and takes out a carton. "Let's get back in before they eat the bowls." He tries for his old, easy smile, falls short.

When we return to the kitchen, George is saying to Mom, "I like this cereal called Gorilla Munch on top of my ice cream. It's not really made of gorillas."

"Oh. Well. Good."

"It's really just peanut butter and healthy stuff." George searches around in the box, tipping it, then heaps cereal into his bowl. "But if you buy boxes of cereal, you can save gorillas. And that's really good, 'cause otherwise they can get instinct."

My mother looks at me for translation. Or maybe salvation.

"Extinct," I supply.

"That's what I meant." George pours milk on top of his cereal and ice cream, then stirs it vigorously. "That means they don't mate enough and then they are dead forever."

Silence falls again. Heavy silence. *Dead forever*. That phrase seems to reverberate in the air, at least for me. Mr. Garrett lying facedown in the rain, that image Jase added to the echo of that sickening thud. Does Mom see it too? She puts down her slice of pizza, her fingers tight on a paper towel as she dabs at her lips. Jase is staring at the floor.

My mother stands up so abruptly that her chair almost overturns. "Samantha, will you come outside with me for a moment?"

Dread snags at me. *She's not going to march me home to face Clay's arm-twisting again. Please no*. I glance at Jase.

Mom bends over the table so she's eye to eye with George. "I'm sorry about your father," she tells him. "I hope he feels better soon." Then she rushes out the door, sure I'll trail after her, even after everything.

Go, Jase mouths at me, lifting his chin toward the door. A look at those eyes and it's clear; he has to know everything.

I hurry after my mom as her sandals click down the driveway. She stills, then turns slowly. It's almost fully dark now, the streetlamp casting a shallow puddle of light on the driveway.

"Mom?" I search her face.

"Those children."

"What about them?"

"I couldn't stay any longer." The words drag slowly out; then, in a rush. "Do you know Mr. Garrett's room number? He's at Maplewood Memorial, yes?"

Melodramatic scenarios crowd my mind. Clay will go there and put a pillow over Mr. Garrett's face, an air bubble in his IV. Mom will . . . I no longer have any grasp of what she'll do. Could she really come over and eat pizza and then do something terrible?

But she already has done something terrible, and then showed up with figurative lasagna. *Here I am, your good neighbor.* "Why?" I ask.

"I need to tell him what happened. What I did." She compresses her lips, her gaze drawn back to the Garretts' house, the light a perfect square in the screen door.

Oh thank God.

"Right now? You're going to tell the truth?"

"Everything," she replies in a small, soft voice. She reaches into her purse, taking out a pen and her tiny "flag this" notebook. "What's his room number?"

"He's in the ICU, Mom." My voice is sharp—how can she not remember? "You can't talk to him. They won't let you in. You're not family."

She looks at me, blinks. "I'm your *mother*."

I stare at her, completely confused, but then I realize. She thinks I meant *she* wasn't *my* family. In the moment, it feels true. And I suddenly know I'm standing somewhere very far away from her. All my strength, all my will, is diverted into defending this family. My mom . . . What she's done . . . I can't defend her.

"They won't let you into the room," is all I say. "Only his immediate relatives."

Her face twists and, with a jerk of my stomach, I interpret her expression. Some shame. Mainly relief. She won't have to face him.

My eyes fall on the van, the driver's-side door. I know who deserves the truth just as badly as Mr. Garrett, though.

Mom's hand moves convulsively to smooth the skirt of her dress.

"You need to talk to Mrs. Garrett," I say. "Tell her. She's home. You can do it now."

Again that snap of a gaze at the door, then a sharp turn of her head, as though the whole house is the scene of the accident. "I can't go in there again." Mom's hand is rigid in mine as I pull at her, trying to urge her back up the driveway. Her palm is damp. "Not with all those children."

"You have to."

"I can't."

My eyes draw back to the door too, as though I'll find the solution waiting there.

And I do. Jase, with Mrs. Garrett standing next to him. His shoulders are set, his arm tight around her.

The screen door opens and they come out.

"Senator Reed, I told my mom you had something to say."

Mom nods, her throat working. Mrs. Garrett is barefoot, her hair sleep-rumpled, her face tired but composed. Jase can't have told her.

"Yes, I—I need to speak with you," Mom says. "In private. Would you—care to come have some lemonade at my house?" She dabs at her upper lip with one knuckle, adding, "It's very humid tonight."

"You can talk here." Jase obviously doesn't want his mother within range of Clay's hypnotism. She raises her eyebrows at his tone.

"You're more than welcome to come inside, Senator," Mrs. Garrett's own voice is soothing and polite.

"It will be just the two of us," Mom assures Jase. "I'm sure my other company has left."

"Right here will be fine," he repeats. "Sam and I will keep the kids occupied inside."

"Jase—" Mrs. Garrett begins, her cheeks flushing at her unaccountably rude child.

"That's fine." Mom takes a deep breath.

Jase opens the screen door, motioning me back in. I stand for a moment, looking from my mom to Mrs. Garrett and back again. Everything about the two women profiled in the driveway is poles apart. Mom's sunny yellow sheath, her pedicured feet, Mrs. Garrett's rumpled sundress and unpolished toenails. Mom's taller, Mrs. Garrett younger. But the pucker between each of their brows is nearly identical. The apprehension washing over their faces, equal.

Chapter Fifty-one

I don't know how my mother said it, if the truth gushed or seeped from her lips. Neither Jase nor I could hear above the clatter of the kitchen, only see their silhouettes in the deepening darkness when we had a moment to steal a look as we cleaned up pizza boxes, shooed the kids into bath or bed or toward the hypnotic mumble of the television. What I know is that after about twenty minutes, Mrs. Garrett opened the screen door of the kitchen, her face giving nothing away. She told Alice and Joel she was headed to the hospital and needed them to come with her, then turned to Jase. "You'll come too?"

When they've gone, and Andy, obviously still suffering from the aftereffects of her Jake Gyllenhaal marathon, falls asleep on the couch, I hear a voice call from the back porch.

"Kid?"

I peer out the screen at the ember glow from Tim's cigarette.

"Come on out. I don't want to smoke indoors in case George wakes up, but I'm chaining, I can't stop."

I step out, surprised by how fresh the air smells, the leaves of the trees shifting against the darkened sky. I feel as though I've been locked in stale rooms, unable to breathe, for hours, days, eons. Even at McGuire Park, I couldn't take a deep breath, not with knowing what I had to say to Jase.

"Want one?" Tim asks. "You look like you're gonna puke." He offers me the crumpled pack of Marlboros.

I have to laugh. "I definitely would if I did. Too late for you to corrupt me, Tim."

"Corrupt" comes back to slap me—the Garretts know now. Have they called the police? The press? Where's Mom?

"So." Tim flicks the lighter open, crushing the previous butt under his flip-flops. "The truth is out there, huh?"

"I thought you'd gone home."

"I booked it outside when you and Grace left. Thought Jase was going to spill it all, and it was a family time and all that shit."

Yes, a nice little family gathering.

"But I didn't want to go home in case, you know, some-body needed me for something. A ride, a punching bag, sexual favors." I must make a face, because he bursts out laughing. "Alice, not *you*. Babysitting, whatever. Any of my many talents."

I'm touched. No Nan, but here is Tim. And after so much time away.

He seems to interpret my feelings, because he rushes to continue. "The sexual favor part is purely self-interest. Also, I fucking hate going to my house, so there's that . . . Where's Gracie?"

Being read her rights?

My eyes fill. I hate this.

"Hell. Not this again. Stop it." Tim waves his hand at my face frantically, as if he can shoo the emotions away like flies. "Did she go to the hospital to 'fess up?"

I explain about the ICU. He whistles. "I forgot about that. Well, is she home?"

When I tell him I have no idea, he drops the cigarette to the ground, mashes it, sets his hands on my shoulders, and turns me toward my own yard. "Go find out. I'll man the fort here."

I walk down the Garretts' driveway. Mom isn't answering her cell. Maybe it's been confiscated by the police who have already patted her down and fingerprinted her. It's ten o'clock. The Garretts left here over an hour ago.

There are no lights on at our house. No sign of Mom's car, but that could be in the garage. I climb the porch steps, planning to go through the side door and check for it, when I find her.

She's sitting on the wrought iron bench by the front door, the one she bought to reinforce the fact that we should sit there and take our shoes or boots off outdoors. She's wrapped her arms around her bent knees.

"Hi," she says, in a quiet, listless voice. Reaching beside herself, she picks something up.

A glass of white wine.

Looking at it, I feel sick again. She's sitting on the steps with chardonnay? Where's Clay? Heating up the focaccia?

When I ask, she shrugs. "Oh, I imagine he's halfway back to his summer house by now." I remember her saying that if I told, she'd lose him too. *Clay plays for the winning team.* Mom takes another sip, swirls the glass, looking into it.

"So . . . did you guys . . . break up?"

She sighs. "Not in so many words."

"What does that even mean?"

"He's not very happy with me. Though he's probably coming up with a good 'resignation from the race' speech. Clay does thrive on a challenge."

"So . . . you kicked him out? Or he left? Or what?" I want to pull the glass out of her hand and toss it off the porch.

"I told him the Garretts deserved the truth. He said truth was a flexible thing. We had words. I said I was going over to talk to you. And the Garretts. He gave me an ultimatum. I left anyway. When I came back, he was gone. He did text me, though." She reaches into the pocket of her dress, pulling out her phone as if it's proof.

I can't read the screen, but Mom continues anyway.

"Said he was still friends with all his old girlfriends." She makes a face. "I think he meant 'previous' girlfriends, since I was probably the oldest. Said he didn't believe in burning bridges. But it might be good if we 'took a little time to reassess our position.'"

Damn Clay. "So he's not going to work with you anymore?"

"He has a friend on the Christopher campaign—Marcie—who says they could use his skills."

I bet. "But . . . but Ben Christopher's a Democrat!"

"Well, yes," Mom says. "I mentioned the same thing in my little text back. Clay just said, 'It's politics, sugar. It's not personal.'" Her tone's resigned.

"What changed?" I point at the bay windows of her office, curving gracefully out to the side of our house. "In there . . . you and Clay were on the same page."

Mom licks her lips. "I don't know, Samantha. I kept thinking of his speech about how I'd done it for you. To protect you and that Garrett boy." She reaches out, sliding her palms down either side of my face, looking me in the eye, finally. "The thing is . . . you were the very last thing on my mind. When I thought of you . . ." She rubs the bridge of her nose. "All I thought was that if you hadn't been there, no one would know." Before I can respond or even let that sink in, she holds up a hand. "I know. You don't have to say anything. What kind of mother thinks that? I'm not a good mother. That's what I realized. Or a strong woman."

My stomach hurts. Though I've thought this myself, though I've just recently said it aloud to Jase, I feel sad and guilty. "You told now, Mom. That's strong. That's good."

She shrugs, brushing off the sympathy. "When I first met Clay this spring, I stalled on mentioning I had teenagers. The truth was just . . . inconvenient. That I was in my forties with nearly grown daughters." She gives a little rueful laugh. "That seemed like a big issue then."

"Does Tracy know?"

"She'll be home tomorrow morning. I called her after I got home."

I try to picture Tracy's reaction. My sister, the future lawyer. Horrified at Mom? Devastated at having her summer interrupted? Or something else entirely. Something I can't even picture? Oh Trace. I've missed her so much.

"What did Mrs. Garrett say? What happens now?"

She takes another big sip of wine. Not reassuring.

"I don't want to think about that," she says. "We'll know

soon enough." She straightens her legs, stands up. "It's late. You should be in bed."

Her motherly, admonishing tone. After all this, it seems ridiculous. But when I see the slump of her shoulders as she reaches for the doorknob, I can only tell her another truth, however inconvenient.

"I love you, Mom."

She inclines her head, acknowledging, then ushers me into the chill of the central air. Turning to lock the door firmly behind her, she sighs, "I just knew it."

"Knew what?" I ask, turning.

"Knew no good would come of getting to know those people next door."

Chapter Fifty-two

Contrary to Clay's predictions, the Garretts don't call a press conference the next day. Or go directly to the police. They do, after all, bring out the talking stick. There's a family conference at the hospital, with all the children down to Duff. Alice and Joel want to report Mom immediately. Andy and Jase argue against it. Ultimately, Mr. and Mrs. Garrett decide to keep the matter private. Mom had offered to cover all the medical bills and the additional expenses of hiring someone to work at the store, Jase tells me, and his parents struggle with that. Mr. Garrett doesn't want charity—or hush money.

For a week, they discuss it as a family. Mr. Garrett is moved from the ICU and Mom goes to visit.

Even Jase doesn't know what passes between them, but the next day Mom resigns from the race.

Just as she said he would, Clay writes the speech for her. "Certain events in my family have convinced me that I must decline the honor of running for office once again in the hope of serving as your senator. Public servants are also private individuals, and as such I must do the right thing for the people closest to home, before I try to serve the wider world."

There's a lot of lurid speculation in the press—I guess there always is, when a politician resigns unexpectedly—but it dies down after a few weeks.

I expect her to take a cruise, that trip to Virgin Gorda, escape, but instead she spends a lot of time at our house, fixing up the garden she used to care about before she got so busy in politics. She makes dinner for the Garretts, and hands it to me to bring over until Duff gets as sick of sun-dried tomatoes, goat cheese, and puff pastry as he'd ever been of pizza. She asks me how Mr. Garrett is doing, averting her eyes. When Jase offers to mow our lawn, she tells me to thank him, but "we have a service."

You'd think, after all the years I've come to the B&T, all the Friday night hornpipe dinners, the holiday festivities, the hours logged in and by the pools, that I would have missed it more since I hung up my uniform and said good-bye to Mr. Lennox. But though Mom decides it's the only possible place to go for a last family dinner before Tracy leaves for college, I don't feel a rush of nostalgia as we open the heavy oak doors to the dining room, just surprise that it's all exactly the same. The soft classical music played low enough to be nearly subliminal, the loud laughter from the bar, the chink of silverware. The smell of lemon oil and overstarched tablecloths and prime rib.

Tracy is leading the way, which is different. Mom follows. We get our usual maitre d', but he doesn't take us to the table that's always been ours, below the sea of harpooned whales and unlucky sailors. Instead he leads us to a smaller corner table.

"I'm very sorry," he tells Mom. "You haven't been here in

a while, and we've become accustomed to giving this table to Mr. Lamont—he comes in every Friday."

Mom looks down at her hands, then abruptly back up at him. "Of course. Naturally. This is fine. Better. More privacy."

She sinks into the chair that doesn't face the rest of the room, shaking out her napkin.

"We were very sorry to hear that you won't be representing us again, Senator Reed," he adds gently.

"Ah. Well. Time to move on." Mom reaches for the bread basket, and butters a roll with enormous concentration. Then she eats it as though it's her last meal. Tracy raises her eyebrows at me. We do a lot of that these days. Our house is a quiet minefield. Trace can't wait to escape to Middlebury, and I can't blame her.

"Speaking of which," Tracy says, "I'm changing up some college plans."

Mom puts down the last bite of her roll. "No," she says faintly.

Tracy just looks at her. Like Mom has lost her right to say no or yes to anything, which has pretty much been her stance since she returned from the Vineyard. And Mom looks away.

"Flip's transferring up to Vermont. To be with me. He's got a great job as a manny for some professors in the English department. We're going to get an apartment together."

Mom doesn't seem to know where to start with this. Finally, she says, "A manny?"

"That's right, Mom." Tracy closes her menu. "And an apartment together."

At first glance, you could mistake this for their old battle: Tracy reserving her right to rebel, and Mom refusing to let her. But these days my mother always blinks first. She looks down at the napkin in her lap now, takes a careful sip of water, then says, "Oh. Well. That *is* news."

Pause while the waiter takes our orders. We are still too well bred or well trained to show visible emotion in front of the waitstaff. When he departs, though, Mom reaches for the silk cardigan sweater she's draped over the back of her seat, fumbling in the pocket.

"I guess, then, it's a good time to show you this." She carefully unfolds a sheet of paper, smoothes it with her hand, and positions it between Tracy and me.

"For sale. Your house of dreams. Nestled on a quiet cul-de-sac in one of Connecticut's most exclusive towns, this jewel of a home features the best of everything—top-of-the-line amenities, prime location near the boardwalk and beach, hard-wood floors, everything of the highest quality. For price, please inquire of Postscript Realty."

I'm staring, not really getting it, but Tracy does, immediately.

"You're selling our house? We're moving?"

"Samantha and I will be moving. You will already be gone," Mom says, with a ghost of her old sharp tone.

It's only then that I actually recognize our house in the picture, caught from a slant, a view I rarely see anymore—the opposite side from the Garretts.

"It makes sense," Mom says briskly as the waiter soundlessly slides her plate of field greens in front of her. "Too much house for two people. Too much . . ." Her voice fades and she stabs at a piece of dried cranberry. "They give it a month to sell, tops," she says.

"A month!" Tracy explodes. "In Samantha's last year of high school? Where are you going to go?"

Mom finishes chewing her forkful of salad, dabs at her lips. "Oh, maybe those new condominiums over by the inlet. Just until we get our bearings. It won't change anything for Samantha. She'll still go to Hodges."

"Right," Tracy mutters. "God, Mom. Hasn't enough changed for Samantha already?"

I don't say anything, but in a way Tracy's right. Who was that girl who trailed in here at the beginning of the summer, with Nan, her best friend, fretting about Tim, baffled by Clay, keeping secret her crush?

But then, that's exactly it, isn't it? Everything big *has* already changed.

Our house was Mom's work of art, her testament to the fact that she deserved the best of everything. But what I loved was the view. And for so long, that was who I was. The girl who watched the Garretts. My life next door.

But I'm not that watcher anymore. What Jase and I have is real and alive. It has nothing to do with how things look from far away and everything to do with how they are up close. That won't change.

Chapter Fifty-three

Now it's early dawn, Labor Day weekend. School starts tomorrow, with its cavalcade of homework and AP classes and expectations. When I open my eyes I can already feel the change, the lazy air deepened now, New England's summer days yielding to the crispness of fall. I bike to the ocean for a predawn swim, focusing on my strokes, then floating in the waves, looking up at the stars fading in the sky. I *will* make swim team this fall.

I'm back home before the sun has fully risen and just out of the shower when I hear him.

"Samantha! Sam!" I rub my towel over my hair and walk to the window. It's still dark but lightening up enough that I can see Jase standing below by the trellis, something in his hand.

"Step aside for a sec," he calls up to me.

When I do, a newspaper swings up and in the window, in a perfect arc.

I pop my head back out. "What an arm! But I don't subscribe to the *Stony Bay Bugle*."

"Look inside."

Snapping off the rubber band, I unroll the paper. Inside is a perfect puff of Queen Anne's lace, fragile and blooming around

392

a center as green as spring, with a note around the stem. *Come next door. Your chariot awaits.*

I climb down the trellis. There, in the Garretts' driveway, is the Mustang, the shredded seats replaced by smooth brown leather, the front part painted a dazzling racing green.

"She's beautiful," I say.

"I wanted to wait till it was perfect, new paint job everywhere. Then I realized perfect could be too long."

"No dancing hula girls yet," I note.

"If you feel like dancing—or doing the hula—be my guest. Although the front seat is kinda cramped. You might have to go for the hood."

I laugh. "And scratch that paint job? No way."

"Come on." He opens the side door with a flourish, ushering me in, then jumps in himself, vaulting easily over the driver's-side door.

"Suave," I say, laughing.

"Right, huh? I practiced. Key to avoid landing on the stick shift."

I'm still laughing as he turns the key in the ignition and the car roars to life.

"She runs!"

"Of course," Jase says smugly. "Buckle up. I've got something else to show you."

The town is still and quiet as we ride through the streets, too early for stores to open, too early for Breakfast Ahoy to unfurl its awning. But the paper boys have already done their job.

We drive down the long shore road and wind up in the beach parking lot, near the Clam Shack, where we had our first date.

"Come on, Sam."

I take Jase's hand and we walk on the beach. The sand is cool, firm, and damp from the receding tide, but there is that shimmer of heat in the air that tells you it's going to be a scorching day.

We walk out on the rocky path to the lighthouse. It's still fairly dark, and Jase holds a steadying hand to my waist as we clamber over the huge crooked stones. When we get to the lighthouse, he pulls me toward the black enameled pipes that form the ladder that takes you to the roof.

"You first," he says. "I'm right behind you."

At the top, we duck into the room where the huge light faces the ocean, then climb out on the gently slanted roof. Jase looks at his watch. "In ten, nine, eight . . ."

"Is something going to blow up?" I ask.

"Shh. Perks of being a paperboy. I know exactly when this happens. Shh, Samantha. Watch."

We lie back, hand in hand, look out over the ocean, and watch the sun rise over the roof of the world.

ACKNOWLEDGMENTS

Though I never thought writing was a solitary job involving the author and a drafty garret, I had no idea before this book just how many people I needed in order to translate the words I wrote into the book in your hands. I've been beyond lucky.

I'll start with my amazing and infinitely supportive agent, Christina Hogrebe of the Jane Rotrosen Agency. She brilliantly balances knowing the marketplace with thoughtful story analysis and nervous-author support. She is absolutely magical.

Meg Ruley and Annelise Robey, also of Jane Rotrosen, who said those magic words—"you definitely have 'it'"—that kept me writing. Carlie Webber brought her YA expertise and her savvy questions behind the scenes, helping more than I can say.

And then there is Jessica Garrison, my editor. It was one of the luckiest days of my life when she read *My Life Next Door* and put her talent and skill behind it. There isn't a page of this book that hasn't been improved by Jess's eagle eye, attention to detail, and creative flair.

"Thank you" is insufficient for the whole team at Dial/Penguin Books for Young Readers. Regina Castillo's supernatural memory for both grammar and plot points saved me from many a mistake. Kathy Dawson and Jackie Engel both believed in this book even during its awkward adolescence. Theresa Evangelista gave me an even better cover than I could have imagined, and Jasmin Rubero gave my words such a gorgeous look.

This story would never have made its way to the final chapter without the patience and honesty of my beloved FTHRWA critique group. They supplied everything from updated teen slang to unstinting hand-holding. Thank you Ginny Lester, Ana Morgan, Morgan (Carole) Wyatt, Amy Villalba, Jaclyn Di Bona, and Ushma Kothari. Plus my hometown friends, who handed on essential knowledge about the innards of cars, the workings of the teenaged mind, and the consequences of medical disasters.

And then there's CTRWA. After the first meeting, I called my husband and said "I've found my people," and you guys have been that and more. An extra shout-out to Jessica Anderson, who honed my pitch, to Toni Andrews, who put up with endless newbie questions.

Like her footwear, Kristan Higgins's generosity toward new writers is rightfully the stuff of legend. Kristan always went beyond the call of duty. I thank her and the talented clones she MUST have. Right?

Finally, Gay Thomas and Rhonda Pollero were utterly unswerving in their kindness all through my trip from their fortunate editor to fellow author. Like Charlotte the spider, they are both rock-solid friends, and amazing writers. I'm honored and lucky to know them.

As for my children—you give me endless laughs, every best moment, and constant reminders of what really counts. I love you more than anything.

My sister, deLancey, held my hand and looked out for me through this whole process. How lucky I am to have a sibling so fiercely protective, fearlessly honest, and fantastically funny. Who never dated blond tennis players. Of course not.

My father—who has always been my hero. And Georgia, my beloved stepmother.

And my husband, John, who took me at my word on our first date when I said "I am a writer" and never stopped pushing me to make that boast real. You are my most faithful fan, my biggest PR agent, and kindest critic.

Turn the page for a look at
Huntley Fitzpatrick's
utterly romantic companion to
MY LIFE NEXT DOOR—

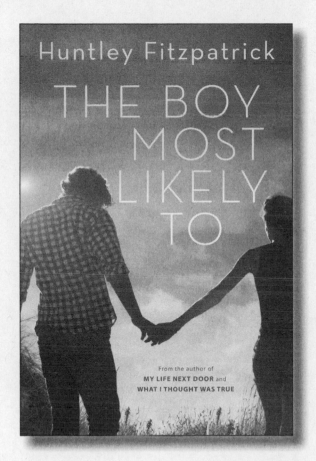

Chapter One

I've been summoned to see the Nowhere Man.

He's at his desk when I step inside the gray cave of his office, his back turned.

"Uh, Pop?"

He holds up his hand, keeps scribbling on a blue-lined pad. Standard operating procedure.

I flick my eyes around the room: the mantel, the carpet, the bookshelves, the window; try to find a comfortable place to land.

No dice.

Ma's fond of "cute"—teddy bears in seasonal outfits and pillows with little sayings and shit she gets on QVC. They're everywhere. Except here, a room spliced out of John Grisham, all leather-bound, only muted light through the shades. August heat outdoors, but no hint of that allowed here. I face the rear of Pop's neck, hunch further into the gray, granite-hard sofa, rub my eyes, sink back on my elbows.

On his desk, three pictures of Nan, my twin, at various ages—poofy red curls, missing teeth, then baring them in braces. Always worried eyes. Two more of her on the wall, straightened hair, expensive white smile, plus a framed newspaper clipping of her after delivering a speech at this summer's Stony Bay Fourth of July thing.

No pics of me.

Were there ever? Can't remember. In the bad old days, I always got high before a father/son office visit.

Clear my throat.

Crack my knuckles.

"Pop? You asked to see me?"

He actually startles. "Tim?"

"Yep."

Swiveling the chair, he looks at me. His eyes, like Nan's and my own, are gray. Match his hair. Match his office.

"So," he says.

I wait. Try not to scope out the bottle of Macallan on the . . . what do you call it. Sidebar? Sideboard? Generally, Ma brings in the ice in the little silver bucket thing ten minutes after he gets home from work, six p.m., synched up like those weird-ass cuckoo clock people who pop out of their tiny wooden doors, dead on schedule when the clock strikes, so Pop can have the first of his two scotches ready to go.

Today must be special. It's only three o'clock and there's the bucket, oozing cool sweat like I am. Even when I was little I knew he'd leave the second drink half-finished. So I could slurp down the last of the scotchy ice water without him knowing while he was washing his hands before dinner. Can't remember when I started doing that, but it was well before my balls dropped.

"Ma said you wanted to talk."

He brushes some invisible whatever from his knee, like his attention's already gone. "Did she say why?"

2

I clear my throat again. "Because I'm moving out? Planning to do that. Today." Ten minutes ago, ideally.

His eyes return to mine. "Do you think this is the best choice for you?"

Classic Nowhere Man. Moving out was hardly my choice. His ultimatum, in fact. The only "best choice" I've made lately was to stop drinking. Etc.

But Pop likes to tack and turn, and no matter that this was his order, he can shove that rudder over without even looking and make me feel like shit.

"I asked you a question, Tim."

"It's fine. It's a good idea."

Pop steeples his fingers, sets his chin on them, my chin, cleft and all. "How long has it been since you got kicked out of Ellery Prep?"

"Uh. Eight months." Early December. Hadn't even unpacked my suitcase from Thanksgiving break.

"Since then you've had how many jobs?"

Maybe he doesn't remember. I fudge it. "Um. Three."

"Seven," Pop corrects.

Damn.

"How many of those were you fired from?"

"I still have the one at—"

He pivots in his chair, halfway back to his desk, frowns down at his cell phone. "How many?"

"Well, I quit the senator's office, so really only five."

Pop twists back around, lowers the phone, studies me over his reading glasses. "I'm very clear on the fact that you left that job. You say 'only' like it's something to brag about. Fired from five out of seven jobs since February. Kicked out of three schools . . . Do you know that I've never been let go from a job in my life? Never gotten a bad performance review? A grade lower than a B? Neither has your sister."

Right. Perfect old Nano. "My grades were always good," I say. My eyes stray again to the Macallan. Need something to do with my hands. Rolling a joint would be good.

"Exactly," Pop says. He jerks from the chair, nearly as angular and almost as tall as me, drops his glasses on the desk with a clatter, runs his hands quickly through his short hair, then focuses on scooping out ice and measuring scotch.

I catch a musky, iodine-y whiff of it, and man, it smells good.

"You're not stupid, Tim. But you sure act that way."

Yo-kay . . . He's barely spoken to me all summer. *Now* he's on my nuts? But I should try. I drag my eyes off the caramel-colored liquid in his glass and back to his face.

"Pop. Dad. I know I'm not the son you would have . . . special ordered—"

"Would you like a drink?"

He sloshes more scotch into another glass, uncharacteristically careless, sets it out on the Columbia University coaster on the side table next to the couch, slides it toward me. He tips his own glass to his lips, then places it neatly on his coaster, almost completely chugged.

Well, this is fucked up.

"Uh, look." My throat's so tight, my voice comes out weird—husky, then high-pitched. "I haven't had a drink or anything like that since the end of June, so that's, uh, fifty-nine days, but who's counting. I'm doing my best. And I'll—"

Pop has steepled his hands and is scrutinizing the fish tank against the wall.

I'm boring him.

"And I'll keep doin' it . . ." I trail off.

There's a long pause. During which I have no idea what he's thinking. Only that my best friend is on his way over, and my Jetta in the driveway is seeming more and more like a getaway car.

"Four months," Pop says, in this, like, flat voice, like he's reading it off a piece of paper. Since he's turned back to look down at his desk, it's possible.

"Um . . . yes . . . What?"

"I'm giving you four months from today to pull your life together. You'll be eighteen in December. A man. After that, unless I see you acting like one—in every way—I'm cutting off your allowance, I'll no longer pay your health and car insurance, and I'll transfer your college fund into your sister's."

Not as though there was ever a welcome mat under me, but whatever the fuck was there has been yanked out and I'm slammed down hard on my ass.

Wait . . . what?

A man by December. Like, poof, snap, shazam. Like there's some expiration date on . . . where I am now.

"But—" I start.

He checks his Seiko, hitting a button, maybe starting the countdown. "Today is August twenty-fourth. That gives you until just before Christmas."

"But—"

He holds up his hand, like he's slapping the off button on my words. It's ultimatum number two or nothing.

No clue what to say anyway, but it doesn't matter, because the conversation is over.

We're done here.

Unfold my legs, yank myself to my feet, and I head for the door on autopilot.

Can't get out of the room fast enough.

For either of us, apparently.

Ho, ho, ho to you too, Pop.

Chapter Two

"You're really doing this?"

I'm shoving the last of my clothes into a cardboard box when my ma comes in, without knocking, because she never does. Risky as hell when you have a horny seventeen-year-old son. She hovers in the doorway, wearing a pink shirt and this denim skirt with—what are those? Crabs?—sewn all over it.

"Just following orders, Ma." I cram flip-flops into the stuffed box, push down on them hard. "Pop's wish is my command."

She takes a step back like I've slapped her. I guess it's my tone. I've been sober nearly two months, but I have yet to go cold turkey on assholicism. Ha.

"You had so much I never had, Timothy . . ."

Away we go.

". . . private school, swimming lessons, tennis camp . . ."

Yep, I'm an alcoholic high school dropout, but check out my backhand!

She shakes out the wrinkles in a blue blazer, one quick motion, flapping it into the air with an abrasive crack. "What are you going to do—keep working at that hardware store? Going to those meetings?"

She says "hardware store" like "strip club" and "going to

those meetings" like "making those sex tapes."

"It's a good job. And I need those meetings."

Ma's hands start smoothing my stack of folded clothes. Blue veins stand out on her freckled, pale arms. "I don't see what strangers can do for you that your own family can't."

I open my mouth to say: "I know you don't. That's why I need the strangers." Or: "Uncle Sean sure could have used those strangers." But we don't talk about that, or him.

I shove a pair of possibly too-small loafers in the box and go over to give her a hug.

She pats my back, quick and sharp, and pulls away.

"Cheer up, Ma. Nan'll definitely get into Columbia. Only one of your children is a fuck-up."

"Language, Tim."

"Sorry. My bad. Cock-up."

"That," she says, "is even worse."

Okeydokey. Whatever.

My bedroom door flies open—*again* no knock.

"Some girl who sounds like she has laryngitis is on the phone for you, Tim," Nan says, eyeing my packing job. "God, everything's going to be all wrinkly."

"I don't care—" But she's already dumped the cardboard box onto my bed.

"Where's your suitcase?" She starts dividing stuff into piles. "The blue plaid one with your monogram?"

"No clue."

"I'll check the basement," Ma says, looking relieved to have a reason to head for the door. "This girl, Timothy? Should I bring you the phone?"

I can't think of any girl I have a thing to say to. Except Alice Garrett. Who definitely would not be calling me.

"Tell her I'm not home."

Permanently.

Nan's folding things rapidly, piling up my shirts in order of style. I reach out to still her hands. "Forget it. Not important."

She looks up. Shit, she's crying.

We Masons cry easily. Curse of the Irish (one of 'em). I loop one elbow around her neck, thump her on the back a little too hard. She starts coughing, chokes, gives a weak laugh.

"You can come visit me, Nano. Any time you need to . . . escape . . . or whatever."

"Please. It won't be the same," Nan says, then blows her nose on the hem of my shirt.

It won't. No more staying up till nearly dawn, watching old Steve McQueen movies because I think he's badass and Nan thinks he's hot. No Twizzlers and Twix and shit appearing in my room like magic because Nan knows massive sugar infusions are the only sure cure for drug addiction.

"Lucky for you. No more covering my lame ass when I stay out all night, no more getting creative with excuses when I don't show for something, no more me bumming money off you constantly."

Now she's wiping her eyes with my shirt. I haul it off, hand it to her. "Something to remember me by."

She actually folds *that*, then stares at the neat little square, all sad-faced. "Sometimes it's like I'm missing everyone I ever met. I actually even miss Daniel. I miss Samantha."

"Daniel was a pompous prickface and a crap boyfriend.

9

Samantha, your actual best friend, is ten blocks and ten minutes away—shorter if you text her."

She blows that off, hunkers down, pulling knobbly knees to her chest and lowering her forehead so her hair sweeps forward to cover her blotchy face. Nan and I are both ginger, but she got all the freckles, everywhere, while mine are only across my nose. She looks up at me with that face she does, all pathetic and quivery. I hate that face. It always wins.

"You'll be fine, Nan." I tap my temple. "You're just as smart as me. Much less messed up. At least as far as most people know."

Nan twitches back. We lock eyes. The elephant in the room lies bleeding out on the floor between us. Then she looks away, gets busy picking up another T-shirt to fold expertly, like the only thing that matters in the world is for the sleeves to align.

"Not really," she says in a subdued voice. Not taking the bait there either, I guess.

I grope around the quilt on my bed, locate my cigs, light one, and take a deep drag. I know it's all kinds of bad for me, but *God*, how does anyone get through the day without smoking? Setting the smoldering butt down in the ashtray, I tap her on the back again, gently this time.

"Hey now. Don't stress. You know Pop. He wants to add it up and get a positive bottom line. Job. High school diploma. College-bound. Check, check, check. It only has to *look* good. I can pull that off."

Don't know if this is cheering my sister up, but as I talk, the squirming fireball in my stomach cools and settles. Fake it. That I can do.

Mom pops her head into the room. "That Garrett boy's here. Heavens, put on a shirt, Tim." She digs in a bureau drawer and thrusts a Camp Wyoda T-shirt I thought I'd ditched years ago at me. Nan leaps up, knuckling away her tears, pulling at her own shirt, wiping her palms on her shorts. She has a zillion twitchy habits—biting her nails, twisting her hair, tapping her pencils. I could always get by on a fake ID, a calm face, and a smile. My sister could look guilty saying her prayers. Feet on the stairs, staccato knock on the door—the one person who knocks!—and Jase comes in, swipes back his damp hair with the heel of one hand.

"Shit, man. We haven't even started loading and you're already sweating?"

"Ran here," he says, hands planted hard his on kneecaps. He glances up. "Hey, Nan."

Nan, who has turned her back, gives a quick, jerky nod. When she twists around to tumble more neatly balled socks into my cardboard box, her eyes stray to Jase, up, slowly down. He's the guy girls always look at twice.

"You ran here? It's like five miles from your house! Are you nuts?"

"Three, and nah." Jase braces his forearm against the wall, bending his leg, holding his ankle, stretching out. "Seriously out of shape after sitting around the store all summer. Even after three weeks of training camp, I'm nowhere near up to speed."

"You don't *seem* out of shape," Nan says, then shakes her head so her hair slips forward over her face. "Don't leave without telling me, Tim." She scoots out the door.

"You set?" Jase looks around the room, oblivious to my sister's hormone spike.

"Uh . . . I guess." I look around too, frickin' blank. All I can think to take is my clamshell ashtray. "The clothes, anyway. I suck at packing."

"Toothbrush?" Jase suggests mildly. "Razor. Books, maybe? Sports stuff."

"My lacrosse stick from Ellery Prep? Don't think I'll need it." I tap out another cigarette.

"Bike? Skateboard? Swim gear?" Jase glances over at me, smile flashing in the flare of my lighter.

Mom barges back in so fast, the door knocks against the wall. An umbrella and a huge yellow slicker are draped over one arm, an iron in one hand. "You'll want these. Should I pack you blankets? What happened to that nice boy you were going to move in with, anyway?"

"Didn't work out." As in: That nice boy, my AA buddy Connell, relapsed on both booze and crack, called me all slurry and screwed up, full of blurry suck-ass excuses, so he's obviously out. The garage apartment is my best option.

"Is there even any heat in that ratty place?"

"Jesus God, Ma. You haven't even seen the frickin'—"

"It's pretty reliable," Jase says, not even wincing. "It was my brother's, and Joel likes his comforts."

"All right. I'll . . . leave you two boys to—carry on." She pauses, runs her hand through her hair, showing half an inch of gray roots beneath the red. "Don't forget to take the stenciled paper Aunt Nancy sent in case you need to write thank-you notes."

12

"Wouldn't dream of it, Ma. Uh, forgetting, I mean."

Jase bows his head, smiling, then shoulders the cardboard box.

"What about pillows?" she says. "You can tuck those right under the other arm, can't you, a big strapping boy like you?"

Christ.

He obediently raises an elbow and she rams two pillows into his armpit.

"I'll throw all this in the Jetta. Take your time, Tim."

I scan the room one last time. Tacked to the corkboard over my desk is a sheet of paper with the words *THE BOY MOST LIKELY TO* scrawled in red marker at the top. One of the few days last fall I remember clearly—hanging with a bunch of my (loser) friends at Ellery out by the boathouse where they stowed the kayaks (and the stoners). We came up with our antidote to those stupid yearbook lists: *Most likely to be a millionaire by twenty-five. Most likely to star in her own reality show. Most likely to get an NFL contract.* Don't know why I kept the thing.

I pop the list off the wall, fold it carefully, jam it into my back pocket.

Nan emerges as soon as Jase, who's been waiting for me in the foyer, opens the creaky front door to head out.

"Tim," she whispers, cool hand wrapping around my forearm. "Don't vanish." As if when I leave our house I'll evaporate like fog rising off the river.

Maybe I will.

By the time we pull into the Garretts' driveway, I've burned through three cigarettes, hitting up the car lighter for the next before I've chucked the last. If I could have smoked all of them at once, I would've.

"You should kick those," Jase says, looking out the window, not pinning me with some accusatory face.

I make to hurl the final butt, then stop myself.

Yeah, toss it next to little Patsy's Cozy Coupe and four-year-old George's midget baby blue bike with training wheels. Plus, George thinks I've quit.

"Can't," I tell him. "Tried. Besides, I've already given up drinking, drugs, and sex. Gotta have a few vices or I'd be too perfect."

Jase snorts. "Sex? Don't think you have to give *that* up." He opens the passenger-side door, starts to slide out.

"The way I did it, I do. Gotta stop messing with any chick with a pulse."

Now *Jase* looks uncomfortable. "That was an addiction too?" he asks, half in, half out the door, nudging the pile of old newspapers on the passenger side with the toe of one Converse.

"Not in the sense that I, like, had to have it, or whatever. It was just . . another way to blow stuff off. Numb out."

He nods like he gets it, but I'm pretty sure he doesn't. Gotta explain. "I'd get wasted at parties. Hook up with girls I didn't like or even know. It was never all that great."

"Guess not"—he slides out completely—"if you're with someone you don't even like or know. Might be different if you were sober and actually cared."

"Yeah, well." I light up one last cigarette. "Don't hold your breath."

Chapter Three

"There is," I say through my teeth, "an owl in the freezer. Can any of you guys explain this to me?"

Three of my younger brothers stare back at me. Blank walls. My younger sister doesn't look up from texting.

I repeat the question.

"Harry put it there," Duff says.

"Duff told me to," Harry says.

George, my youngest brother, cranes his neck. "What kind of owl? Is it dead? Is it white like Hedwig?"

I poke at the rock-solid owl, which is wrapped in a frosty freezer bag. "Very dead. Not white. And someone ate all the frozen waffles and put the box back in empty again."

They all shrug, as if this is as much of an unsolvable mystery as the owl.

"Let's try again. *Why* is this owl in the freezer?"

"Harry's going to bring it in for show-and-tell when school starts," Duff says.

"Sanjay Sapati brought in a seal skull last year. This is way better. You can still see its eyeballs. They're only a little rotted." Harry stirs his oatmeal, frowning down at what I've tried to pass off as a fun "breakfast for lunch" occasion. He upturns the spoon, shakes it, but the glob of cereal sticks, thick as paste, stubborn as my brother. Harry holds the spoon out toward me, accusingly.

"You get what you get and you don't get upset," I say to him.

"But I do. I do get upset. This is nasty, Alice."

"Just eat it," I say, clinging to patience with all my fingernails. This is all temporary. Just until Dad gets a bit better, until Mom doesn't have to be in three places at once. "It's healthy," I add, but I have to agree with my seven-year-old brother. We're way overdue for a grocery run. The fridge has nothing but eggs, applesauce, and ketchup, the cabinet is bare of anything but Joel's protein-enhanced oatmeal. And the only thing in the freezer is . . . a dead bird.

"We can't have an owl in here, guys." I scramble for Mom's reasonable tone. "It'll make the ice cream taste bad."

"Can we have ice cream instead of this?" Harry pushes, sticking his spoon into the oatmeal, where it pokes out like a gravestone on a gray hill.

I try to sell it as "the kind of porridge the Three Bears ate," but George and Harry are skeptical, Duff, at eleven, is too old for all that, and Andy wrinkles her nose and says, "I'll eat later. I'm too nervous now anyway."

"It's lame to be nervous about Kyle Comstock," Duff says. "He's a boob."

"*Boooooob*," Patsy repeats from her high chair, the eighteen-month-old copycat.

"You don't understand anything," Andy says, leaving the kitchen, no doubt to try on yet another outfit before sailing camp awards. Six hours away from now.

16

"Who cares what she wears? It's the stupid sailing awards," Duff grumbles. "This stuff is vomitous, Alice. It's like gruel. Like what they make Oliver Twist eat."

"*He* wanted more," I point out.

"He was *starving*," Duff counters.

"Look, stop arguing and eat the damn stuff."

George's eyes go big. "Mommy doesn't say that word. Daddy says not to."

"Well, they aren't here, are they?"

George looks mournfully down at his oatmeal, poking at it with his spoon like he might find Mom and Dad in there.

"Sorry, Georgie," I say repentantly. "How about some eggs, guys?"

"No!" they all say at once. They've had my eggs before. Since Mom has been spending a lot of time at either doctors' appointments for herself or doctor and physical therapy consults for Dad, they've suffered through the full range of my limited culinary talents.

"I'll get rid of the owl if you give us money to eat breakfast in town," Duff says.

"Alice, look!" Andy says despairingly, "I knew this wouldn't fit." She hovers in the doorway in the sundress I loaned her, the front sagging. "When do I get off the itty-bitty-titty committee? You did before you were even thirteen." She sounds accusatory, like I used up the last available bigger chest size in the family.

"Titty committee?" Duff starts laughing. "Who's on that? I bet Joel is. And Tim."

"You are *so* immature that listening to you actually makes *me* younger," Andy tells him. "Alice, help! I love this dress. You never lend it to me. I'm going to die if I can't wear it." She looks wildly around the kitchen. "Do I stuff it? With what?"

"Breadcrumbs?" Duff is still cracking up. "Oatmeal? Owl feathers?"

I point the oatmeal spoon at her. "Never stuff. Own your size."

"I want to wear this dress." Andy scowls at me. "It's perfect. Except it doesn't fit. There. Do you have anything else? That's flatter?"

"Did you ask Samantha?" I glare at Duff, who is shoving several kitchen sponges down his shirt. Harry, who doesn't get what's going on—I hope—but is happy to join in on tormenting Andy, is wadding up some diapers from Patsy's clean stack and following suit. My brother's girlfriend has much more patience than I do. Maybe because Samantha only has one sibling to deal with.

"She's helping her mom take her sister to college—she probably won't be back till tonight. Alice! What do I do?"

My jaw clenches at the mere mention of Grace Reed, Sam's mom, the closest thing our family has to a nemesis. Or maybe it's the owl. *God. Get me out of here.*

"I'm hungry," Harry says. "I'm starving here. I'll be dead by night."

"It takes three weeks to starve," George tells him, his air of authority undermined by his hot cocoa mustache.

"Ughhh. No one cares!" Andy storms away.

"She's got the hormones going on," Duff confides to Harry. Ever since hearing it from my mother, my little brothers treat "hormones" like a contagious disease.

My cell phone vibrates on the cluttered counter. Brad again. I ignore it, start banging open cabinets. "Look, guys, we're out of everything, got it? We can't go shopping until we get this week's take-home from the store, and no one has time to go anyway. I'm not giving you money. So it's oatmeal or empty stomachs. Unless you want peanut butter on toast."

"Not again," Duff groans, shoving away from the table and stalking out of the kitchen.

"Gross," Harry says, doing the same, after accidentally knocking over his orange juice—and ignoring it.

How does Mom stand this? I pinch the muscles at the base of my neck, hard, close my eyes. Push away the most treacherous thought of all: *Why* does Mom stand this?

George is still doggedly trying to eat a spoonful of oatmeal, one rolled oat at a time.

"Don't bother, G. You still like peanut butter, right?"

Breathing out a long sigh, world-weary at four, George rests his freckled cheek against his hand, watching me with a focus that reminds me of Jase. "You can make diamonds out of peanut butter. I readed about it."

"Read," I say automatically, replenishing the raisins I'd sprinkled on the tray of Patsy's high chair.

"Yucks a dis," she says, picking each raisin up with a delicate pincer grip and dropping it off the side of the high chair.

"Do you think we could make diamonds out of this peanut butter?" George asks hopefully as I open the jar of Jif.

"I wish, Georgie," I say, looking at the empty cabinet over the window, and then noticing a dark blue Jetta pull into our driveway, the door kick open, a tall figure climb out, the sun hitting his rusty hair, lighting it like a match.

Fabulous. Exactly what we need for the flammable family mix. Tim Mason. The human equivalent of C-4.

Read Huntley Fitzpatrick's
hauntingly raw and beautiful
story of first love—

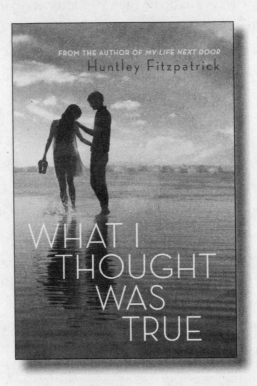

"Utterly luminous . . . deftly balances the shimmering promise of summer, first love, and yearning in an emotionally charged, beautifully written book."

—Kristan Higgins, *New York Times* bestselling author